WORLD TOUR

World Tour

MIKE SHERER

Ink & Quill Press

For more excellent works of fiction, visit Inkandquillpress.com

To my wife Connie, my loving traveling companion to geological wonders such as these.

Chapter 1

Kilauea

Uzmahndey was skipping rope when the door to his future opened. Actually, it was the door to his office that opened. Also, skipping might be too childish a term for what his five-foot-eleven inch, one-hundred and ninety pound frame (a muscular BMI of 28 with 6% body fat) was doing. The rope was a blur as it whipped around his glistening gym short clad black frame. His fresh skin fade buzz-cut brushed the acoustic ceiling tiles with his double-unders. His boxer steps were nearly as good as the Ali Shuffle. His mummy kicks made Boris Karloff look like a dead guy.

Still skipping, Uzmahndey rotated to see who had entered. A plain washout of a young woman in a not-very-sunny sundress stood in the doorway, holding an infant car seat by the handle. Uzmahndey decelerated. "May I help you?"

"I'd like to book a tour." Her voice held no betraying accent to help him place her origin. It was as toneless as a robocall.

Uzmahndey slowed to a halt. She was a tourist, of course. Way too pale to be a native. Besides, what other reason would she have for being in his office? Maybe she spoke in such a monotone because English wasn't her first language. He set his GoxRunx aside. "Please come in."

The young mother took two strides and crossed to his desk. Uzmahndey noted for the umpteenth time he needed a bigger office. He had shoved everything easily moved—which meant everything; he really needed to get better furniture when he got a bigger office—out of his way to jump rope. He was surprised she had stepped up so close to him. He had been jumping for a half-hour. His cure for a hangover. The best way to recover was to get the blood pumping and the sweat flowing. He sniffed on the sly to see how bad he was. Not *that* bad. The blank face so close before him didn't register any displeasure. It didn't register much at all. But if she didn't mind, he sure didn't. He was an athlete. He was used to sweating. "Any particular destination in mind?"

"Kilauea."

"Of course. In Hawaii Volcanoes National Park. The most active volcano in the world. You're in luck. There's an eruption going on now." Uzmahndey glanced down at the car seat she held. In it was a tiny baby wrapped in a pink blanket. She looked to be only a few months old. He was surprised the woman had flown so far with such a young child. It wasn't a short jaunt to reach Hawaii from any departure point. Also in the car seat was a huge stuffed Tyrannosaurus Rex. It seemed way too large for such a small baby. Most likely a gift from some well-meaning boob.

He looked up from the baby to smile reassuringly at the mother. "It's nothing to worry about. Only at alert level 3. A minor volcanic eruption. You and your baby will be safe." He walked behind his desk. "Excuse me."

The young woman stepped back, and Uzmahndey shoved the desk back where it belonged. He then scooted a chair up before it for her. Plucking his shirt off his office chair, he indicated his bare, sweat-streaked chest. "Do you mind? It's pretty casual here on the Big Island."

The woman shook her head as she sat.

"Good. I like to cool down before I put a shirt back on." He tossed the tee shirt on top of a file cabinet, then rolled his office chair up behind his desk and sat across from her. He massaged his forehead, attempting to dispel the echoes of his hangover.

"Is that you?"

Uzmahndey looked to see she was referring to the framed photo of an action shot of him in his Las Vegas Raiders uniform snatching a contested pass out of the hands of a Cincinnati Bengals defender. He smiled. He had scored on that play. "Yes, it is."

"Your hair was longer." In the photo, long, tight braids whipped about out of the back of his helmet.

He smiled, sweeping a hand over his close-cropped hair. "I was projecting an image. Establishing my brand." He lowered his hand, losing his smile. "Those days are over."

"Were you good?"

Uzmahndey choked back a laugh. Direct question, he liked that. "Played for LSU on a full scholarship. A sixth round draft pick for the Raiders. But I didn't have much of an NFL career. Messed up a knee my rookie season."

The woman sat across from him and lowered the car seat to the floor. "Your knee looked okay jumping rope."

"There's a big difference between jumping rope and playing receiver in the NFL. My knee was reconstructed. Three different surgeries. I rehabbed ruthlessly." He chuckled. "They always say that when they're talking about an injured player working to come back. It's never just *rehabbed.* It's always rehabbed *ruthlessly.*" He paused for a response to this insight. Receiving none, he plunged on. "But it never healed right."

He opened a program on his laptop. "Enough about me. Let's see what kind of a tour I can line up for you." Uzmahndey looked up from the computer screen. "Are you traveling with anyone else? Besides your baby? A husband? Companion? Family? Friends?"

She shook her head.

"So it would just be the three of us?"

She nodded yes.

"Let me bring up some packages."

"I don't want a package. I want you to take us to Kilauea. I'll pay whatever it costs."

Words never before uttered in his office. With his best poker face, he quoted an outrageous sum. She agreed. No hesitation, no haggling. It suddenly felt like his mouthpiece was in place.

The woman reached down into the car seat and picked up the stuffed dinosaur. "How close can you get us?"

Uzmahndey spit the imagined mouthpiece out.

"You're not planning on jumping in, are you? This isn't some human sacrifice thing?"

Fiddling with the toy, she gave a deadpan reply. "No."

Uzmahndey broke into a wide grin.

"I was joking. Besides, Pele prefers virgins." He glanced at the baby. "Unless you were planning on sacrificing *that* virgin."

With still no reaction from this stoic customer, his grin faded as he looked back up at her.

"Moving right along then. Time to get serious. We'll do the Rim Trail. That's easy walking. If you want to descend into a caldera."

He paused for effect.

"An *inactive* caldera." He glanced down at the baby. "That won't require any sacrifice." He looked back up to her. "Or if you want to walk through the lava tubes, you should wear sturdy shoes. No sandals. No stroller, either. I hope you have a good baby carrier. Maybe a BabyBjorn?"

The woman returned the stuffed toy to the car seat. "I'll be prepared."

"I can see you are fair skinned." Uzmahndey smiled, indicating his black bare chest glistening with sweat. "Unlike me. Be sure to use a high SPF, for you and your baby. The sun can be brutal here in Hawaii."

Receiving nothing but a blank-face stare, he plowed on.

"When would you like to go? The park is open twenty-four seven."

"Before daybreak tomorrow."

"Good idea. Beat the heat. And the sunrise is beautiful there. Juxtaposed against an active volcano, it can be stunning." He scrolled through the program open on his screen. "I'll provide food and drinks. I'll pack a cooler. Any preferences? Or food allergies? You or your daughter?"

She shook her head no.

"I'll pick up a sampling of local fare. I know a place." He surreptitiously rubbed his right knee. It was stiffening. He hadn't had a chance to do a proper cool-down. "Are you staying here in Hilo?"

"The Wild Ginger Hotel."

"Beautiful place. I'll be by at four-thirty tomorrow morning. We'll reach the park well before sunrise." He handed her some papers. "If you'll look these over and sign. It's just the usual tour contract and release."

He watched the woman sign without reading.

"Angela. What's your daughter's name?"

"Charlie." She motioned toward the stuffed Tyrannosaurus Rex. "That's Snugglesaurus."

Uzmahndey smiled. "They're both cute." He glanced at her signature. "About mode of payment."

"I've already taken care of that." When Uzmahndey merely stared, Angela continued. "Check your bank account."

After Angela walked out with her baby, Uzmahndey did just that. It was there, deposited several minutes ago. How did she do that so quickly? He had no idea, but that outrageous amount was really sitting there in his account. Whatever scraps of headache were still clinging to the inside of his skull lost their grip. He slapped on his stereo. IDK blasted, and he danced across his office. He sang along with their lyrics for a verse, then started making up his own.

"Whoop! I got children NOW, at least one little custoMER. And I sure ain't got no money problems NOW, not after this TOUR."

Once Uzmahndey calmed a bit, he yanked on his shirt, jammed feet into sandals, and dashed several doors down the strip mall where his office was located to the Moon & Tortoise, a small restaurant specializing in Hawaiian cuisine. Being the middle of the afternoon, it wasn't busy.

A young Hawaiian cook stepped out of the kitchen at the sound of the door chime. "Who's Your Mama! What can I do for you?"

Uzmahndey's good mood soured. "You can start by calling me by my real name. Uz-mahn-dey. It's not that hard to pronounce. I don't mangle your name."

"That's because you don't use it. You call me Neo."

The smile returned. "Is it my fault your mother named you Keanu? I never even knew that was a Hawaiian name until I met you."

"You mangle other names. Like Pe'epe'e Falls."

"I know what the real name is. But I show a lot of foreigners around our beautiful island, and it's a lot easier for them to say Pee Pee Falls. And they get a chuckle out of it."

"So what can I do for you, Who's Your Mama?"

"Go ahead and have your fun. I'm in too good a mood for it to bother me today."

"Did the lights put you in such a good mood?"

"What lights?"

"The other night. Everybody saw them. They were coming from the northwest."

"Don't know what you're talking about."

"Were you blitzed by then? That early? Man, Who's, you've got to quit drinking so much."

"What about the lights?"

"They were off toward Keck. There must have been something going on at the Observatory. They were fantastic."

"Didn't see them. And how much I drink is my business." He shifted his weight off his gimpy leg. He might have overdone the rope work. "I need some food for a tour tomorrow."

Keanu picked up an order pad and pen. "How many?"

"Just two, besides me. And one of them doesn't eat solid food." When Keanu arched an eyebrow, he continued. "She's still on milk."

Early the next morning, Uzmahndey loaded up his cooler with what Keanu had prepared for him: panko crusted mahi, oyster sauce veggies, wild boar mac and cheese with a sweet potato sauce, and a Japanese-style potato salad. For sweets, Keanu had prepared brown sugar-grilled pineapple and pot kulolo. For drinks, his friend had filled Uzmahndey's gallon thermos with mango lemonade. Plenty for him and Angela to picnic on. The baby was on her own.

It was a short drive in his Dodge Grand Caravan from his condo near the strip mall to the Wild Ginger Hotel. As Uzmahndey rattled across the empty streets along the waterfront at four in the morning, he daydreamed about upgrading his rusty drive. With the money from this score he had enough to put a good down payment on some respectable wheels. Everyone assumed NFL players were rich. A few big names were awarded big contracts, but the vast majority just made a living. The average NFL career was only three years. His had lasted way less than average. The injury settlement he'd made with the Raiders was long gone after he sank most of it into his tour business.

Pulling into the parking lot, Uzmahndey chuckled at the notion of the Wild Ginger Hotel advertising an ocean view. Maybe from up on top of the roof. If you stood on a stepladder. Walking into the old blue and white two-story stucco building, he found Angela seated in the lobby with the baby asleep in her lap. She didn't appear any more animated than the day before, with the same glazed expression on her face. But she was dressed appropriately. Comfortable lightweight tan slacks, a white tee shirt with a print of Keck Observatory on the front, a bucket hat with a tropical design, and good hiking shoes. At her feet were the carseat and a backpack with the stuffed dinosaur sticking up out of it.

"Good morning, Angela."

"Good morning." Same unexcitable monotone as before.

"I see by your shirt you like Keck. Have you been to the observatory?"

"Yes. It was the first place we saw when we came here."

"I heard they had a light show up there several nights ago. Did you get to see it?"

She merely stared without replying, offering no feedback at all. This was going to be a long day. But a highly-profitable one. He strove onward.

"There are plenty more sights on the Big Island you shouldn't miss. I'd be happy to take you around."

"I hope you will continue our tour. If today goes well."

"Then let's get started." He picked up her backpack and car seat while she rose with her baby. "If you need any help with your baby, don't hesitate to ask."

"I don't need help. Taking care of Charlie is what I was made for."

Uzmahndey led the way out to his Caravan. He was glad it was still dark. "It runs better than it looks. The salt spray in Hawaii is rough on vehicles."

Angela paused briefly after Uzmahndey slid open the cargo door. Was she having second thoughts? He quickly scanned his van. It didn't look unsafe. Did it? He knew she had a baby to consider. He looked back at her. She wasn't even looking at the van. She was looking at him. But not in the face; lower. Was the barn door open and the critter running loose? He glanced down. No, securely corralled. She seemed to be looking at the stuffed dinosaur sticking out of the backpack he held. His eyes shot back to her. "Is anything wrong?"

"No. Your vehicle is functional."

Uzmahndey set the backpack down and got busy installing the baby seat. "These can be tricky, but I'm good at this. Done it plenty of times. For my customers. I don't have a baby myself. Charlie will be perfectly safe." Once finished, he leaned out. "Check it out if you like. It's in there right."

Angela didn't inspect it. Instead, she once again looked att the stuffed toy. Without another word, she strapped her baby in and climbed in over her.

Uzmahndey handed the backpack in to Angela, then tugged the door closed. Sometimes it hung up. Better to close it by hand. He sure didn't want to give this prize customer any further doubts about his mode of transport. He climbed in behind the wheel and turned the key. Nothing. He expelled his breath in a silent curse. Not today! He depressed the brake pedal and jiggled the gear shift. Sometimes it didn't settle into park all the way. He glanced in the rearview mirror. Angela sat patiently still, impassive as ever, watching him. He turned the key again. The engine started. Yes! Thank you, Pele.

Uzmahndey took the Mamalahoa Highway up to the park. He turned on to Crater Rim Drive and headed directly toward Kilauea. The new eruption going on wasn't at a dangerous stage, yet was still impressive in the dark of early morning. Pulling into the parking lot at the trailhead that led to the viewing site, he glanced into the back seat. Angela had already undone her seat belt.

"Do you need help with anything?"

"No. Charlie needs to eat before we get started."

"Have you got a bottle in the bag? If you'd said something I would have put it in the cooler. It can get really hot in the car..." He never finished his sentence. He was distracted by the sight of Angela pulling her tee shirt up to her shoulders. He remained speechless as she leaned forward and reached around to undo her bra. "Oh." Uzmahndey finally managed to avert his eyes. He had no idea how to react to this. He had not spent much time around young mothers.

His eyes were drawn back to Angela as she lifted Charlie from the car seat. She relaxed back and nestled the baby to her breast. Once she began to suckle, Angela looked up at Uzmahndey with an expression as blank as ever. "Thank you for your patience."

Uzmahndey finally forced his gaze forward. "No problem." He glanced down at the in-dash monitor displaying what the cabin camera was seeing. The baby was placidly feeding. Then he looked away out the side window. Unable to resist, he looked back at the monitor. This time, Angela was staring directly into the camera back at him. He swore under his breath and switched the key off. This was not a good way to start what could develop into a lucrative relationship. "I'll wait outside." He opened his door and climbed out.

A few minutes later Angela emerged with her clothes in order and a placid Charlie settled into the baby carrier. She slipped her backpack on with ease. "We're ready."

They hiked the short distance along the Kau Desert Trail from the parking lot to the viewing platform, where they had a good view of active Kilauea glowing hellishly in the dim predawn sky. Uzmahndey was about to show her the best place on the platform to see the soon-to-be-rising sun positioned against the caldera when Angela abruptly stepped off the platform, heading directly for the volcano.

"Angela! That's not safe!" She paid no heed. Damn, maybe this *was* a human sacrifice thing.

Uzmahndey chased after. "We should stay on the trail!" She didn't stop. "It's not safe for the baby! It's too dark! You can't see where you're walking! The ground is rough off-trail!"

She never faltered. Damn, she was getting away.

"Slow down! You'll trip and fall and hurt the baby!" She continued to pull ahead. Uzmahndey broke into a jog. "That's an active volcano! We shouldn't get any closer!"

She was moving at a fast clip over treacherous terrain. Uzmahndey lengthened his strides, growing more perturbed with each one . She could do whatever the hell she wanted, but she had no right to endanger her baby like this.

He finally caught up with her and grabbed her by the shoulder. When she turned to face him he expected to see an insane person. Instead, her expression was as vapid as ever. She shoved him in the chest with one hand. It seemed to be a mere flick of a wrist, but he ended up on his butt.

She continued on.

Uzmahndey had never encountered an unruly customer before. Should he let her go? Should he try to stop her? She was a lot stronger than she appeared to be. He'd been hit by linebackers and safeties without going down. This little woman had felled him with no effort at all. What the hell was she wanting to do, anyway? Snap selfies of herself doing yoga poses on the rim of a volcano? While holding her baby? Genesis' 'Dance On A Volcano' began playing in his head.

He stood and walked after her. He couldn't stop her. The only way would be to tackle her, and he couldn't do that with the baby strapped to her chest. All he could do was trail after her so he could help if she got into trouble.

Uzmahndey sighed with relief when Angela halted half a football field length from the edge of the caldera. So maybe she wasn't going to descend into it. Or pitch her baby in. Instead, she unslung her backpack and extracted a small Tupperware container filled with what looked like Cheerios, or some kind of cereal ring. He assumed it was a snack for the baby. Until she took one out and flung it high into the air. She must have a hell of a throwing arm, Uzmahndey speculated, as he watched it sail far out over the caldera. That was a toss Tom Brady would have been proud of. If that really was a Cheerio it should have been too light to travel that far. But it disappeared into the thick billowing smoke.

Angela turned back, unsurprised to see Uzmahndey behind her.

"Are you okay?"

"I'm good. Let's get out of here before a park ranger shows up."

Angela brushed past him.

He started to follow, but stopped when something caught his eye. In the fiery smoke swirling up out of the volcano a dark shape formed. Just an outline. Something big, with wings, hovering above the caldera. Just for an instant. Then it dissipated into a formless ash cloud, leaving no discernible trace. What the hell? Uzmahndey shook his head and turned away.

On the way back to the viewing platform he had difficulty keeping up with her. She certainly didn't appear to be so nimble, or even athletic. And she was loaded down with a baby strapped to her chest and a pack strapped to her back. How was she doing this?

Uzmahndey was lagging ten feet behind by the time they got back to the viewing platform. She was as serene and composed as ever when he scrambled up into her face.

"What was that about?"

"Something I needed to do."

That calm uninflected speech was driving him nuts. "What did you throw into the volcano?"

She stared, mute.

"It looked like a Cheerio. Can I see?"

Another moment of silence. Then she handed the Tupperware container to him.

Uzmahndey looked it over. It was filled with little brown rings. He popped open the lid. They looked like cereal rings. He sniffed. And smelled like them. They sure didn't look dangerous, so that probably hadn't been an act of terrorism. But why would she do that? How had she done that? He picked out three and weighed them in the palm of his hand. They weren't heavy at all; they weighed about what he would expect three Cheerios to weigh. How had she thrown them so far? He held them up to his nose and sniffed again. They smelled like original flavor Cheerios.

He saw she was watching him closely. Bv "What you just did could be considered an act of vandalism."

Still no reaction. Damn, the woman was infuriating. And she didn't seem the least interested in the sunrise. Had she wanted to come in the dark so no one would see what she had just done?

He popped the three little cereal rings into his mouth.

"What are you doing!?"

Uzmahndey smiled as he chewed and swallowed, despite them tasting as bad as he remembered Cheerios tasting. He had finally provoked a response. Was she really upset with him for eating three of her precious Cheerios. He'd buy her a whole box when they got back to Hilo.

Angela snatched the Tupperware container.

"We need to get back to the van. Now." She stalked off down the Kau Desert Trail toward the parking lot.

She sure sounded upset. So what? He did not like dealing with an unruly customer. He had his business to consider. He wanted to stay on good terms with the local officials. She had already paid for this tour. If she was going to go rogue on him like this he wanted nothing else to do with her. She shouldn't be throwing stuff into volcanoes.

There was nothing for Uzmahndey to do but follow. But he wasn't running after her again. She could move as fast as she wanted, she would just have to wait at the van for him.

By the time he reached the parking lot he was feeling light-headed. What was going on? He had just been walking, and he hadn't run all that hard before when he chased after her. He was in better shape than this. And his knee wasn't even bothering him.

Angela, waiting beside the Caravan, appeared more concerned with his condition than angry at what he had done.

"Are you okay?"

Chapter 2

Sailing Stones

Uzmahndey opened his eyes to see a toddler sprawled on the floor staring solemnly up at him. She had curly brown hair and a chubby face. The stuffed dinosaur he had seen before was clutched to her chest. It didn't appear so oversized now. "Hello."

She stared blank-faced in response. Looking beyond her, he saw he was in a strange bed in a strange bedroom. Not actually *that* strange of a situation, he had to admit. He had awakened like this before, even with strange children staring at him like now, just never without a hangover.

As his searching eyes swept the room they settled on an elderly man in traditional Hawaiian garb standing in a corner. Uh-oh. Enraged husband? The guy didn't look enraged. He was smiling. And he was kind of old for Angela. As he faded away. What the hell? This immediately brought to mind the incredible form he had seen hovering above Kilauea. Had that been a hallucination, also?

Uzmahndey sat up. When the cover fell down into his lap he realized he was naked. And that Angela was sitting in a chair across the room staring at him. He pulled the cover up to conceal the necessities. "Where are my clothes?"

"I cleaned them." She motioned across the room. His shirt and pants were hanging in an open closet, his undershorts and socks folded on a dresser. "You were sick."

"I threw up?" He looked his body over.

"I cleaned you up, too. You swallowed something you shouldn't have."

"The Cheerios?"

"They may have looked like Cheerios, but they had something inside them."

She had drug-infused cereal? With her baby around? Whatever it was, it packed a punch. Uzmahndey looked over the room again. Where was her baby? His gaze settled on the silent little girl still in a limp heap on the floor. "Who is this?"

"Charlie."

He stared at the child in disbelief. Had he pulled a Rip van Winkle? "How long have I been asleep?"

"A day and a night." Angela glanced at Charlie. "She has a thyroid condition."

"No way." He looked back at Angela. "How did we get here?"

"I drove your van."

Uh-oh. The gig was up about his wheels. "Did you have any trouble starting it? Sometimes it's difficult. There's a certain routine."

"No problem. Snugglesaurus told me what to do."

Uzmahndey glanced at the stuffed animal in the little girl's arms. "That stuffed toy. Told you how to start my van."

"And how to drive it."

His eyes shot back to the woman. "You don't know how to drive? Do you have a license?"

She shook her head twice.

Oh boy. This was worse than he thought. The crazy lady was not only claiming her child grew years overnight, but she was also taking driving instruction from a toy dinosaur.

Uzmahndey looked all around. "Then you dragged me into your room at the Wild Ginger?"

Angela nodded once again.

"How do you feel?"

He took a deep breath, considering. "Okay." Actually, he felt great. He stretched, flexed. Not even a headache, only a well-rested sense of well-being. "Did you give me some medicine?"

"No. It must be the xenobots. They were inside the cereal rings you ate. That was a foolish thing to do."

Angela's expression and tone of voice didn't sound like she was admonishing him, merely commenting.

"I've done worse. Like going up for a pass with Logan Wilson closing on me. He hits like a bulldozer doing fifty miles an hour. But I held onto the ball." At last, Uzmahndey felt calm enough to, if not smile, at least relax his frown. "Would you two mind leaving? So I can get dressed?"

Angela picked up the little girl clutching the toy dinosaur from the floor and walked out.

Uzmahndey crawled out of bed. He held onto the headboard until he was sure he was steady. Which, surprisingly, he was. What the hell were xenobots? If they were so powerful to make him sick and knock him out for twenty-four hours, what was Angela doing with them around her baby? Babies were notorious for putting stuff in their mouths that shouldn't go in there. What had happened to her baby, anyway? She couldn't have grown like that overnight. Thyroid condition my ass.

He looked to the corner where he had seen that old Hawaiian guy. No sign of him. He must have been dreaming, or the xenobots - whatever xenobots were - were making him hallucinate. Had that winged monster he'd seen above the volcano been a hallucination, too? But he'd seen that *before* eating the Cheerios. Realizing he wasn't dizzy at all, he let go of the headboard and dressed. So the chick had stripped him naked. Fair play, since he had watched her nurse her baby.

Uzmahndey emerged from the bedroom to find Angela and that little girl out on the veranda. No way was this the baby he had seen the day before, no matter what the crazy lady said. He joined them. Damn, there *was* an ocean view, from the second floor. Which meant Angela had dragged him up a flight of stairs. The Wild Ginger, old enough to be grand-fathered, didn't have an elevator. How strong was this woman? He didn't see much in the way of muscles. She must have had help.

"Are you thirsty?"

Uzmahndey saw his thermos and a glass on a table beside an empty chair.

"Yes." He filled the glass, then offered some to Angela. "Keanu's mango lemonade is good."

She declined. "I put your food in the refrigerator. Let me know when you want it."

Uzmahndey set the glass down. He was hungry. Ravenous. But there were more pressing matters. "Tell me what xenobots are, and if I need to have my stomach pumped."

"You already emptied your stomach. Besides, it's too late for that. They've settled into your body."

"What will they do to me?"

"I'm not certain. You are the first person to ingest one. But it seems like they have assessed your physical condition and already begun repairing whatever needs repairing."

"Like my knee? They can fix my knee?"

"They might already have. They will also enhance your natural abilities."

"I was a professional athlete. An NFL receiver. My natural abilities are speed, agility, endurance, and spatial coordination. Are you saying all that has been enhanced?"

"Exert yourself in some way."

Uzmahndey was always willing to show off his athletic prowess to the fairer sex. He dropped and gave her twenty. Effortlessly. He went to one hand and did another twenty push-ups. He switched to his other hand for twenty more. He did twenty clap push-ups. He never broke a sweat, nor was he even breathing hard. He caught himself with one hand while the other checked the vein on the side of his neck that should have been throbbing. It wasn't.

"You're not sweating like you were the other day from jumping rope," Angela noted.

Uzmahndey popped up off the floor and sat down. "Why did I get so sick?"

"The xenobots weren't intended for human consumption. But they are of high intelligence. They have adapted to their unanticipated environment."

"So I'm over it." When Angela nodded, he relaxed. "That's cool. The NCAA really pushed Covid vaccination. Inoculation for the football team at LSU was something like ninety-seven per cent. It knocked me off my feet. Sick as a dog. But only for a day. Next day I was fine. Swallowing those xenobots must have been like that shot."

Uzmahndey picked up his glass and drank, then relaxed back into his chair. "How much do I owe you for this miracle cure?" When Angela didn't respond, he continued. "If they really helped my knee then maybe I can get back into the NFL. That's wonderful. Thank you. So how much?"

"I hope you will go a different path."

Uzmahndey's elation dimmed. "Like what path?"

"We need a guide."

His smile returned. "Don't worry about that. I can refer you to a good agency."

"I want you."

"Why me?"

"For one thing, you have my xenobots inside you."

Uzmahndey's face fell. "Do you want them back? I didn't steal them. I thought I was eating Cheerios. I had no idea I was swallowing those things."

"You can keep them. If you agree to continue as our guide." When he merely glared at her, she went on. "You will be well-paid, also."

Uzmahndey considered. Money seemed to mean nothing to her. She threw it around like she had an endless supply. Maybe she did. No telling whose daughter this was. And the baby, wherever she went, could be some billionaire's granddaughter. So Angela was a little kooky. Many rich people were. This was an offer he couldn't refuse, and it didn't involve being in bed with any bloody animal heads. He could possibly get back in the NFL once this gig was over. Waiting one more season wouldn't hurt. Especially if he was in the kind of shape he seemed to be in. He was twenty-six. Brady had played at a high level well into his forties.

"What do you want to see?"

Angela had an extensive world tour planned out. The Sailing Stones in Death Valley, California, was to be their first destination. Having played in nearby Las Vegas, Uzmahndey had heard of these curiosities. They settled on his fee. Or rather, she stated a sum and he caught his jaw to keep it from hitting the floor. She promised the same amount again as a bonus upon completion of the tour, plus all travel expenses.

The first thing Uzmahndey did after leaving the Wild Ginger was to stop by a branch of his bank and request an account balance. A wide-eyed teller informed him what it was. Wow. The money was for real. He didn't know how it had gotten deposited into his account—the teller went on about electronic transfers and routing numbers—but it was really there. The teller immediately started pitching investment schemes. Uzmahndey told him later. He would deal with that when he got back.

The second thing Uzmahndey did was go online to find out what xenobots were. This was what he read on Wikipedia: *Xenobots are synthetic life forms designed to perform some desired function, and built by combining biological tissues with artificial structures. Whether xenobots are robots, organisms, or some hybrid of the two remains a subject of debate among scientists.*

So he had three semi-synthetic living creatures inside him. He had learned in high school that there were numerous natural life forms existing inside his body, like the bacteria in his gut that helped with digestion. He did another search on Google to find out what else he was carrying around. He came across this article: *The Human Microbiome: Everything you need to know about the 39 trillion microbes that call our bodies home.*

Oh my God. Thirty-nine trillion? He hesitated about reading on. He needed to get a good night's sleep before starting this trip. He gritted his teeth and continued: *Your body is crawling with bacteria and fungi. But don't worry, most of them are there to keep you alive. Welcome to the wonderful world of the human microbiome. In any human body there are around 30 trillion human cells, but our microbiome is an estimated 39 trillion microbial cells, including bacteria, viruses, and fungi that live on and in us.*

You mean they outnumber us? Hell, *we're* hitching a ride with *them*. Enough. He really needed to get a good night's sleep. He already had images of a multitude of horrid things crawling around inside of him. Thirty-nine trillion! Damn, those three little xenobots he'd swallowed weren't going to make any difference.

But how were they doing what he had felt them doing while he was doing push-ups? He had heard about nanobots under development that could be injected into the bloodstream to remotely treat health conditions. Were these xenobots some experimental medical technology? If so, how had this crazy woman gotten hold of them? With the sums of money she was throwing around, he guessed she had the means to buy something like that on the black market. Or maybe the xenobots were part of a clandestine government experiment. He wouldn't be the first black man to be used like that. He should admit himself to a hospital and get checked out. Only this could be his ticket back into the NFL. Besides, it was too late, they were already inside him. And he felt so good. They couldn't possibly be harmful. So he would closely monitor his physical condition and just wait and see what happened.

Uzmahndey got busy preparing for the trip. Angela had told him tickets had already been purchased for their flight the next day to Los Angeles. One detail he didn't have to deal with. He canceled all his scheduled appointments. He paid up the lease on his office for the remainder of the year. He paid up his rent and condo fees for the rest of the year, too. None of this was a problem with that small fortune now sitting in his bank account. He also dealt with the utilities and other loose ends he needed to tie up before leaving on this globe-spanning odyssey. He locked up his office and ran the keys to it and his condo down to Keanu, who promised to look after everything while he was gone. He found his passport, since Angela said at some point they would be leaving the country.

Then he packed.

Once everything was taken care of, Uzmahndey settled down with a shot of whiskey. He didn't finish it. It didn't taste right. Probably because he had been sick earlier. So he climbed into bed, hoping to get a couple hours of sleep. But he couldn't stop imagining those trillions of tiny creepies crawling around inside him.

Uzmahndey's too-vivid imagination wasn't the only thing holding sleep at bay. He didn't know what to make of the little girl. She was not the same girl he had taken to Hawaii Volcanoes National Park the day before. That girl had looked to be about three months old. The girl he saw today looked to be about three years old. Yet Angela claimed it was the same girl. Which was impossible. Why was the woman playing this game?

Why should he care? She had already paid him a fortune and was offering to double that if he completed this world tour. That more than compensated for her unruliness at Volcanoes National Park. But that wasn't the decisive factor. He had a way to get back into football. From the first time he had strapped on a helmet to play pee-wee at the age of five, he had never enjoyed anything else nearly as much. Football had been the focus of his entire life. It had been ripped away from him by a knee that wouldn't heal right. Here was an opportunity—incredibly tenuous, yes, but, by how he had felt while doing pushups on the veranda of the Wild Ginger Hotel, all so convincingly believable—to get back in the game. How could he walk away from that? He didn't know what was going on with the little girl. Or those xenobots. He didn't care. This time next year he could be playing in the NFL again. Of course he was taking the job.

Uzmahndey awoke early the next morning refreshed. He had slept only a couple hours yet felt well. Was that the xenobots' doing? He collected Angela and this older Charlie at their hotel. He half-expected to find a teenage girl with Angela, but she hadn't changed any; she still appeared to be about three years old. Angela informed him that her growth happened in spurts. Thyroid condition, sure. The woman had ditched the baby somewhere. For the money he was making on this gig and the opportunity to play in the NFL again, he wasn't going to ask too many questions. So off to the airport they went. He parked the van in long-term. Angela promised to pay the tab, as part of covering his expenses. The airport could keep the damn thing, for all he cared.

In Los Angeles, Uzmahndey rented a Jeep Wrangler (with Angela's money). He drove, while Angela sat in back with this new Charlie strapped into a bigger child seat. Uzmahndey Googled the nearest sporting goods store in the direction they were headed. At a Big 5 they stocked up on camping gear: a small tent, three sleeping bags, backpacks, and sundries. Angela had insisted on an adult sleeping bag for Charlie. Was she anticipating more growth spurts? Uzmahndey bit his tongue nearly clear through and didn't ask. Their next stop was a Ralphs to buy food and drink suitable for camping. Then he drove off to the northeast.

During the long drive to Death Valley there was ample opportunity to talk. Only they didn't. Angela was content to watch the passing scenery without commenting, while Charlie either played with Snugglesaurus or dozed, like she had the entire flight from Hawaii. Yet she was more active than she had been. The day before, she had been so sluggish he had feared she was sick. Today she seemed okay.

At first Uzmahndey tried to give value for the money he was being paid by delivering a spiel about Death Valley, but after ten minutes he realized neither of his passengers were listening. So he fell silent. He kept glancing back at Charlie in the rear view mirror. This could not possibly be the Charlie he had seen at Angela's breast. How would that even be possible? Growth spurt? He shrugged. Sure, he was good with that. Whatever the crazy lady who talked to stuffed dinosaurs said. He wouldn't press her on it. If he pissed her off she might demand the xenobots back.

Driving in silence gave Uzmahndey way too much time to brood. Yet he felt too good to brood. He had worked well past midnight preparing for this trip. He had gotten up early that morning to get them to the airport in time for their flight. Then the long flight itself. Then the hassle of renting the Jeep, shopping for supplies and food. And now this long drive. After just recovering from an illness so serious he had tossed his cookies and passed out.

Yet he felt great. Not even jet lag. He had kept in good shape since quitting the NFL. But shouldn't he at least feel tired? He didn't. Was this because of the xenobots? They must be everything Angela said they were. A wide smile broke out. When he got back in the game he would lay waste to Logan Wilson.

It was late afternoon when they turned off 395 onto 190 at Alancha. At the park boundary they turned off the paved road and headed north on gravel. After more than an hour of bouncing across this rough track they arrived at the smooth desert expanse of Racetrack Playa.

Pulling into the Grandstand, Uzmahndey hopped out from behind the wheel. It was in the nineties, which wasn't bad for Death Valley. The record was 134 degrees Fahrenheit. He saw that the first thing Angela did upon exiting the Jeep was to slather suntan lotion on Charlie. She put away the bottle without applying any on herself. "You need some, too."

"No, I don't."

It was her funeral. He wasn't chasing after her any more, like he'd done at Kilauea. He was sure she would change her mind later. He just hoped it wasn't too late by the time she did.

The trio approached a wooden frame laden with all manner of curious metal oddities. He started to explain what he had read online about this. Angela wasn't interested. She breezed past it onto the desert playa, stopping at the first curious rock she came to. Behind the small unremarkable stone was a track in the sand.

Uzmahndey looked to see a dozen similar stones spread out across the flat expanse with similar twisty tracks behind them, some short and some long.

"They figured out what makes them move. This is an old dry lakebed. When it rains it fills with shallow water. The water can freeze at night. It gets that cold here in the winter. The next morning the ice breaks up as it warms, and the strong winds that blow through here push the ice fragments, which in turn nudge the stones along. This leaves tracks in the sand. Later in the day the ice melts and the water is absorbed into the sand, leaving no trace of what had caused the stones to move, only the tracks they made."

"That's one explanation." Angela kneeled beside a rock and buried a Cheerio in the sand beneath it.

"What's that for?"

Angela declined to answer as she rose. Without a word, she took Charlie's hand and led her back toward the Grandstand.

Uzmahndey was stunned. "That's it? We came all this way for you to leave a Cheerio here? Why?"

"Is there a campground nearby?"

Homestake Day Camp was a short drive beyond Racetrack Playa. They set up camp and had a bit to eat. At least Uzmahndey and Charlie did. Angela fasted. "You need to eat something," Uzmahndey insisted.

"No, I don't."

Uzmahndey hadn't seen her drink anything, either. She was going to collapse if she continued this way. She also hadn't relieved herself. He had merely walked off a ways and turned his back to them, while Charlie hadn't even bothered to do that much. Uzmahndey had purchased a Luggable Loo at Big 5, but the composting toilet remained unchristened. Was this some kind of Zen thing—mastering your bodily functions? He had not even seen any sweat on her brow.

It came to a head as they settled down for the night in their tent. Uzmahndey stayed outside to let them get into their sleeping bags. This he didn't object to at all. Out here in the desert with no light pollution the brilliant black night sky was ablaze with an infinity of dazzling constellations. He was getting a stiff neck from gazing up at them for so long.

"Who are you?"

Uzmahndey looked all around for the person who had asked that question. He could see no one nearby in the dark. Several other tents were pitched, with small campfires before them, but none close. He did a quick walk around their tent, but found no one lurking.

When he looked back up to the sky he saw something. Not the dark outline of a flying creature like back in Hawaii, but rather a lack of something. Some of the stars were blotted out, some constellations half-gone, replaced by a dark shape of a huge human form looming directly above him. It was almost as if he could reach up and touch it, which he had no inclination to do. What was up there? And speaking? To him? A moment later the thing disappeared, and all the brilliant desert night stars blazed back. Whatever had obstructed his view of them was gone.

Angela called out to him to come in. He found her in her sleeping bag in the middle, with Charlie swallowed up in an adult sleeping bag to one side of her and his still rolled-up sleeping bag on her other side. "Wouldn't it make more sense to put the kid in the middle?"

"No."

That did it. Her dull toneless one-word answer. She wouldn't even consider it. He and Angela would be sleeping practically on top of each other. Then he saw her and Charlie's clothes folded at their feet. Including their underwear. Were they sleeping naked? Angela turned over onto her side, away from him, to give him a bit of privacy. "Now wait a minute."

Angela looked back over her shoulder, but Charlie didn't budge. Was the kid asleep already? She had slept most of the flight from Hawaii, then had slept in the car with Snugglesaurus in her arms nearly the entire drive to Death Valley. Was that a result of her growth spurt? No, dammit, kids can sleep anywhere at any time. There was no such thing as a three-month to three-year growth spurt. Thinking of that just made him more irritable.

"We need to talk."

Angela awaited his words.

"I need to know what's going on. I mean, you could be a Russian spy. Or Chinese."

"Why would a spy come to Death Valley?"

"Then what's going on? What did you do with the baby? Why are you claiming she aged nearly three years overnight? Why did you toss a Cheerio into a volcano? Why did you come all the way out here just to bury a Cheerio in the sand beneath a rock? How can you go without eating or drinking or relieving yourself? Or even sweating? In one of the hottest places on Earth?"

<u>She's a robot.</u>

Where had *that* come from? Angela's lips hadn't moved. Charlie was asleep. He cast a frantic gaze around the tent. No one else was in there with them. Had the voice come from outside? Had that dark form blotting out the stars returned and spoken to him again?

Angela noticed how upset he had grown. "What's the matter?"

She hadn't heard the voice? It had sounded plain as day to Uzmahndey. "I just heard someone say something ridiculous."

He unzipped the tent and crawled out. He looked up to the sky. No dark outline, like he had seen before. He searched all around outside the tent. No one.

"What are you doing?"

Uzmahndey turned back to the open tent flap. Angela stood directly before him. Naked. Her pale form glowed like a ghost in the brilliant night. Damn, she was beautiful. He could only blabber. "I heard something. Someone. Say something. Something stupid."

"What?"

She pierced him with her stare. At least *she* had no problem maintaining eye contact. When he didn't reply, she took off to search around the tent.

Wouldn't you like to jump that?

Damn! There it was again. Only it was different. A different voice. This one sounded sassy, where the previous one had sounded dull. He looked all around. No one. The closest other tent was twenty yards distant. The voice hadn't shouted, it had sounded like normal conversation. When Angela came back around the tent to face him, he babbled some more. "You shouldn't be out here barefoot. There are scorpions out at night."

She didn't seem concerned about scorpions. "What did you hear?"

"Nothing that makes any sense. I must be hearing things. It's been a long day. I'm tired. Recovering from a serious illness that knocked me out for twenty-four hours. Let's go back in and get some sleep."

Angela crawled back into the tent, her shapely tail rolling wondrously under Uzmahndey's lustful gaze.

Do you really want to make love to a robot?

Damn! Another one! Could eating those xenobots cause him to lose his mind? Uzmahndey took a long calming breath. During which time none of the voices said anything else. When he climbed back into the tent he saw Charlie sitting up in her bag. Angela got her settled back down then climbed into her own sleeping bag.

Once that beautiful body was safely covered and zippered up, Uzmahndey released a long breath. The notion of Angela being a robot was crazy. She didn't look like any robot he'd ever seen. He'd not heard of any robot looking and behaving so human-like. He had seen her nurse a baby, for Christ's sake. No robot could do that. Yet Angela was hardly acting normal. He'd not seen her eat or drinkanything, or go to the bathroom.

And Charlie sure wasn't normal. No one aged three years overnight. What kind of freaks had he gotten involved with?

"You need to rest. The xenobots need down time to recharge."

Uzmahndey spit out a bitter laugh. He couldn't leave himself out of this freak show. He had three little monsters roaming around inside his body. He stripped down to his undershorts and climbed into his bag. He and Angela were pressed together on their sides, faces inches apart.

She smiled. For the first time since he'd met her. It wasn't much of one, a mere upturn of the corners of her mouth. But a smile, all the same. Could a robot do that? Uzmahndey ground his teeth. He was way too manic to fall asleep, he didn't care what the xenobots needed. And his dick was hard.

"Are you a robot?"

Angela rolled over onto her other side to face away from him.

Now he'd done it. He'd pissed her off. A beautiful young woman was lying naked practically on top of him and he'd called her a robot.

<u>She's not angry.</u>

"Who are you?"

Silence. Now that Uzmahndey was ready to talk to whoever it was talking to him, the voice clammed up.

Angela rolled back over to face him. To his surprise, she didn't appear angry, just like the voice had said. She appeared concerned.

He shook his head. "I wasn't talking to you."

She continued to stare with her perfect blue eyes.

"Can I touch you?"

"Yes."

He placed his hand on her bare shoulder, caressed it, squeezed it. It sure felt real. No way was she a robot. He released her.

"I'm sorry. It's been a long day." Uzmahndey rolled over away from her and struggled for sleep. To his surprise, it wasn't a long struggle.

Chapter 3

Mono Lake

Uzmahndey awoke the next morning feeling great. Normally, the first night of a camping trip spent sleeping on the ground left him stiff and achy. Was this because of the xenobots?

The other two sleeping bags were empty, and there were no clothes other than his in sight. Good. Somewhat. He took a moment to recall how beautiful Angela had looked. A robot? No way. A person would have to be crazy to believe that. Did hearing voices in his head mean he was? He grew quiet, listening. Not a word. He squirmed into his clothes, feeling way too good to be pondering his sanity.

Uzmahndey emerged from the tent to be staggered by a stunning blow to his sanity. A young girl much older than the one he had spent the previous day with. Yet who looked eerily familiar. "That can't be Charlie."

"She had a growth spurt last night." Angela poured hot water into a cup from a tin pot on a Coleman gas stove and stirred in instant coffee. She handed it to him.

Uzmahndey had to clutch the cup with both hands since they were trembling so badly. The girl seated before him in a camp chair frowning off into the distance looked like a years-older version of the three year old that had gone to sleep in the tent with him the night before. The growth spurts were for real. How was that possible? What wasn't possible was to deny the resemblance of this older girl to the younger from just the day before. It was Charlie. How could she be growing like this? There was no condition he knew of that could cause this to happen. But it had happened. He was staring at it. Could she have escaped from some secret government experiment that even QAnon hadn't heard about? Like Eleven, in Stranger Things?

Uzmahndey slumped into a camp chair, spilling half his coffee. When Angela offered a towel, he just stared at her. If Charlie could grow like that, was it beyond the realm of possibility that Angela really could be a robot? Like the voice in his head had told him. One of three different voices. Which made a weird sort of sense. Three xenobots, three distinct voices. But there were no robots like Angela he had ever heard of. That didn't mean there weren't. The government had a lot of secret programs going on. Had the two of them escaped from one? And now he was mixed up with them. What had he gotten himself into?

Uzmahndey spilled the rest of his coffee when Angela began mopping up what he had already spilled from the front of his pants. He tossed down the coffee cup and shot to his feet, overturning the camp chair as he stumbled back away from her.

Angela froze, staring.

What was in that stare, Uzmahndey wondered, staring back in fright? Nothing. At. All. It was as blank as a new document in Word. And like that blank page, there could be all kinds of hidden codes beneath the surface. Just what was he looking at? "Are you a robot?"

"Yes."

"Show me."

Angela merely stared.

"Show me some wiring or something. Peel back your skin so I can see some circuitry."

"No."

"Why not?" Another silent stare. "Assuming you are not bonkers, since that bonkers thing you told me about Charlie's growth spurts seems to be true, who made you?"

"Father."

"Okay. So who is your father?"

"You've met him. He was in the room back in Hawaii when you came to."

Uzmahndey recalled the old Hawaiian guy. It hadn't been a hallucination? "Where'd he go?"

"Back to his lab."

Uzmahndey swore to himself. This was going nowhere, just more idiotic rambling. He looked to Charlie. She sat slumped in clothes that swallowed her, with the stuffed dinosaur in her lap, staring dully at them. "Is she a robot, too?"

"No."

His gaze shifted back to Angela, who hadn't moved a muscle. If she had flesh and blood muscles. "What are you doing with those xenobots?"

"Sealing portals to the interior of the planet."

"Sure you are." Uzmahndey released an exasperated sigh. More idiotic rambling. He turned his gaze back to Charlie. She hadn't moved, except for some drool that had run from her slack mouth down her chin. "What's wrong with her?"

"A growth spurt is hard on her. It takes about a day for her body to adjust to its new dimensions."

He looked back to Angela. "If you are a robot, how do I know you won't murder me in my sleep? I've seen Westworld. I know what happens when robots go rogue."

"I will not harm you. I need you."

Uzmahndey took a long calming breath. "I'm hearing voices. Do you know anything about that?"

"Those are the xenobots. They have adapted to their new environment well enough they are now able to communicate with you."

She will not harm you.

She needs you.

She'll do anything you ask. Man, you sure landed in a sweet deal.

The voices were talking to him again. He looked to Angela. "Did you hear what was just said?"

"No. The voices of the xenobots are inside your head."

Uzmahndey decided he might as well talk back to them. What good were having voices in his head if he just ignored them? "How do you figure I'm in such a sweet spot?"

You are being paid a small fortune to visit some of the most interesting places all over the world.

After which we will help you realize your dream of getting back into the NFL.

All while in the company of a beautiful babe who'll do anything to keep you happy. If this isn't a sweet deal, I don't know what is.

"You three aren't going to take me over?"

All we want is what's best for you. We will keep you healthy and strong.

If you thrive, we thrive.

Just wait until you see what we can help you do to Logan Wilson.

That last remark brought a bark of a laugh from Uzmahndey before he could repress it. He sighed, relaxing. He hadn't realized how tense he had become.

But if we were really good, how would you know?

Suddenly Uzmahndey wasn't so relaxed. "Know what?"

If we were controlling you or not.

Uzmahndey was distracted from further introspection when, reaching for the towel Angela still held, their hands touched. Damn, she felt soft and warm. Mopping coffee off his pants, he turned his dark gaze back to Charlie. "How old is she now?"

"Eight."

"Packing for her must be a trick."

Charlie scowled at him then looked away.

"She's wearing my clothes. We'll stop today and buy her some clothes that fit. Are you hungry?"

"Starving. But I'm sure you have your hands full taking care of Miracle Growth girl here. I can take care of myself."

He walked away to the Jeep and rooted through their stuff in the back to find the box of protein bars.

That was crude.

"What was?"

Asking Angela to show you her inner workings. It's like asking a woman to show you her uterus.

She wants you to think of her as a woman, not prove to you that she is a machine.

"I'll believe it when I see it. All I've seen so far is a good-looking woman."

You've seen Charlie. Do you now believe she's the same baby you met back in Hilo?

"I'm having a conversation with three different voices I'm hearing in my head. So I honestly don't know what to believe." He dug out a half-dozen bars and turned back to Angela. "Where are we headed now?"

"Mono Lake."

This time Uzmahndey had no idea what to expect. He had never heard of Mono Lake. He and Angela tore down the camp and packed it all up in the Jeep, while eight-year old nearly-comatose Charlie sat slumped in a camp chair watching them. By keeping busy he didn't dwell upon what he had agreed to take part in. Guide a supposed robot and a freakishly-growing girl to weird places all around the world. All the while sharing his body with three xenobots he had swallowed. Thankfully, the voices kept quiet. Assuming they really did have his best interests in mind, they probably wanted to give him time to sort all this out, while not stressing him out any more than he already was.

Then there had been that *other* voice. 'Who are you?' That had been different. That had sounded like it had come from up in the sky, not inside his skull. All these voices, all the weirdness with Angela and Charlie. Could he be losing his mind? That was always a concern for football players. He'd had a concussion at LSU, and one in his rookie season with the Raiders. Neither had seemed that bad at the time, and he had recovered fully from both, but who knew what the cumulative long-term effects could be.

Damn Logan Wilson.

He slipped covert glances Angela's way while she was busy stowing gear into the Jeep. He *must* be losing his mind to believe she could be a robot. He didn't know what her game was, but she was as human as he was. He had let a golden opportunity slip by last night. He wouldn't let *that* happen again.

He glanced at Charlie. She hadn't moved, she was still staring out across the desert. If she was this moody now, what would she be like when she was a teenager? Which could be tomorrow.

During the drive north up 395 they stopped at a Wal-Mart to buy some clothes that fit an eight-year old girl. Angela had insisted he come in and help pick out appropriate items. Neither female seemed to have any idea what was in style. He chose three outfits he wouldn't be embarrassed to see on Charlie while he was with her.

They didn't stop again until reaching Lee Vining, California, where they had lunch at the Basin Café. Charlie had not wanted anything, but Angela ordered her a grilled cheese and fries, and insisted she eat it. Uzmahndey ordered a Chicken Ortega sandwich. He loved the way California food was smothered in chili. Angela ordered nothing.

"You have to eat something," Uzmahndey said. "You'll collapse if you don't."

She responded with only a hollow stare.

"Order something. You might get hungry if you smell food. You don't have to eat it. Just order something."

Her mouth twisted into what might be considered a grin.

"So you can eat it?"

Uzmahndey smiled in return. "I wouldn't let it go to waste."

"What would you like?"

He indicated his sandwich. "Another one of these would be good."

"The xenobots require a lot of energy. You'll notice your appetite increasing."

Her grin, no matter how ill-formed, made Uzmahndey feel better. The woman was not a robot, despite what she and the voices in his head claimed. A robot couldn't grin like that. Or look so sexy. Damn, he couldn't get the memory of her prowling around the camp naked last night out of his mind. But this was business, he had to keep insisting to himself. The hands on the purse strings to his future should not also be on his dick.

After lunch they drove to Mono Lake Tufa State Natural Reserve. Uzmahndey parked in the small lot, and they walked to the waterfront on a boardwalk. Stepping off the end of it onto a dirt path, he noticed the ground was swarming with little black insects, some of which took to the air as they were disturbed by his passing. "I hope these don't bite."

Angela glanced down to Snugglesaurus, which Charlie held at her side. "They don't."

Why was she always looking at the stuffed animal like that? "What are they?"

Following another glance at the toy T. Rex, Angela replied, "Alkali flies."

Still distracted by all the buzzing, Uzmahndey was amid the tufa towers before he even noticed them. He stopped to look them over. Jagged, twisty, irregular spires of gray and brownish stone rose from knee-high up to thirty feet tall, randomly scattered around the water's edge and out in the lake. "They're weird. It's like Dr. Seuss' sandbox."

"Originally the lake was underwater," Angela said. "This is one of the oldest lakes on the continent. All these tufa towers were built up from mineral deposits expelled over millions of years from hot springs on the lakebed. In recent years the water level of the lake went down and many of them were exposed."

"How do you know all this stuff, but you don't realize how many eight year old girls are wearing clothes with Disney characters printed on them?"

Angela glanced at the Encanto tee shirt he had picked out that Charlie was wearing. He let it go. "Why are we here?"

"To go swimming."

Angela pulled off her tee shirt. She was wearing a one-piece swimsuit underneath her clothes. Charlie did the same, and the top of the two-piece he had selected for her came into view.

"You could have warned me we were going swimming."

"Swim in your underwear." Angela stepped out of her shorts. "It's not like we haven't seen you with your pants off before."

Was that levity in her voice? And a rumor of a grin? Not things a robot would do. Maybe she was warming to him. Uzmahndey looked around before peeling off his tee shirt. There weren't many people present, and no one close. He saw Angela remove a Cheerio from the Tupperware container, while Charlie, having already shed her shorts, watched with dull interest as he stripped down to his undershorts.

Uzmahndey followed the two into the lake. He stopped when some tiny animals swarmed his feet. "What's that in the water?"

Angela took Snugglesaurus from Charlie and placed it upon a dry perch on a tower at the water's edge. "Brine shrimp. There's trillions of them here."

"Trillions?"

"Don't worry, they won't bother you." Angela took Charlie's hand and led her out into deeper water.

Uzmahndey followed them. "Can she swim? She was only a baby last week."

Angela stopped where the water came up to Charlie's waist. "No, she can't. Stay with her." Angela swam out toward a cluster of tall towers in the middle of the lake.

Uzmahndey stood next to Charlie, ignoring her while he watched Angela's sleek form slice across the placid surface.

Until Charlie bobbed up next to him afloat on her back. Seeing him watching her, she mumbled. "Snugglesaurus says the water is real salty. It's easy to float."

So she talked to the stuffed animal, too. No big deal, a lot of kids had imaginary friends. Uzmahndey kicked his feet up and floated on his back beside her. "The T. Rex is right. And the water at the top is warmer. My toes were getting numb."

It also felt slick, like there was a skim of oil on top of the water. He assumed that was because of the high salinity. This water seemed much saltier than the ocean.

He glanced at Charlie floating contentedly beside him. She probably couldn't drown if she wanted to. He could relax, too, if only there weren't so many of those little critters swimming around in the water. Trillions? Damn, the only time he'd heard that word used before this week was in relation to the federal deficit.

Charlie went under. Suddenly. Like someone had grabbed her and dragged her down. A huge mass of the tiny shrimp swarmed where she had been floating, obstructing his view. He couldn't see her at all.

Uzmahndey lunged to his feet and looked for Angela. She was swimming back toward them from the middle of the lake. "Angela!" He waved both arms. "It's Charlie!"

He dove after her into the maddened throng of brine shrimp.

Uzmahndey was ensnared by the swirling multitude. He opened his eyes, but the water was so salty it stung so much he could see nothing but the dark chaotic mass of tiny bodies darting all about him. He couldn't find Charlie. The water itself pulled at him, like he was caught in a rip tide. Was Charlie caught in one?

<u>Yes. We'll clear your eyes.</u>

His eyes suddenly stopped stinging and he could see again.

<u>She's right below you. Go get her.</u>

He dove, fighting through the strong current and teeming shrimp toward the bottom.

<u>Grab her. She's drowning.</u>

He saw Charlie. She was splayed motionless on the lake bottom. He forced his way down to her. He had never been a good swimmer, but his muscles seemed to know what to do. He grabbed her with both hands and tried to lift, but the water seemed to pin her to the bottom. He planted his feet and strained with all his might. She slipped through his hands. The water was so slippery he couldn't keep a good grip on her slick skin.

Uzmahndey saw something in the murky currents of brine shrimp. A gray-bearded old man with horns coming out of his head. No, not horns. Crab claws?

"Let her go."

How was the old man talking underwater?

Uzmahndey was knocked aside as Angela dove down to Charlie. She seized the girl with both hands, planted her feet on the bottom, and pulled up on Charlie with all her might. The current was still pulling her down, threatening to tear Charlie from her grasp. Angela managed to lift the girl up off the bottom, but no further.

Uzmahndey dove down to squat beneath Charlie. He planted his feet on the bottom and pushed up on her, straining with all he had. He and Angela together forced the young girl up through the killer current and attacking shrimp, up to the surface.

As soon as they lifted Charlie's limp form up out of the water the current eased and the storm of brine shrimp dispersed. Angela carried a limp Charlie to the shore. He staggered after. He could hardly move, and it wasn't because of any current. He was exhausted. By the time he stumbled up out of the lake Angela had stretched Charlie out on the ground flat on her back.

Uzmahndey dropped to his knees beside Charlie and began mouth to mouth. He sucked a brine shrimp out. Sitting her up, he performed the Heimlich. Five more brine shrimp shot out, along with an immensity of water.

Charlie began coughing. Angela snatched her out of his arms. He collapsed, spent, watching as Angela pounded on Charlie's back. More water was ejected. The girl collapsed crying into Angela's arms. Uzmahndey slumped to the ground and closed his eyes.

He opened his eyes to find himself flat on his back on the ground, with Angela sitting on one side and Charlie sitting on the other cradling Snugglesaurus. He looked to Charlie. "Are you okay?"

She smiled, and nodded.

He looked to Angela. "What happened?"

She smiled down at him, a big bright glowing warm human smile. "You saved her life."

"It took both of us." He looked back to Charlie. "How did you go under? We were floating so easily."

Angela answered for her. "She was pulled under."

"There are warnings posted on Hawaiian beaches about dangerous currents. Why are there no warnings posted here?"

"That wasn't a current. That was something else."

"I saw something. Someone. On the bottom." He had Angela's riveted attention. "It was an old man with crab claws on his head. He spoke to me. Said, 'Let her go'." Uzmahndey shook his head. "A crazy hallucination. I was panicked and oxygen deprived." He shook the eerie image from his head. "Why am I so tired?"

"The xenobots gave you a double shot of adrenaline so you could fight through the water. Can you get up? If you can, we'll leave. We're done here." After he nodded, Angela and Charlie scrambled to their feet. Angela easily pulled him upright. He was still surprised by how strong she was. She held him up while Charlie wrestled his pants onto him.

Uzmahndey looked to Angela. "You are so strong."

"So are you." She produced that glorious smile again.

Charlie fastened and zipped his jeans. "I'll get our clothes." She gathered them up, while Angela led a stumbling Uzmahndey back to the parking lot.

Chapter 4

Old Faithful

Uzmahndey drove back to Lee Vining and stopped at the first motel they came to. He was in no condition to search for a campground. He was dozing at the wheel when he parked the Jeep. Angela secured a room then dragged him into it. He fell asleep with his head inches above the pillow of the bed she dropped him onto.

It was dark by the time Uzmahndey came to. He saw Angela and Charlie had already cleaned up. Charlie seemed livelier. He could understand how nearly dying could affect a person like that. Or was she just better adjusted to her eight-year old body? Of more import, he saw there were two more Chicken Ortega sandwiches waiting for him. He gobbled them down. His next imperative was to get rid of the salt that encrusted his skin.

When he emerged after his shower he found Charlie lounging in bed with Snugglesaurus and Angela sitting erect in a chair staring down at her. He interposed himself between the two. "What happened today?" Getting no reaction from either, he continued. "I've never heard of such a strong current in such a small lake. And I thought you said those brine shrimp were harmless. They attacked me."

When neither responded, he formed a capital 'T' with his hands. "Time out. We need to get serious. We all nearly drowned today."

"The xenobots wouldn't let you drown," Angela said.

"And you can't drown. Since you're a robot." That made a crazy kind of sense. Her not eating, not drinking, not relieving herself, not even sweating in the desert, for Christ's sake. And how strong she was. He shook his head in dismay. "You sure don't look like a robot. You don't act like a robot."

"What is she supposed to do?" Charlie smiled. "Swing her arms around in circles and say, 'Danger, Will Robinson, danger'."

He turned on her. "You sure know a lot about an old TV program for someone who is supposed to be only weeks old."

"Snugglesaurus instructs her," Angela said.

"Her stuffed toy." Disbelief oozed between the syllables of those three words. Getting no reaction from either with that tone of voice, Uzmahndey attempted sarcasm. "For some reason I have a hard time believing what you tell me." Still no reaction from the supposed robot. Uzmahndey gave up and asked a serious question. "Then what is she? She's certainly not normal."

Charlie burst into tears.

"I know I'm not normal!"

Angela hugged Charlie, while giving him a dark look. "Do not attack her."

"Or what? *You'll* attack *me*?"

"I told you I was designed to take care of her."

"Yeah, but I figured that was just something mothers said."

"Will you two stop it?" Charlie broke free of Angela's embrace. "I'm okay."

Uzmahndey eyed Angela warily. She was strong as hell. She could probably beat the shit out of him. "Just give me some straight answers. I was okay with the situation before on account of all the money and the opportunity to get back into football, but today I could have died. That changes the equation. Now I need some straight answers."

He looked from one to the other. "Why were we attacked? By whatever it was."

<u>Enough.</u>

<u>You're exhausted. You need to rest.</u>

<u>You're ranting, buddy.</u>

He collapsed onto the bed, asleep before he could wonder why.

Uzmahndey awoke the next morning to find himself tucked in beneath the covers of the bed he had collapsed on. He glanced at the other bed. Charlie was asleep, with Angela curled up behind her, staring back at him over the girl's shoulder. Seeing his eyes open, Angela, careful not to wake Charlie, eased out of bed. Naked.

Uzmahndey couldn't help himself. She claimed to be a machine, but what a beautiful design. When she turned down the covers to climb into bed with him, he saw he was naked, also. "Whoa, whoa, whoa."

Angela ignored him and slid in, pulling the covers up over both of them.

"What are you doing?" Uzmahndey scooted back.

<u>She wants you.</u>

"But she's a robot."

<u>You can't tell that by looking.</u>

<u>Or by touching. Just go with it.</u>

"Are you having a conversation with your xenobots?" Angela attempted an alluring smile. She nearly succeeded.

"How are you doing this if you are a robot? Behaving so much like a real person?"

<u>She has a learning program. The more she interacts with people, the more she adapts to become more like them.</u>

<u>She has interacted with you more than anyone.</u>

And right now she wants to interact with you in a big way.

Uzmahndey thought back to when she had first walked into his office. She had behaved much like a robot that day. Since then she had been changing all along, but the process had been so gradual he hadn't noticed. He had thought it normal, the way people warm to each other as they spend time together. "It's just a computer program?"

You shouldn't say *just* a computer program. It's actually very elegant.

"How do you know this? Where are you getting all this information?"

Snugglesaurus.

He couldn't keep the incredulity out of his voice. "The stuffed dinosaur talks to you?"

That toy dinosaur has a computer stuffed inside it.

Uzmahndey was jerked out of his conversation with the xenobots by Angela's touch as she stroked his chest.

"Don't you like me?"

"Yeah, I like you. I like the 'vette I bought my rookie NFL season, too."

"Then drive me." Her hand slid lower.

He intercepted it. "Is this part of you taking care of Charlie? Do you think if I get hung up on you, I'll stick around to help her?"

"I'm designed to learn how to be human. You can help me learn."

And have one hell of a good time teaching her.

"Shut up!"

Angela jerked away.

"Not you." Uzmahndey rubbed his forehead. "Give me a minute." He closed his eyes. "Are you three going to be watching me all the time?"

Yes.

Except when you sleep.

It gets boring then.

"I'll never have another private moment in my life."

Sorry.

Privacy is overrated. Ask Zuckerberg.

But we *can* keep our mouths shut.

"You have mouths?"

Virtual mouths.

"Let's make a deal, then. You don't speak unless spoken to. Okay?"

Okay.

Uzmahndey waited. Silence. Would they stick to this arrangement? Would it be enough for him? He knew they were in his head, watching his every move. But at least they weren't in his ears.

He opened his eyes. Angela stared expectantly at him. He lifted the cover and looked her over.

"Are you fully functional? Even down there?"

"Yes."

He stared a moment longer. Then let the cover drop. "I can't. I'm sorry. Knowing what you are, what you claim to be, and with the xenobots watching and a little girl in the room, I just can't."

He scooted across the bed to get out the other side then froze, gazing down at the cover bunched in his lap.

"Go ahead and get up. I want to see what it looks like in an upright position."

"It's not called an upright position." He scowled at her. "It's called an erection."

"It got that way just by you looking at me?" Angela tossed the cover off. "Then take a good look."

Hearing laughter, he looked to see Charlie, who was now wide awake and watching. "Go ahead and get up. I want to see it, too."

Damn. He was trapped. "I am not exposing myself to a child." He threw the cover back over Angela. "And you shouldn't, either."

Angela seemed intrigued. "I thought it was okay, since we are the same sex."

"She doesn't have a sex. She's eight. And I don't know what to call what you have." He grew still, awaiting a snarky response in his head. There wasn't one. Could he really order the xenobots to be quiet?

"You know less about children than you do about women." Charlie laughed again. "I've got a sex."

"I know plenty about women. Now will you two turn your backs and let me get dressed?"

Angela turned away, as requested. "Turn your back, Charlie. This is upsetting him."

Once both backs were turned, Uzmahndey climbed out and found his undershorts. "I understand children, too. It's mannequins I don't understand."

Angela turned to face him. "I am no mannequin."

Uzmahndey turned his back on her. He had his undershorts up, but they didn't fit right. "You don't have to do this, Angela. I'll stick around, at least a little longer. For Charlie's sake." He looked to Charlie, who was now watching him, also. He tried to turn his back on both of them. "She could have drowned yesterday."

Angela's second attempt at a sexy smile was more successful. "How long will it remain like that?"

Uzmahndey snatched up the rest of his clothes without answering and stalked off to the bathroom to finish dressing in peace.

They checked out and were on the road by daybreak. Their route took them northeast out of California, across Nevada, across Idaho, and into Wyoming. A day-long drive during which not a lot was said. Uzmahndey roamed the airwaves, searching out music he could tolerate. Angela was content once again, watching the passing scenery from the back seat. Charlie, also in back, spent all her time playing with, and supposedly being tutored by, Snugglesaurus. From time to time, Uzmahndey glanced at her image in the rearview mirror. "Does that thing have games on it?"

Charlie ignored him, engrossed with the stuffed animal.

"Instructional games," Angela said.

"What are they instructing?"

"It's actually uploading. All the information a normal child would have learned by eight years of age."

"She's learning all that in a couple of days?"

"While her conscious mind is involved with a game, the AI is uploading to her subconscious mind vital information she needs to function. This instructional process is even more intense while she sleeps. Another reason she is so drowsy the day after a growth spurt."

"You say she's not like you. But then she's not like me, either. So what is she?"

"Of course she's not like you. She's an eight-year-old girl."

"Can we stop soon?" Charlie said. "I need to use the bathroom."

"You're right, Angela. She sounds like an eight-year-old girl."

"And don't drag out that bucket with a toilet seat on it. Can we find a real bathroom?"

It was growing dark when they arrived at Jackson Hole, just south of Grand Teton National Park. They stopped at the Mangy Moose for dinner. Uzmahndey had recovered sufficiently from his ordeal in Mono Lake that a single Buffalo Super Burger sufficed.

Being too late to find a campground, they checked into a motel. As soon as the door to their room closed, Uzmahndey proclaimed the ground rules.

"You two stay in your bed; I stay in mine. Alone." Both female heads nodded in agreement. "We give each other some privacy. I know that's difficult, the way we are traveling, but we make an effort." More nods. "Anything either of you would like to add?"

"Yes," Charlie said. "No snoring."

Uzmahndey smiled. "If I do, throw a shoe at me."

Despite the ground rules, no shoes were thrown during the night. They got underway early the next morning. Uzmahndey drove north through Grand Tetons National Park. Charlie split her attention between Snugglesaurus and joining Angela in gazing at the passing splendor. They continued out the north entrance of Grand Tetons National Park through the south entrance into Yellowstone National Park.

It was late morning when they parked at Old Faithful. Uzmahndey headed for the lodge to check the eruption schedule, but Angela said she wasn't interested. "Then why are we here?" was his exasperated reply.

"There are other geysers here. Ones we can get closer to."

Uzmahndey didn't like the sound of that, but he followed her lead. They bypassed the crowd awaiting Old Faithful's next eruption to stroll along the Upper Geyser Basin Trail, passing many other hot springs, sulfur pools, and small geysers. Both Uzmahndey and Charlie were so distracted by the sights, neither realized Angela seemed to be searching for something.

Until they came to Grotto Geyser. This miniature volcano boiled with thick billowing steam and spitting hot water. Angela took the Tupperware container filled with Cheerios from her backpack. She removed one and tossed it toward the geyser. It disappeared into the steam. Under the disapproving glares of nearby tourists, she put the container back into her backpack.

One irate young couple stepped forward. "This is a natural treasure you are defacing," the woman said.

Angela turned away without replying.

The woman's equally offended partner stepped into Uzmahndey's face and hissed a single word. "Traitor."

Traitor? To what? Yellowstone? Uzmahndey forgot all about the accusation when the woman lunged at Charlie. Before he could make a move to stop her, Angela was there blocking her. The dangerous look on her previously inanimate face made the woman back off.

Uzmahndey stepped up alongside Angela, with Charlie behind them. "You two had better leave the child alone." The two young people were nearly snarling as they backed away.

Uzmahndey tried to lead Angela and Charlie off, but Angela wasn't done. "If any of you ever touch her, I'll kill you."

He pulled Angela along. "They thought you were littering in one of America's crown jewels."

"The xenobot won't hurt anything. It's helping the Earth."

"Why did they come after me?" Charlie asked. "I didn't do anything."

"Who knows. Nowadays, people are ready to fight over anything." Uzmahndey slipped an arm around each of them. "I drove all day yesterday to get here. Let's enjoy the rest of these geysers."

Charlie was in agreement, and she accompanied him down the boardwalk. Angela had no option but to follow. As they walked on, Uzmahndey cast one last glance over his shoulder. The two fuming young adults were still glaring at them. Why had the man called him a traitor?

"What else do you want to see here?" Uzmahndey asked Charlie several hours later, back at the Jeep.

"Anywhere we can drive to. No more walking. I'm worn out."

He looked at Angela. "It's late. Can we spend the night?"

"Snugglesaurus already reserved us a campsite."

He glanced to the toy dinosaur. "Handy guy."

"You have no idea."

Uzmahndey drove to Norris Campground, and they set up camp. Angela offered to stay outside the tent. "You two need to rest, and I don't. I'll stay out here and keep watch for bears."

"What will you do if you see one?" Uzmahndey asked.

"Dissuade him from bothering us."

He and Charlie crawled into the tent and stretched out on their sleeping bags. He studied her face. No matter what she really was, she looked like a tired eight-year-old girl. "Are you doing okay, Charlie?"

She smiled. "I bet she could take a bear."

He smiled in return. "I bet she could, too."

A few seconds later, her eyes closed. His followed soon after.

That evening, they walked over to see Norris Porcelain Basin. Another trail through geysers, pools, and hot springs, although not as large a collection as at Old Faithful. They had stopped to admire the placid pale blue of Veteran Geyser when behind them, steam and water shot a hundred feet up into the air. Steamboat Geyser, which had been dormant when they passed it just minutes ago, was erupting. With a squeal, Charlie ran back the way they had just come. Angela dashed to catch up with her, while Uzmahndey walked after.

He joined the two on the viewing platform. Charlie stood before Angela, who held her close from behind with both arms wrapped around her. The pair were thoroughly soaked from the spray, as Uzmahndey soon was. It wasn't unpleasant. The water was steaming hot when it came out of the ground, but by the time it had traveled high into the air, dispersed, then drifted back down as a heavy mist, it had cooled to an agreeable warmth.

A sudden, powerful gust of wind surged up out of nowhere. It directed the spray emerging from the ground horizontally at the viewing platform. People screamed from the scalding water, and a mad scramble to escape was on. Angela spun

Charlie around, placing herself between the girl and Steamboat Geyser.

The hot water wasn't the only peril. The spray turned noxious. The sulfur content had increased tremendously. Uzmahndey gasped for air, sulfur burning his lungs. He couldn't draw a breath of oxygen. Angela swept Charlie up in her arms and fled. He staggered after. The boardwalk was slick, and his feet flew out from under him. He crashed hard, hardly able to breathe.

"Abandon these two or you will die!" Uzmahndey looked up at the voice roaring from above the spewing horizontal geyser. In the sun-sparkled spray, he saw a huge, dark male form flickering with flame. "I will imprison you in torment!"

Suddenly, his lungs stopped burning. He could breathe. He was still gasping for air, but the sulfur content seemed to have lessened. As his stinging eyes cleared, he saw the threatening giant in the air disappear, its fearsome form dissipating in sparkling droplets. The torrent from the geyser righted itself to its natural vertical direction. Uzmahndey struggled to his feet on the slippery boardwalk. He located Angela with Charlie half-way to Emerald Spring. "Is she okay?"

Angela hugged the crying girl. "Yes. Are you?"

"Yeah." He glanced around to see who was close. Everyone was distracted with recovering from what they believed was a freak occurrence and paying him no mind. "That was another attack. I saw another monster."

Angela nodded.

"Let's get back to our site."

Not much else was said on the walk back to Norris Campground. Angela supported Charlie, and Uzmahndey followed. He kept a close watch on every geyser they passed, but there were no more incidents. Charlie's sobs soon subsided under Angela's soothing.

Arriving at their camp site, Uzmahndey remained outside while Angela took Charlie into the tent to get her into dry clothes. He plopped down into a camp chair to consider what to do. Charlie was definitely in danger. Whatever attacked her at Mono Lake had followed them to Yellowstone. Most likely, they wouldn't give up. Angela had led them into danger twice and would probably do so again. He was an ex-NFL player turned tour guide, not a bodyguard. But there was that small fortune he was being paid to consider and the xenobots that could get him back into the NFL. And he *liked* Charlie. He knew she was extremely weird, growing like she did. He had never heard of any medical condition causing anything like what she was going through. Yet she still behaved like any other young girl. He *wanted* to protect her. But if he was to continue with whatever it was they were doing, he needed to understand what they were doing.

"Uzmahndey, wake up."

Uzmahndey stirred to see Angela squatting before him, with Charlie standing right behind her. He sat up straight and tried to rouse his senses. "I fell asleep."

"Your body's reserves need to be restored every time the xenobots use them up. Rest is necessary." She smiled. "Go in and put on some clean clothes. You stink of sulfur."

He saw Angela and Charlie had changed. Uzmahndey hoisted himself up and went into the tent. Angela had smiled at him. Again. It was happening more frequently. Was it authentic? Or a stage smile? One she presented him because she had learned he liked seeing it? He had been so delighted when she first smiled at him. Was she merely acting? And if she was, was that any different than why other women smiled? He shook his head. Interacting with a robot was making him question other people's humanity.

When he emerged in clean clothes, he saw Angela cooking on the Coleman stove. She smiled at him. Again. The same smile? Or had it improved even more? "Hungry?"

It wasn't the same. Her smile was better every time he saw it. Her facial expressions and body language all seemed so real. He had difficulty remembering how bland and monotone she had been that first day she walked into his office in Hilo. When Charlie had been three months old. Had that really been less than two weeks ago? He sighed. He could drive himself batty trying to make sense of all this. So he forced his thoughts to basics, such as his rumbling stomach. "Starved."

"We've got to keep feeding those xenobots if we want them to keep saving your life. So you can keep saving Charlie's life."

"*We* have to talk."

"Of course. But can it wait until after dinner?"

"Sure. What are you whipping up?"

"Fried potatoes and onions, with bacon bits."

"Smells delicious."

"Snugglesaurus says it is. That's where I got the recipe."

Uzmahndey glanced at Charlie, who was seated in a camp chair clutching Snugglesaurus. What was that stuffed toy? He opened up another camp chair and sat next to the girl. "How are you doing?"

"That was scary."

"She's getting traumatized." He looked at Angela.

"After dinner." Angela stirred the hash browns.

After dinner, the three sat around a fire Uzmahndey had started. It was getting dark, and campfires had ignited all around.

"We're getting low on clean clothes. We'll go to Canyon Village first thing tomorrow. They have laundry facilities there. You two can all get showers there, too, while your clothes are washing. Get this sulfur off."

Uzmahndey had to suppress a smile. Angela sounded like any other mother organizing her family. He stirred the fire. "The laundry isn't what I want to talk about."

"Let's go for a walk. We'll talk about anything you want."

Another voice in his head! Different from the other three. Only this one sounded familiar.

Angela noticed his discomfort. "What's wrong?"

"I've got someone else in my head! And it sounds like someone I know."

"Who?"

"I can't place it. But it's definitely someone I know." Uzmahndey shot to his feet and bolted away down a lane through the campground. Numerous campfires blazed in the crystal clear wild country night. The full moon was so brilliant he had no problem walking.

A middle-age man dressed in cargo shorts and a tee shirt with a print of Keck Observatory stepped up alongside him.

"Who are you?"

"The person Angela calls Father."

"Are you a robot, too?"

"No. A hologram." When Uzmahndey appeared skeptical, the man offered an open hand.

Uzmahndey reached out to shake, but his hand passed through it. He jerked his hand back in fright. "Why do you sound so familiar?"

"I thought hearing a familiar voice would reassure you."

"You thought wrong. Whose voice is it?"

"Your head coach at LSU. I found his voice in your memories."

"Coach Orgeron?" Damn, it *was* the voice of his old college head coach. "You're sure you're not one of the xenobots? Disguising its voice? Messing with me?"

"I am not another xenobot. The xenobots will never deceive you or, as you say, mess with you."

"They all seem different. Why is that?"

"They each reflect a different aspect of your personality. One speaks to your best side. One plays Devil's Advocate. One moderates between the two."

"Enough about the xenobots. Tell me what Angela is doing."

"Sealing portals."

"Portals to where?"

"The realm beneath the surface of the Earth."

"What's that mean?"

"Kilauea volcano. The dry lake bed beneath the sailing stones in Death Valley. The hot springs at the bottom of Mono Lake. The massive caldera here at Yellowstone. These ancient geological formations are all connected to the interior of the Earth."

"Are you one of those Hollow Earth nuts?"

"The Earth need not be hollow to support life within it. Life blossoms under the harshest conditions."

"So you are saying there are beings living inside the Earth."

"From the time Australopithecus afarensis first came down from the trees."

"What are these beings?"

"Extremophiles I don't have a name for. But their worshippers have given their leader a name. Gaia."

"This Gaia has worshippers?"

"Yes."

"Why are these beings attacking us?"

"They feel threatened. As well they should."

"*They* feel threatened? Angela is a robot. Charlie is a human with a serious aging problem. Snugglesaurus is some kind of a computer..."

"Artificial intelligence."

"...tucked inside a stuffed toy dinosaur. You are a ghost..."

"Hologram."

"...who sounds like my old college coach. I've eaten three artificial life forms who talk to me. *I* feel threatened." Uzmahndey took a deep breath. "What do all of you want?"

"To save you from your planet."

That stopped Uzmahndey in his tracks. "That's nuts."

"This is a lot for you to take in at one time. Why don't you sleep on it and see how you feel in the morning."

"Just one more question."

"Shoot."

"Angela says I get to keep these xenobots. Do I?"

His companion laughed.

"Hey! It's a serious question. These things saved my life twice already." Uzmahndey sucked in a deep breath and let it out. "And they repaired whatever damage the sulfur fumes did to my lungs. These things are incredible."

"Yes, you may keep the xenobots. If you complete the tour you signed up for."

"How long will they last?"

"As long as you live. Once you die, they will decompose along with the rest of your body."

"So they won't keep me alive forever?"

"Correct. They won't make you immortal. They won't interfere with your normal aging process." The hiker stepped off the lane and disappeared behind a tree.

Uzmahndey wound his way through the campground back to his site. Angela sat alone by the fire. "Charlie turn in?"

"She's exhausted."

He sat in a camp chair. "I just spoke with your father."

"Did he answer your questions?"

"Some of them." He picked up a stick and poked the fire. "Are we really going all the way around the world?"

She nodded.

"You've got enough money for that?"

"Snugglesaurus takes care of the finances."

"Where is he getting the money?"

"I don't know." When Uzmahndey gave her a skeptical look, she continued. "The money is just there when we need it."

"What happens when this trip is over?"

"You get to play football again."

"If I survive."

"You'll survive. No one is attacking you. It is Charlie who is in danger."

"Why should I believe you?"

"Because I cannot lie."

Really? That's interesting.

"Why don't you turn in?"

"What about you?"

"I'll be in after the fire is out." She smiled at him. "I don't sleep, but I need to keep up appearances."

Uzmahndey hauled himself up and crept into the tent. Charlie was asleep in her bag. He undressed down to his undershorts and climbed in his bag on the opposite side of the tent, leaving Angela's bag in the middle. She'd be in later, since to keep up appearances she had to pretend to sleep. And she might want to make another pass at him.

Would he let her? She certainly didn't seem artificial. Nothing he had seen hinted at her being a robot. She seemed more and more human by the day. Was she, or was that wishful thinking on his part? What if it was? People projected their own hopes and fears onto other people all the time. He had to watch himself. He was coming to want Angela to be human so badly he might fool himself into believing she was.

Chapter 5

Spotted Lake

Angela dragged Uzmahndey from his sleeping bag well before dawn. He found a cup of coffee and a stack of protein bars awaiting him on the picnic table, which he stuffed and slurped down while Angela took down the tent. She had no trouble working in the dark. Upon washing down the last crumbs with the last dregs of coffee, he rose to help. After dropping several tent poles, which clanged in the early morning quiet, he was accused by Angela of waking up the whole campground, and dispatched to go sit in the Jeep. There he found Charlie curled up with Snugglesaurus asleep in the back.

It was still dark when Uzmahndey eased the Jeep out of Norris campground, on the lookout for wild animals on the road. Critters of all sizes roamed the night. Luckily, not all of them were awake. They passed a field full of bison Uzmahndey could hear snoring.

They made it to Canyon Village without hitting anything. While Uzmahndey and Charlie took showers, Angela did the laundry. Once it was done she began changing into clean clothes in the middle of the washing machines, startling an elderly couple waiting for their clothes to dry. Uzmahndey shoved her into the women's shower room to finish dressing. He apologized to the startled spectators. "She's French."

The sun was shining through the pine trees when they carried their clean clothes out to the Jeep. They doubled back to Norris campground, then turned north on Grand Loop Road. Uzmahndey could drive faster in the daylight. Still, he had to slow to a crawl when he came up behind a bear strolling down the middle yellow stripe. Charlie had awoken in a pensive mood, an aftereffect of the attack at Steamboat Geyser, but she broke out a big grin at seeing the bear. Eventually the bear ambled over to the side of the road, and Uzmahndey drove around it. They didn't stop to see monumental Mammoth Hot Springs. After what had happened no one wanted to explore any more hot springs.

They exited Yellowstone through the northwest entrance, soon crossing out of Wyoming into Montana. At Livingston, they turned west on I-90, which took them through Bozeman and Missoula into Idaho. They continued west to Coeur d' Alene, then on into Washington. At Spokane they left the interstate and continued west through more forests and mountains. After crossing the Columbia River they turned north into even more rugged terrain, traveling north through the Cascade Mountains all the way to the Canadian border.

During this yet another day-long drive, Angela merely stared out the window and Charlie communed with Snugglesaurus. Which left Uzmahndey to stew behind the wheel. He had nearly been killed twice. Was the money and the chance to play again in the NFL worth the risk? He was encountering beings people had nightmares about, and enough voices in his head to drive a crazy man sane. He was also seeing ghosts, or holograms, he didn't know what the difference was. This Ghost, who could appear as different people, Uzmahndey guessed so he could blend in wherever he found himself, and who had the voice of his old college coach, seemed to be in charge. He said he had come to save Uzmahndey, and everyone else, from the Earth. Did he mean from those monsters supposedly living inside the Earth? Uzmahndey was prone to believe him since he sounded like the person who had done more to promote his football career than anyone else in his life? Hearing that old commanding voice again had had a soothing effect on him. Had that been the intention?

Then there was Angela. Uzmahndey had never heard of a robot so advanced. And the AI hidden inside the T. Rex toy seemed to be so powerful it could bring on the Singularity. He had no idea what all the three xenobots that had taken up residence inside his body could do. All this advanced technology was beyond anything he knew of. Could it be alien tech? And he was tangled up in all of it. He should park the Jeep and run for his life.

"I will imprison you in torment," the ethereal being hovering above Steamboat Geyser had threatened.

But that was a hollow threat. He was already imprisoned in torment. The cart ride off Allegiant Field had been like riding a hearse to his own grave. He had lived and breathed football since pee wee league. Of course, at the time of the injury he hadn't known it was the end. Like a cancer patient undergoing chemo after chemo after chemo, doggedly pursuing a fruitless struggle against death, he had endured surgeries and rehabs and exercise regimens that would have brought a corpse back to life. All for nothing. He had finally thrown in the towel. Moved to Hawaii, opened his tour business. At least the ring of Inferno he had been consigned to was Paradise. Then Angela had walked into his office and offered him a chance to play in the NFL again. A chance at another life. How could he walk away from resurrection?

At the end of an endless day of stewing behind the wheel he arrived at the Oroville-Osoyoos border crossing. Uzmahndey knew his passport was current, but he didn't know what

Angela and Charlie had. Apparently, theirs were good, too. The only questions asked were concerning their purpose for entering Canada and what their destination was. Angela spoke up. "Vacation. Spotted Lake."

The Canadian border agent was skeptical. "I hope you are aware Lake Kliluk is not a tourist destination. It is on Okanagan land."

Angela told the border agent she was well aware of this, and they proceeded. It was a short fifteen-minute drive, which Uzmahndey filled with questions. "So we can't get to it?"

"We can."

"I'm not breaking any laws. I don't know what Canadian jails are like and I'm not anxious to find out."

"You worry too much," Charlie joined in from the backseat. "Snugglesaurus says Canadians are civilized people. Their jails can't be that bad."

When the lake came into view Uzmahndey was underimpressed. It was a small body of water, as much pond as lake, whose surface was covered with different-sized circles of pale colors.

"Pull up to the gate," Angela instructed.

There was a wire fence alongside the two-lane road they were on, with a small dirt pull-off before a wooden arch proclaiming 'ktlil'x Spotted Lake Okanagan Nation'. There was a young man standing just inside the gate.

"See. It's guarded. We can't trespass."

"Just park." Angela was adamant.

When Uzmahndey did, to his amazement the young man swung the gate open. Charlie hopped out and followed Angela through. Uzmahndey reluctantly joined them. "What's going on?"

Angela smiled back. "Snugglesaurus made a donation to the Okanagan Nation."

Charlie's smile mirrored Angela's. "See? You worry too much."

It was a short walk down a dirt track from the gate to lakeside. Their guide filled them in as they went. "This is sacred land to the Okanagan. Each of the 365 spots possess specific and unique healing properties."

"You're kidding me." When the guide glared at him, Uzmahndey hurried on. "I'm not disrespecting you, it's just 365 spots? Really? That just happens to be how many days in the year there are."

He smiled. "Yes, that has been noted."

"That's amazing," Charlie chimed in. "It can't be a coincidence."

Their guide turned his smile on her. "We think not, too."

Reaching the edge of the lake, all the many circles of color came into focus. There were varying shades of yellow, brown, green, and blue.

"What causes all these colored circles?" Uzmahndey asked their guide.

"Do you want folklore or science?"

"Science, please."

"The lake contains many highly concentrated minerals. As the water evaporates during the dry season, all the minerals remain and crystallize to form the polka-dot pattern you see. The colors constantly change as the mineral composition of the lake changes."

Angela kneeled at the edge of the water in a reverent pose and bowed her head. Their guide bowed his head also, indicating Uzmahndey and Charlie should do the same. Charlie did, but Uzmahndey snuck a glance at Angela. He saw her slip a Cheerio into the water.

He also saw a woman in a flowing white robe arise from out of one of the colored circles. She was blindfolded, with a scale of justice in one hand and a sword in the other. But she remained in the lake. She didn't brandish that impressive blade, or make any threatening move. But she did address Uzmahndey. "Why do you help the alien attack our world? Why do you betray your own people? We have protected you for millions of years. Why do you fight against us? You will be enslaved by the alien."

Before he could respond, the figure sank back into the lake out of sight.

Angela stood a moment later and thanked their guide. He escorted them back up the hill to the gate. Uzmahndey was past ready to leave. He was getting used to these weird apparitions appearing and disappearing. At least this one hadn't tried to kill Charlie. He doubted any security cameras hidden in the brush around the lake had recorded the woman in white. He seemed to be the only person seeing or hearing these incredible beings. But Angela might have been filmed tossing something profane into this sacred water. They needed to get back across the border fast.

"I can't believe you did that," Uzmahndey growled as soon as he pulled out onto the road and raced back the way they had come.

"It won't cause any harm."

"It will if what you did shows up on security camera footage. Besides, it shows disrespect for their customs." Getting no response, he continued in a different vein. "Did you see that blindfolded woman in the lake? With the big sword?"

"No."

That little performance had been for him only. The Ghost who sounded like his college coach must be the alien the woman of the lake referred to. The Ghost said he was saving the human race from the Earth. That didn't make sense. Unless these monstrous people who kept showing up were what he considered to be the Earth. What if the Ghost was lying? What if he, Uzmahndey, was aiding and abetting an alien conquest of Earth, just like the woman in white said? Is that why that young man in Yellowstone called Uzmahndey a traitor? A traitor to Earth? But then how had he known what was happening? Who were those two?

Once the three crossed back into the United States, Charlie spoke up. "I kept waiting for one of the spots to jump out of the water and grab you, Mom."

Uzmahndey had been so focused on hurrying back into the U.S. he hadn't paid any notice of her, but she must have been holding her breath until they were safely across the border. "I was waiting for that woman in the lake to take her blindfold off and attack us with that sword."

Uzmahndey was so unnerved he couldn't drive any further. At the first gas station they came to he stopped to inquire about camping. Learning of an RV park a little ways south that had tent sites, he drove there and secured a site.

Chapter 6

Devil's Tower

The following morning they were once again up and gone before dawn. Another grueling day-long haul, from just below the Canadian border in north central Washington across the upper neck of Idaho and across southern Montana into the northeast corner of Wyoming, was scheduled. Like in Yellowstone, this was dangerous territory to be driving in the dark. Deer, elk, bear, mountain lion, perhaps even moose could be out wandering along, or on, the road. Angela and Charlie both kept a keen watch until daybreak. After the sun came up Angela continued to keep watch from the back seat, while Charlie curled up with her head in Angela's lap and Snuggle-saurus in her arms and went to sleep.

Once they made it to Spokane and headed east on I-90, Uzmahndey relaxed. He refused to dwell any longer on what he was involved in. Was he helping to save the human race? Was he betraying it? He didn't care. He was getting back into the NFL. That's all that mattered. If he had to ally himself with an invading alien and battle inhuman creatures living inside the Earth to do so, so be it. As a receiver he had been adept at blocking downfield as well as catching passes. If anything got in his way of his returning to football he would knock it on its ass.

By the time they pulled into the KOA next to Devil's Tower it was once again dark. He'd been driving for over fifteen hours, so was beyond exhausted, bordering on comatose. When Angela suggested he relax while she and Charlie set up camp, he wrestled open a camp chair and collapsed into it without argument. As soon as the tent was up he crawled into his sleeping bag and passed out.

Uzmahndey awakened early the next morning to find Angela lying beside him with eyes open and a smile all over her face. Damn, he'd have to tell her to work on this if she wanted to pass as real. No real woman looked so good in the morning. She put a finger to her lips and nodded behind her. He raised up to look. Charlie, flat on her back staring straight up, was also wide awake. And much bigger. She was starting to fill that adult sleeping bag he had gotten her in Los Angeles. He dropped back down and whispered. "How old is she now?"

"Twelve."

"She'll be an old woman by the time we finish this trip."

"Her growth will slow down soon. Humans stop growing in their teens."

"But we don't stop aging."

"That should slow, also."

"Should? You don't know?"

"She's the first."

"First what?"

Angela refused to answer. Uzmahndey was too tired to press her. He was stiff and sore and felt like crap. In the last week he had flown from Hawaii to Los Angeles, then driven through five states into Canada, and then all day to get to Devil's Tower. He must really be pressing the limits of the xenobots' ability to rejuvenate him.

Uzmahndey planted himself in the camp chair he had opened up the night before while Angela whipped up breakfast on the Coleman stove. Charlie sat at the picnic table staring into the ground. She was having a difficult time adjusting to her bigger body, just like when she had aged overnight from three to eight. She held Snugglesaurus close. Uzmahndey assumed the data transfer was taking place, filling her in on what she had missed by skipping ahead four years.

Following breakfast, Angela was ready for them to hike over to the monument for her to place a xenobot so they could then depart for the next destination. Uzmahndey balked. He was worn out and Charlie was out of it. "Let's just rest up today. Neither I or Charlie are up to traveling all day again. We can drive over to Devil's Tower this afternoon for you to do your thing, spend another night here, then pack up and leave first thing tomorrow morning."

Reluctantly, Angela relented.

Later that morning Uzmahndey called Keanu. "How is everything going?"

"No problems. How is your tour going?"

"It's wild. But highly profitable."

"Where are you at now?"

"Devil's Tower."

"Seen any aliens?"

That was a shocker. How did Keanu know he was dealing with aliens? Then Uzmahndey realized what Keanu was referring to. "That was just a movie, Neo."

"Yeah, like 'JFK' was *just* a movie."

"I appreciate you looking after my stuff. Let me know if anything comes up."

That afternoon they drove over to the monument parking lot. Devil's Tower was even more impressive up close. The brochure Uzmahndey picked up informed him it was a laccolith, an igneous intrusion where magma welled up from the mantle between chunks of sedimentary rock. The exterior had been weathered away, leaving the fluted granite core presently seen. It was 867 feet from base to summit, 800 feet wide at the base, tapering to 300 feet wide at its acre and a half flat top. The trail that encircled the monument was a mile and a half.

Looking up from the pamphlet, Uzmahndey saw three different people scaling the flutes of the nearly-sheer sides at three different places. He turned to Angela. "I hope you don't expect me and Charlie to do that."

Instead, they hiked the encircling trail. Halfway around, Angela ventured off trail. Uzmahndey wasn't concerned at first since many people were doing this to pose for photos. He grew concerned when Angela began scrambling up a side. "Don't you need a permit for this?"

She continued climbing.

"You don't have any equipment. Are you free-climbing to the top?"

Charlie shaded her eyes as she watched Angela ascend. "What happens to me if she falls and kills herself?"

"Technically, if she's a robot she can't kill herself." He watched her climb higher. "But I suppose she could break."

Despite his flippant remark, Charlie's question struck a chord. What *would* he do about Charlie if something happened to Angela? The proper thing would be to turn her over to children's services. What would happen to her once they witnessed one of her growth spurts? Charlie would disappear into a government lab for study. She might never see the light of day again. Uzmahndey wouldn't wish that fate on anyone. Yet what else could he do? He wasn't about to adopt a young girl, although she wouldn't be so young for long. All he could do was hope nothing happened to Angela.

Angela's climb attracted a crowd of spectators. Her rapid ascent halted half-way up. The other spectators couldn't tell what she was doing, but Uzmahndey knew. She had found the right niche to insert a Cheerio into. Angela nimbly scrambled back down.

When she rejoined them on the trail, Uzmahndey admonished her. "That was stupid."

"You could have done that." She responded with a smile.

He stormed off down the trail without answering.

Angela followed, with Charlie right behind. "You have never tested what the xenobots can do. You'd be amazed."

"Can I fly like Superman?"

"No, but you can climb."

"Like Spiderman?" Charlie asked.

"I'll be happy if I can run like Flash when I get back into pads."

That night Uzmahndey sat outside. Another location that observed dark sky protocol. The stars were amazing. Eventually, he forsook stargazing to focus on the huge dark rock formation stabbing high into the clear sky. It blocked out an immense swath of the sparkling heavens, a mute black presence looming above the campground.

Angela had taken Charlie into the tent to get her settled for the night. The poor discombobulated girl had been tripping over pebbles on the trail earlier. Normal teenage growth could scramble your coordination badly enough. He couldn't imagine what it was like for her growing three, four, five years at a time.

When Uzmahndey finally tore his gaze away from the dark form of Devil's Tower, he noticed a man several camp sites distant staring at him. Once the man saw Uzmahndey looking, he turned away.

<u>He was watching you.</u>

"Yeah? What does he want?"

<u>We don't know. But we'll keep an eye on him.</u>

"You mean you'll keep *my* eye on him."

You don't keep an eye on anything. Your eyes see everything while seeing nothing. Go back to daydreaming about all those touchdowns you are going to score. We got this.

A little later Angela emerged from the tent. "We need to stop tomorrow and get Charlie some new clothes."

"Are you ever going to tell me what she is?" Getting no response, he continued. "You said she was the first. The first what?"

When Angela failed to respond, he looked back off to Devil's Tower.

"There's a movie I don't suppose you've seen. 'Close Encounters of the Third Kind'. It's about encounters with aliens. The climax of the movie was filmed here. An alien spaceship lands on top of Devil's Tower." He focused on Angela sitting beside him. "The blindfolded lady with the big sword in Spotted Lake told me you and Charlie and Snugglesaurus are aliens. Are you?"

"Charlie is human. I've told you that."

"How about you and the stuffed Tyrannosaurus?" No reply. "Ghost told me you can't lie. You can withhold information apparently, but you can't lie."

Still no reply.

"If you want to become a real woman, you've got to learn how to lie."

Her eyes flashed to him at that. He had struck a chord. She wanted to become a real woman.

Uzmahndey continued to appraise her. "Since you aren't going to answer my question, I'll tell you what I surmise. You are from another world. You arrived on Earth the night there was a big light show up near Keck Observatory. That's what the lights were, you arriving from space."

Angela remained stone-faced.

"I just can't fit Charlie into the equation. You insist she is human. If you really can't lie, it must be so. But she's far from normal. So what is she?"

That question remained unanswered.

But Angela did respond to one of his statements. "You are wrong about one thing. I am not from another world. I am from this world."

That surprised Uzmahndey, supposing she couldn't tell a lie. He pressed her, yet she would say nothing else on the subject.

Chapter 7

Interlude One

The next morning Charlie was fully functional once again. But she definitely needed clothes. The tee shirt she wore rose up above her navel like a crop top, and since she could no longer fit into her pants she was forced to wear a skirt with an elastic waist, which was way too short. When she climbed out of the tent, Uzmahndey began singing, "I see London, I see France."

"What does that mean?"

"It means you're going to be driving all the teenage boys crazy today."

Charlie laughed, flipping up the front of her short skirt to flash her panties.

Which made Uzmahndey laugh. "I can also see you're in a better mood today."

Leaving the KOA, they embarked on their longest drive yet. A short jaunt south put them on I-90, upon which they headed east out of Wyoming into South Dakota. They exited at Rapid City to take Charlie shopping. Since Angela had no notion of teenage fashions, and Charlie only vague notions that Snugglesaurus had imparted to her, Uzmahndey's expertise was called upon. He tried to beg off, claiming he had no idea what teenage girls wore. Angela insisted, claiming when he took families with teenage girls on tours of Hawaii he must have noticed what they had on. His last line of defense was that dressing for the tropics of Hawaii and dressing for the high plains of South Dakota were two totally different things, but she wasn't buying it. So they drug him into a mall. He suffered through the torturous trek, offering honest advice, but put his foot down at selecting appropriate underwear.

After a meal at the fast food court – the food was fast, not the meal, considering Uzmahndey wolfed down enough to feed two offensive linemen – they climbed back in the Jeep and resumed their eastward journey on I-90 through South Dakota. As they crossed into Minnesota the countryside morphed from open range to verdant farmland. Angela spent the day gazing out the window, and Charlie communed with Snugglesaurus. While Uzmahndey daydreamed of leveling Logan Wilson.

Once they crossed the Mississippi River into Wisconsin, the countryside grew more urban, which meant more traffic. After another two hours Uzmahndey was shot. When he pulled off I-90 in Madison, he was way too tired to fool with another campground. They checked into a motel by the Interstate. He limped down to the lobby so Charlie could shower and Angela could take care of whatever maintenance she required. With time to kill, he called Keanu. "How's it going, Neo?"

"Busy night here. Can't talk for long. Where are you at now?"

"Madison, Wisconsin."

"You're getting around. Where are you headed?"

"To see something called the Eternal Flame."

"The Olympic torch? Don't they keep that burning in Athens? Greece?"

"I don't think we're driving to Greece. Though I don't put it past Angela to think we can. This must be something else."

"So how's it going between you two?"

"Ha! She's crazy as a bedbug."

"Then you two are suited for each other."

"No way."

"You're spending a lot of time together in close quarters."

"It's a business relationship."

"If you say so. I've got to go, Who's. The Moon and Tortoise is hopping tonight."

Uzmahndey ended the call, but kept the phone pressed to his ear. Not having slain many minutes talking with Keanu, he decided to check in with his xenobots, and the phone gave him cover for talking to himself. "Anything to report, guys?"

<u>No one here is acting suspicious.</u>

<u>So you were probably not followed from Devil's Tower.</u>

<u>Can I ask you a question for a change?</u>

"Go for it, Bad."

<u>Why haven't you jumped Angela's bones yet? She's willing and able.</u>

"I'm not about to have sex with a machine. If she is a machine."

<u>Why not? Some of the females I've seen seem more mechanical than Angela.</u>

"Can we discuss something important?"

<u>You think sex isn't important?</u>

<u>Ignore him. What do you want to discuss?</u>

"What is your take on Ghost?"

<u>He seems sincere.</u>

"So I should believe what he tells me?"

<u>He's an alien. Difficult to judge such an unfamiliar being.</u>

"So since I don't understand him I shouldn't trust him?"

<u>How much did you understand about these beings inside the Earth before you met Ghost?</u>

"The same as now. Nothing at all."

<u>But you never imagined they were for real?</u>

"Not in my wildest dreams."

<u>So Ghost has revealed this truth to you.</u>

"But are they evil? Enemies of Earth? Like he claims?"

How many times have they tried to kill Charlie?

"Point taken. Thanks, guys. You've given me enough to think about for now."

So quit thinking and go have some fun with Angela.

Not long after quieting the voices in his head, Uzmahndey judged it was safe for him to come up to the room. He found Charlie in new pajamas splattered across one bed with Snugglesaurus, while Angela sat in a chair in her underwear watching the girl. Uzmahndey frowned. "Why are you in your underwear?"

"I told you it would bother him," Charlie crowed.

"I took my dirty clothes off and didn't want to put clean clothes on," Angela answered. "I left something on. Since me being naked seems to upset you."

"Seeing you in *that* underwear upsets me. When is the last time you changed?" Receiving a blank expression, he continued. "I know that if you are a robot as you claim to be you don't sweat, or do anything else to soil your clothes, but they are still bound to get dirty."

Angela looked over her panties and bra.

"Even if they are spotless, if a man sees a woman wearing the same clothes day in and day out he assumes she is dirty. Especially the same underwear."

Charlie laughed.

"You should have kept your mouth closed, Uz." When he gave her a questioning look, she said, "This means another shopping trip, to find her some pajamas."

The next morning they stayed long enough to partake of the motel's free breakfast, which Uzmahndey cleaned out, then hit the road, not stopping until late afternoon. They exited I-90 just west of Buffalo, New York. This was a shorter trip, a little over ten hours. Campgrounds weren't so plentiful in this part of the country, so they checked into another motel.

Since Uzmahndey was too tired to leave the room this time, he merely stripped down to his undershorts, climbed into the bed furthest from the bathroom, and rolled over onto his side away from the two females.

Yet he couldn't help himself, even as tired as he was. He looked back over his shoulder to find the other two watching him, Charlie with a grin and Angela with the cool appraising gaze he had become way too familiar with. He turned back away and forced his eyes closed, but he couldn't close his ears to their diabolical whispering.

Chapter 8

Eternal Flame Falls

When Uzmahndey pried open his eyes the next morning he saw Angela didn't look as fresh and lively as she had previously looked in the morning. "Did you have a bad night?"

She appeared puzzled. "No."

"You don't look as chipper as you've been looking in the morning."

"You said that wasn't normal."

"So you purposefully made yourself look worse?" When she merely stared at him, he shook his head. "You really take what I say to heart." He looked beyond her to see Charlie sprawled across the middle of the other bed, still sound asleep. "What do you do all night? Since you don't sleep."

"I have a sleep mode."

"When you merely become inactive?"

She nodded.

"But you are still on."

"You are still on when you sleep. Your heart still beats, your lungs still pump air, your mind dreams."

"Do you dream of electric sheep?" Seeing her puzzled expression, he said, "Ask Snugglesaurus." He climbed out of bed and dressed. "I'm going down for coffee while you get the princess up."

In the lobby with coffee, Uzmahndey got on his phone to look up information about their destination. Eternal Flame Falls was in Chestnut Ridge Park outside the small town of Hamburg to the south of Buffalo. It was accessed by a half-mile hike rated moderately-difficult. The flame was caused by natural gas escaping from an underground pocket, which burned behind the falling water. There was some disagreement about the cause of the flame. A scientist from Indiana University claimed the shale under the waterfall wasn't hot enough or old enough to cause the formation of gas pockets. It should not be able to produce much gas at that temperature, yet it was still coming and was not being depleted. The scientist posited there must be a different mechanism responsible for continuous gas generation at that depth. Such as Gaia and her co-horts, Uzmahndey posited himself.

He turned off his phone. Another weird place connected to the interior of the planet. That's what this Bizarro world tour was all about. This gas pocket feeding the flame was yet another portal into the realm of ancient aliens posing as mythological creatures dwelling in the interior of the Earth.

Charlie had a frown for him when she came down with Angela for the complimentary breakfast. "I'm not a princess."

"You heard that? I thought you were asleep."

"I told her what you said." Angela sat at the table with him, while Charlie went off to find something to eat.

He laughed. "You're learning. That is typical female behavior. Ganging up with another woman against an outnumbered male."

"You are happy I told her?"

"Impressed at how you are behaving more and more like a real woman. Your learning program is good."

"You can help me become more of a real woman."

"Ewww." Charlie returned with donuts and milk and a sour face.

"And Snugglesaurus is doing a good job teaching you. That is a typical teenage reaction to the notion of adults having sex."

"*Who* taught *you* how to be such a jerk?" Charlie scowled from one face to the other. "If you two ever do it make sure I'm not in the room."

After breakfast they checked out and made the short drive to the trailhead parking. The first part of the hike was easy. The moderately-difficult part came when they made a steep descent down into a ravine. At the bottom a twisty trail followed a narrow creek, which they had to cross and re-cross several times as they struggled through a hemlock grove.

Rounding a bend, Eternal Flame Falls came into view. The waterfall was about thirty feet high, and was running well. Near the bottom of it, set back within a little grotto, was the flame. It flickered about a foot high behind the curtain of falling water. Angela extracted a Cheerio from the Tupperware container and approached the flame, while Uzmahndey and Charlie stood back and watched.

The flame went out. Angela froze, then looked back at them as if uncertain how to proceed.

"I read this happens," Uzmahndey said. He produced a book of matches. "You have to relight it." He stepped up to do this.

Angela blocked his way. "Stay back with Charlie." She took the matches from him. Holding the book tight inside a clenched fist to keep it dry, she thrust her hands through the falling water far back in the grotto to strike a match.

The explosion knocked her fifty feet through the air. From out of the huge burst of flame a dazzling male figure clad in leather armor and brilliant light swelled out of the grotto through the rushing water to tower in midair above Uzmahndey and Charlie. A fireball formed in his upraised right hand. He hurled it at Charlie. Uzmahndey dashed to shield her, twisting his body as he timed his leap perfectly. The fireball struck him in the back, setting him ablaze.

Uzmahndey opened his eyes to see the Raiders head coach kneeling over him. "Just lie still. Don't try to get up, don't move. The cart is coming."

"Chucky?"

The head coach grinned just like the possessed puppet of the movies. "You know I don't like to be called that."

"Sorry, Coach Gruden."

The cinematic grin faded. "That's better."

"My back feels like it's broken. What happened?"

"You went up for a high pass. You were fully extended when Logan Wilson drilled you."

"Damn Logan Wilson." Uzmahndey closed his eyes.

"Uz! Uz!"

Uzmahndey opened his eyes. Jon Gruden was gone. Logan Wilson towered above him. He appeared concerned. "Get up, Uz. Get back in the game."

Logan Wilson stepped aside as Charlie kneeled at his feet. What was she doing out on the playing field? She was crying. "Can you move?"

Good question. But Coach had told him not to. Where was that damn cart?

"Angela's hurt."

Damn, *he* was hurt. How did Angela get hurt? Then he remembered seeing her fly backward through the air. The blazing monster had emerged from the falls. Thrown fire at Charlie. He had run to protect her, deflecting the fireball away from her, just like he would tip an errant pass away from a defender trying to intercept it. Damn, he had run fast. He had never moved so fast in his life, or jumped so high. Then Logan Wilson had leveled him.

No. It wasn't Logan Wilson. It had been the fireball. He was badly burned. Could he move? He moved his legs. Good, he wasn't paralyzed. "Tell Coach I don't need the cart. I can get up."

"What cart?" Charlie asked.

Uzmahndey stirred. It hurt. Then he remembered. "You said Angela's hurt?"

"Yes. She's hurt bad."

He peered into Charlie's face. "Are you hurt?"

"No. You saved my life. Again."

"That's what we do. We're teammates. We've got each other's backs." *His* back was in agony. He slowly, slowly, crawled to his feet. Charlie supported him, helped him up, steadied him once he was upright. The rush of pain nearly leveled him.

Charlie hugged him.

"Not so tight," he gasped. "Don't hold me so tight."

"I'm sorry!" Charlie eased up, tears flowing.

After several more gasping breaths, the darkness cleared. He didn't think he'd pass out again. He looked around. Angela lay motionless in the creek twenty yards downfield. He shook his head, trying to clear it. He wasn't on a field. In a stadium. He was beside a creek. Soaking wet. "Why am I so wet?"

"You were on fire. I rolled you into the creek."

"Help me get to Angela." He leaned heavily on Charlie as she escorted him to the unmoving form. By the time they reached her he was nearly walking on his own. Charlie started to ease him down, but she lost her grip and he tumbled down on top of Angela.

"I'm sorry." Charlie bawled. "I'm so sorry."

Uzmahndey rolled off Angela. He had just tackled her and she wasn't moving. Not a good sign. They might need to bring the cart out after all.

Stop acting goofy. You're not in a game. You didn't tackle her. She's off. You need to restart her.

Uzmahndey looked her over. She didn't appear too badly burned. On her upper right arm he spied a small blackened patch of skin that had peeled away. He leaned in for a closer look. A dim light flashed just underneath the burn. Circuitry?

"Angela." Her eyes were closed, her face lax. "Are you okay?" No response.

Charlie was frantic. "We've got to get her to a hospital."

"We can't. They'd take her apart to see what she is."

"Then what do we do?"

Uzmahndey shrugged Charlie's hands off when she tried to help him up. He made it to his knees by himself. He was feeling stronger, and the pain was less. This brought a smile. "You guys are working fast."

<u>You have a high tolerance for pain.</u>

"Of course I do. I'm a football player."

"Are you okay?" Charlie asked. "You keep talking to yourself."

"It's a habit of mine." He looked Angela over. "What do you think is wrong with her?"

"Maybe she's in shock," Charlie suggested.

<u>She was knocked off-line.</u>

"What do I do?"

"I don't know."

Uzmahndey glanced at Charlie. "I'm not talking to you. I'm talking to myself."

<u>You need to reboot her.</u>

"How do I do that?"

<u>Snugglesaurus says there is a bone at the top of her spine at the back of her neck. Press on it for ten seconds.</u>

Uzmahndey slipped his hand behind her neck. He found the protruding bone, and pressed. After ten seconds Angela's eyes closed.

"You killed her," Charlie whispered.

"Have I?"

<u>No. Have patience.</u>

After thirty tense seconds, her eyes opened. She looked up at Uzmahndey. "What happened?"

Uzmahndey was so overjoyed she had spoken he didn't notice how she had spoken. Or how she looked. But as Angela continued to stare blankly up at him, the pitch of her monotone voice sank in. "She's like she was."

"What do you mean?" Charlie asked.

"That first day when she walked into my office back in Hilo. She was expressionless, and her voice had no inflection to it."

"I don't remember her like that."

"Of course not. You were three months old."

Angela looked around. "Where are we?"

"At Eternal Flame Falls. You were knocked off line. I had to reboot you."

After helping Angela to her feet, Uzmahndey looked to Charlie. "She's lost everything she learned about being human. She's back to square one."

Angela turned away.

"What are you doing?" Not receiving an answer, Uzmahndey started after her.

She stopped to stare at him. "Stay with Charlie." Angela walked up to the falls and reached through the curtain of water into the grotto and around the flickering flame to place a xenobot in the portal.

Charley held her breath. "Will she get blasted again?"

"I don't know. Guys?"

Maybe not. That explosion and fireball could be all that fiery guy had.

Angela withdrew her unclenched hand from the grotto and turned away.

So far so good. Keep your fingers crossed.

"My fingers aren't crossed."

"Mine are." Charlie held up both hands.

Angela rejoined them. She took one of Charlie's upraised hands. "Come." She led her up the creek away from the falls.

Uzmahndey fell into step behind.

"Where are we going?"

"Skaftafellsjokull Glacier."

"Never heard of it. Where's it at?"

"Iceland."

With each step Uzmahndey took on the trail back to the Jeep the pain eased. Pain was nothing new to him. Throughout his football career he had endured blows that would have incapacitated most men. It seemed like he would recover from this, too, at least physically.

Mentally was another matter. Why had he done that? Sacrificed himself for someone he had known for only a couple of weeks? Charlie, walking ahead alongside Angela, who had a secure grip on her hand, kept looking back at him shuffling along behind. She seemed scared. He supposed that was a natural response for a twelve year old girl to what had just happened.

Had his response been natural? Or had the xenobots seized control of his body at the moment of crisis? To carry out the prime directive, which seemed to be to protect Charlie? Had they forced him to risk his life to save hers? It had all happened so fast. He had reacted so heedless of his own well-being. Had he had a choice?

No, you didn't. But not for the reason you think.

You don't stop to consider your options while you're playing football. Things happen so fast in a game you don't have time to think. Your reflexes take over.

That's what happened back there, big guy. What you did was a result of your reflexes taking over. Not us controlling you.

You are in total control of your body. We've told you that.

It has to be that way. Can you imagine the four of us hashing out every move? Someone has to be in control. It would be chaos otherwise.

Besides, who says we all agreed with what you did?

That took Uzmahndey so by surprise he blurted aloud.

"What?"

Angela and Charlie both looked back at this. "Are you alright?" Charlie asked.

She still looked so frightened. Why? The danger was over. But he had other things on his mind at the moment. "I'm good. Keep going."

<u>I agreed.</u>

<u>I had my doubts.</u>

<u>*I thought we were dead. Talk about prime directives. My prime directive is to stay alive. You do realize that when you die, we three die, too.*</u>

<u>Now you need to stop distracting us.</u>

<u>We have a lot of work to do.</u>

<u>*So leave us alone and let us fix you.*</u>

When they reached the Jeep, Angela dug through the suitcases to find clothes she and Uzmahndey could replace their burnt rags with. While she was busy, Charlie pulled him aside. "Is she okay?"

"No. But she doesn't seem to realize that."

"What do we do?"

"What we've been doing, I guess. Our world tour."

"With her in this condition?"

"I'm sure Snugglesaurus will continue to help."

Charlie glanced down at the stuffed dinosaur in her grasp. She hugged it close with one arm. With her other she hugged Uzmahndey. "You'll help, too. Right?"

"Of course." When Uzmahndey hugged her in return he was surprised it didn't hurt too badly.

<u>*You're welcome.*</u>

After Uzmahndey eased out of his burnt clothes down to his undershorts, Angela looked his back over. Some of the burns had already healed, many more were in the process. "You'll be okay." She then stripped off her own scorched rags, not stopping at her underwear like Uzmahndey had.

Several nearby parties gawked while she dug through a suitcase for clean clothes, in no particular hurry. Charlie hid out in the Jeep. Uzmahndey glared all around. Failing to deter several young men from watching, he turned to Angela. "Will you hurry up."

He then stared, too, but not for the same salacious reason as the young men. She should have been injured much worse than him, the explosion had hit her right in the face. Damn, she was rugged.

Angela finished dressing, at last. She and Uzmanhdey joined Charlie in the Jeep, and they were underway.

Chapter 9

Skaftafellsjokull Glacier

Uzmahndey opened the in-dash navigation program to plot a course from Eternal Flame Falls trailhead parking to the nearest Wal-Mart to buy cold weather clothes for the trip to Iceland and pajamas for Angela. When he next went to plot the best route to New York City, he was surprised to discover a route to Newark Liberty International Airport had already been plotted, and that three tickets for a flight to Iceland the next morning had been purchased in their names. Snugglesaurus had been busy. Along the way they stopped at a Goodwill to donate their camping gear.

During the hours-long drive Uzmahndey had ample time to dwell on his primary problem. Angela. He had gotten a glimpse of her innards, but that wasn't definitive proof that she was a robot. She could have a prosthetic arm. Prosthetics were becoming incredibly advanced. So she could still be a real woman. Who wanted to make love to him. He had been tempted. Yet he believed her, even if fully human, to be either delusional or Machiavellian. Despite that he had been tempted, he couldn't deny. She was gorgeous. If she really *was* a robot, she was a more advanced model than anything he had ever heard of. Also, whoever had written her learning program was brilliant. She had started out so cold, yet had become so likable. So fuckable. Uzmahndey had been seriously conflicted.

He looked in the rearview into the back seat. Angela sat upright with perfect posture, rigid as a statue, staring blank-faced out at the passing scenery. Who was he trying to kid? She was definitely a robot. He had rebooted her. Like a computer. Now she was back to being a nonentity. She was behaving like he imagined a robot would behave. The attraction was gone, the sexual tension dialed down. So the matter was settled. For a while, at least. She had learned to be human once. Would she learn again? Would she ever become as alluring as she had been before the explosion at Eternal Flame Falls?

Having no one else to talk to, he muttered under his breath, "Do you three have names?"

<u>No.</u>

"Then I'll give you names. How about Good, Bad, and Ugly?"

<u>Which one is which?</u>

"You three figure it out."

<u>*I am definitely not the ugly one.*</u>

Arriving at the airport, Uzmahndey turned in the Jeep to the rental company, collected the tickets, then caught a taxi to the nearby hotel Snugglesaurus had booked them into. After a subdued dinner, they went to their room.

Charlie dragged Uzmahndey into the bathroom and shut the door. "Am I supposed to sleep with her?"

Uzmahndey tried to ease her near-panic. "You've been sleeping next to her this whole trip."

"Not with this zombie."

"Charlie, she's the same person." He sighed at her scowl. "The same robot. She is still looking out for you, trying to take care of you, protecting you. She will definitely not harm you."

"Maybe not on purpose. But she's not in her right mind."

"She was in this same state of mind when she nursed you."

Charlie appeared doubtful. "She breast-fed me? When I was a baby? You saw her do this?"

He smiled, nodding.

"How does a robot breast-feed a baby?"

"I don't know how a *real* woman does it. I'd never seen it take place before I watched Angela nurse you."

"Did you get a thrill out of watching?"

"No!" Damn, teenagers could be mean. Uzmahndey ran his fingers across burn scars that were mere hints of what they had been. "What if I sleep with her? And you get a bed to yourself?"

There was no problem when Uzmahndey insisted Angela get into her new pajamas. To his consternation, she began undressing immediately instead of going into the bathroom like he had expected her to do. So he turned his back until she finished changing.

The problem arose when he suggested she climb into bed with him instead of Charlie. She insisted on sleeping with Charlie so she could guard her during the night. When Charlie insisted on sleeping by herself, it was Angela who came up with the solution. She pulled a chair up beside Charlie's bed and planted herself in it. This was as much a relief to Uzmahndey as it was to Charlie. She wouldn't be sleeping with him, either. Angela didn't sleep anyway, so why did she need a bed?

All during the night he kept waking up and glancing over to the other bed. Each time he found Angela sitting unmoved in the same rigid upright posture staring down at Charlie. At least Charlie seemed to be getting a good night's sleep. Somehow.

In the morning Uzmahndey gently probed Angela, trying to ascertain if any changes had taken place during the night. She seemed as stoic as ever since the explosion at Eternal Flame Falls. He couldn't remember how the humanizing learning program had gone before. It had been so gradual, and at first he hadn't realized the program was running. Now that he was aware of it, and watching for it, it seemed not to be working at all. Which was more disturbing? When she behaved like a woman or when she behaved like a robot? He honestly couldn't decide.

After that, the usual bustle of boarding an airplane occupied his attention. The flight itself wasn't bad. Even with the time difference, it was still morning when their plane touched down in Iceland at Keflavic International. Yet by the time they passed through customs, collected their luggage, grabbed lunch, and caught a tram to a car rental it was early afternoon.

Uzmahndey was happy to learn people drove on the right side (which meant the correct side as far as he was concerned) of the road in Iceland. A five-hour drive along the south coast went as their travels across the United States had gone, with Uzmahndey in front by himself driving, Angela in back engaged with watching the passing scenery, and Charlie next to her, only not as close as before, engaged with Snugglesaurus.

This time Uzmahndey didn't lose himself in thought, or fruitless scanning of the radio dial. He was too caught up with the passing scenery. He had never been in such a northern clime. His eyes veered from the snow-covered mountains on one side of the two-lane highway to the open expanse of Atlantic Ocean on the other, an ever-changing wonderland of jagged snowy white peaks and robust whitecaps.

They drove past Skaftafellsjokull Glacier. The end of this huge tongue of ice sliding down out of the mountains toward the sea could be seen from the road. Google directed them a little ways further to the town of Hof. The lodging Snugglesaurus had selected was the Adventure Hotel, which was next to a curious structure. The Hof Turf Church was a small one-story building with a roof covered in grass. It seemed like the structure was melting into the green landscape. In the adjoining churchyard graves burbled up out of the ground like grim grassy bubble wrap.

The Adventure Hotel was an ordinary unimposing lodge in an extraordinarily imposing setting. Outside in its backyard stunning mountains rose to great snow-covered heights, while inside was unadorned functionality. Which presented a problem. Their tight little room had one double bed, and didn't have a private bathroom.

Uzmahndey was too tired to worry about it. After dropping off their suitcases, they went to the restaurant for dinner. Angela watched Uzmahndey and Charlie devour a local favorite suggested to them, plokkfiskur, described by their waiter as a mashed fish stew, while she pretended to nibble on rye bread. By the time they finished it was dark, so they ventured outside to view a glorious performance put on by the northern lights. The xenobots kept Uzmahndey comfortably warm in the frigid night, while Charlie never complained of the cold.

They eventually went back to their room to prepare for bed. Everyone turned their backs to each other as they undressed. Modesty went out the window after Uzmahndey was down to his undershorts. Angela and Charlie, having donned pajamas, both examined his bare back. "It's nearly healed," Charlie marveled.

Angela poked at it.

"Ow. Take it easy, it's still tender."

Charlie gently traced the outlines of scars. "You saved my life."

"Stop it. You're making them itch."

Uzmahndey and Charlie climbed into bed back to back, positioning themselves as far apart as possible. Just before turning off the light, he glanced over his shoulder. Angela was poised erect in a chair on the other side of the bed, staring at Charlie. How could that poor girl sleep?

The next morning they rose early and drove to Skaftafell Visitor Center. Uzmahndey picked up the three tickets Snugglesaurus had reserved for a tour with Arctic Adventures. They joined a small group of a dozen or so. The tour company outfitted them with what they needed to hike on the glacier, such as crampons for their hiking boots and a straight-hilt pickaxe that could be used for a walking stick as well as for climbing. Their guide assured this was the easiest hike offered and didn't require training, yet they would get to walk on Skaftafellsjokull Glacier as well as see Svartifoss Waterfall.

Uzmahndey abandoned his many worries and gloried in the wonderland of ice he ventured into. For once someone else was the guide, so he could relax and experience the adventure without responsibilities. They hiked a dirt trail up into a craggy heath then took an even rockier trail descending into a ravine down to a creek. They followed the narrow winding creek to the base of the falls. Water plunged over a cliff sixty-six feet high before a sheer wall of black basalt columns.

After everyone in the group had taken all the pictures they desired, the guide led them back out and onto the trail to the Skaftafellsjokull. This foot path became more treacherous and rocky as it ascended on its approach to the glacier. They hiked parallel to the ice behemoth, crossing rickety wooden foot bridges and ducking through shallow ice caves. At an easily-accessible point the guide led the group up onto the glacier. They carefully made their way across the ice, maneuvering around crevasse after crevasse.

At one large crevasse Angela kneeled as if attending to a hiking boot. Aware of what she was up to, Uzmahndey positioned himself to shield her from view of the guide. He watched her toss a Cheerio into the crevasse. As it disappeared into the inky depths he caught a glimpse of something deep within - red glowing eyes in a large shadowy form. He wondered what it would do. The creature at Eternal Flame Falls had hurled fire at them. Would this monster attack them with ice? Hurl icicle spears at them? Split open the ice under their feet so the glacier would swallow them? But Angela turned away without incident. Uzmahndey remained vigilant through the rest of the tour, expecting the ice monster to rise up out of one of the crevasses they passed by to slay Charlie. But the rest of the hike was uneventful.

On the hike back to Skaftafell Visitor Center, Uzmahndey pulled Angela aside. "I saw something in the crevasse where you tossed the Cheerio."

"Another of Gaia's children."

"Why didn't it attack us?"

"We've proven ourselves not so easy to kill. They will pick their battles more carefully."

Back in their room they followed the same procedure as before, turning their backs on each other while undressing for bed. Charlie climbed in and turned onto her side away from Uzmahndey, while he stretched out on a precarious perch upon his side with his back to her on the opposite edge of the bed. Angela scooted her chair up next to Charlie and positioned herself for the night's vigil.

Uzmahndey felt Charlie scoot her back up to his back. "Stop it."

Charlie giggled. "I like sleeping with a man."

"We're not sleeping together. We're sharing a bed." He bumped her away with his butt.

"Stop it. You're going to knock me out of bed."

"Then stay on your side."

"Is there a problem?" Angela asked.

"Charlie is being a brat."

"It's a small bed."

"I could change places with Uzmahndey," Angela suggested.

That settled Charlie down. She scooted away to the edge of her side, her rigid back as far from Uzmahndey as the bed would allow.

Uzmahndey wondered if that light-hearted threat Angela made was a sign of progress. Was the learning program beginning to run again? Or was he grasping at straws? He missed the woman Angela had become. He wanted her back. Only for companionship, of course. There were other uses for her besides sex.

"Angela?"

"Yes?"

"Charlie made my scars itch." The cover was pulled down from his shoulders, and Angela's nails lightly grazed his back. He sighed with contentment. Five minutes later, he said, "You can stop now."

She did.

"Thank you, Angela." There was no reply as she drew the cover back up over his shoulders. He knew without looking she had taken her seat and resumed her watch over Charlie. Uzmahndey drifted contentedly off to sleep.

Chapter 10

Fingal's Cave

Uzmahndey awoke the following morning with his nose itching. He opened his eyes to stare into a pair of glass eyes. Snugglesaurus was on his face. That was because Charlie was practically on top of him. She was still sound asleep. He tried his best to extricate himself without waking her. Surprisingly, he succeeded. Angela sat in her chair by the other side of the bed staring down at Charlie. Her stony expression seemed unchanged from the day before. Damn.

Turning his attention back to Charlie, he saw why she had invaded his space during the night. It was because she required much more space. She had grown again. Damn, and damn. That's all he needed. Now he had *two* zombies to lead around. Since Charlie was still asleep, and Angela was ignoring him and focused on her charge, he grabbed his shaving kit and headed for the common bathroom down the hall.

Upon his return nothing had changed, except that Charlie, still asleep, was sprawled across the entire bed. In tight pajamas that no longer fit, he could tell she was now well into her teens. He turned to Angela as he dressed. "How old is she now?"

"Fifteen."

"Can you get her up? We need to get going." When Angela started to rouse her, he dropped off his kit and bolted out the door. "I'm going for coffee."

Uzmahndey checked his phone while drinking coffee in the lobby. Snugglesaurus had booked them on a flight out of Keflavik to Glasgow. When he wondered why they were headed for Scotland, classical music began playing. He checked to see it was 'Fingal's Cave', from The Hebrides Overture by Felix Mendelssohn. Such weirdness no longer seemed so weird anymore. He assumed this was being accomplished by Snugglesaurus for his edification. He listened while finishing his coffee.

Just as the strings were whipped into a frenzy at the climax, to be replaced at the very end by a haunting melody played on a lone flute, Angela led Charlie into the breakfast nook. Charlie looked more like a robot than the robot did. On their last shopping trip he had wisely insisted she get pants with an elastic waist. Still, the bottoms of the legs were way up past her ankles. He swore silently as he realized another shopping trip was in his immediate future.

Angela settled Charlie into a chair at Uzmahndey's table then went to find her something to eat and drink. Charlie clutched Snugglesaurus with both hands while examining the tabletop. Despite everything, he couldn't help but smile at her slack face. "Good morning, princess."

She looked up at Uzmahndey, needing a moment to focus on him, frowned, then looked back down at the tabletop.

Angela returned with donuts and milk. "Don't irritate her."

She had heard what he'd said to Charlie? From across the room? He hadn't spoken that loudly. He needed to keep in mind how sharp her hearing was. To escape from the two grim faces, he went for a second cup of coffee.

Upon completing the morning-long drive back to Keflavik airport, they went through the same routine as before: turn in the rental car, collect their tickets, check their luggage, grab a bite for lunch. Then wait.

At Glasgow airport they caught a bus for the west coast, then a ferry to the Isle of Mull. It was nearly dark when their taxi dropped them off at Glengorm Castle. Uzmahndey's face beamed as he gazed upon the magnificent fairytale castle situated on rolling lush green hills overlooking the ocean. "I've never stayed at a castle before."

"We're in the stables," Angela replied, as monotone as ever.

Uzmahndey's nose unwrinkled when he realized the building that had housed the stables was no longer used as a stable. The Steadings housed four modern suites within the remodeled old structure. Uzmahndey was very pleased as he conducted a walk-through, until he came to the bedroom. "One bedroom," he declared in a dour voice. "With one bed."

"For you and Charlie," Angela declared without interest.

"Charlie is fifteen now. She's too old for us to be sleeping together."

"Definitely," Charlie chimed in.

Uzmahndey stooped to confront Snugglesaurus, clutched by Charlie. "From now on take Charlie's age into consideration when making arrangements for us." He turned to Angela. "So what's the plan?"

"We have tickets tomorrow morning for a tour of Fingal's Cave."

Uzmahndey turned toward the door. "This is my first stay in a castle. I'm exploring."

"Be careful," Angela said.

Uzmahndey studied her face. Did she care about his safety? Or only how her mission could be impacted if something happened to him? Could she be concerned for him, or was he merely projecting his hopes onto her? Still, her tone of voice hinted at a slight thawing. Or was that more projecting on his part? That humanizing program could be running again, if slower than before. He smiled at her. "Sure thing, babe." Then walked out.

Uzmahndey strolled about the grounds. The castle had been restored to a pristine condition it surely never possessed when first constructed. It was set on a hilltop with an incredible view of the ocean. The Hebrides, of which Mull was one of many isles, were stark green rocky gems arrayed all across the vast dark waters.

Uzmahndey walked inside and roamed through the main hall, the library, and the sitting room. At the front desk he learned there was a walking path that passed by some standing stones en route to the ruins of Dun Ara Castle.

He set off across gentle rolling green pastures. No other hikers were encountered, although he did see several grazing sheep, and pigeons flying about. The portentous standing stones he passed were sleek and spear-shaped, not large and blocky like the ones at Stonehenge he had seen so many images of. Stark and somber, they stood alone, or in rows, or in groups of three encircled with smaller stones. Mysterious mystical patterns from out of the unfathomable pre-legendary past.

Not much remained of Dun Ara Castle, which sat atop a cliff directly above the ocean. He could vaguely make out the outline of the foundation. Below he saw a bathing pool. From the top of the high cliff he gazed down upon the waves crashing into the rocks far below, as he imagined knights of old had done.

Uzmahndey wasn't tired, although he had risen before dawn to drive five hours to the airport in Iceland, spent several hours waiting for then embarking on a flight to Scotland, taken a two-hour bus and ferry ride to Mull Island, and hiked a mile to the cliff he now stood atop. The xenobots were amazing. He couldn't get this world tour over fast enough. When he got back in the league he would set records.

Then a nasty thought popped up. "Can you three be detected?"

"No," he heard his old LSU head coach say. "They have fully integrated into your system."

Uzmahndey had become so accustomed to hearing voices in his head, even that of his old college coach, he hardly missed a beat. "So they are not producing a performance-enhancing drug, or anything that will show up under testing?"

"No one will be able to detect them, not with the present level of human technology."

"What all are they doing to me?"

"They are not harming you in any way. In fact, they will defend you as best they can. As they have already done on several occasions. Their survival depends upon your survival."

"So what was their intended purpose? Why is Angela placing them everywhere?"

"They have many functions. One I already told you about. Another is to explore and communicate their findings. Much like the robot space ships NASA sends out."

"So the xenobots inside me are communicating with you?"

"They can, but they are mostly communicating with the AI. Even though you put them to a use they were not designed for. They have adapted well." A young bearded man in light armor carrying a broad sword stepped out from behind a section of castle wall that still stood.

"You're a knight now?"

"I have adopted the form of one who once lived here in this castle."

"Who are you really?"

"I am sentient information. Information can take any form, from cave art to quantum bits. This is a form you can comprehend."

"You said you were a hologram."

"I can fashion holograms. Such as this one. Would you prefer a little green man?"

"No, this is good. Can others see you? You're not just inside my head?"

"I'm not inside your head. Others can see me."

Uzmahndey gazed all around. "If someone saw you they would probably assume you were a ghost haunting these old ruins." He focused on the young knight. "What is generating this image? Snugglesaurus?"

"No. The AI works the Internet to produce wealth, manipulate financial accounts, purchase plane tickets and bus tickets, reserve rooms. It generally takes care of whatever business can be accomplished remotely, which is practically everything."

"Even through encryption and firewalls?"

The knight chuckled. "There is nothing that can obstruct Snugglesaurus. It is exponentially more powerful than the quantum computers your scientists are struggling to create."

"Charlie clings to it."

"That is because it downloads cultural information it gleans from the Internet directly into her brain so she can function somewhat normally."

"Where do you come from?"

"I'm not of your world. Does where really matter?"

Uzmahndey studied the broadsword. "Will that blade cut me?" When the Ghost raised it up toward him, Uzmahndey reached for it. His hand passed through without resistance.

"Don't think that I'm unreal, like this sword. Immaterial, but real."

Uzmahndey lowered his arm.

"Where are you projecting this image from?"

"I *am* this image, which is standing right here in front of you." Uzmahndey started to object, but Ghost spoke up first.

"We can finish this conversation another time. You need to start back. It is getting late."

"Wouldn't the xenobots take care of me?"

"You wouldn't get lost. They could guide you back in the dark. But it's tricky for people to walk at night through unfamiliar terrain."

"If I twisted an ankle they could heal it, couldn't they?"

"Yes. They can repair your body. Like they have your injured knee."

"I'm counting on that. I can get banged up pretty bad playing football."

The knight shook his head. "Such a wasteful use of this technology."

"But they are mine to use?"

"Yes. If you complete this mission you can keep them."

"Then let's keep this show rolling." Uzmahndey set off for the castle. "The sooner we finish, the sooner I get back in pads." When Ghost didn't respond, he looked back over his shoulder. The young knight was gone.

It was pitch black by the time Uzmahndey returned to their suite in the Steadings. He was surprised to find Charlie wearing shorts.

"Angela cut the legs off," she exclaimed, pleased. "This is better than wearing jeans way too short for me."

Uzmahndey frowned. "You can't help them being tight, but did they have to be so short?"

Charlie looked to Snugglesaurus. "This is the style on the Internet."

"Most of the women you see on the Internet are either models or Photoshopped to look like models. Not many images of real people are on the Internet." He looked up to the ceiling. "Ghost, this is the problem with Charlie getting her education off the Internet. She'll get a warped version of the world."

Angela looked up to the ceiling. "Who are you talking to?"

"A knight I met at Dun Ara Castle. But he's not answering." He looked back to Charlie. "We'll get you some decent clothes first chance we get."

Uzmahndey couldn't believe he had just offered to go on another shopping trip. He must really be frazzled. He sat down to remove his shoes. "I'm ready for bed."

Angela stood. "You and Charlie can go to bed. I'll sit up."

"I and Charlie are not going to bed. Charlie is fifteen now. Charlie is going to bed and I'm taking the couch."

The next day they checked out and caught a taxi to the tour company Snugglesaurus had booked them with. A brief boat ride took them to little Staffa Island, half a mile long and a quarter-mile wide. Their group disembarked near the entrance to Fingals Cave. A narrow stony path took them along the shore around the base of hexagonal black basalt columns. Well aware of how clumsy Charlie could be following a growth spurt, Angela held her hand, while Uzmahndey kept a close watch on both females.

The path led them into the cave on fractured columns that formed a walkway just above the sloshing water. Where it became even narrower a metal railing was there to hold onto, while in other places there was a cable secured to the wall. The group proceeded carefully on the slick rock. The opening was wide, allowing waves to rush into the cave, and ample light to flood in and illuminate the musty interior. Much of the cave walls were made up of six-sided pillars similar to the hexagonal black basalt columns outside.

It took only a few steps for the light to fade into shadows. A dense dancing gloom permeated the moist misty atmosphere, shifting shadows performing on the glistening jagged stone walls. Uzmahndey understood the mysterious attraction this cave had engendered in people over the centuries. Felix had gotten it right with his music.

Charlie brought the other two to an abrupt halt. "Listen."

Uzmahndey and Angela stopped to listen. The wind blowing into the cave hummed a low melody, barely audible, haunting. The wind, water, shadows, stark sharply-shaped rock all combined to impress a spiritual presence in the narrow dark dank confines. Had Stone Age people ventured there? Ancient Druids? Medieval Scottish monks? Vikings?

There was a splash. A woman in their group had slipped and fallen into the water. Several people slipped on the wet rock, also, nearly falling in themselves. What was going on? Everyone had been progressing so smoothly before. Now they were jerking about like spasmodic puppets on tripwire strings.

Uzmahndey, with an assist from his xenobots, lifted the woman out and back up onto the path. She was soaking wet and cold, but otherwise appeared unharmed. Yet the expression on her face was panicked. Uzmahndey tried to reassure her. "You're okay now."

She lunged away out of his grasp without a thank you, nearly falling back in the water. The guide ushered everyone toward the cave entrance in a rush. Several other people lost their balance and slipped, although no one else fell in.

Angela entrusted Charlie's hand to Uzmahndey then ventured deeper into the cave. While the two of them hung back and watched, Angela, from as deep into the cave as it was possible to go, tossed a Cheerio even deeper. It disappeared into the gloom. She rejoined them, and they made their way out.

Emerging from the cave, Charlie was still awed by the experience. "That was incredible."

"Yes, it was," Uzmahndey agreed.

"You think so because you didn't see the hideous creature producing that music." When he and Charlie both turned questioning faces to Angela, she continued. "It was hidden deep in the shadows."

"Why didn't it attack us?" Uzmahndey asked.

"It did. Its music was its attack." Angela twisted her lips into a grotesque sliver of a smile. "It didn't work. On us. Everyone else seemed disturbed by it."

"What in the living hell are you talking about?" Uzmahndey asked.

"It didn't affect me because I'm not human. It didn't affect you because the xenobots buffered your ears. And it didn't affect Charlie. This is certainly good to learn."

"Why do you say that?"

"Because most likely the Schumann Resonances won't affect her any more than that music did." Angela turned away, the automated mask back in place.

But he had seen that brief smile flicker across it. Angela had enjoyed thwarting the creature she claimed was lurking in the cave. The program was working. The ice queen was thawing. Which meant relationships between the three could soon get complicated once again. That was a concern for later. At the moment all he could think was, what music? He had heard nothing but the humming of the wind blowing through the cave. And what the hell were Schumann Resonances?

Chapter 11

Giant's Causeway

The tour boat dropped them back on the Isle of Mull, a ferry took them back to the mainland, and a bus transported them back to Glasgow. As Uzmahndey had insisted, Snuggle-saurus had this time secured them a hotel room with two beds. Charlie collapsed on one, and Uzmahndey kicked his shoes off and stretched out on the other.

"We need to go shopping for Charlie," Angela said before he could even uncurl his toes.

"Can't you go without me?" he growled. "The sales clerks can help you more with styles and fashions than I ever could."

"We need to stay together."

With a moan, Uzmahndey was up. Despite all his complaining, it wasn't a bad evening. He'd never been to Glasgow before. It was an ancient city crammed with historic gothic architecture in several little knotted-up neighborhoods overflowing with sensory delights. They spent most of the evening in the medieval Merchant City district, strolling down Trongate Street viewing well-preserved gems such as Tollbooth Steeple and St. Andrews-by-the-Green, while stepping in and out of quaint well-stocked little shops along the way. The clothes shopping didn't take that long. Charlie was easy to please. Uzmahndey was pleased to see her out of those tight hacked-off short-shorts and into some decent slacks that fit.

Afterwards, they sat down to a nice dinner. Ever the courageous eater, Uzmahndey was eager to try what was advertised as Scotland's national dish, also known as Burn's Supper, in honor of Scottish poet Robert Burns – haggis, neeps and tatties. Charlie, not so brave, inquired of Snugglesaurus what these oddly-named foods were. With a turned-up nose, she related to Uzmahndey that haggis was a boiled mix of sheep's pluck. "I like lamb. What is pluck?"

"Chopped liver, heart, and lungs." Seeing the smile fade from his face, she went eagerly on. "Neeps are mashed turnips, and tatties are mashed potatoes."

Uzmahndey picked the menu back up. "Moving right along."

Charlie, also scanning a menu, burst out laughing. "Here's a good one for you. Rumbeledethumps."

"What the hell? I thought they spoke English here."

"Snugglesaurus says its sautéed cabbage and onions with mashed potatoes."

"That doesn't sound bad."

"How about Cock-a-leekie?"

"Sounds like a venereal disease."

Charlie snorted. "It's not what it sounds like. It's a chicken broth with barley, onions, leeks, and prunes."

"Prunes? That must be where the leaky comes in."

"Then there is Cullen Skink."

"I'm not eating anything that stinks."

"Skink, not stink. It's a chowder with smoked haddock." She continued scanning the menu. "You could try stovies. That's potatoes stewed in dripping and mixed with mincemeat and onions."

"Dripping what?"

Charlie once again consulted Snugglesaurus. "Dripping is either lard or butter."

Despite all his protestations, Uzmahndey ate heartily. Including a double helping of Cranachan for dessert that looked and smelled and tasted so good he forbade Charlie from informing him what was in it. Their waiter suggested they finish their meal with a good whiskey. Uzmahndey took one sip and nearly gagged. What was going on? He liked whiskey, and Scottish was some of the best. But this turned his tongue. He excused himself from the table and stepped outside to find a quiet corner. "What's going on, Good?"

Am I the one you are addressing?

"You are the one who answered to Good. Why can't I drink any more?"

It's not healthy for you.

"I enjoy drinking."

We are charged with maintaining your health.

"That's not the point. You shouldn't control me like this."

You could be attacked at any time. You need to be alert, not impaired.

"I'm willing to take that risk."

But you are also putting Charlie at risk.

"Does that mean once this trip ends I'll be able to drink again?"

If you insist.

"Did you just sigh? Was that a sigh I heard? You can sigh?"

Want to know what was in that Cranachan you just ate two helpings of?

"No, Bad, I don't!"

Another sigh. Does that mean I am to be stuck with the name Ugly?

"If the face fits, wear it."

We don't have faces.

Uzmahndey ignored Good's remark and stomped back in to the table.

Angela appeared worried. "Is everything okay?"

"Looks like I'll be staying sober this whole trip. Damn those busybody xenobots."

"You haven't had a drink since we left Hawaii?"

"No. And it looks like I won't have a drink until I get back there."

"Were you a heavy drinker?" Charlie asked.

"It's none of your business." She continued to stare, until he relented. "Sort of."

"Hold out your hand," Angela said.

He merely stared back. As did she. Until he held his hand out above the table. There was no staring down a robot. Uzmahndey examined his steady hand. "It's not shaking."

"If you were a heavy drinker and you quit cold turkey, shouldn't you be a little shaky?" After Uzmahndey dropped his hand, she said, "It's the xenobots. They will take good care of you, if you let them."

Uzmahndey surreptitiously glanced down to where he held his hand up under the table so the other two couldn't see. It was still motionless. "Damn."

You're welcome.

Uzmahndey dropped his hand and grinned at the other two. "Do you know what this means?" Receiving blank stares, he rushed on to deliver the good news. "No more hangovers when I *do* get back to Hawaii. If they can stop the DT's then they can prevent hangovers." He sat back in his seat, his entire body a satisfied grin. To the sound of a sigh in his head.

Back at their hotel room, Charlie went into the bathroom to change into the new pajamas they had bought. Uzmahndey turned his back to Angela and began undressing. "Is it okay if I join you in bed?"

He looked over his shoulder as he laid his pants aside. Angela stared at him, as blank-faced as ever. Or maybe not quite as ever.

"Charlie says me sitting up staring at her all night bothers her."

"You're in charge of this operation. What does it matter what I prefer?"

Her granite face never flinched.

He sighed. "It's okay, Angela. I don't mind. As long as you put on your pajamas." He climbed in beneath the covers.

When Charlie emerged from the bathroom and encountered Angela waiting to go in to change into her pajamas, she looked at Uzmahndey in consternation.

"It's none of your business."

Uzmahndey studied Angela's not quite blank face as moments later she emerged from the bathroom. "What?"

The vulnerability of her question was not robotic. She was undeniably becoming what she had been before. Which made her attractive to him once again. Too attractive. He felt stirrings from below. "Maybe you should go back to your chair."

"If that's what you want." She turned away from the bed.

"I don't know what I want." He saw her stiffen, half-way between bed and chair. "Come to bed."

She turned back to him. "It makes no difference to me."

"It does me. It's unnatural for you to sit up in a chair all night long. It bothers me, too. Sometimes when I wake up during the night it spooks me to see you sitting there, right beside the bed, staring at Charlie while she sleeps."

Angela settled into bed.

Uzmahndey rolled over away from her. "Besides, I like having you in bed with me."

Angela cuddled up to him from behind.

"Just not too close."

Angela scooted away.

He lay still for a moment. Unable to settle down, he looked over his shoulder. Angela was on her side facing him, eyes wide open, staring. "Close your eyes, Angela."

She closed them.

"Goodnight." He only peeked once after that. To find her eyes still closed. He was then able to go to sleep.

The next morning they boarded a bus for Cainryan, where they caught the ferry to Larne on the east coast of Northern Ireland. It was a pleasant day, so they spent the passage on deck watching the passing scenery. The water was choppy, but Uzmahndey didn't suffer. "Thank you."

<u>No problem.</u>

At Larne, Snugglesaurus had a rental car waiting for them. Uzmahndey wasn't as lucky as he had been in Iceland; in Northern Ireland they drove on the left side of the road. Despite his misgivings, he had no difficulty. Once again, he quietly gave thanks.

<u>No problem.</u>

Since Uzmahndey had never been to Ireland before, Northern or Republic, he insisted on the scenic route. Hugging the east coast as they headed north made it a longer drive. Having spent a full day traveling, they took a room Snugglesaurus had reserved them at Smuggler's Inn, outside of Bushmills.

While they were preparing for bed, Uzmahndey drug Charlie into the bathroom and closed the door. "Are you feeling okay about Angela by now?"

"No! The thought of sleeping with her is still scary."

"She's getting back to how she had been before Eternal Flame Falls."

"I don't care. I don't want to sleep with her."

Uzmahndey studied her face. "You're a terrible liar. I bet her watching you sleep all night doesn't really bother you, either. You manipulative scamp."

Charlie lost control of the smile she was trying to suppress. "You and Angela should be sleeping together."

"You said you didn't want to be in the room if we ever did it."

"I was twelve then."

"That was three days ago."

"Just go ahead and do whatever you want to do." Charlie walked out of the bathroom.

When Uzmahndey emerged he found Angela already in her pajamas standing beside a bed. She appeared puzzled. "Why haven't you two changed?"

"You thought we went in there to put our pajamas on? Together?" Charlie made a face. "Eww, gross." She snatched up her pajamas and ducked back into the bathroom.

"I don't own any pajamas," Uzmahndey said as he undressed. "I could never stand to wear any."

"You wear your underwear to bed."

"Not when I'm sleeping by myself."

"Eww, gross!" came from behind the bathroom door.

"Eavesdropper!" Uzmahndey barked back.

Angela watched with her usual stony expression as he approached the bed. "Don't let me crimp your style. I'm only a machine. You wouldn't think twice about getting naked in front of your car. That's what you compared me to once. Your 'vette."

"Just like a woman. Never forget a slight." Despite the banter, Uzmahndey was pleased. Not only was she becoming more conversant, she had remembered something he had said before Eternal Flame Falls. He walked around the bed she stood next to. "You are way more than a machine."

"I am? Then what am I?"

Uzmahndey climbed in and turned over onto his side away from her facing the wall. "I haven't figured that out yet."

Angela climbed in and scooted up to his back. This time he didn't protest.

The next morning they checked out and drove the short distance from Smuggler's Inn up Causeway Road to the visitor center on the northern coast, where they picked up the passes Snugglesaurus had reserved for them. From there it was a three-quarter mile hike on the Blue Trail to Giant's Causeway; an easy stroll on a kerb stone footpath. To the right rose a sheer rock cliff, to the left the open North Atlantic. A powerful surf sent four-foot waves crashing ashore.

Charlie pulled them aside at a vista, which gave a good view out over Portnaboe Bay. "Do you see Humphrey?"

"Who is Humphrey?" Uzmahndey asked.

"The camel."

Uzmahndey squinted. "I see something. It doesn't look much like a camel."

"He's sitting down."

Suddenly, Humphrey the Camel came into sharp focus for Uzmahndey. "Yes. I see him. Now."

"Your eyesight is getting some help," Angela said, smiling.

He scowled at her. "The xenobots?"

"How can you still be surprised at what they can do for you?"

Charlie nudged him with an elbow. "Just wait until you and Angela are intimate. I bet they improve that experience, too."

Uzmahndey abruptly turned away. "What do you know about that?"

"You think Snugglesaurus hasn't filled me in on that?"

He glared at the stuffed dinosaur in her arms. "What all is it filling her head with?"

"Don't be upset with Snugglesaurus," Angela said. "Age-appropriate sex education is a good thing."

"People have different opinions on what is age appropriate." Uzmahndey took off down the path, and Angela and Charlie fell into step behind. Turning a sharp corner at Windy Gap, the Giant's Causeway stones came into full view. Somewhat-circular columns of all heights, from ground level up to several feet tall, dotted the ocean front. There were thousands, perhaps tens of thousands, up and down the coast. Uzmahndey froze, staring all around. "What caused this?"

Charlie mimicked the Native guide in Canada who had escorted them to see Spotted Lake. "Do you want science or folklore?" When Uzmahndey glared at her, she went on without his answer. "Volcanic activity sixty million years ago. Lava oozed up through the chalk beds, then cooled to form these interlocking basalt columns, each nearly perfectly hexagonal in shape."

"Now the folklore," Angela said.

Uzmahndey looked to her. She appeared anxious to hear the story. Human curiosity? He couldn't help but smile.

"The Irish giant Finn McCool built the Causeway as a bridge to join Ireland to Scotland. He did this to confront the Scottish giant Benandonner, who had been threatening Ireland. Once Finn saw how big Benandonner was, he retreated back to Ireland where, with the help of his wife, he disguised himself as a baby. When Benandonner arrived in pursuit and saw how large Irish babies were, not wanting to confront any full-grown Irish adults he fled back to Scotland, destroying the causeway as he went. There are similar basalt columns on the coast of Scotland to support this story. We saw some of them at Fingal's Cave."

People were scrambling all over the hexagonal stone pillars. Charlie hurried down a gravel path to join them. "Let's go see the Giant's Boot." She hopped across the pillars toward an odd-shaped rock by the water's edge. Angela rushed after, not wanting to let Charlie get too far away.

Uzmahndey followed at a more leisurely pace.

Look out to sea.

Uzmahndey looked, but saw nothing amiss. "I thought I told you guys not to speak unless spoken to."

It's an emergency, dumbass.

"I don't appreciate your attitude, Bad."

<u>Forget about his attitude. You have better eyesight than you are used to having. Look again.</u>

Uzmahndey shaded his eyes with an open hand and focused his gaze far out to sea. He saw a wave. "What is that?"

<u>A rogue wave.</u>

<u>*And you know where it's headed, bright guy? The shore.*</u>

<u>Charlie and Angela are in danger.</u>

Uzmahndey located the two. Charlie was at the water's edge climbing on the Boot, while Angela knelt next to the rock formation, apparently placing a Cheerio at the base of it.

"ANGELA!!"

He bound with furious but sure-footed strides across the slick columns toward them. When she looked up at his charging approach, he pointed out to sea.

Angela turned her eyes to that direction. Seeing what he had seen, she snatched Charlie off the Boot and ran toward Uzmahndey.

Other nearby people heard Uzmahndey's booming cry, and saw the three of them fleeing. They, too, looked out to sea, but their eyesight wasn't as keen as his or Angela's, and they couldn't yet make out the onrushing danger. "Rogue wave!"

Uzmahndey shouted over and over as he ran. As the call spread up and down the coast, people began retreating.

The wave hurtled toward the shore at amazing speed. And grew to an amazing height. Angela, with Charlie in her arms, joined Uzmahndey, and they sprinted away. He looked back. It was coming in too fast. They might not gain the top of the cliffs in time, and all the others who hadn't had as early a start and could not run as quickly definitely would not. This monster could be over a hundred feet high. A lot of people were going to be battered against the rocks or swept out to sea. Reaching the base of the cliff, they scrambled up.

Looking back once more, Uzmahndey saw a large creature riding atop the wave. He appeared human from the waist up, but instead of legs he had the tail of a serpentine fish, and there were bull horns on his head. Yet another ally of Gaia's? How many of these monstrosities were there?

Yet something even more amazing happened before his eyes. Basalt pillars of the hexagonal stones rose from below the water, higher, higher, forming a towering wall. Atop this enormous new causeway structure was a giant bearded long-haired warrior in a green cape brandishing a broadsword.

"Finn McCool," Charlie whispered, in awe.

The tremendous onrushing rogue wave crashed into the wall. Some of the water passed right through, but most subsided, dispersed, or evaporated into spray shooting high into the sky and falling harmlessly as a heavy mist. The half-man half-fish creature riding atop it evaporated along with the rogue wave. The pillar wall, and Finn McCool, dissipated into a heavy fog which moved inland up and down the coast.

Still, the three didn't pause their mad scramble until they reached the top of the cliff. Angela set Charlie down on her feet. Uzmahndey looked out to sea, but the fog was so heavy there was nothing to see. "What just happened?"

Charlie consulted Snugglesaurus. "A rogue wave, like the one a hundred and fifty-four feet high that struck the coast of Ireland in 1985."

"I know what a rogue wave is. I'm talking about all that crazy stuff." He peered into the eyes of Charlie, then Angela. "You did see it. Right? It wasn't just in my head, like before?"

Charlie smiled. "I saw it. Finn McCool just saved Ireland again." When Uzmahndey glared at her in disbelief, she pointed. "If you don't believe me, ask him."

Uzmahndey spun around. The giant he had seen atop the pillar wall now stood behind him. Only this time he was of human proportions. Big, but hardly a giant. He leaned on the hilt of his broadsword as his green cloak billowed in the swirling fog. Uzmahndey was too stunned to speak.

Until Finn McCool did. "That was Oceanus. Another child of Gaia's." The large man did not have an Irish accent. He sounded like his old coach at LSU. It was Ghost.

"How did you do that?"

"By creating a convincing hologram."

"That wall wasn't real?"

"It was real. Holograms are real. I told you that. It just wasn't what it appeared to be. A stone wall."

"But it stopped the rogue wave."

"No, it didn't. Much of the water got through. But it confused Oceanus. He *thought* it was real. I tricked him, like the real Finn McCool tricked Benandonner. Oceanus was so befuddled he lost control, and the rogue wave fell apart. Trouble is, I don't think a ruse like that will work again."

The fog thinned, and the foursome on the cliff top began to draw a crowd. Finn McCool turned to Angela.

"Is Charlie okay?"

After Angela nodded yes, Uzmahndey spoke up. "I'm okay, too, in case you're worried."

Finn McCool smiled at him. "I'm not. You've got three xenobots taking care of you." Looking around at the gathering crowd, he turned back to Angela. "I better go." Fog swirled around the legendary Irish warrior, and he disappeared.

By this time the fog had thinned sufficiently for Uzmahndey to see down to the Giant's Causeway all the way to the water's edge. Most people had gained the cliff top. A few had slipped and fallen on the wet pillars in their mad flight from the rogue wave and been slightly injured. Perhaps a twisted ankle or a wrenched knee, but no one looked too bad off, mostly drenched. Sirens could be heard in the distance.

"We better go," he urged. The three set off for the parking lot.

Uzmahndey was intercepted by a manic man. "Did you see that?"

"Yeah. It looked like a tsunami, but it never reached the shore."

"No! All that crazy stuff. The sea monster on top of the wave. The pillars rising to make a wall. And that giant with a sword on top of it."

Uzmahndey shrugged. "It was foggy, and I was running for my life. I didn't see a whole lot." He abandoned the astonished man and hurried after Angela and Charlie.

Back at the car, Angela told Uzmahndey to open the trunk. When he did, she opened Charlie's suitcase.

"What are you doing?" Charlie asked.

"Finding you some dry clothes."

"We already checked out. Where am I going to change?"

"Right here."

"No way."

Angela turned to Uzmahndey for help.

"People change clothes at their car all the time," he offered.

The fog-shrouded parking lot was not crowded. Most people were still milling about the cliff top. Charlie focused on Uzmahndey. "Turn your back."

When he did, he saw a man passing by stare as Charlie stepped out of her slacks. "She's a little young for you, mister!" Embarrassed, the man hurried on. Angela laughed.

"Just remember you are a lot stronger now than you are used to. If you punch someone you could really hurt them."

He glanced back at Charlie to see how she was doing. She was snapping and zipping a dry pair of slacks, but hadn't put on a shirt yet. He noticed Angela had bought her a bigger bra the night before in Glasgow. He stopped gawking before he could be accused of gawking. "I'm not an NFL player anymore. I'm allowed to punch people."

Once Charlie finished, Angela put her wet clothes into a plastic bag. "Now it's your turn."

"No, I'm good." He started to climb in behind the wheel.

"You need to get out of those wet clothes."

"The xenobots will keep me from getting sick."

"What a hypocrite," Charlie brayed. "It's okay for me to change clothes in public, but you won't do it."

Looking from her mocking face, with an irritated shake of his head he yanked off his shirt.

Charlie laughed. "I'll pick you out something," diving into his suitcase.

Angela took his wet shirt, and his wet pants, too, after he peeled them off.

Charlie offered her selections with a grin.

Uzmahndey scowled at her. "*I* didn't watch *you* change clothes."

Angela smiled. "Yes you did."

This information didn't upset Charlie. "This is too funny not to watch."

"I'm leaving my underwear on."

"Thank God. *That* might get us arrested."

Uzmahndey realized what was happening. They were all releasing a little tension after surviving another attack. Even Angela. She had smiled, for the first time since Eternal Flame Falls. Robots shouldn't need to release tension like this, but humans do. Encouraging. Once everything was packed away in the trunk, they climbed in the car and drove away.

Chapter 12

Long and Black Lakes

Uzmahndey took the direct inland route to Belfast. After what had just happened at Giant's Causeway they were no longer interested in the scenery. At the airport they turned in the rental car then lounged around until it was time for the flight Snugglesaurus had booked them on to depart.

Not much was said during this time, or during their flight to the Azores. Two of them were badly shaken by how close to death they had come. Charlie sought refuge with Snugglesaurus, as usual. Uzmahndey didn't even listen to music on the car radio, or turn on his phone once at the airport. Instead, he stewed. Was this really worth the money? The chance to play in the NFL again? He could have been swept out to sea and drowned. Perhaps the xenobots could have saved him from that. Perhaps. But this wasn't his fight. He was helping who he suspected to be an alien from God-knew-where invade the Earth. Angela claimed Ghost was benevolent, that he was here to save humanity *from* the Earth. But she was a robot built by him. What else *would* she say?

How was that supposed to work, anyway? Saving humanity from the Earth? The accusation of 'traitor' made by that young man in Yellowstone still rang in his ears. Good had told him he was being followed at Devil's Tower, too. How did these people know anything about what was going on? And was he a traitor? Something from inside the Earth, this Gaia and her mythological cohorts, were determined to stop them. It had nearly succeeded at Giant's Causeway, if not for Ghost. He needed to learn more about this powerful creature of sentient information. And how did *that* work, sentient information?

Their flight from Belfast landed at Ponta Delgada Airport on Sao Miguel Island in the Azores late in the afternoon. Since Snugglesaurus couldn't get them a connecting flight to Flores Island until the next morning, the AI had booked them a room at the Azoris Royal Garden. True to Uzmahndey's demand, their room had a double and a twin bed. Charlie promptly claimed the twin by curling up on it with the stuffed Tyrannosaurus. Angela sat down to watch over her. Uzmahndey was too upset to settle down, so he went for a walk.

The lobby was set in a modern tropical motif, well-lit with natural light streaming in through generous windows. Uzmahndey was too distracted to take in much else of what he strode through. He had to make up his mind how much longer he was doing this. He could buy himself a ticket back to Hawaii. But was that what he wanted? Beyond the small fortune, beyond the xenobots that could not only get him back in the NFL but also put him in the record books, what of the others? He had grown to like Charlie. He wasn't sure just what she was exactly, although Angela insisted she was human. And Angela was starting to seem more like a real person again. How good did a simulation need to be before you accepted it as more than a simulation? If it felt like water and tasted like water and nourished like water, wasn't it water?

Uzmahndey's meanderings brought him to a pool table. A game was going on, with several onlookers standing around. Maybe this would ease his stress. He watched the game. They were good. He had no idea what language they were speaking, Portuguese most likely, since the Azores were a possession of Portugal. Once the game ended he indicated he would like to play the winner. Heads nodded assent, and the loser handed him his pool cue. Uzmahndey sank two balls on the break. Then ran the table.

The loser knew enough English to call him Fast Eddie as he opened his wallet and offered a fistful of bills. Uzmahndey hadn't realized they were playing for money. "I only play for fun," he said. He set the wad of foreign bills down on the pool table. "Let it ride." He handed off the pool cue to the next player and walked away.

Several inches above the floor! If that was a hint of what could happen on the football field, he couldn't wait to get back into uniform. He was definitely in this adventure to the end.

Uzmahndey burst outside into the Zen garden. Boardwalks led through a maze of angular pools amid stands of bamboo and other greenery, and beds of carefully combed stone, and pleasing wood constructs. He could feel the tension ooze out through his pores. Maybe there was something to this Zen stuff. Nah, it was the rush from the masterful game of pool he had just played that was ballooning his spirits.

<u>Billiards is just geometry and physics.</u>

<u>Same as football.</u>

<u>*Simple stuff.*</u>

"Be quiet, guys. You're spoiling the Zen." Receiving curious looks, he pulled out his phone for cover. It went off in his hand. He was so startled he nearly dropped it.

And you call yourself a receiver? That bobble was nearly as bad as the San Diego game.

He secured his phone in midair on the third grab. "How do you know about that?"

We have access to your memories.

Now be quiet, Bad, and let him talk to Keanu.

Keanu? He checked. It was Keanu. "How's it going, Neo?"

"Where are you at now?"

"The Azores."

"In the middle of the Atlantic?"

"I commend you on your knowledge of geography."

"So you're not in Northern Ireland."

How did he know about Northern Ireland? "I was this morning."

"I *knew* that was you!" Keanu was exultant.

"What do you know?"

"There's a video going viral of you talking to some guy in a green cape with a big sword." When Uzmahndey was too stunned to respond, Keanu went on. "There's video of this same guy, only a lot bigger, on top of a stone wall out in the ocean confronting a sea monster riding a huge wave. People who were there posted about a wall of rocks rising up out of the water that saved a lot of people from being drowned by a rogue wave. They are calling the guy Finn McCool, and saying that he saved Ireland for a second time. Then a smaller version of this same guy was filmed talking to you. What was going on?"

"I've got to see these videos. I'll call you back."

"I'll send you a link. But wait. There's something else. I caught someone prowling around your office."

"What did he want?"

"He wouldn't say. Just asked some questions about you."

"What did you tell him?"

"I didn't tell him shit. I told him to stay away or I'd call the police. I haven't seen him since. I just thought you'd like to know."

"Thanks, Keanu. I really appreciate you looking after my place. But I've got to watch that video." He sprinted back into the hotel.

When Uzmahndey dashed into their room, he found Charlie sound asleep with Snugglesaurus in her arms, and Angela sitting in a chair staring at her. "Wake Charlie up. You both need to see this."

"What's going on?" Charlie opened puffy eyes.

"We've gone viral." Uzmahndey sat on the edge of the bed and clicked on the link Keanu had texted.

All three watched the video on Uzmahndey's phone of a giant Finn McCool riding the stone pillars up out of the water to a hundred feet height, and the wave bearing a sea monster seeming to dissolve before it. Then another video of a smaller version of Finn McCool standing on top of the cliff conversing with Uzmahndey, with Angela and Charlie in the background.

Once the last of the videos played, Uzmahndey turned to the other two. "What do you think?"

"I was soaking wet," Charlie complained. "My hair looked awful."

"I don't care about your stupid hair. Are you aware of the kind of facial recognition software being used nowadays? Whoever investigates this incident will identify us real quick. Me, at least. I played in the NFL. There are images of me all over the Internet. They'll track me down in no time."

The laughter Uzmahndey heard in his head sounded like Bad. *All over the Internet? Really? You didn't even complete one season. And it wasn't like you were Offensive Rookie of the Year. How many passes did you catch?*

"Shut up!" Both women stared at him. "Sorry. Bad is being an asshole."

"We haven't done anything," Charlie said.

"We were involved with a person who could have been an accomplice to a fantastic terrorist incident that might have killed a lot of people." Seeing this sparked no reaction from Angela, Uzmahndey snapped, "Aren't you worried?"

"Snugglesaurus can keep anyone from finding us."

Uzmahndey looked to the stuffed dinosaur. "Is that true?"

"He's not going to tell *you*. He talks to me." Charlie looked at the toy she held, then smiled. "He's already taken care of it. No one will track us down."

"Yeah? Someone is already looking for *me*." When both females stared back without replying, he went on. "Keanu caught someone lurking around my office."

Angela was dismissive. "It was probably just a thief."

"He was asking questions about me."

"He was probably just a *stupid* thief," Charlie said. "Play those videos again."

They all three settled down to watch.

That night after Charlie climbed into the twin bed she turned away from the double bed. "I'm not watching you two. And I've got ear plugs in so I won't hear a thing."

"Good," Uzmahndey said as he undressed. "Then the snoring won't bother you."

"I've got a shoe right here by the bed where I can reach it."

Uzmahndey climbed in then looked up to Angela. "Are you coming?"

When Angela returned from the bathroom wearing her pajamas she climbed in on the side facing Charlie.

"So I can keep an eye on her. Someone might have followed us from Ireland."

"Of course."

Uzmahndey was too hopped up by all that had happened this long day to go to sleep. The attack at Giant's Causeway, and the video of him talking with Finn McCool, and the pool game that teased what was in store once he got back in the NFL. And now this warm beautiful body that had just climbed into bed with him. Was it human? Why should he care? He snuggled up from behind. "There's not a lot of room."

She pulled his hand to her breast. "Something to hold onto. So you don't fall out of bed."

Uzmahndey gently squeezed. "I'm seriously conflicted."

"Really?" Angela wriggled her butt into him. "It doesn't feel like it."

He sighed. "I might be a long time falling asleep."

"I could help you with that."

"This is good. This feels good. This is enough. Tonight."

Uzmahndey opened his eyes to the dim light of early morning. Angela was up and dressed, and he could hear Charlie in the shower.

Angela spoke to him matter-of-factly, making no reference to last night's cuddling. "We've got an early flight."

He rose and hurried Charlie out of the bathroom so he could clean up.

It was a short bumpy flight to Flores Island on a small prop. The little airport where they touched down was on the eastern edge of the island, and the sight of the sparkling blue of the Atlantic crashing onto the rugged dark bluffs as they descended put Uzmahndey in a vibrant mood. "This is more like it. Reminds me of Hawaii. I've had my fill of cold water."

"We're not going to the beach," Angela informed him.

"That's good," Charlie said. "I don't want to be attacked by another monster wave."

Uzmahndey frowned at both of them. They were bringing him down. "Where are these Black and Long lakes we're headed for?"

"In a forest reserve in the interior on the other side of the island."

They rented a Jeep, since once they entered the reserve they would be on dirt roads. A short drive through verdant pasture land brought them to the subtropical forest. Once they entered the reserve Uzmahndey drove onto a narrow rutted twisty dirt road that kick-backed up the side of a mountain through dense jungle terrain. Fir trees abounded, bedecked with vibrant blue and pink hydrangeas lining the road.

Two other vehicles were present at the small lot where the dirt track ended, but their occupants were not in sight. The lush green foliage of tall ferns and dense holly and blueberry shrubs seemed nearly impenetrable, the air steamy in the haunting mist of the cloud forest. Uzmahndey parked the Jeep with a smile.

"This reminds me of the Big Island." He hopped out from behind the wheel. "Looks like we're off on a hike through paradise."

He led the way into the moist swirling fog, with Charlie behind and Angela bringing up the rear, onto a narrow rocky trail overarched with evergreen trees and towering scaly fern trees.

A short trek led them up to the crest of a hill overlooking two side by side lakes, one long and narrow, and the other smaller and round. Several waterfalls tumbled down from all sides into the depression formed by the lakes. Charlie consulted Snugglesaurus. "These lakes are water-filled calderas created by the ancient volcano that raised this island up from the ocean floor."

Uzmahndey peered through the mist that hung over the water. "Why is one of them so black?"

"One is much deeper than the other. It's about three-hundred feet."

"That's the one we want." Angela set off down into the caldera.

Charlie, having been attacked several times by monsters lurking in water, hung back. "Is it safe?"

"Yeah, Angela," Uzmahndey seconded. "What if we just wait here while you go do your thing?"

She stopped to look back up at them. "We stay together."

Uzmahndey took Charlie's arm. "Come on, kid. We'll take care of you."

"We?"

"Me and Good and Bad and Ugly."

"You are getting as weird as my mother."

Uzmahndey led her down to Angela, and they all three descended to the water's edge. He watched Angela take off her shirt. "Going for a swim?"

"Yes. You stay here with Charlie." She stripped down to skin then waded in.

"You two are sure comfortable with each other now." Charlie frowned.

"Disapprove?"

"No. I just need to find a boyfriend so I can have some fun, too."

Another problem for another day. Uzmahndey turned his attention back to Angela's pale body slicing across the dark water as she swam out to the middle of Black Lake. She dove. They lost sight of her right away. Three hundred feet, Snugglesaurus had told Charlie. How long would it take Angela to swim that deep?

Charlie fidgeted. "Sure is taking her a long time." Then, "Do you think she's alright?" She looked all around. "If something happened to her we'd never know."

Uzmahndey checked in with the xenobots. "Do you know what's going on, Good?"

<u>No.</u>

"Did you just call me good?"

"Be quiet. I'm talking to my xenobots."

How would any of us know what's going on in that black water?

"How about it, Ugly? Should I go in for her?"

Why have I been designated Ugly? You've never seen me to know what I look like.

"It's just the name of an old movie. 'The Good, the Bad, and the Ugly.' I'll watch it with you guys sometime."

You don't need to. Snugglesaurus already played it for us.

The AI was streaming movies in his head? Without him even knowing? Damn, what else could that AI do to him without him being aware of what it was doing?

Yet another worry for yet another day. "What should I do about Angela?"

You could jump in and save her, Tarzan.

No. She would want you to stay with Charlie.

That's right. Stay here.

Uzmahndey started pacing. "She's been under too long." He paced before Charlie a half-dozen more times. "Damn. I'm going in." He began yanking off clothes.

He was down to his undershorts and heading in when Charlie yelled.

"She's up!"

Uzmahndey looked to see Angela had surfaced in the middle of the lake and was swimming toward them. He waded in to his knees to help her out.

She slung his hand away. "Why did you come in?"

He was too stunned by her appearance to answer. She was battered and scarred all over. "What happened to you?"

"There was a welcoming party waiting for me."

"Are you okay?"

"Of course I'm okay." She strode past Uzmahndey onto land then turned to glare at him as he waded out. "Don't ever leave Charlie alone near a portal."

"No matter what happens to you?"

"Yes. I can be rebuilt. Charlie is irreplaceable." Angela snatched up her clothes and began trekking up the side of the caldera. Charlie fell into step behind her.

Uzmahndey jammed his feet into his shoes. "Aren't you getting dressed?"

"I need to dry off first," she tossed back over her shoulder.

He snatched up the rest of his clothes and scrambled uphill in pursuit.

Uzmahndey caught up to the pair at the top of the caldera. A gang of four men blocked the trail. Angela had dropped her clothes and positioned Charlie behind her.

One of the men turned to Uzmahndey's approach with a leer. "What have you three been up to?"

"It's none of your business." Uzmahndey dropped his clothes and charged up toward them.

"Wait." Angela held out a restraining hand. She turned back to the four. "Will you let us pass?"

One whose lecherous gaze had never left Angela answered.

"What's your hurry, sweet meat?"

"Looks like you've already been through the grinder," another added.

"You must like to play rough," a third said. "So do I."

"You can have her," the fourth man said. "I'll take the young chick."

It was the last remark that did it for Angela. She dropped her restraining hand. "Go ahead."

Uzmahndey advanced on the one who had threatened Charlie. The other three must have assumed their companion could handle him since they all hung back to watch. Uzmahndey juked to the right, as he would in a game to get his opponent to commit, then lunged back to the left. The guy totally bought the move. A certain amount of hand-play is allowed between players contending for a pass, so he was skilled at using his hands in close quarters. But this was too easy, and the guy wasn't even wearing a helmet. A short hard uppercut to the jaw leveled him. This surprised Uzmahndey nearly as much as it had surprised the guy now sprawled on his back at his feet, out cold.

Angela said you'd be surprised at what we can do.

Don't stop now. You've got three more coming to tackle you.

Just picture Logan Wilson.

Three Logan Wilsons charged him. Except it wasn't much of a charge. They seemed to be moving in slow motion. Uzmahndey dodged, feinted, parried, and punched at twice the speed of the trio. In less than a minute all three joined their friend on the ground, two of them out cold. The two still conscious watched him warily from the dirt, making no move to get up.

Uzmahndey stopped, gazing around with wonder at the carnage he had inflicted. He held up his hands to stare. They weren't even sore. He had heard bones crunch, but none of them had been his. He looked to Angela. "They don't even hurt."

She was smiling. "I told you. You have no idea what all those xenobots can do for you." She led Charlie on up the trail.

Uzmahndey picked up his clothes. "Logan Wilson, I am coming for you!" He chased after them. Not a move was made to stop him by the two still awake.

By the time they reached the parking lot Angela was dry enough to put on her clothes. Uzmahndey tossed his shirt and socks into the back of the Jeep, too energized to finish dressing. Charlie stared at him with fascinated eyes. "You were a blur."

"Talk about a blur, just wait till you see me run a crossing pattern over the middle when I get back in the league."

On the drive down the mountain he continued ranting about how good of a football player he was going to be. "I'll get the two of you Super Bowl tickets."

Charlie laughed. "So now you are going to the Super Bowl."

"Has Snugglesaurus told you about the Super Bowl?"

"He's told me a lot about American football, since I'm traveling with a football player."

"Good for him. Of course I'm going to the Super Bowl. Whatever team I'm on will go to the Super Bowl."

Hitting pavement at the boundary of the reserve, Uzmahndey swerved, nearly going off the road.

"Be careful!" Angela barked.

"Why?" Uzmahndey closed his eyes.

"Uz!" Charlie screamed.

Angela smacked him on the back of the head. "Stop it!"

Uzmahndey opened his eyes. "We're still on the road. The xenobots were driving."

"Don't test them like that. For no good reason. Not with Charlie in the car."

Uzmahndey settled down at last, and the rest of the drive back to the other side of the small island was uneventful.

It was still early afternoon, and their flight back to Sao Miguel wasn't until the next morning, so they checked into the Hotel Occidental in Santa Cruz. It was above the ocean at such a height to make them feel safe from a rogue wave, yet provided a nice view out over the Atlantic. Although none of them had any inclination to visit one of the nearby beautiful white sand beaches, there was a pool just outside their room. Uzmahndey stepped outside onto their balcony to give Charlie a chance to change. He gazed down at the waves crashing into the towering rocky bluff he stood atop.

Still too worked up from the fight for merely staring off to the horizon, he initiated a conversation. "Thanks, guys."

<u>No need for that. We were protecting Charlie.</u>

That was stupid, closing your eyes while driving.

I concur. Don't assume we can do everything.

"Duly noted. I was still worked up from the fight."

And you were still worked up from watching Angela parade around naked.

Uzmahndey chuckled. "Yes I was."

When are you going to do something about that?

"Good? You are being awfully quiet. Don't you have anything to say?"

He doesn't go in for bawdy talk.

Yeah, the sap is too noble.

The patio door slid open and Angela emerged. Her conservative one-piece swimsuit concealed most of the new marks on her skin she had acquired at the bottom of Black Lake. "You can come in to change now."

Uzmahndey beamed at the sight. Until Charlie walked out wearing a much more revealing bikini. His beam dimmed. "Is that appropriate for a fifteen-year old girl?"

"Yes it is, Daddy!"

"I'm not your daddy."

"Then don't act like it." She sashayed away.

Angela followed her. "Put your trunks on and join us."

Charlie is one hot dish.

"That's not funny, Bad." Uzmahndey entered their pool-side room and began undressing. "I've heard enough for a while." The xenobots fell silent.

Uzmahndey joined the other two at the pool. They were the only ones there. Charlie was in swimming, while Angela stood at the side in water up to her shoulders. "Lifeguard duty?"

Angela nodded, never taking her eyes off Charlie.

He stretched out on a pool lounge and dozed in the warm soothing sun.

That evening they took a stroll through Santa Cruz. The city wasn't very big, so it wasn't much of a walk. They dined at the

Macau. It was traditional Chinese, nothing adventuresome like in Scotland.

They walked back to their hotel in the dark. Charlie went into the bathroom to change into pajamas, which gave Uzmahndey a chance to strip down to his undershorts and climb into bed, while Angela changed into her pajamas. As before, she took the side facing Charlie's bed so she could keep an eye on her during the night. Uzmahndey snuggled up to her from behind, as before.

Charlie emerged from the bathroom. "You two behave yourselves tonight." She took Snugglesaurus to bed with her, then closed her eyes to commune with her stuffed dinosaur.

Angela leaned back to whisper. "Want to go exploring?"

"What do you have in mind?"

She guided his hand down inside the front of her pajama bottom. "You seem frightened of me. Like I'm some kind of Frankenstein monster." She pressed his hand into her pelvic bush. "I'm constructed like any woman on this planet. No different." She urged his fingers down between her open legs. "There is nothing dangerous inside me. Nothing to harm you. See for yourself."

Uzmahndey slid two fingers into her. She was soft and warm and very wet. She was right. Nothing to be scared of. He probed deeper. Yes, everything seemed to be in order. She squirmed at his touch. "Am I hurting you?"

"No," came her breathless reply.

"Are you enjoying this?"

"Yes. My body responds like any woman's would." Her squirming grew more pronounced. She wriggled her butt back into him. "I can feel you responding, too."

"Yes." Uzmahndey tugged at her pajama bottom with his free hand.

"Wait." Angela pulled away.

"What's the matter?" Uzmahndey released her.

"I just wanted you to know I'm put together like any other woman you've known. That I won't hurt you."

Uzmahndey heaved a heavy sigh. "Duly noted."

"Don't be upset."

"I'm not."

"Just a few more nights. When we are in a better location. This island is remote."

A better location? What did she mean by that? He decided not to press her. "Okay. Gives me something to look forward to." Uzmahndey hugged her from behind. "What *is* our next location?"

"The Richat Structure in Mauritania."

Chapter 13

Richat Structure

Flying from Flores Island to San Miguel Isle the next morning, and a layover there for a connection from the Azores to
Nouakchott, Mauritania, made this leg of the tour the longest
yet. Yet this leg was far from over. Upon stepping off the airplane in Africa, they were taken to a government office to
apply for travel visas. In this less-digitized country it had to
be done in person. They also had to declare who in Mauritania
was sponsoring their visit. Snugglesaurus had foreseen these
difficulties and had dealt with them, but there were actual
paper forms to be filled out. At long last free to continue, they
collected their bags and walked out of the terminal.

The heat slapped Uzmahndey in the face. His body was
getting jerked around by all the jet-lagged climates he passed
through, from the freezing glacier in Iceland to the cool
clammy coasts of Scotland and Northern Ireland, to the tropical humid warmth of the jungles of the Azores. Now, this blazing dry heat on the edge of the Sahara desert. Even with the
three xenobots, his body had difficulty moderating the effects
of being yanked from one extreme climate to another.

A short taxi ride from the airport north of the city took them
to the Al Salam Resort on the Atlantic coast. It was a modern

jewel, with the desert on three sides and the Atlantic Ocean at its front. Uzmahndey ignored the travel brochure scenery as he hurried past the large pool and many palm trees into the comfort of the air conditioned lobby. They were shown up to a room with a double bed, and the promise of a cot for Charlie. Uzmahndey and Charlie were so weary they flopped down onto the bed side by side, while Angela took a seat to watch over them.

Uzmahndey awoke late in the afternoon. Alone. His dazed gaze located Angela's and Charlie's clothes on the cot that had been delivered and set up without disturbing his deathlike slumber. Since he didn't hear the shower running, hence they couldn't be taking a shower together, though why they would ever take a shower together he didn't know, and he had yet to see Angela take a shower, though he wouldn't mind seeing this, but then there was a lot he didn't know about Angela, or about Charlie, for that matter... His plodding mind finally worked out they must be swimming. So he changed into his trunks.

Passing through the lobby, he saw several people gathered around a flat-screen TV. He assumed they were watching a football match, and so was drawn to the screen. He hadn't gotten to watch much sports lately.

He was wrong. On the screen stood Finn McCool atop the wall of hexagonal columns a hundred feet high facing off against the sea monster riding atop the hundred-foot rogue wave. Amid the swirling fog and heavy mist the action was sketchy. You couldn't really tell what all was happening. Until the image switched to one of Uzmahndey and a human-sized Finn McCool talking on top of the cliff. In this his face was plain as day.

Uzmahndey hurried away. Snugglesaurus might be blocking facial recognition programs, but what could the AI do to prevent him being recognized in person? He kept his face down as he rushed back up to their room. To settle his nerves, he turned on the TV and found a football match to watch.

By the time Angela and Charlie walked in, Uzmahndey was in a foul mood. The bikini on Charlie seemed to have shrunk. "You do realize we are in a Muslim country?"

"As long as we're on the resort there is no need to don a hajib," Angela said.

Charlie sat by the window and gazed out. Uzmahndey joined her to look out over an infinite expanse of blinding white sand and sparkling crystal blue ocean spread out before them. "This place is beautiful."

"And dangerous."

Angela stepped up to look out, also. "The whole planet is dangerous."

"To you. Because you are invading it." He turned to confront her. "Haven't I earned the right to be told what is going on?"

"I've told you. We are rescuing the human race."

"Rescuing us from our own world. What does that mean?"

"The xenobots I'm placing in the portals Gaia and her family use to reach the human world will deny them access to the surface."

"Then why do they seem more intent on killing Charlie than stopping you?" Uzmahndey glanced back at Charlie. She had turned away from the grand vista outside and was following their discussion with a frown. "Don't worry, Charlie, I won't let that happen, and neither will Angela."

"I know," was Charlie's soft-spoken, doe-eyed response.

Uzmahndey turned back to Angela. "So why?"

"Because Charlie is the future. Half-human, half-alien. She and her kind will inherit the Earth. Gaia does not want that to happen."

Uzmahndey turned his gaze back to Charlie. "She doesn't seem half-alien. She looks totally human to me."

"Really? Has she grown the way humans grow?"

His head snapped back to Angela. "Is there a reason for her doing this?"

"Childhood is a vulnerable time. Humans are basically helpless for the first ten years or so. Her alien ancestors have nearly evolved this vulnerability away."

"At the cost of her missing her childhood." He glanced at the stuffed dinosaur Charlie hugged. "I know the AI fills her in on what she has missed, but she has still missed it."

"What she loses on the front end she will more than make up on the back end."

He looked back to Angela. "What does that mean?"

"Charlie's life expectancy is at least two hundred, possibly as long as three hundred years. Father is not sure."

Uzmahndey was stunned. "Three hundred years? Charlie could live to be three hundred?"

"Will you two stop it!" Charlie shot to her feet. "You're talking about me like I'm not even here. I know I'm a freak. I know no one else on this planet ages like I do. I know no one else has a robot for a mother and an AI for a tutor." She snatched up her clothes from the bed and dashed into the bathroom. She tried to slam the door, but didn't pull it off.

"You are the future of your people," Angela called after. She turned from the muffed slam to face Uzmahndey. "Humans will become stronger and more resilient than ever before because of what they inherit from the alien race they will be cross-breeding with. They will be free of their enslavement to Gaia and her kind, which they have endured since before they walked upright. They will stop warring so much with each other and unite for their own betterment. That is what you are fighting for."

"But will we still be human?"

"Are you still like you were a hundred thousand years ago? Is it a bad thing that you are not?" Angela turned away and began taking off her swimsuit.

That broke the tension. Uzmahndey laughed as he watched her get naked. "No fair. You're distracting me."

Angela turned to face him, holding her damp suit at the side. "All's fair in love and war."

"You sound and behave more like a real woman every day."

"You are teaching me how to be a real woman." She set her swim suit aside and began dressing.

The bathroom door opened and Charlie emerged in slacks and shirt. She stopped when she found Angela in her underwear.

"I'm not interrupting anything?"

"No. We've got more pressing problems." Uzmahndey picked up the remote and flipped through the satellite stations.

"Good," Charlie said as Uzmahndey switched away from the game he had been watching. "Football is so boring."

"You mean soccer. My kind of football is not boring." Uzmahndey found a news channel that was playing a video from the Giant's Causeway. "This isn't boring, either." They all fell silent to watch.

"It's so foggy," Angela said. "No one can tell what's really going on."

"My face is plainly visible," Uzmahndey responded. "I need to stay out of sight as much as possible, give this a chance to die down."

"That's cool." Charlie picked up the hotel directory. "We'll order room service for dinner."

That night when Uzmahndey and Angela climbed into bed, she scooted back into him. "Still mad at me?"

He snuggled up to her. "I'm not mad at you. I just don't like being kept in the dark."

"Do you think I know everything? Father tells me only what I need to know to carry out my mission."

"And he installed that wonderful learning program. You seem as real as any woman I've ever known."

Is that an indication of how good the learning program is? Or of the kind of women you have known?

"Shut up, Bad." Uzmahndey tugged at her pajama bottom. "Is this a good location?"

"No." She pulled his hand away. "We'll be in a good location soon."

Uzmahndey scooted back from her in irritation. "We're in bed. What better location is there?"

"Please be patient. Just a little longer."

"Fine. Just let me know when we're there." He rolled over away from her.

"I will."

Damn, she could be infuriating. He sighed. Just like any woman. Any real woman. He took a deep breath. Patience, Ghost had said. He needed to be patient.

The next morning Uzmahndey skipped shaving. "Time for me to grow a beard, maybe let my hair grow out. I've got to change up my look." He studied his companions. "But I'm more concerned with how you two look. We're going off the resort into the interior."

Angela looked herself and Charlie over. They were wearing concealing baggy slacks and shirts. "This should be okay."

"You two need to cover your heads."

After conferring with Snugglesaurus, Angela concurred. When they went downstairs to the lobby, she and Charlie went into the gift shop to purchase head scarves, while Uzmahndey went outside. The cool desert night air lingered in the soft morning light. He located the taxi Snugglesaurus had summoned. Uzmahndey blabbered in English, and the driver responded in Arabic, and all they could agree on was Nouakchott as a destination.

When the other two emerged with their new scarves on their heads, Angela took charge. As usual, she spoke the local dialect. Their driver didn't seem happy about having to deal with a woman, but he bit his tongue with the few teeth remaining in his mouth and they were off.

On the way south to Nouakchott they passed through barren desert, with the Atlantic a distant sight to the west. The city itself was a maze of shops and homes and mosques tangled up with a multitude of cars jamming twisted alleys and narrow lanes.

The taxi wormed through this snarl to the Garage Atar on the eastern edge of the urban sprawl. Although Snugglesaurus had appraised them of the bus schedule, it had been unable to purchase tickets. All transactions in Mauritania took place with cash. So Angela told Uzmahndey where to go and what to say, and let him buy their tickets. Which actually made it easier, as the Mauritanians preferred dealing with men. They boarded a crowded bus and headed northeast out of the city.

The urban landscape was quickly left behind as they traveled into the desert. The region they passed through was on the fringe of the harshest part of the Sahara. Flat sand stretched from horizon to horizon. Even the occasional home or shop was left behind. Along with the sun, the heat made a steady ascent. The flailing air conditioning on the bus was soon overwhelmed. Uzmahndey wasn't too uncomfortable. There was sweat on his brow, but not overmuch. The xenobots were moderating the effects of the heat on him, but they must have decided him not sweating at all would be noticed.

He knew Angela would be okay, so he checked with Charlie. Like him, she seemed unbothered by the rising temperature. This new human-alien crossbreed was made of tough stuff. Perhaps Angela was right. These alien genes would benefit the human race.

What did seem to bother Charlie were the young girls seated nearby who kept laughing and pointing at the stuffed dinosaur she held. Uzmahndey had to admit it was a strange sight to see a fifteen year old girl with such a childish thing. Charlie would just have to grin and bear it.

Since the government of Mauratania was dealing with the Jamaat Nusrat al-Islam wal Muslimeer terrorist group, military checkpoints were set up along this major highway. Passing through the first one went smoothly. At the second one, the three of them were pulled aside. Uzmahndey could read Angela well enough to know she was about to detonate over the way the men were treating Charlie. One of the soldiers yanked Snugglesaurus from her and squeezed it hard, trying to determine if anything was hidden inside. Angela was tensing like a spring.

<u>You need to do something.</u>

<u>This could get ugly fast. Give him some money.</u>

<u>Three bills of the largest denomination you have</u>

Uzmahndey pulled out five. The soldier with Snugglesaurus scowled at him.

<u>I said three! Now he's suspicious why this toy is worth so much.</u>

The soldier pulled out a knife and cut the dinosaur open. He poked around in the stuffing. Finding nothing, he tossed Snugglesaurus down and snatched the bills.

Charlie picked up the stuffing and tried to jam it back into the dinosaur.

The soldier motioned for them to rejoin the other passengers on the bus.

"Is it ruined," Uzmahndey asked Angela as they walked.

"No. The AI is not so easily damaged."

Once the bus was underway, an old woman motioned for the T. Rex. Charlie shook her head no, until the woman produced a needle and thread. She did an expert job sewing up the dinosaur. When she handed it back to Charlie, Uzmahndey offered payment. The old woman shook her head no.

"Alhamdulilah," Angela said.

The old woman smiled in return then turned away.

The rest of the bus ride was uneventful. Although the desert remained as barren as before, they passed a shopping strip out in the middle of nowhere. And, of course, there were mosques. The little town of Akjouit had a single-runway airstrip and a military base. Then it was down out of the hills and back into flat desert landscape. At Ain Ehel Taya, with two mosques, they ascended into another mountainous region. This was as barren as the desert lowlands had been. They wound their way through these dry heights until they arrived at Atar.

Six hours after leaving Nouakchott they disembarked in the middle of this small town. They walked to a supermarket, where they bought some drinks and snacks. A Jeep pulled up before they had a chance to finish them. The driver was a young man covered from shoulders to feet in a flowing white robe.

"Our guide," Angela said. She began to address him in Arabic.

He shook his head. "No, no. Learn English. Practice." He turned to Uzmahndey. "Black Moor?" He pointed to his own chest. "White Moor. How trip?"

"Interesting."

He laughed. "Soldiers." He puffed up and pranced about the sidewalk. Which made Charlie laugh. He turned serious as he faced her. "Okay? No bother?"

Charlie held up the ragged dinosaur.

Their guide made a sad face. "Animals." He turned back to Uzmahndey. "Sidi," the man said, gesturing to himself.

Uzmahndey responded with their names, pointing to each in turn.

Sidi herded them into the Jeep, Uzmahndey in front, and Angela and Charlie in back. Sidi climbed in behind the wheel. "Bathroom?"

Uzmahndey shook his head. "No, we're good."

Sidi pulled away from the curb. "Jeep okay? Prefer camel?"

Uzmahndey might have said yes if he'd realized how Sidi was going to drive. In the city he was okay, but once he left it and descended from the mountains onto flat desert he kept the pedal just off the metal. The road was straight as an arrow, and there was little to no traffic, but the pavement wasn't in as good of shape as the road from Nouakchott had been. With the roar of air through the open Jeep it was hard to talk, but Angela leaned up to Sidi's ear and made her displeasure known in Arabic. Uzmahndey didn't believe she was quoting the Qaran this time by how quickly Sidi slowed down.

"I've not seen any animals," Uzmahndey shouted, trying to take their guide's mind off whatever Angela had said.

His strategy worked, as Sidi broke into a broad smile. "No camel caravans. No nomadic Berbers. All gone. Berbers in city now."

"Nothing lives out here?"

"Drought bad for many years. Leopards, gazelles, all hunted, gone."

Not long after ascending into more mountains, Sidi pulled over at a scenic location. "Nouatil." They were in a high narrow pass the road twisted through, offering a good view of the desert all around. They got out to stretch their legs. Sidi motioned ahead. "Bandits."

Uzmahndey smiled in return. "Bandits don't want to mess with us."

Sidi was impressed with the bravado. He smiled. "No more. Soldiers chase off."

Uzmahndey turned to Charlie. "Are you doing okay?"

"Yes." She smiled at Sidi. "This is so much better than the bus." When Sidi mimicked some expressions and behaviors of people they had seen on the bus, she laughed. "He's funny."

Uzmahndey leaned in close. "Not boyfriend material. Don't flirt."

Charlie took offense. "I'm not flirting. Can't I be nice to someone without flirting?"

"Not in this country."

After a brief rest they got underway. They passed no signs of civilization the rest of the way to Ouadane, the culmination of their dash in Sidi's Jeep. "Much to see here," Sidi said. "World Heritage site. Medieval ruins, stone age relics, winding alleys..."

"We have no interest in Ouadane," Angela said. "Take us to the Richat Structure."

"Eye of Sahara. Yes. Ouadane is on edge of it." He drove to the end of the road then off pavement onto a dirt track leading out of town. He followed a dry wash northeast for ten miles or so, then stopped. "We are here."

Uzmahndey scanned the barren landscape. There were no features to distinguish it from the desert they had been traveling through all day. "Where is it?"

"All around you," Charlie answered. "Snugglesaurus says the Richat Structure is a thirty-mile diameter collapsed geological dome."

Uzmahndey got out and walked around. His eyesight sharpened in a way he was growing accustomed to. He saw they were inside a distant ring of sand dunes. The land was so flat it was impossible to determine how distant they were, or how high. These rings they were in the middle of *could* be thirty miles across.

Charlie exited the Jeep and stepped up beside him. "The pictures taken from the air are much more impressive. Like crop circles. They don't look like much, either, from ground-level."

"Are you getting all this from Snugglesaurus?"

"Of course. Like I get everything."

"So the AI is undamaged? Like Angela said? You are communicating with it now?"

"Yes. He's robust." She held up the stuffed toy for him to see. "It's components must be woven into the material it is stuffed with."

She turned her attention back to their surroundings. "This site was undiscovered until the Gemini astronauts saw it from space back in the sixties. Images of it taken from orbit are impressive."

Sidi joined them. "Not Gemini. Ouadane on caravan route. Berbers found. Thought it lost city Atlantis."

"In the middle of the desert?" Charlie asked. "No way." She continued in a more serious vein. "It was originally thought to have been caused by a meteor. But there was no evidence of a collision other than its circular shape, so that was ruled out. Now it's believed to have happened when the ancient super-continent Pangea pulled apart."

Angela walked up behind Sidi. "Can you drive us to the center."

"Yes. Maybe."

Uzmahndey looked at him. "Maybe?"

"Hard to find. On ground." He led them back to the Jeep. "I do it."

After wandering around for a half-hour, Charlie cried out, "Stop!"

Sidi stopped, looking at her. "Here?"

"Yes. Snugglesaurus says."

"Who is Snugglesaurus?"

Ignoring the question, Angela climbed out. "I need to find the very center." She walked off in search of it.

"Uzmahndey."

Uzmahndey turned to find a bare-chested man in a blue robe draped over one shoulder, with large round eyes, long wavy black hair, and a long wavy beard standing before him. He had broken shackles on his wrists and an owl perched on his shoulder. Apparently neither Sidi nor Charlie had heard him call Uzmahndey's name. The man backed away, motioning for him to follow.

"Stay here," Uzmahndey ordered Charlie. "Watch her," he ordered Sidi. They both watched him walk away, seemingly alone. Twenty feet distant, he stopped. "This is as far away as I get from Charlie."

"Why do you believe her?"

"Charlie?"

"No. The machine." When Uzmahndey said nothing in reply, he continued. "It lies to you. It entraps you. It tricks you into destroying your own world."

"Why should I believe *you*?"

"Because I am from this world, same as you."

"You and the others are monsters."

"We have cared for mankind since the dawn of humanity."

"Ghost says you have dominated us, and he is here to liberate us."

A deep chuckle. "And you believe this off-worlder? He wants to imprison us, so he can enslave you."

"Uzmahndey!"

He turned to find Angela had rejoined Charlie and Sidi. He looked back. The bearded man was still there. He looked back to the other three. They all stared at him with questioning eyes. "You don't see him?" He pointed to his companion.

Angela grew alarmed. "Get back here. Now."

"Go back to your machine. You have betrayed your race for a shiny toy." The man dissolved before his eyes, the owl flying away as his robe fell to the ground. Where it dissolved into the sand, while the owl merely faded away in mid-air.

Uzmahndey joined the others.

`"What did you see?" Angela asked.

"A bearded man with long hair in a blue robe."

"That is Arab," Sidi said. "Not Moor."

"I didn't see anyone," Charlie said.

Sidi stopped laughing. "You see ghost. Let's go. This sacred ground. You offend spirit." He tried to shepherd them back to the Jeep as he spoke.

Angela stepped up to Uzmahndey instead. "You left Charlie."

"She was never out of sight."

"You cannot let Charlie out of reach when we are near a portal. Never."

Angela refused to say another word to Uzmahndey all the way back to Atar. Sidi spoke to him, though. "Bad time on bus?"

"Definitely," Uzmahndey answered.

Sidi looked back at Angela. "See what Eye of Sahara really looks like?" She nodded in response. Sidi glanced at Charlie. "Have good time?" She smiled. Sidi turned back to Uzmahndey. "I know somebody."

Sidi drove to a small airport outside Atar. An acquaintance with a small prop plane offered to fly them to Nouakchott, with a detour to see the Richat Structure from the air. Charlie walked around the plane with Snugglesaurus. Completing the circuit, she nodded yes to Angela. Who negotiated a more than fair price with the pilot, high enough to sooth his displeasure at dealing with a woman. Uzmahndey climbed in front with him, Angela and Charlie climbed in back, and Sidi waved them bye.

The Richat Structure was impressive seen from above. It consisted of huge, concentric rings of different shades of dark rock spread out across the sand for thirty miles, encircled by a ring of low sand dunes. The prominent ring structure spiraled in to a blue bulls-eye. Sidi was right. Eye of the Sahara was a more suitable name.

The day had darkened by the time they touched down in Nouakchott. A taxi took them back to Al Salam Resort. Charlie called dibs on first shower. Uzmahndey collapsed in a chair to watch Angela take off her clothes.

She glared at him when she was down to her underwear. "Don't bother me tonight."

"Do you have a headache?"

She took off her bra. "I don't have headaches. You shouldn't have left Charlie with Sidi."

"You should."

She paused with her thumbs hooked in the waistband of her panties.

"Have headaches. That's the typical excuse a woman uses to punish her man by denying him sex when she is mad at him."

Intrigued, Angela stared at him as she stepped out of her panties.

"And then she parades around naked in front of him to rub his nose in it. She's saying, 'see what you're not getting tonight', without actually saying it."

Angela stood naked before him, covered in dirt and grime from the day's grueling adventure, her unscarfed hair a tangled mess. "Real women do that?"

"Yes. It drives men crazy."

"So I'm becoming more like a real woman?"

"God, yes."

She smiled, for the first time since the Richat Structure. "Good." The smile quickly disappeared. "I'm still mad at you for leaving Charlie. I'm counting on you to watch over her while I'm busy at a portal. The portals are dangerous places. That's where we are most likely to be attacked."

Once Uzmahndey emerged from his shower, he found Angela in her pajamas seated in a chair beside Charlie's bed. Apparently she was still angry with him. No bed mate tonight. He turned his back on the two of them. The hell with patience. He didn't want to make love to a robot anyway.

Liar.

Not wanting Angela to hear him arguing with his xenobots, he let Bad's accusation slide. Besides, he was right.

Chapter 14

Eisriesenwelt

Early the next morning the three travelers caught a taxi to the airport for their flight to Szalzburg, Austria. After suffering the sapping Sahara heat, walking out of the terminal into the brisk Alpine air chilled Uzmahndey, despite the xenobots' intervention. Following another full day of travel and yet another jarring climate transition, a depleted Uzmahndey relished crashing in their hotel room.

Crawling from the taxi, he confronted the Lachensky Hof, an expansive three-story chalet-style structure beyond which snow-capped Alps rose to rugged heights. He limped inside into an airy lobby of wide-plank blond wood with a high-gloss finish, open and high-ceilinged. The storybook exterior contrasted sharply with its airy clean-cut modern interior. The three were ushered up wide wooden stairs into a suite on the second floor. Even in his dazed condition, Uzmahndey could appreciate that Snugglesaurus had outdone himself this time. He and Angela had an entire room to themselves, while there was a separate kinder room for Charlie.

Or so he thought.

"Charlie has not left my side overnight on this trip yet," Angela said. "That won't happen here, either."

Uzmahndey couldn't believe what he was hearing.

"I'm to sleep in the children's room? Are you still mad at me over what happened in Mauritania?"

"Yes, but that has nothing to do with it." She turned her back on him. "In a hotel like this I'm sure the single bed is comfortable."

Uzmahndey stuck his head in the kinder room. Bunk beds. He headed straight for the door.

"Where are you going?" Angela asked.

"To find the playground." Uzmahndey stormed back down the stairs he had just come up. His anger overpowered his exhaustion. He walked without deviating straight through the lobby and out the back.

Where beautiful gardens froze him in his weary tracks. Amid the spacious greenery he had lunged into were four different bodies of water – a sauna, a cold water pool, a natural swimming pond, and a brine pool. Even amid this splendor, his eyes were irresistibly drawn up to take in the magnificent Alps they would be venturing into.

He collapsed into a pool-side chair. Austria was the sixth foreign country he had been to in less than two weeks. It had been a tiring but amazing experience. His head should be spinning. But it wasn't, because of the xenobots. He was some kind of a freak now. And the woman, female, *thing*, he was traveling with was even freakier. The machine had its priorities, and number one was Charlie. Angela was well on her way to becoming a real woman. She was certainly learning fast how to be as infuriating as the real thing. One night she invites him to explore her body, the next night she strips in front of him then gives him the cold shoulder, the night after that she sends him off to sleep by himself in the kid's room.

Damn! Uzmahndey shot to his feet. How could he let a machine get under his skin like that? He paced aimlessly across the grounds, his mind in turmoil. Until…

<u>Look up.</u>

Uzmahndey jerked to a halt, looking up as ordered. "What?"

You are being watched.

Uzmahndey discovered his irate meandering had led him out of the garden to the front of the hotel. The sidewalks on this major boulevard was teeming with pedestrians. He scanned the faces, surprised to see the details so clearly from this distance. The xenobots were good.

We are, but you're not. See the man wearing the stupid gift shop Alpine hat? With a feather in it, for Christ's sake.

Uzmahndey spotted him. "I see him."

<u>He was watching you.</u>

"Yeah? Maybe he recognized me. Even with my beard and long hair. He might have seen me play. On TV. The NFL is big in Europe."

Yeah, but you weren't. He's been tracking you since you came outside.

If you've been located, then so have Angela and Charlie.

Uzmahndey walked in the front entrance and bee-lined across the lobby and up the stairs. He had to knock since in his haste he hadn't grabbed a key card.

Angela opened the door. Her expression was complex. This was a robot? And it's face could convey anger, remorse, uncertainty, confusion, and probably a lot more he wasn't catching? All at the same time?

"I've been talking with Charlie."

"That will have to wait." Uzmahndey slipped inside and closed and bolted the door. "Someone is following me."

Angela's face congealed into apprehension. "Where is he?"

"Out on the street in front of the hotel."

Charlie, with the stuffed animal, joined them just inside the door. "Snugglesaurus says no government agencies have tracked your identity down from those videos."

"*Someone* is tracking me."

"Are you sure?" Charlie asked.

"The xenobots are." He turned to Angela. "Now what were you and Charlie talking about?"

"Charlie wants to take the children's room. She says I should sleep with you in the double bed." Angela dropped her eyes. "But if someone is following us."

"It's okay. I get it." When she looked back up, he managed a smile. "You need to protect Charlie. That is your prime directive. I should know that by now." He smiled at Charlie. "Thanks for trying, kid." He dropped his smile and turned away from both of them. "I'm still too worked up to settle down. We've got free use of the sauna?"

Charlie consulted Snugglesaurus. "Yes. Of the entire wellness area."

"I need to let off some steam." He paused for a reaction, but none was forthcoming. "Let off some steam? In the steam room?"

Charlie groaned. "Dad joke."

"When did you learn *that* expression?" Uzmahndey saw Snugglesaurus wink at him. With a glass eye? Impossible. No, improbable, maybe. Nothing seemed impossible with Snugglesaurus. Did that mean the AI had a sense of humor? Uzmahndey tried to keep it on a humorous level. "Can I use an *adult* robe?"

Charlie's groan morphed into a laugh. "Of course. The kid robe wouldn't even fit me."

"We'll all go." Angela was adamant. "We need to stay together."

Uzmahndey located a robe and went into the kinder room to undress. Wanting to give the two females plenty of time to do the same, he sat down on the bottom bunk. It didn't feel that bad.

"What do you think, guys?"

<u>The AI has discovered a religious sect of devoted Gaia worshippers.</u>

She is mobilizing them to oppose you.

We're good, Snugglesaurus is powerful, Angela is strong, and Charlie is tough, but they outnumber us.

"What about Ghost?"

<u>We know next to nothing about him.</u>

The AI will not divulge any information.

"So you have no theories for what his actual intentions are for the human race?"

We'll let you know the minute we figure something out. We're part of the human race, too, you know. We live in you, and you're human. Whatever the alien intelligence has planned for Earth affects us as much as anybody.

The sauna wasn't crowded. Although everyone was wrapped up in towels, Charlie was surprised to see both men and women present. Uzmahndey reminded her they were no longer in a Muslim country, that Europeans were much more casual about the sexes mixing. Angela found a quiet corner for them to settle into.

Uzmahndey sighed, leaned back, and finally relaxed. This felt wonderful. The hot steam leeched concerns out through his polluted pores. Until a burly middle-aged man sat beside him. Uzmahndey was instantly alert. What now? But the xenobots hadn't raised an alarm, so it was probably nothing.

Or so he thought, until the man spoke in the voice of his old LSU head coach. "Don't get so upset with Angela. She has made great progress."

Recognizing the voice, Uzmahndey didn't miss a beat. "That wasn't a smart move approaching me at Giant's Causeway like you did. We are all over the Internet now."

"You're probably right. But Snugglesaurus is handling the problem."

"So you are not infallible."

The heavyset man smiled. "Far from it."

"Coach was. Infallible."

"I'm not really him."

"Then what are you?"

"I've told you. Information."

"How does that work? Sentient information?"

"The Universe is a hologram. Surely you've heard that theory."

"Nah, I don't watch Marvel movies."

"It's not comic book material. It's the way the Universe is."

"That's hard to believe."

"Reality is a projection on the walls of your existence. That idea has been around since Plato. Like shadows on a cave wall, or images projected onto a movie screen in a theater. The action takes place on the surface of the screen, the theater itself is a void. I can project you through the void to anywhere on this wall. In fact, I'm projecting your image right now."

"What are you talking about?"

"Look at Angela and Charlie."

Uzmahndey did. They were sitting quietly side by side.

"Don't you think it strange Angela would allow a total stranger to join you three without reacting in a defensive way?"

"You're right. What's going on?"

"She can't see either of us. All she sees is you sitting still with your eyes closed. That is the hologram of you I am projecting." The heavyset man focused his gaze on Angela. "Angela is my creation. I'm extremely proud of her."

"You should be. You did a good job. It's hard to remember she's a robot."

"Thank you."

"Is it okay for us to be intimate? That won't damage her, will it?"

Ghost chuckled. "You sound like a suitor asking permission of his girlfriend's father to court her."

"I'm just wondering if it's a good idea."

"It will bond you two in ways you don't foresee."

The faint outline of a frown crossed Uzmahndey's face. "Is that a good thing?"

"It will be a wonderful thing. But don't press her. She is still evolving."

"Okay." Uzmahndey nodded his acceptance. "I was also wondering about Charlie. Must she grow up so quickly? She is missing so much."

"Her rapid growth is an expression of her alien genes. It is imperative she reach adulthood as quickly as possible. Once she does, her growth spurts will cease, and from then on she will age the normal human way."

He looked Uzmahndey over. "You've been in here quite a while. It's not healthy to stay in here too long, especially if you aren't used to the sauna."

Uzmahndey began stirring. "Wow, you're right. I feel as limp as a noodle."

Ghost smiled as he stood. "Being a noodle does no one any good. You need to get out of here." He walked away into a bank of steam.

When they returned to their rooms, Uzmahndey and Charlie were so deliciously enfeebled by the sauna they were ready for bed. He stumbled into the kinder room, where he pulled his robe off and tumbled naked onto the bottom bunk.

Angela looked in on him with concern from the open doorway. When the look evolved into a stare, he at last asked what the problem was. She retreated from the room without responding and closed the door.

The next morning they rose early and dressed warmly. The ice cave they were going to was high up in the mountains and would be below freezing, perhaps well below considering the winds howling up there. But first things first. They hit the breakfast buffet. Or rather Charlie hit it, while Uzmahndey tackled it. The xenobots had been working hard lately.

They took a taxi to Salzburg Parsch train station. After boarding, Uzmahndey scanned the passengers for the feathered Alpine hat, but didn't see it or the person who had been wearing it. All three xenobots assured him they had noticed no one following them from the hotel. So he relaxed and enjoyed the excursion. They rode through the city to the Salzach River, which they followed out into the countryside. After crossing the river and passing by a quarry they entered a long tunnel, emerging from it in the mountains. The train followed the river's twisting course far up into the Alps.

More than an hour of breathtaking Alpine scenery brought them to Tenneck. They disembarked and caught a bus up to the Eisriesenwelt visitor center. From there a short walk took them to the cable car loading platform. A stunning nearly vertical much-too-brief climb up cliff face after cliff face provided heart-stopping sights of the valley far below. They disembarked at the top for a half-hour hike on a covered walkway along the bald face of a mountain. All these stunning views were unlike any Uzmahndey had ever witnessed before.

The covered walk led them to the mouth of the cave, secured by a steel door. Once everyone was inside, the tour guide distributed gas lanterns. He led the group deep into the cave along a paved path with guardrails. Eisriesenwelt was the largest ice cave in the world. The flowing walls and stabbing spires of ice just kept coming. They passed through one high-ceilinged cavern after another of monumental icy landscapes filled with exotic natural ice sculptures that sparkled in the soft glow of lantern light. For over an hour they hiked through this frozen wonderland.

Throughout the tour Uzmahndey remained on guard. Determined to regain Angela's trust, he kept Charlie within arms reach the entire time. The dark recesses of the vast cave gave limitless opportunity for ambush, but no monstrosities attacked. Uzmahndey never saw any creatures lurking in the shadows. None even tried to persuade him to abandon the quest, like they had done at Spotted Lake and the Richat Structure. He watched Angela's back when she dropped back from the group to place a Cheerio, but there was no need. What was going on?

After safely emerging from the cave without incident, Uzmahndey pulled Angela aside. "Why weren't we attacked? Why did none of them try to turn me?"

Angela merely shrugged. "I do not know what their strategy is."

He turned inward. "Any ideas, guys?"

Gaia may be trying to lull you into a false sense of security.

You are expecting them to try something at the portals, so maybe they'll attack you somewhere else.

Or maybe they've given up and are packing their bags.

"Not very helpful, guys."

Back at their hotel all three went into their separate bedrooms to strip out of their clothes, wrap towels around their still-chilled skin, pull their robes on, and head for the sauna. When it was time to leave, Charlie was so limp she slid off the bench and had to be dragged out. They returned to their room to dress, then went to the restaurant to once again feast on hearty German fare.

It was late by the time they returned to their suite. Without a word, Charlie carried Snugglesaurus into the kinder room. Uzmahndey stood stock still watching the door close in his face.

Angela took his hand and pulled him into the larger bedroom. "I detected no one following us today. Snugglesaurus will notify me if he detects any danger tonight. If there is I'll be sure to wake you." The largest smile ever to grace an artificial face appeared. "If you are asleep."

Angela closed the door, and they both undressed. Once naked, she didn't reach for her pajamas. She merely stared at Uzmahndey after he climbed in under the covers.

She's waiting for you to take your underwear off.

Uzmahndey wormed them off and tossed them to the floor. When Angela climbed in he pulled her close. While he stroked her back and shoulders with soothing caresses, she wasted no time, reaching below the covers for him.

Uzmahndey was okay with Angela taking charge. He was nervous, as he was every first time with a new partner. And this was far from a normal first time. His new partner was not human. Yet he had spent so much time with Angela, been through so much with her, by this point he was more curious than worried. How would the xenobots react? How would *he* react to sharing the experience with three others? To making love to a robot? He had seen 'Westworld', of course. In that show the men had seemed to enjoy it. But they had used and abused the robots. He would not do this. Angela was so dear to him that his feelings for her were real. He sincerely wanted this to be a real relationship.

Once Uzmahndey slid into her, all altruistic thoughts disappeared. This was as good as any sex he'd ever had with any woman. Better. As it went on and on. Were the xenobots holding him back? Were they prolonging the act, trying to make this better for him? Better for themselves? Better for Angela? Angela's lips and hands and legs wandering all over him were as warm and human as any he had ever felt. Her hips matched his rhythm, her fingers digging into his butt urged him faster, harder, deeper.

Until, at last, release.

Uzmahndey collapsed on her. "That was incredible."

Angela stroked his hair, rubbed his back, petted his bottom. "Yes, it was."

"Really? For you? You're not just saying that?"

"You've made me a real woman tonight."

"You are a real woman. I don't care who made you."

She rolled out from beneath him. "Now sleep."

He did just that.

Uzmahndey woke during the night to find himself alone in bed. He felt Angela's side. Not even warm. He rose to look into the kinder bedroom. Angela was in the top bunk, awake of course, above Charlie sleeping with Snugglesaurus in the lower bunk. He walked up to kiss her, to let her know he was okay with this. Then he went back to bed.

Chapter 15

Interlude Two

Uzmahndey was shaken from a pit-mine deep sleep. He pried his eyes open using a lump of coal as a fulcrum to find Angela, fully dressed, bending over him. "We've got to hurry. There's not much time."

The room was dark, except for light coming from the kinder room. "What's going on?"

"It's been five hours already. Get up, Uz."

"Five hours since what?"

Angela yanked the covers off him. "Since we made love."

Uzmahndey stretched every extremity to the max. "It feels like five minutes."

She shoved him out of bed. "Get dressed. An Uber driver is coming."

Uzmahndey landed in a heap on the floor. Before he could yell how angry he was at Angela for doing that, Charlie popped through the open door already out of her pajamas and into her underwear. "She's pregnant." She popped back out.

That landed on Uzmahndey's head like a hopper full of coal. "How can you know? It's only been hours."

"Five hours." Angela threw the clothes he had worn the day before at him. "Get dressed or I'll carry you down to the curb like that."

Uzmahndey scrambled to his feet. He had no doubt she could do that, never mind the xenobots. "How can you even be pregnant?" he asked as he stepped into his pants. "You're a robot."

"I told you everything was functional down there."

"Really? I was asking about your woman parts for sex. I wasn't asking about your woman parts for making babies. You're a robot. How can you make a baby?"

Charlie popped in once again, snapping and zipping her pants. "She gave birth to me." She ducked back out.

"Okay. So you're a robot who can give birth. Somehow. What's the rush? You've got nine months."

Charlie entered once again, this time slinging on her shirt. "She's nearly two months already." She ducked back out.

It finally erupted within Uzmahndey's sleep-addled brain that, just like Charlie, the baby Angela was carrying wasn't growing at a normal pace. He shifted into high gear. "How much time do we have?"

Charlie rushed in buttoning her shirt. "Snugglesaurus says a little over one day. Every three hours the baby ages one month."

Uzmahndey paused to tally up the math.

Twenty-seven hours, dimwit. Get a move on.

Angela wheeled the suitcases up to the door. She had already packed everything. "Come! On!"

Uzmahndey jammed his feet into shoes, jammed his pocket articles into pockets, snatched up his phone, and ran.

In addition to summoning the half-asleep Uber driver awaiting them before the hotel, Snugglesaurus had also found a nearby condo for them. There hadn't been time to rent one, so the AI had located an empty unit. Charlie punched in the security code Snugglesaurus gave her, and they were in.

As they hauled their suitcases inside, Uzmahndey proved to be as frantic as any first-time father. "Shouldn't we get you to a hospital?"

"She's only into her third month," Charlie said.

"But this isn't a normal pregnancy."

"I can handle it myself," Angela said.

Charlie smiled. "She's already been through it once."

Uzmahndey moaned his way down into a stiff couch. "Why didn't you tell me this would happen? Protection didn't even cross my mind. You're a robot. How could you get pregnant?"

"You shouldn't upset an expectant mother," Charlie snapped.

"He's not upsetting me." Angela was as calm as ice. "I carry biological material from another world. Charley will be half-alien and half-human. Same as Charlie."

"So you're like a Petri dish." Uzmahndey glanced at Charlie. She seemed to be taking this well. But he had way more urgent worries than Charlie's emotional state. He looked back to Angela. "You know it's a boy? And you are naming him Charley? Won't that get confusing?"

"I like Charley."

"Let me see."

Angela pulled up her shirt. Her stomach looked a little puffy.

He stroked it. "My God. My son is in there. My half-human son."

Angela stood. "I need to get out of these clothes. They are starting to feel tight." She unbuttoned her shirt.

"What are you going to wear?"

Charlie produced a hotel robe from out of a suitcase. "We swiped one."

Angela pulled her shirt off, unfastened her bra. "You two need to get busy."

"Doing what?" Uzmahndey asked.

"Getting ready for the baby."

Charlie held up Snugglesaurus. "He's already been busy. He located a store that has everything we need. Medical supplies and baby stuff. He's ordered it all online. He paid premium so they'll deliver it as soon as they open."

Uzmahndey was shocked that he could still be shocked, but he was. "You're having the baby here?!"

"I did it before, with no one but Snugglesaurus to help." She looked from Uzmahndey to Charlie as she unsnapped and unzipped her slacks. "This time I'll have plenty of help."

Uzmahndey scowled all around. "It's not sterile."

"Half of the baby will be extremely hardy." She smiled as she stepped out of her slacks. "And you seemed healthy even before swallowing the xenobots. So the human half will be strong, too."

"Won't it be, I don't know, kind of messy?"

"I'll give birth in the bathtub." She stepped out of her panties, then took the robe Charlie handed her. "Besides, it won't be that messy. I'm a robot, remember?" She slipped the robe on.

Uzmahndey shot toward the door. "I need some coffee."

"You're not abandoning us, are you?" Charlie asked.

"Of course not. Angela is giving birth to my son. I just need to clear my head." Uzmahndey burst out the door and down the hall. That was a joke. His head would never be clear ever again.

Yeah, baby, you got us in here.

We are being as unobtrusive as we can be.

"Maybe you could be a little *more* intrusive. Why didn't you warn me Angela could get pregnant?"

We did not know. We are not omnipotent.

That's right. We only know what you know, or what Snugglesaurus tells us.

Or what we learn through your senses. We sure learned a lot last night.

Uzmahndey barged out of the building onto the sidewalk. It was still dark, but traffic was heavier than when they had arrived. He checked the time on his phone. Six a.m. Angela was nearly four months. He put his phone away and strode down the sidewalk.

Are you okay?

"I've not been okay since the day that woman walked into my office."

Don't you want a son?

"A human one. When I'm ready. I don't like being tricked into it. Angela knew she would get pregnant and said nothing about it. That's why she wanted to wait for a 'good location'."

Austria is a modern high-tech country that has everything we need readily available. That makes it a good location.

"She could have warned me."

What's done is done.

Uzmahndey stopped in his tracks. "I know what's been done, Good. It's my child. No matter how weird. If he was born with a physical or mental handicap, I'd accept him. So what if he's half-alien? He's half-human, too. Half me."

A middle-aged man approached on the sidewalk. He gave Uzmahndey a strange look as he stopped and addressed him. "Bist du deppert?"

"What did he just say?"

Are you crazy. Nod your head yes and say 'Ich glob ich spinne'.

He nodded his head at the man and massacred the line Bad had given him. The man walked on, shaking his head.

Uzmahndey returned to the condo with an orange juice and the kind of pastries he'd seen Charlie eat at hotel breakfast buffets. She sat at the dining room table and gobbled them down. He sat with her to finish his coffee. "How long have you known about all this?"

"Snugglesaurus filled me in this morning."

"You seem to be handling it well."

She shrugged. "What choice do I have?"

"Do you know who *your* father is?"

"A tourist from California," Angela called out.

Damn, he'd forgotten how good her hearing was. Uzmahndey turned toward her. "How did you meet him?"

"He was about to pass out in a bar."

Uzmahndey laughed. Then glanced an apology at Charlie. "Sorry."

Another shrug. "I'm not. I'm glad to be alive."

"It's not been much of a life. You're really, what, about a month old?"

"With the body and the knowledge of a fifteen year old," Angela added.

Uzmahndey turned to her. "Has Snugglesaurus filled her in on her alien culture?"

"Not yet. It's not as imperative she learn that, since she is living here and not there."

"Where is there?"

"I don't know. Father hasn't told me where he comes from. Right now I've got other things to deal with."

"Is everything going okay?"

"So far."

He turned back to Charlie. "So you are going to have a half-brother."

"No, she's not. Your son Charley is from a different stock."

Back to Angela. "He won't inherit anything from you?"

"I'm not organic. I am only a container for organic material. A Petri dish, like you said. Charley has a different mother from who his sister has."

"Why do you insist on naming him Charley? That will be so confusing." Angela showed no sign of yielding to reason. "How about Charles?"

"His name is Charley," Angela said.

"Fine. But I'm calling him Charles."

Charlie, having finished the pastries and juice, stood, snatched up Snugglesaurus, and walked off into a bedroom.

Uzmahndey turned back to Angela. "Maybe this is upsetting her more than she let's on."

Angela looked to the closed bedroom door. "I hope you can help her."

"Me?"

"You are the only human influence she has."

"So now I am supposed to be a role model? An alcoholic-ex-NFL-athlete-washed-up-at-twenty-six role model?"

"You didn't mention your most important roles."

Uzmahndey jerked around at the sound of his old college head coach's voice. A middle-aged man in medical scrubs stood before him.

"What are you supposed to be now?"

"An obstetrician." Ghost raised both arms. In the blink of an eye the condo transformed into a maternity ward. "You were upset that Angela wasn't going to a hospital. So I brought a hospital to her. Satisfied?"

When Charlie emerged to see what the commotion was, Ghost asked,

"Want to be my nurse?"

She nodded dumbly, and was immediately clad in scrubs.

Ghost turned back to Uzmahndey. "Will you be attending the birth? Most modern fathers here do."

"You mentioned something about my most important roles."

"Besides being father to the second alien ever born on this planet, you will be Earth's ambassador to an alien race."

"Wow." Charlie grinned. "That's an impressive resume."

Uzmahndey shook his head. "All I ever wanted to do was play football."

By the time the ordered supplies were delivered early that afternoon, Angela was in her fifth month. After Uzmahndey and Charlie feasted on the food the Austrian version of Grubhub delivered, they prepared the bathroom for delivery. Every so often Uzmahndey asked Angela how she was doing, and every time she opened her robe to present an ever larger stomach.

By that evening Uzmahndey was convinced the record-breaking pace of the pregnancy wasn't endangering his son, so he was able to divert his mind to other matters. He cornered Ghost in the kitchen. "Tell me about my son's ancestral home."

"We left it eons ago. It was used up. It is nothing but a barren rock."

"Where do you live now?"

"Interstellar space."

"How can you exist in outer space?"

"As information."

"You don't have bodies?"

"Not until we arrive at a planet that supports life. Like yours. We recreate the recorded patterns of our biological essence with the native material on hand, which we then mix with the dominant life form. Once we are established on a planet, we move on."

"You've done this before?"

"Many times."

"How do you travel between planets?"

"I told you, as information. When I arrived in Hawaii..."

"At Keck Observatory?"

"Yes. When they trained their telescope on us, I followed the track back to the source."

"Someone at Keck *saw* you?"

"Saw what we did. We set off high-energy bursts in deep space. Something to attract the attention of beings technologically advanced enough to react to them. Like shooting off a flare. Once we detect their reaction, we track their focus back to its source."

"No matter how far away?"

"No matter."

"How can you reach us so quickly? From deep space?"

"You are limited by the speed of light. We are limited only by the speed of thought."

"How fast is that?"

"Instantaneous."

"Impossible. Nothing moves faster than the speed of light."

"Nothing *physical* can travel faster than the speed of light. Information is not physical."

"You are giving me a headache."

"Really? I've not even gotten started yet. Information can be faster than instantaneous. Information can travel so fast it can precede itself and influence how it came about."

"You're talking about time travel now?"

"In a sense. Your own physicists have done experiments where the reaction to a decision has preceded the decision itself. You can react to a thought before the thought is conceived."

"That's impossible."

"No, that's information."

Uzmahndey collapsed in a chair.

"You got the wrong guy for this ambassador position. You need an Einstein."

"That's exactly who we don't need. Scientists have too many rigid preconceived beliefs. You are a blank slate."

Uzmahndey scowled up at him. "Is that supposed to be a compliment?"

"Take it any way you like." The doctor beamed down at him. "So I had the plans and your planet supplied the materials."

"To recreate your genetic code?"

"And to construct Angela, the AI, and the xenobots. When I first arrived here I encountered Gaia and her ilk. A race of highly-advanced extremophiles living inside the Earth influencing you humans, and not in a good way. They are vicious parasites, with no compassion for their hosts."

"Why have I never heard of them?"

"You have, in myths. What you probably haven't heard about is the Schumann Resonance."

"What is that?"

Ghost shook his head. "We can't go into it now. There is too much going on. But I *will* tell you that the network of xenobots you three, soon to be four, are establishing around the planet will free humans from Gaia's dominion."

"That is why Gaia is fighting back."

"Yes. As we complete more of the net we are trapping them in, they will fight ever more fiercely."

"Why are you doing this for us?"

"We don't want our progeny living under Gaia's dark sway. Freed from her over-lordship, this planet will blossom as never before. Now excuse me. I need to see how your son is doing." The doctor walked out of the kitchen.

By the time Uzmahndey collapsed with exhaustion, Angela was into her seventh month. It was only seven p.m., but he had been up since three that morning and needed to catch a nap before the delivery.

Charlie roused him at eleven, when Angela was going into her ninth month. He found her sprawled naked in the bathtub. Her stomach was huge. "Charley can come at any time now," she blithely informed him.

"Scrub up," Ghost instructed. "It's up to you and Charlie to deliver the baby."

Charlie scrubbed first, while Uzmahndey stewed behind her. "She did this before by herself?"

"Yes," the doctor answered. "But this time she will have your help."

"It's psychological," Angela spoke up from the tub. "I'm perfectly able to do this alone. But if you are engaged with the birth then you will feel more attached to the baby."

Uzmahndey noticed the glare Ghost gave Angela. Apparently she wasn't sticking to the program. Was she telling him something Ghost didn't want him to know? Was she favoring him over her father? She could do that, and would?

Angela continued, ignoring the glare from Ghost. "Human fathers normally have nine months to become attached to the baby growing inside the mother's womb. You only have twenty-seven hours."

This warmed his heart more than anything she had yet done. She was defying Ghost and preferring him. She had grown more human beyond even what she had been before the explosion at Eternal Flame Falls. While Ghost was still merely information. Cold hard facts could be exactly that – cold and hard.

The birth went off without a hitch. Snugglesaurus instructed Charlie how to care for the newborn. She cleaned the baby up and bundled him in a blue blanket. While this was going on, Angela cleaned herself up. She didn't seem to be discomfited whatsoever, same as she had been all during the delivery. Charlie held the baby until Angela put her pilfered robe back on.

She carried Charley out of the bathroom into the condo. The hospital delivery room was gone, along with the doctor. She settled into a recliner and began nursing. Charlie, exhausted, went to bed. Uzmahndey pulled a chair up beside the recliner to watch his son take his first meal. Not long after the baby finished feeding and dozed off at Angela's breast, Uzmahndey dozed off on the couch.

Awakening late the next morning, he found Angela gone and the baby asleep in the baby seat that had been delivered the day before. He got up to look the infant over, taking care not to disturb him. If he was half-alien it didn't show. No eyes on stalks, no tail, no antennae. He looked as human as any baby.

Angela's emergence from a bedroom interrupted Uzmahndey's contemplation of his son. "How did he do last night?"

"He slept, ate, and pooped. That's all any baby does."

"So he's okay?"

"He's heartier than any other baby born yesterday."

"He looks beautiful." Uzmahndey hugged Angela. "You are beautiful."

She returned the hug. "You're not angry with me?"

He peered into her eyes. "I should be. But you are the mother of my child."

"Technically…"

"I know. You're a surrogate mother. Not the biological mother. If there is a biological mother?"

"Of course there is. Half his genetic code came from an actual being other than you."

Uzmahndey released her. "Are we taking a break from our trip? To care for the baby?"

"I was planning on us leaving today, but something else has come up." Angela glanced to the closed bedroom door she had just passed through. "Charlie is now eighteen."

Uzmahndey shrank back. "Oh no. Besides having a newborn to deal with, we also have a teenage zombie."

"This is her final growth spurt. She is now an adult. She will age in a normal human fashion from now on."

"That's good to hear." He glanced down to the sleeping newborn. "Will Charles go through these same growth spurts?"

"Approximately the same."

"This is a lot for me. I need to clear my head." Uzmahndey put his shoes on. "I'm going for a walk. I'll bring back some breakfast for Charlie."

Uzmahndey headed down the sidewalk toward the pastry shop he had found the day before. On the street traffic was heavy but, early on a weekday morning there were not many pedestrians.

You are being followed.

"Damn it!" Uzmahndey wheeled around to scan the few people on the sidewalks.

That was smooth. A spy you will never be.

"Who is it?"

That woman walking a dog.

And that old man sitting on the bench.

"I've got *two* people following me?"

Four. There's also that middle-age couple in front of the clothing store.

This could be the reason you weren't attacked in the ice cave. Gaia is giving her believers a chance to mass.

Uzmahndey located all four. None of them seemed to be paying him any attention.

"Sure you guys aren't just being paranoid?"

They aren't watching you now, you're looking. They are better at this than you.

"I'll shake them."

To what purpose? I'm sure they already know where you're staying.

"What do they want?"

We don't know.

Start walking again, Double O Zilch.

Uzmahndey continued toward the pastry shop.

"Why don't I beat the shit out of one of them and find out what's going on?"

In the middle of Salzburg? In broad daylight? Come on, James, you're smarter than that. Maybe.

When Uzmahndey returned to the condo he informed Angela he had been followed. Before he could say much else, Charlie emerged from the bedroom, her slack body still in ill-fitting pajamas. He couldn't help but grin. "I've had mornings where I felt as bad as you look."

Charlie grunted as she slumped into a chair at the kitchen table.

They spent the rest of the day in the condo. If enemies were closing in, they needed to stay out of sight. Angela cared for the infant, who spent most of the day sleeping. Charlie never changed out of her pajamas. She spent most of the day curled up in bed with Snugglesaurus.

Uzmahndey was left alone to fret the day away. He had this trip around the world to complete. With an eighteen-year old who had been alive for a month. And a robot he was not only romantically involved with but was also the mother of his son, despite what she claimed. And with his half-alien newborn son. Also, he couldn't forget about the three xenobots living inside him. And this holographic information guy who kept popping up in different guises spouting science babble with the voice of his old college coach. And they were all battling this alien creature and her host of monstrous minions living inside the Earth who had dominated mankind since the dawn of history. And they were being followed by fanatic worshipers of these beings. Plenty enough to keep him stewing all day.

Snugglesaurus ordered dinner to be delivered that evening so they wouldn't have to venture outside. They all bedded down shortly after. Charlie with Snugglesaurus in what had become her bedroom in the two-bedroom condo. Uzmahndey could have taken the other bed, but Angela sat up in a recliner in the living room to care for Charley all night, so he stretched out on the couch like he'd done the night before. He liked being near his son, and he'd gotten used to spending the night with Angela, even if she never slept. It was amazing what all he had gotten used to since leaving Hawaii. All this strangeness bounding about his mind should have kept him wide awake, but the xenobots lulled him into a deep dreamless sleep.

Chapter 16

Babele

The train from Salzburg out of Austria across Hungary into Romania to Brasov was yet another exhausting day-long journey. Charlie napped on the train. This was easy for her, as she was still recuperating from her latest, and mercifully last, growth spurt, so could sleep anywhere anyhow anywhen. They hadn't taken the time to buy new clothes for her before boarding the train. The best she could find to wear was another elastic waist skirt which, like the last one, was way too short. She was too out of it to care, but every time she dozed off in her seat Uzmahndey tugged the hem as far down her longer legs as it would go.

One surprising development was when Angela took Snugglesaurus from out of Charlie's grasp as she slept and put it in the baby carrier with the newborn. "He needs it now more than Charlie."

"Snugglesaurus will help his development like it did Charlie?"

Angela nodded. "Snugglesaurus is doing it now."

Uzmahndey glanced up at sleeping Charlie. "But she just had a growth spurt. Doesn't she need him?"

"Charley is the most vulnerable. He is my focus now." She rearranged the stuffed dinosaur, which once again looked huge next to a newborn. "You must look after her."

Uzmahndey tugged her hem down.

Later during the trip he pulled out his phone and walked down the aisle of the train to find a quiet corner. "Keanu?"

"I've been trying to call you."

"We're in and out of coverage. What's going on?"

"Someone broke into your office. And your condo."

"What did they take?"

"Nothing I can tell. Looks like they were looking for something."

"Damn. I've got people following me here."

"Think it's got something to do with those videos from Northern Ireland?"

"Could be."

"I filed a police report on both break-ins."

"And?"

"They don't have a clue. What have you gotten yourself into?"

"Fatherhood."

"Really? Congratulations. Who is the unlucky mother?"

"Angela."

"That woman you're taking on the extended tour?"

"Yeah."

"When is the baby due?"

"He was born yesterday."

"What? Are you adopting?"

"I might be. Her daughter. But the boy is mine." He rushed on before Keanu could ask any more awkward questions. "I'll tell you all about it when I get back. Be careful, Neo. These people could be dangerous."

"I'm cool. I'll let you know if anything else happens here. I'm dying to see your kids."

"My son's not green, thank God." Silence. Did he lose the connection? "Keanu?"

"Was that some kind of racist joke?"

"What?"

"You're black, and you told me Angela is white, so you're glad your kid didn't turn out green?"

Uzmahndey broke out in stress-relieving laughter. "No. Not a racist joke. It was a bad alien joke. Forget it. I'm goofy from jet lag."

"You're goofy, period."

Although Uzmahndey was beyond exhausted and approaching comatose by the time the train pulled into Brasov, the xenobots gave him a jolt of adrenaline to get him going. The two children had slept most of the trip, and Angela was Angela, so they were ready to go. While Angela carried Charley, Uzmahndey and Charlie rolled their luggage across the parking lot to the Unirea Shopping Center.

"Last one," Uzmahndey exulted. "Right? Charlie grows at a normal pace from now on?"

"Your son will start his growth spurts soon," Angela reminded him.

The exultation faded. "How soon?"

"I don't know. There is not an exact schedule."

A torturous hour later a taxi took them from the shopping center to the Victoria Boulevard Hotel, where Snugglesaurus had reserved a room for them. They crashed for what remained of the day. The adrenaline had worn off, and Uzmahndey was asleep on his feet before his feet left the floor.

Waking late that afternoon, Uzmahndey soon grew restless. He scanned the hotel brochure. "I see there is a spa here. Can Snugglesaurus set up an appointment for me?"

"Can I get one, too?" Charlie asked.

Angela's acquiescence surprised him. "Charlie doesn't have to stay by your side anymore?"

"She's grown. She needs to socialize more. Besides, she's under your supervision now."

Uzmahndey and Charlie changed into robes and headed for the spa.

"Pretend I'm talking to you," he said as they walked down the hall. "I'm going to check in with the xenobots and I don't want people thinking I'm crazy."

"It's too late for that. You are crazy." She smiled. "But I like you anyway."

When had that smile turned so dazzling? "I couldn't tell it by the way you treat me."

"I like the way you treat me. I saw you tugging on my skirt on the train, trying to keep me decently covered. That was sweet."

"You may be grown now, but you are still a child to me. It seems like just last month you were in a baby seat like the one Charles is in. Because it was."

"I don't know if it's been a long time or not. I've nothing to compare it to."

"Believe me, your childhood was brief. Moving right along." Uzmahndey turned his thoughts inward. "Were we followed on the train from Salzburg?"

<u>No.</u>

"And no one is following us around Brasov?"

<u>We will tell you if we detect anyone.</u>

<u>Just remember we are not perfect.</u>

<u>Yeah, especially since we rely on your eyes for input. And that hollow space between your ears to process it.</u>

"What's that like?"

Charlie's question jarred his focus. "What?"

"Having those xenobots inside you. In the Azores I saw how they can help you fight."

"I could fight pretty good before I had them. I was in the NFL."

Yeah, you were real good at getting pancaked.

"Butt out!"

Charlie froze. "I'm sorry."

Uzmahndey turned back to her. "I wasn't talking to you." He rubbed his forehead. "It's too difficult carrying on two conversations at the same time."

And chew gum.

"That's it. New rule. *You* keep quiet. If I need to know something then Good or Ugly can tell me."

Charlie laughed. "Good or Ugly? You've got names for them?" When Uzmahndey merely glared at her, she continued. "What's the other one's name?"

"Bad. The Good, the Bad, and the Ugly is the name of an old Western movie. The names fit them."

Except for mine. I am not ugly.

"Ugly, I'm warning you. I'll restrict your speaking privileges, too."

Charlie burst out laughing. "You can restrict their speaking privileges!?"

Uzmahndey cast a final glare at her then charged ahead on down the hall.

"Ugly!" Charlie called out as she chased after. "Tell him to slow down. I can't keep up."

Charlie did catch up by the time they reached the spa. Where Uzmahndey received another shock. When asked by a masseuse if they required separate rooms, Charlie blurted no before Uzmahndey could get yes out. She pulled off her robe and stretched out naked upon her stomach.

Uzmahndey just stared. When another masseuse came in and urged him to remove his robe, he stepped back. "We're not doing this."

Charlie looked up at him with poorly-performed innocence. "Doing what? Getting a massage?"

Uzmahndey focused on the masseuse. "I require a separate room."

"Why, Uz? I'm eighteen now."

The masseuse led Uzmahndey into a different cubicle. "She is not your wife? Or girlfriend?"

"She is my daughter. Adopted daughter. Sort of."

The young woman smiled. "A Lolita?"

"No. And if you want a tip you'll wipe that smirk off your face."

The masseuse did, and Uzmahndey removed his robe.

When he and Charlie returned to their room, he called a conference. "We've got to set some ground rules." He focused on Charlie. "I am not your father, but I have watched you grow up from a baby. I have feelings for you, but they are in no way sexual."

Charlie smiled at Uzmahndey, in no way innocently. "Snugglesaurus says there are cultures on Earth that allow a man to have more than one wife." She glanced at Angela. "Or a wife and concubines."

Angela shrugged. "We can not make love again, not unless you want another child. Take a concubine if you want." Her face darkened. "Just not Charlie."

"I don't want Charlie. In that way. Or another child, at least right now. Or multiple wives. Or a concubine." He let loose a long sigh of exasperation.

Angela stood. "Are we done here? It's time to feed Charley."

Uzmahndey moaned. "So now I get to see those beautiful breasts. Which I can no longer touch."

Angela picked up the baby. "Want me to go in the other room?"

"No. I enjoy watching you nurse." He glanced at Charlie. "But not in a sexual way."

"That sure sounded sexual to me," Charlie said.

"It's complicated. It's all complicated. At eighteen you cannot understand how complicated."

Angela sat in her recliner. She opened her robe and lifted the infant to a breast. "This isn't complicated. Baby is hungry, baby eats." She looked up to Uzmahndey. "If you want to be more involved with your child, you could help with changing his diapers."

The look of unease that crossed Uzmahndey's face at the suggestion wasn't complicated at all. Even Charlie could read it. She burst out laughing.

Early the next morning they all three dressed warmly since they would be hiking in the mountains. After checking out they took a taxi to the train station, where they caught a southbound train for Bustini. Charlie was much more alert on this trip, and busied herself watching videos, while Angela watched the passing countryside, as she always did when they traveled. Uzmahndey wondered what she was seeing? Was she trying to learn about the planet? Could she be genuinely impressed by what she saw? Was she learning, or enjoying, or some combination of the two? Since she had given birth to his son he had grown much more interested in what made her tick.

The train whisked them through a mix of open fields and small towns. Soon after they were in a valley following the Timis River through the heavily-forested Carpathian Mountains. They emerged from a tunnel into the city of Predeal. From there it was a short distance to Bustini.

After checking their luggage, they walked out of the train station carrying only what they would need for the day. Uzmahndey and Charlie each bore backpacks, while Angela had Charley and Snugglesaurus. She pointed skyward. "That is where we are headed."

Uzmahndey and Charlie looked up. A large cross emerged from out of the shifting low clouds atop the highest peak to the west. "This is different," Uzmahndey said. "A man-made destination. We've always visited natural locales before."

"We're not going to the Heroes Cross. Babele is near it, so we're taking the same route up."

The cable car they stepped into was old and creaky. It started with a jerk, and shook everyone up whenever it passed over a support tower. Charlie clutched Uzmahndey's hand. She squeezed even harder when half-way up they were enveloped in fog. Nothing but swirling gray could be seen. Circulation didn't return to Uzmahndey's hand until the cable car reached the top and Charlie let go to scramble out.

Angela led the way to the trailhead for the Babele rock formations. Heavy clouds obscured the view below in all directions. Charlie was disappointed. "You can't even see the town."

Angela voiced no sympathy for her. "We're not here to sightsee." She walked off with the baby into the fog.

Uzmahndey escorted Charlie from one weird eroded rock shape to another. The mountaintop was dotted with all sizes, mysterious distinctive forms shrouded in vaporous fog.

A young man appeared out of the fog. "English?" After Uzmahndey nodded, the young man smiled. "Yes. English. Good." It immediately became clear to Uzmahndey it was Charlie the man was interested in. "Have you heard story of Babele?"

Enjoying his attention, Charlie smiled and shook her head no.

"An evil old woman named Dochia who lived on this mountain tormented her daughter-in-law. On the first day of March, way too early in the year, she sent the young woman up to this mountaintop to pick wild berries. Seeing her search desperately in the snow, God took pity on her and appeared to her as an old man. He gave her some fresh berries to take back to her wicked mother-in-law. Dochia, seeing the fresh berries, thought winter must have ended early, so she took her sheep up onto the mountain to graze. The warm weather made her throw away nine coats in nine days. But then the weather suddenly changed, and she and all her sheep froze. The ice formations they made transformed into the strange stones you see here."

Uzmahndey was relieved to see Charlie attracted to some man other than him. This was a healthy development. "Why don't you let him show you around, Charlie? He might know some more interesting stories about Babele."

They both gave Uzmahndey wide smiles of appreciation, then he led Charlie off.

Angela joined Uzmahndey. "Is she safe with him?"

"I'll keep an eye on them. It's good for Charlie to meet other people. Like you said, she needs to learn to socialize." To his surprise, Angela nodded in agreement. "Go ahead and do what you need to do."

He accompanied Angela to the largest rock formation. "That's impressive." Noticing a sign in Romanian, he asked, "What does it say?"

"Sphinx." Angela took the Tupperware container holding the Cheerios from her backpack. The swirling mist helped conceal her as she planted a xenobot at its feet. Raising up, she looked all around. "Where is Charlie?"

Uzmahndey's sharp xenobot-enhanced eyesight pierced the light mist and he pointed to the outlines of the young couple standing nearby before a mushroom-shaped rock. "Can we give them some more time together? She seems to be enjoying the young man's company."

The three of them wound their way through the exotic rocks on a roundabout route to join the couple. "Tell me more about where you come from."

"I come from here." When Uzmahndey scowled at her, she continued. "I was created here. Fashioned of material from here. Earth."

"So you know nothing about where Ghost comes from." When she shook her head no, he probed further. "Is he here to liberate us, like he says, or is he here to colonize us?"

"He is here to help us."

"Help can mean different things to different people. Missionaries thought they were helping Native Americans when they destroyed their indigenous culture and forced them to adopt European ways." Yet Uzmahndey was struck by Angela including herself with humanity with her simple 'us'. She was brought into existence on Earth, made of materials from the Earth. So she considered herself an Earthling? "What do you know about Gaia?"

"Only what Father has told me. That she came to this planet several million years ago and has oppressed humanity since humans descended from the trees."

<u>Charlie is in trouble.</u>

Uzmahndey quickly scanned the bank of wispy mist enshrouding the hillside. He immediately located the struggling couple. He dashed across the mountain to them.

The young man held Charlie from behind with a large blade to her throat. "Gaia resists the invaders!"

Charlie screamed as the knife slashed her.

There was no blood. The astonished young man raised his hand to slash again.

He never got the chance. Uzmahndey leaped forward and grabbed his arm. It snapped like dry kindling. The knife fell to the ground as the man screamed.

Charlie broke free of his other arm and stumbled away.

Uzmahndey pinned the man to the dirt as he moaned.

"Who are you?"

Angela charged up out of the fog.

"Leave him."

Uzmahndey looked up in disbelief.

"He tried to kill Charlie."

"The fog has concealed his actions. And so far yours. We can't get involved here. Let's go."

Uzmahndey gave the broken arm a savage twist.

The young man emitted a blood-curdling scream then passed out.

Angela grabbed Uzmahndey and pulled him away. "Was that necessary?"

"He won't ever use *that* arm again." Uzmahndey rushed to Charlie, huddled on the ground sobbing. He pulled her to her feet and inspected her throat. There was a scar, but no blood.

"She's okay," Angela insisted. "We have to go. Now."

Uzmahndey towed Charlie along as they followed Angela back toward the cable car platform. "Does your throat hurt?"

Charlie merely shook her head no as she pressed herself into his side as tight as she could.

Uzmahndey called up to Angela. "How is she unharmed?"

"The alien half of her is hardy. I told you that."

"She's invulnerable?"

"No. Just a lot tougher than pure-bred humans."

By this time they had reached the line to take the cable car back down. "What is the commotion back there?" one of the operators asked.

"I don't know," Angela said. "But my baby is worn out. I need to get him down off this mountain."

The operator looked at Charlie sobbing in Uzmahndey's arms. "Is she okay?"

"Just a lover's quarrel." Uzmahndey smiled, hugging her. "She'll be fine."

Chapter 17

Pumakkale

By the time Charlie got off the cable car at the bottom she was somewhat composed and steady on her feet, although in no hurry to abandon Uzmahndey's protective embrace. They walked directly back to the Bustini train station and reclaimed their luggage. Snugglesaurus had already booked them passage to Bucharest. The train ride was a chance for all of them to recover.

Only Angela wasn't ready to. She glared at Uzmahndey. "I have my hands full with the baby now. You have charge of Charlie. You need to take better care of her."

"He did," Charlie insisted, leaning into him.

Angela wasn't placated. "Next time it won't be a knife. They know now it will take more to kill her. Next time it will be a gun. Or a bomb."

"Would that do it?" Uzmahndey asked.

"Don't be an idiot. The new half-breeds will be hard to kill, but not indestructible." Her demeanor softened, but her rant wasn't over. "I agree she needs to socialize, now that she's turned eighteen. She needs to meet men other than you. But under strict supervision." Her tone sharpened again as she glared at Uzmahndey. "I am counting on you to provide that."

Uzmahndey took Charlie's hand. "I'm sorry. He seemed nice."

Charlie laid her head on his shoulder. "Can we stop talking about it? I don't want to think about it any more." She closed her eyes.

"If we don't think about it, next time could be the death of you." After saying this, Angela let it go and turned her attention to the baby.

It was late afternoon by the time they reached the North Railway Station in Bucharest. They disembarked and took a taxi to the Orhideea Residence and Spa. The Orchid Sky Restaurant on the top floor offered a stunning view of Bucharest, but no one much noted the Romanian cityscape, or the fine fare they were served.

After dinner, they went directly to their room. The only one Snugglesaurus had been able to secure was one with just a double bed. When Uzmahndey objected, Angela cut him short. "Don't be foolish. We are a family. You two take the bed. I'll sit up with the baby." While Angela settled into a chair for the night with Charley, Charlie went into the bathroom to change into pajamas.

Uzmahndey undressed down to his undershorts and climbed into bed. At eighteen Charlie was no longer a child. She was legally able to choose who to share a bed with. If both women were okay with it, why should he object? He really did not enjoy sleeping on a couch. Besides, he wasn't about to take advantage of his charge.

Charlie laughed when she found him perched on one side on the very edge with his back to her. "You're going to fall out of bed." She climbed in the other side. "Relax. I won't bite you."

Uzmahndey scooted back a little to a more comfortable position. When Charlie snuggled up to him from behind, he erupted. "No!"

She burrowed in closer. "Please. I feel so safe with you. Just until I fall asleep. Just for a little while."

<u>She needs this.</u>

<u>*And it feels kind of good.*</u>

<u>We'll lull you to sleep.</u>

Uzmahndey released a long sigh and closed his eyes. The xenobots were true to their word, or however they were communicating with him. He was asleep within a dozen breaths.

He awoke during the night with Angela looming over the bed. "What's wrong?"

"How could you sleep through all that thrashing and yelling?" Angela towered above him in the dark. "Charlie had a nightmare."

Uzmahndey could now hear Charlie's ragged breathing. He rolled over to find her flat on her back staring wide-eyed at the ceiling. He touched the side of her face. "We've got you, Charlie. No one is going to hurt you."

"It wasn't the man with the knife. On the mountaintop." She rolled over into him. "I don't know where I was. Somewhere scary. On another planet? In deep space? And those creatures."

Instead of scooting away, he pulled her close and stroked her hair. "You're okay. You are here with us. With your family. Go back to sleep." Eventually she did, with Uzmahndey close behind.

The next time Uzmahndey awoke it was early morning, this time to Angela shaking his shoulder. "What now?" he growled. But she was smiling. "Damn, Angela. I told you real women don't look so good in the morning."

She shushed him, then whispered. "I've got something to show you."

Uzmahndey found that he and Charlie had separated during the night. She was still asleep, curled up away from him. He slipped out, trying not to disturb her.

Angela was waiting with the baby in her arms. She handed Charley to him.

Uzmahndey found him heavier. And bigger. "He had a growth spurt?"

"His first."

"How old is he now?"

"Three months."

"That's not much of a spurt."

"It is. A human baby more than doubles its size in its first year."

"Let me see." Charlie had awakened.

He handed the baby down to her.

"You're right. He's so heavy." She laid Charley on the bed beside her, and Uzmahndey and Angela sat at either end of him. Charlie smiled all around. "We really are a family."

Another lengthy train ride took them from Bucharest out of Romania through Bulgaria into European Turkey to the Halkali Station. The exhausting trip was made even more exhausting for Uzmahndey by Charlie. She hardly left his side. This wasn't healthy.

Once while she was off to the bathroom, Uzmahndey asked Angela what he could do about her.

"You're asking me? About human behavior?" She snorted. "You are the expert on that."

"Expert? I know nothing about teenage girls. What I do know is she needs to meet some young man to take her mind off me. Someone who won't try to kill her." Getting no help on that front, he asked Angela to pass a request on to Snugglesaurus. "Tell him to send a link to my phone to whatever Internet sites he found on Gaia and her followers. I need to learn more about them."

Snugglesaurus did, and Uzmahndey spent much of the train ride perusing the information. 'Chaos was the origin of everything and the very first thing that ever existed. It was a primordial void from which everything was created. In ancient Greek, chaos is translated into 'the gapping void'. In the beginning, Chaos was a state of random disorder existing in primordial emptiness. Soon after a Cosmic Egg formed in its belly and it hatched, producing the first deities into the darkness.'

He looked up at Charlie, draped all over him reading over his shoulder.

"That Cosmic Egg sounds a lot like the Big Bang."

He resumed reading off his phone. 'Gaia was the first deity to emerge out of Chaos. Her name essentially means earth or land. Some refer to her as the ancestral mother and claim that she gave birth to all the elements of the world. Chaos came before everything else. It was made of Void, Mass, and Darkness in confusion, and then Earth in the form of Gaia came into existence. From Gaia sprang the mountains, plains, seas, and rivers that make up the Earth as we know it today.

'Tartarus was the next immortal. He was not only a primordial force, but also a place, a deep abyss far below Hades, where Gaia and all the rest came to exist. Eros was the next primordial force born out of Chaos. Uranus, the heavens, also emerged out of Chaos. Pontus emerged from Chaos to become the primordial force of the sea. The Ourea were the nine children of Gaia. They were elemental powers who controlled natural aspects of the world. Cronus, the leader of the twelve Titans, was the son of Gaia and Uranus.'

Uzmahndey looked up to complain to Charlie. "All this is just Greek Mythology."

"Early Greek Mythology," Charlie added. "Preceding the Olympian gods."

"Are all these beings supposed to be real?"

"Gaia and all the others are real." Uzmahndey and Charlie both looked up at Angela. "All this mythology is just how the ancient Greeks comprehended them."

<u>Like the Standard Model of Particle Physics is the mythology physicists have created to account for a world they cannot experience directly.</u>

Angela continued. "They are an ancient race of aliens who came here long before the evolution of homo sapiens. They may have directed that evolution. They live beneath the surface because they need to be near the molten core, the generator of the planet's magnetic field. It's their power source. From there these aliens influence everything people do."

"I hope this all connects to that weirdo who tried to cut Charlie's throat." Feeling Charlie shiver at his side, he apologized. "Sorry."

Charlie squeezed his arm. "Keep reading."

'The ancient Greeks, especially the Mycenaean, revered these creatures. But as Greek civilization advanced they were mostly forgotten, replaced by the gods of Mount Olympus, such as Zeus and Hera and Poseidon and Hades, more humanized gods people could more easily relate to. But a few continued the old worship. There have been no shrines to Gaia discovered, but that supposedly is by design. The Gaia cult has remained hidden over the millennia. Their members today are most likely few, but the actual number is unknown.'

Uzmahndey turned his phone off. "So I don't know much more than I did before. Just a lot of weird names."

At the Halkali Marmaray train station they found the driver Snugglesaurus had lined up waiting for them. He knew little English, but Angela had no difficulty conversing with him in his native language. He drove them through Istanbul across the Faith Sultan Mehmet Bridge over the Bosporus into Asia. Once out of eastern Istanbul, they ascended from the coast up onto the central plateau that made up most of Anatolia. They passed back and forth between developed farms and dense forests until they reached Eskisehir, where they turned south and descended from the plateau.

Unable to follow the conversation between their driver and Angela, or the few stabs the driver took at English, Uzmahndey dozed through much of the long trip.

He woke up as they made the final leg of their journey into farmland near the Mediterranean coast. "Is that cotton?" he asked, looking out at the passing fields of white.

"Yes," their driver answered. "Good to wake up. In Denizli." In a good mood since the long drive was nearly over, he rambled on in English. "Denizli known for three things. Kiz, toz, and horoz."

Not having a clue, Uzmahndey glanced to Angela.

"Girls, dust, and roosters," she translated.

"Yes," the driver continued. "If you want fight, pick one with horoz. Not as mean as kiz." He pointed to the fields they were passing. "Tobacco, figs. Have fig malted?"

Uzmahndey shook his head no, but their driver nodded yes.

"Try. Get very hot here. Cool and refreshing."

They were soon beyond farmland and into the city, with the driver, Uzmahndey, and Charlie all drinking fig malteds.

"Denizli big city. Everything here. Much to see here." Angela directed him to the ANIM Boutique Hotel. Receiving an enormous tip, on top of what Snugglesaurus had already paid him, he drove away a happy man.

Uzmahndey was also happy. The dazzling white exterior of the hotel oozed luxury. He was even more entranced upon entering the lobby. "Snugglesaurus has outdone himself this time." His good mood carried him right up to the point where he walked into their room. "One bed?"

"A second one is being brought up," Angela told him. "Also a baby bed."

Uzmahndey looked around the rest of the room. There was a sitting area, with a desk. He walked over to peek into a small yet ornate bathroom. "This place is nice." He collapsed upon the bed. "After two days of hard traveling."

Charlie flopped down beside him. "Yes. Can we rest up here?"

"No," Angela replied. "We must keep moving."

"We're exhausted," Uzmahndey said.

"We just took a day off after Charley was born. We must finish shutting down the portals as quickly as possible." Angela extracted Charley from the carrier strapped to her chest and handed him off to Uzmahndey.

"I know," Uzmahndey said as he watched her remove the baby carrier. "Charles is hungry."

Charlie sat up in bed. "Can I have him?"

"Gladly." He handed the baby off to her. "While you have him see if he needs changing."

After short naps and long showers, they went down to the Loca Ristorante. "Italian?" Uzmahndey exclaimed in disappointment. "I was hoping to try the local cuisine."

Following a long relaxed meal, which for Uzmahndey, and his starving xenobots, included a double order of lasagna, a second basket of breadsticks, and for desert two servings of torta della nonna and one of chocolate-pistachio biscotti, they made their way back up to their room. To his joy, the extra bed had been set up in the sitting area, and a baby bed was set up next to the double bed.

After Angela laid Charley down in the baby bed, Charlie took her by the hand and dragged her into the bathroom. "Why don't you get in bed while we're in here." Charlie shut the door.

Uh-oh.

Women behind closed doors. Never a good sign.

What do you think they're cooking up in there?

"I do not care. I am so tired and full I could sleep for the next two days."

He undressed and climbed under cover. When the two women emerged from the bathroom, Uzmahndey did not like the way Angela was looking at him.

"Why didn't you tell me?"

A dread blossomed deep in his belly. "Tell you what?"

Charlie merely laughed as she extracted her pajamas from her suitcase.

"That there are things we can do to keep me from getting pregnant."

"Charlie!" Uzmahndey yelled as she retreated back into the bathroom and closed the door. He turned back to Angela. "How detailed is the sex education she's been getting from Snugglesaurus?"

"Very detailed." Angela began undressing. "Now that she is eighteen."

"It's your fault. I was so shocked at making a baby I've been afraid to touch you again."

"When you talked about 'protection' I had no idea what you were talking about." Angela donned pajamas and climbed into bed.

"We're in Turkey now. I don't even know if I can find 'protection' in a Muslim country."

"Snugglesaurus told Charlie condoms are popular in Turkey."

Charlie called out from behind the bathroom door. "Is it safe to come out now?"

"No!" Uzmahndey yelled back. "Troublemaker! Just sleep in there tonight!"

The door opened and Charlie emerged in pajamas. "I'm sure Snugglesaurus can tell me where to buy them."

"For us. You won't be needing any."

"Of course not," Angela agreed. "We *want* her to get pregnant."

The next morning Uzmahndey awoke when Angela got up to pluck Charley from the baby bed. "Time for breakfast."

Uzmahndey and Charlie went down for their own breakfast. Not being too hot yet, they sat outside in the Garden Restaurant. Uzmahndey scanned the surrounding streets. "Are we safe here, guys? No snipers taking a bead on Charlie?"

<u>We haven't seen any danger.</u>

<u>Relax and eat your breakfast.</u>

<u>*All you are doing is scaring Charlie.*</u>

Uzmahndey glanced at her. She was craning her neck trying to see in all directions. "We're okay. Good, Bad, and Ugly are standing guard."

"*You* are not the one they are trying to kill." Still, Charlie calmed.

Now was a good time to take her mind off her troubles and get her thinking about his. "Do you think I'm weird? For having sex with a robot?"

Charlie's worried frown dissolved into a smile. "I might if my mother was a robot."

"She is artificial."

"She gave birth to your son. And to me. That makes her real."

Uzmahndey looked away with fidgety eyes. "I just don't want you thinking I'm some kind of pervert."

"For making love to your son's mother?"

"She says she's not really his mother."

"She gave birth to him." Charlie took his hand. "I never would have suggested the condoms to her if I thought something was wrong with it."

"What all did you suggest to her?"

Charlie laughed. "How much do you think I know? Besides, it's all second-hand." She cast a wandering gaze around the sidewalks. "I need to gain some first-hand knowledge."

"No you don't. Not until we complete our world tour and you're somewhere safe. No more wandering off with young men who want to slit your throat."

Charlie touched her scar and nodded in agreement.

After breakfast, they returned to their room to prepare for the day. Angela directed everyone to wear swim suits under their street clothes. At the front desk Uzmahndey collected the keys for the rental car that had been delivered to the hotel for them.

It was a short drive to the World Heritage Site at Pamukkale. To Uzmahndey's surprise, Angela headed for the Hierapolis ruins first. "I thought we came to see the Cotton Castle?"

"We will. But business first." Angela, with Charley strapped to her chest, led the way through the ruins of the second century Roman spa resort. Many of the stone arches were still upright. What brought Uzmahndey to stock stillness was the amphitheater. It rose fifty tiers high, with an original capacity to seat fifteen-thousand spectators. The stage, and the several large statues amid the columns behind it, was intact. A truly impressive structure, preserved through nearly two millennia, in much better condition than the famous one in Rome.

"What are you looking for?" Uzmahndey asked.

"The Gate to Hell."

"You're joking? Right?"

"No, she's not." Charlie plucked Snugglesaurus from Angela's backpack. "Ancient Romans believed there is a portal to the underworld here. The toxic breath of the three-headed hellhound Cerberus flowed out of the ground to kill unsuspecting victims on behalf of his master, Pluto. Sacrifices were held here. Priests would enter the cave with animals, who would fall dead, while the priests remained unharmed."

"How did the priests survive when the animals didn't?"

Duh. Maybe they held their breaths, genius.

Guessing Uzmahndey had had his question answered by Bad because of the scowl that graced his face, Charlie laughed and let it go.

They arrived at the Plutonian. It had been excavated and restored to what was believed to be its original form. There was a long rectangular enclosure filled with sparkling clear water, with a small arched entrance on one side. Above the arch was stone seating for spectators, and a replica statue of Pluto.

Angela handed Charley off to Uzmahndey then shed the baby carrier and her outer clothes. In her one-piece swim suit she dropped down into the pool. The arch was gated, with warning signs posted about toxic air, but, of course, this wasn't a concern since she didn't need to breathe.

"Watch out for the three-headed Hell Hound," Uzmahndey warned.

Neither Cerberus nor any other mythological creature attacked. She flung the Cheerio deep into the gloom of the cavern.

"Now we can go see the pools." She climbed out, leaving her clothes off so she could air dry as they made their way back through the ruins.

Arriving at the travertine pools, Angela dressed and took Charley. All three removed their shoes as the sign directed. Most of the many crystal-blue pools cascading down the hillside of sun-dazzled bleached white limestone were small and shallow. Although fed by hot springs, the ones they walked barefoot through were cool. The dazzling white hillside set with sparkling blue gems of water were mobbed with people. Some were lounging in the larger pools, or sitting in the smaller ones, or merely soaking their feet in the smallest.

After trekking down to the bottom then back up to the top, they abandoned the swarming hillside for Cleopatra's Pool. It, too, was crowded, with rude jostling people. Angela was wary. "I don't know about this. There are a lot of people here."

Uzmahndey peeled off his tee shirt. "Good, Bad, and Ugly say it looks okay to them."

"You two go on. I'll stay out with Charley." She glowered at Uzmahndey. "Keep a close eye on Charlie. Stay within reach of her."

Charlie stripped down to her bikini. "Snugglesaurus says this is not a natural travertine pool, like all the others. This is man-made. It was a gift from Marc Antony to Cleopatra. There once was a temple to Apollo here, with an ornate roof held up by Doric columns, but an earthquake toppled them."

Uzmahndey stepped out of his pants. "Turkey has had a lot of bad earthquakes."

She pointed. "Those columns are still down on the bottom."

Uzmahndey followed her into the Pool. "This water is warm."

"It's fed by a hot spring. Can you feel the bubbles?" On their way to the surface, little fizzing air bubbles released by the mineral springs below danced across their skin. "It's champagne water." She floated above the toppled columns.

Uzmahndey floated beside her. "Be careful. Remember the last time you floated on water? At Mono Lake?"

"Can't you just relax and enjoy?"

"After someone tried to slash your throat? I don't think so."

After a half-hour Charlie grew weary of the jostling mob in the water. While Uzmahndey grew weary of staring down every man who admired Charlie's bikini-clad eighteen year old form. The xenobots helped by making his muscles bulge to twice their normal size whenever he glared at someone.

Angela was more than happy when the pair climbed out of the pool. The two were mostly-dry by the time they arrived back at their rental car. While beside it they donned their outer clothes then drove back to their hotel in Denizli.

Chapter 18

White Desert

Before dawn the next morning the four checked out of the ANIM Boutique Hotel and took a taxi to the Denizli Cardak Airport. Snugglesaurus had booked them a flight to Cairo. Upon landing, they checked into the room at the Novotel Cairo Airport Snugglesaurus had lined up for them. After dropping off their bags, they took a bus to Giza and spent the remainder of the day behaving like any normal tourists seeing the Pyramids and the Great Sphinx.

Back at their hotel room that evening, Uzmahndey cornered Angela while Charlie was in the bathroom changing into her pajamas. "Why haven't we been attacked by the zealots again?"

"The knife attack on Charlie failed. Perhaps they are still trying to figure out their next move."

"Or they are waiting for a chance when we're not in a crowd. Which will be tomorrow, when we're going out in the Western Desert. People here at the hotel have warned me it could be dangerous."

"That's why we're not going alone. We'll have a personal guide."

"Who will guide us, not protect us."

"I need to get to the White Desert. We'll just stay on high alert."

They fell silent when Charlie emerged from the bathroom. "Were you guys talking about me?"

"Yes," Uzmahndey covered. "About what a charming young lady you have become."

"You are a terrible liar, Uz."

"Yeah, I can trash talk with the best of them."

Early the next morning the guide Snugglesaurus had secured picked them up at their hotel. His English was excellent. "Not the most comfortable of vehicles," he said as they settled into his Jeep, Uzmahndey next to him in front, and Charlie and Angela, with the baby in her lap, in back. "But you need four-wheel drive in the desert."

As he drove them through Cairo he described everything they passed. Reaching the east bank of the Nile, they paralleled it southward for miles, finally crossing at the Tahya Misr Bridge. They continued west. Once away from the city, they drove into the fertile Nile farmland Egypt is historically known for, then on further west into the desert.

Even there Uzmahndey saw fields scattered about. This piqued his interest. "What can you grow in the desert?"

"A lot of potatoes," their driver answered. "Corn, wheat. Tea plants."

The four-lane blacktop took them ever deeper into the desert. Soon there were no farms, no fields, and few structures to see, merely desolate white sand. The dearth of variable scenery didn't deter their driver from talking. "This road was built upon an old caravan route. Traders have been passing this way on camel for thousands of years."

"I am surprised such a good road as this was built out here in the middle of nowhere."

"This is not the middle of nowhere. There are iron mines out here. Ore is transported across this road to the steel mills in Cairo."

Rounding a sharp bend in the road, a small settlement came into view. "Bahariya," their guide proclaimed. "The Northern Oasis. It took three days for traders on the old caravan route to reach Cairo from here. We made the trip in less than four hours."

When the Jeep breezed past the little town, Charlie whined. "Aren't we stopping?"

"There is nothing to see here. We will stop at the oasis." Just beyond the small collection of homes and palm trees, he turned off pavement onto a dirt lane. This took them down into a depression ringed by black basalt rock columns. They drove through a grove of palm trees and around the end of a narrow contorted body of water. He parked at the water's edge.

"This is Salt Lake. A resting place along the old caravan route where travelers could escape the sun in the cool shade of the palm trees. It is a good place to stretch your legs."

Uzmahndey and Charlie took his advice. They strolled in the shade of the palm trees beside the lake dotted with small sandy knolls.

"It's a good place to stretch *your* legs," Uzmahndey said. "They keep getting longer."

"My legs are hot right now. I'd sure like to pull my pants off and jump in that water."

"Don't even think about it. I insisted you wear slacks for a reason. We're in a Muslim country, far from cosmopolitan Cairo. Out here women keep their bodies covered. You need to respect the local culture when you are traveling."

Charlie smiled at him. "I bet you were a good travel guide in Hawaii."

"I was a good slot receiver in the NFL, too. I'll show you how good next season." He studied her face as she gazed out over the water. There was no sweat beading on it. She didn't look as hot as she professed to be.

Her mix of human and alien blood can tolerate extremes much better than pure-bred humans.

The planet is getting hotter. She and Charles and their kind will not be stressed by higher temperatures.

Yeah, Uz, you are standing next to the future of the human race. I can see now how Ghost plans to save them.

For once Bad speaks wisely. The world is growing harsher. It requires hardier beings to survive on it.

Such as the one standing right next to you.

That's why Angela is anxious for Charlie to develop her social skills, even if it puts her in physical danger. So her genes can propagate.

Before Uzmahndey could object to this remark, they were joined by their driver. "Your wife needed to feed your son. I give her privacy."

Charlie choked back a laugh. "I don't think Angela worries much about privacy."

"But I do," Uzmahndey said. "Thank you."

"How much further are we going today?" Charlie asked.

"As deep into the White Desert as you desire. We'll pitch camp whenever you get tired."

Uzmahndey smiled. "I'm looking forward to that. We haven't camped since Devil's Tower."

Their guide gave him an odd look. "That does not sound like a good place to camp. Here is much better. A night in the desert is like a Thousand and One Arabian Nights fantasy. Beautiful."

By the time the three returned to the Jeep, the baby was sound asleep with a full belly. They drove out of the oasis and turned off onto another dirt road that led ever deeper into the desert. The terrain turned darker.

"We are entering the Black Desert," their driver said. "These hills are black because of the dolerite and iron quartzite covering them. The few white hills you see are because of limestone."

"Limestone?" Uzmahndey questioned. "Isn't that formed on sea bottoms?"

"Yes. Northern Africa used to possess an inland sea. Where the Sahara Desert is now. There used to be plenty of water. Now it is scarce. Amazing how much the Earth has changed through the ages."

Here they got their first glimpse of unusual rock formations jutting out of the sand in fantastical shapes. "It's like a Doctor Seuss playground," Uzmahndey said.

At the el Haiz Oasis their driver pulled up to a small café. "We stop for lunch." He pointed to a rectangular pool. "A hot water spring. You can bathe there. With swim suits. It is permitted."

Angela declined, taking Charley into the relative cool of the adobe building. So Uzmahndey and Charlie, after taking turns changing into swimsuits inside the Jeep, went in on their own. The dip, even in warm water, was resuscitating. Their rumbling stomachs eventually drug the rest of their bodies out of the pool back to the Jeep to don clothes.

They joined Angela and their guide at a table inside the café. He shrugged at their approach. "Your wife won't eat."

"She eats like a bird," Uzmahndey said. "Me, I eat birds."

After lunch, they left all trace of civilization behind as they drove deep into the White Desert, where they found an even higher concentration of incredible rock formations.

"We are going to the Valley of Agabat," their driver announced. "The most beautiful part of the White Desert." The many shapes they passed suggested a chicken, a Sphinx, a camel, a tent, and various mushrooms.

"I'm looking for a rabbit," Angela said.

"Yes, yes," their driver said. "I will take you there."

Descending to the valley floor, they ventured into a labyrinth of fanciful natural creations. Their driver crept around them, giving his passengers a chance to take them all in. Until he pulled up to the rabbit-shaped rock. "It is getting late. A good place to set camp."

Charlie wandered off amid the formations.

"Keep an eye on her," Angela admonished as she walked over to the rabbit rock with Charley.

Uzmahndey split his attention between following her command and helping their guide set up the tent. He called out to Charlie when she slipped out of sight behind a large mushroom-shaped rock.

Her agitated form reappeared right away. "I'm right here."

"I've got her."

Uzmahndey saw Angela returning from the rabbit rock. "Did you take care of business already?"

"Yes." She joined Charlie, and with the baby they wandered away to view other formations.

Once the tent was up he joined them. "Strange place for a portal."

"This used to be a seabed. There are still ancient subterranean connections."

"But there are many other places that could provide access much deeper into the Earth. Such as the Marianas Trench, the deepest place on the surface. I hope there isn't a portal there."

"There's not. The portals were created where Gaia and her people would have easy access to where humans lived."

Their guide called them to the fire once he had dinner prepared. They ate a meal of flatbread with mashed chickpea hummus, and also mahshi stuffed with eggplant, zucchini, bell peppers, cabbage, and tomatoes.

After the fire died down, they all stretched out flat on their backs on bedrolls beneath a crystal clear night to sky gaze. The black heavens sparkled with a brilliant multitude of stars. Eventually, they all crawled into the tent and settled down for the night.

<u>The wind is picking up.</u>

"Damn," Uzmahndey muttered in his sleep.

<u>Wake up.</u>

"Damn damn," Uzmahndey muttered, by then half awake.

Something is happening. Go out and take a look.

When Uzmahndey stirred, their guide spoke in the dark.

"Don't leave the tent. Sand is blowing."

The tent rocked. "Isn't it blowing pretty hard?"

"Yes, it is." Angela said. "It's been getting steadily stronger."

"What's going on?" Charlie asked with a grump.

"Kahmsin," their guide said in the dark. "We are safe inside the tent."

A singularly powerful gust yanked one tent peg out of the ground.

"It's getting too strong." Angela gathered the baby to her chest.

"The Jeep," the guide, still calm, said. "Keep your head down. Keep your eyes closed as much as you can. Hold hands. I'll lead the way." He snapped on a flashlight.

A second stake came free just as he unzipped the tent flap. With the nylon thrashing wildly about in the gale, their guide led them out into the open. He took Uzmahndey's hand, who took Charlie's, and she took Angela's. They staggered single-file into the silica blizzard.

The blistering grains stung Uzmahndey's exposed skin. His face felt like the flesh was being flayed off. Until it didn't. He knew damage was still being inflicted, but the xenobots were moderating the pain. He doubted Charlie was suffering. If a knife couldn't cut her, then this sand blasting shouldn't cause much harm. And Angela was nearly indestructible. The one to worry about was their guide. Especially after he stumbled and fell to his knees. Uzmahndey strained with one arm to pull the Egyptian to his feet, still gripping Charlie's hand.

"You can't save all."

The roaring wind filled his ears, but Uzmahndey could still hear the soft feminine voice clearly. A dark female form stood before him in the madly-swirling sand. His eyes were closed, but he still saw the black body draped with a diaphanous black-gown flapping in the fierce wind.

"Save your guide. You are all lost in the desert without him. Let go the devil girl and pull the Egyptian to his feet."

The demon was trying to make Uzmahndey choose between saving himself and his son, and saving Charlie. He wouldn't panic and do so. He leaned back to yell into Charlie's ear. "Hang onto my belt!" Once she did, he let go of her hand to sweep their guide up in his arms. He turned his face toward where the dark woman had stood.

Her image had vanished. Uzmahndey dared not open his eyes to search for her. He would be blinded by the sand. He turned his head from side to side. He had seen her before with his eyes closed. Not this time. Now Uzmahndey was disoriented. Which way had they been going?

Don't worry about it. Your guide was leading you the wrong way.

Turn thirty degrees left.

Have no idea what thirty degrees is? Can you manage left? Then turn left, left, keep going. There. Now walk straight.

Since to reply would have meant a mouth full of sand, Uzmahndey bit down on his irritation at the snarky remarks and did his best to follow Bad's directions. Five staggering steps later he bumped into the Jeep. At that, he heard a flapping of wings from above. He turned his face up to the sound, but no image appeared on the backs of his eyelids. Uzmahndey felt his way to the front passenger door, opened it, and deposited their guide. The Egyptian scooted over behind the wheel.

Uzmahndey felt a hand give him a powerful shove, and he toppled into the front passenger seat next to their guide. He looked back to see Angela slam the door in his face. Then the back passenger door opened and Charlie scrambled in. Angela leaned in to hand the baby to her, sand swirling all around her into the car.

"Get in!" Uzmahndey stopped coughing enough to hack out. "And shut the door."

Instead, Angela withdrew and slammed the door.

"What the hell," he wheezed, and opened his front passenger door. The door slammed shut on him before he could stick a leg out, which was a good thing because it would have been broken. Was that the wind? Or Angela?

A moment later the back passenger door opened and Angela, in a burst of blasting sand, lunged in. The door slammed shut behind her. "What were you doing?"

"It doesn't matter," their guide said. "If this wind keeps up we'll be buried in sand. Either die now or die later by suffocation."

"I choose later." He turned back to Angela. "What were you doing out there?" Angela didn't answer.

He expected her to take their son back from Charlie, but she didn't. Instead, she stared out the back passenger window at the swirling demonic sand. But the baby seemed content in Charlie's lap, and she seemed content holding him. He didn't know why Angela was too angry with him to speak, but he couldn't deal with it now. He had done his duty. He'd gotten Charlie safely out of the storm.

A powerful gust rocked the Jeep. That distracted him from worrying about Angela's mood. He turned to their guide. "How long will this last?"

"Hours? Days? There's no telling."

"Will they come look for us?"

"After the storm ends. Until this wind stops? No way."

"What do we do?"

"Pray to your God. Excuse me while I pray to mine." He bowed his head, closed his eyes, and intoned softly in Arabic.

Uzmahndey looked into the back seat. Charley had drifted off in Charlie's lap. Bless his soul, like his dad he could sleep through anything. Charlie wasn't far behind, her eyes drooping. Angela continued to stare out the side window into the stormy black night. She hadn't budged. She often got like that, especially at night.

Uzmahndey turned back around. He was exhausted. The way he had picked up a full-grown man and carried him through the raging wind and shifting sand like a rag doll meant the xenobots must have given him a shot of adrenaline. Now he was feeling the aftereffects. He leaned his head back and closed his eyes.

When Uzmahndey next opened his eyes it was gray inside the Jeep. There was a coat of sand on him, on everything. Stillness. Silence. No sound of wind. Was he dead? Were they all? The Jeep didn't rock. And no sand was coming in. He and their guide had cracked their windows the least bit to let some air in for as long as they could before being buried. It had let sand swirl in, too, but they had desperately needed the air. Now no sand, no wind, was blowing in. Were they entombed? Not completely, he could see daylight through the slit at the top of his window.

Uzmahndey looked into the back seat. Angela sat same as before, the exact same posture, staring at the sand-caked passenger window. Charlie was asleep, her breathing ragged but deep. Charley was awake, but placid. He stared dully back at Uzmahndey from Charlie's lap. He couldn't believe Angela had let Charlie hold the baby all night. He turned his gaze back to Angela's still form.

Do not speak.

We have to tell you something and you cannot talk back.

We mean it. Don't open your mouth. Nod your head if you understand.

Uzmahndey nodded.

Try forming words in your head.

You're wasting your time, he'll never do it.

WHAT?

That was good.

Try not to react when we tell you this.

Just go on and tell him. If he blows it, he blows it.

That is not Angela in the back seat.

WHAT?! He stared at her. She sat, same as before, unmoved from the previous night, still staring out the window.

This is too difficult. Get out of the car and we can talk.

Uzmahndey opened the door. It moved a half-inch. He pushed hard with both hands. Sand had banked up against the Jeep, but the vehicle wasn't completely covered. The door opened enough for him to wriggle out.

The wind had died. He took a deep breath of fresh air. He hadn't realized how stale the air inside the Jeep had become. He gazed all around at the quiet unmoving surreal landscape through a sparkling haze. There was a multitude of sand grains suspended in the air. The drifting sand had been rearranged into new dunes totally different from what he remembered seeing the day before. There was no sign of their camping gear.

Close the door.

Uzmahndey did.

"Now tell me what you are talking about? Angela is sitting right there in the back seat."

<u>That is not Angela.</u>
<u>**We can read her body language.**</u>
<u>*Yeah. She doesn't have any.*</u>

"Is she off again?" Damn, she had become such a warm loving woman. A mother to his child. Now she needed to be rebooted again? She was going to have to start over again?

"It's worse this time." Uzmahndey jerked around at the voice of his former LSU coach. A man dressed in classic Berber robes stood a foot away.

"What you saw in the back seat is a hologram I created."

That's why the baby was still in Charlie's lap. "Then where's Angela?"

Ghost pointed at sand banked up against the front of the car. "Dig her out."

Uzmahndey flew into action, A dozen scoops uncovered a foot. He drug her out of the sand. No kidding it was worse this time. She had been sandblasted beyond recognition.

"She was out here all night. She kept digging the car out. If not for her, you would have been buried alive, and it would have been a long time before anyone found your corpses."

"Can I reboot her?"

"No. The damage is too extensive."

Uzmahndey hugged her broken body and began sobbing.

"I didn't say I couldn't fix her."

Uzmahndey looked up.

"I'll take her to my lab."

"Where is that?"

"I set it up on a remote section of the Mid-Atlantic Ridge."

"At the bottom of the ocean?"

"The perfect location. Seclusion, and a plentiful easily-accessible thermal energy source. In the meantime, you and Charlie and Charley need to continue."

"What about our guide?"

"Oh, he's okay."

"Won't he miss Angela? He started out with four customers, now he has three."

"He'll see Angela in the back seat. Same as you. But since I need to get to work on her, I won't be able to animate the hologram. I can't be two places at once. Tell him she's in shock from the storm and can't talk."

"What about the Jeep? Will it run?"

"Not until you get the sand out of the engine."

"I'm no mechanic."

"Snugglesaurus will tell you how to do it. Or rather, he'll tell Charlie, and Charlie can tell you. He'll also tell her where your next destination is."

"We're going on without Angela?"

"For a while. I'll get her back to you as quick as I can. In the meantime, you've got to keep going. Now move Angela away from the Jeep." When Uzmahndey stooped to gather her in his arms, Ghost laughed. "Just drag her. She's a robot. You won't damage her any more than she already is."

"She is the mother of my child." Uzmahndey carried her away from the Jeep and tenderly spread her out on the ground behind a newly-blown bank of sand.

She and Ghost began to shimmer away, but he suddenly returned. "I almost forgot to tell you something. Charley is now three."

"No, he's not. I just saw him."

"Another hologram. We can't have our guide seeing a three-year-old back there, where yesterday there was a three-month-old baby. The poor man has had enough shocks."

"Hell of a time for him to have a growth spurt."

"A hell of a *good* time. That's why I forced it to happen."

"Why would you do that?"

"Because Angela won't be with you." Seeing Uzmahndey still hadn't thought it through, he went on. "How were you going to feed him? Certainly not the way Angela did."

When Uzmahndey glanced down at his flat chest, Ghost chuckled.

"It's not healthy to force a growth spurt to happen, but it was necessary. Your son will be more dazed than usual. Be sure he keeps Snugglesaurus close." Ghost faded away for good this time, accompanied by Angela's mangled form.

When Uzmahndey climbed back into the Jeep, he saw their guide was awake. He turned his terrified visage on him.

"Is the demon gone?"

"What demon?"

"I heard things last night. All night long. And saw things. Something was out there last night. In the storm."

"You were hearing the wind." Seeing their guide was not persuaded, he added, "Nothing could have survived out there last night."

"Nothing human."

Not wanting to concede that something not human *had* been out there all night, he turned around to the back seat. The hologram of Angela was unmoved, as before. The hologram of three-month old Charley appeared to be awake but still lax and motionless. The real three-year old Charley the image concealed was sure to be lax and motionless, also, on account of the growth spurt. The only animated one in the back seat was Charlie. "Good morning."

She stretched. "Is it over?"

"Yes. We survived."

She shifted in her seat. "Charley feels so heavy." She tried to rearrange him in her lap, but couldn't budge him. "He *is* heavy." She looked the three-month old hologram over. "He didn't have a growth spurt." She looked up at Uzmahndey. "What's going on with him?" She looked at Angela. "What's wrong with Angela?"

"Step out and I'll tell you what's going on."

Charlie climbed out of the Jeep with three-year old Charley in her arms. Uzmahndey explained to Charlie all Ghost had explained to him. Once her panic passed, he opened the driver door and roused their guide from his funk. The Egyptian produced a tool box. He and Uzmahndey, under Snugglesaurus' instructions relayed to them by Charlie, cleaned the air filter, and everything else fouled with sand.

The guide made no comment about the amount of mechanical knowledge the eighteen year old girl seemed to possess. He also only nodded when Uzmahndey informed him Angela was in shock from the night of terror they had gone through. He, too, was in bad shape from that, and was sympathetic to how a woman might react. He didn't give the immobile hologram of the baby he saw, since the real baby was just as immobilized by the forced growth spurt, in Charlie's arms a second glance. To their guide he appeared to still be three months old, and sleeping soundly.

Once they got the Jeep started, their guide made a beeline for the paved highway they'd left back at the Bahariya Oasis. The drive back to Cairo seemed to take half the time as the drive out. When he dropped them off at their hotel he made no mention of the fact that he had not seen Angela get out of the Jeep, that he did not see her with the others on the sidewalk, or that he no longer saw her sitting erect as a mannequin in the back seat. He merely jumped in behind the wheel and sped away without looking back.

Chapter 19

Well of Barhout

As soon as their guide pulled away from the hotel, the hologram of three month old Charley in Uzmahndey's arms disappeared, replaced by the actual three-year old Charley in shredded rags way too small for him. This real face appeared as lax as the hologram face, and the real boy remained just as motionless. Still, this was Uzmahndey's first glimpse of his son at three years of age. He was transfixed.

Charlie urged Uzmahndey into motion. "Let's get him inside." She collected their backpacks, and they went up to their room. Receiving concerned looks along the way because of their bedraggled appearance, she took time to explain. "We were caught in a sand storm out in the desert."

As soon as Charlie closed the door to their room, Uzmahndey shot her a worried look. "Is he okay?"

"Probably." She looked him over. "He's just dazed from the growth spurt. He needs Snugglesaurus."

Passing on the baby bed, Uzmahndey laid him down in the middle of the double bed.

Charlie placed the stuffed dinosaur in his limp arms. "He should recover, but it might take longer without Angela here to soothe him."

Uzmahndey sat on the bed beside him. "I'll watch him. Go take a shower and get all that sand off you."

"Gladly."

Once Charlie was showered and in clean clothes, Uzmahndey took his turn. Then the two of them peeled the rags off Charley and put him in the tub. Charlie smiled at Uzmahndey as they kneeled side by side in the bathroom to scrub the boy. "We'll both be taking care of him."

"At least he can eat real food now."

Charlie laughed. "I'd like to see you try to breast feed him."

"No, you're the one with breasts. That would have been your job."

She glanced down. "I didn't think you'd noticed."

"I noticed. Along with every young man in the last three countries."

"We're lucky he had a growth spurt last night."

"It wasn't luck." Now that they were alone, Uzmahndey related to her everything he had not had the chance to in the White Desert.

"So Angela is coming back?"

"Yes. Ghost seemed sure he could fix her. It will just take time."

"What are we supposed to do until then?"

"Keep going. Ask Snugglesaurus what our next destination is."

A moment later Charlie said, 'The Well of Barhout."

Once Charley was out of the tub, Charlie cut off a tee shirt of hers and put it on him. It fit him like a sack, but at least he was covered. The three made a dash to the nearest clothing store.

Since Charley was still out of it that evening they ordered dinner from room service. At bedtime Charlie insisted on sleeping with her younger brother, so Uzmahndey gave them the double bed and he took the single.

Early the next morning they awoke to find Charley more animated. They went down for breakfast as soon as the hotel restaurant opened. Uzmahndey was oblivious to the stares. All he had eyes for was his beautiful son. Uzmahndey was worried about him since, although Charley seemed happy, he was having a difficult time expressing his joy.

"Don't worry about that," Charlie told the worried father watching his son babble nonsensically. "Snugglesaurus will catch him up on his verbal skills." Not oblivious like Uzmahndey, she looked all around at the other early risers. "You know people are taking us for a family. Husband and wife with our young son."

Uzmahndey frowned at that notion. "You could be my daughter."

"Yeah, if you had me when you were eight." Meeting his glare with sparkling eyes, she continued. "You're only eight years older than me now. A lot of older men have young wives."

"Twenty-six is not old. And you are not my wife."

"I might have to pose as your wife. Until Angela rejoins us."

"You are two months old."

"Chronologically. Biologically, I'm eighteen." She beamed at Charley. "Our son is adorable."

"He's not your son. He's your half-brother."

"Angela said he's not. She says his genes come from a different stock than mine."

"I don't know how Angela works. Or you."

"Or Charley, then, because he's half-alien, too."

"He's my son. And you are under my protection. I signed on for that, and I will finish the job."

"What happens to me after this is over?"

"I have no idea. Let's just get it over."

"Are you going to abandon me? Who else do I have? Besides you and Charley?"

"Your mother, Angela."

"Once she completes this mission she'll abandon me, too. I'll be a freak, all alone in this world." Charlie was on the verge of tears.

Uzmahndey took her hand. "I will not abandon you." This caused her to sniffle back the tears. "For one thing, I'll get you season tickets to the Las Vegas Raiders, or whatever team signs me." He looked down at his son. "You and Charley."

The next morning they took a taxi to Cairo International Airport to catch their flight to Salalah, Oman. Charley was occupied with Snugglesaurus the entire trip. Charlie was occupied with behaving like a wife. She adjusted Uzmahndey's clothes, discussed their 'son' seated between them, ordered a drink and snack for her 'husband'. Uzmahndey scowled through it all, trying his best to ignore her attentions. Like many a husband would.

I'd take her up on it. If she really wants to be your wife. She's a dish.

"Shut up!"

Charlie, aware of what was going on, burst out laughing, while nearby passengers shifted in their seats away from Uzmahndey. He closed his eyes and tried to sleep.

It was late afternoon when they touched down. Snugglesaurus had booked them into the Atana Stay Salalah, next to the airport. Uzmahndey was happy to see upon rolling his luggage into their room there was a king bed and a twin. He tossed his bag up onto the twin. "Perfect."

Charley scrambled up onto the king. "My bed!"

Charlie stretched out on the twin. "It'll be kind of tight."

"No it won't." Uzmahndey moved his bag onto the king. "I'm happy to sleep with my son."

Charlie rose up on elbows. "I saw a pool."

"Yes!" Charley rose up on his elbows, too, mimicking her. "A pool!"

Uzmahndey scowled at her. "Have you got something decent to wear? This is a Muslim country. Respect the culture, remember?"

"Angela's one piece should fit me."

They changed into swimsuits. Uzmahndey and Charlie donned bathrobes, and all three went down to the pool. When Charlie took her robe off, Uzmahndey looked around to see if there were any negative reactions. None of the male guests or Omani attendants stared. While on the plane he had read on his phone that Omanis were conservative yet extremely polite, and so long as you didn't intentionally insult their culture they would overlook minor gaffes. Seeing no one seemed offended by how Charlie comported herself, he stretched out in a lounge chair and relaxed. Apparently, Snugglesaurus had instructed her how to behave while in Oman, and she was accordingly decorous. Charley, on the other hand, was quite exuberant in the water, but then he was a three-year old boy. His behavior elicited nothing but slight smiles and shy nods, directed at Uzmahndey.

Charlie stayed at Charley's side while they were in the pool. She was as protective of him as Angela had been of her. After a time, Uzmahndey joined them. Before Charley was worn out they had him swimming between his father and sister. "He's a fast learner," Charlie said. "And that doesn't come from you."

"I don't know about that," Uzmahndey protested. "I can learn a playbook really fast."

They had a late dinner at the hotel restaurant. Always eager to try new foods, Uzmahndey went with mutton majboos and harees, and the country's national dessert, halva. Charlie was delighted to see sliders on the menu. Of course, no alcoholic drink was offered, which suited Uzmahndey. Whiskey had become a distant memory, one he no longer missed. He felt only slightly irked at the xenobots' manipulation. Was his docile acceptance even more manipulation? By this point he no longer cared.

Charley fell asleep on his father's shoulder on the way back up to their room. He tucked the boy into the king bed, while Charlie took her pajamas into the bathroom. Uzmahndey undressed and climbed in beside his son. He wondered what was taking Charlie so long, until he realized she must be giving him plenty of time to get beneath the covers. He smiled at that. She might tease, but she didn't want to stress this new family dynamic with Angela absent. She finally emerged in her pajamas. She came around to Uzmahndey's side of the bed. "Good night."

He shushed her. "He's sound asleep."

"Sound is right. I don't think a diesel truck coming through the room would wake him up." Charlie kissed him on the cheek, then pecked Uzmahndey's. She cut the lights off and climbed into the single bed.

Uzmahndey was awakened early the next morning before dawn by a knock at the door. He looked to see Charlie was sitting up in bed and watching. He eased out of bed, so not to disturb his still-sleeping bed mate, and slung on his robe. Cracking the door, he found a hotel employee before it. "Mister Uzmahndey?"

"Yes."

"Your guide is waiting for you in the lobby."

<u>Just say okay.</u>

<u>Do not act surprised.</u>

Fat chance of him acting.

Despite Bad's doubt, Uzmahndey followed the xenobots' advice. "Tell him I'll be right down." He closed the door and turned to Charlie. "Do you know anything about this?"

"Oops. I forgot to tell you. Snugglesaurus arranged for a guide to take us across the border into Yemen to visit the Well of Barhout."

Uzmahndey was astounded. "It's in Yemen?"

You need to bone up on your geography.

It's just across the border.

Nearly all of the trip will be through Oman. This is a prosperous peaceful country. You'll be safe.

"Oman might be safe, but there's a war going on in Yemen. I am not taking my children into a war zone."

Leave them here.

Uzmahndey turned to confront Charlie. She was beaming. "You called me your child."

"I just woke up. I'm confused. This took me totally by surprise. Thanks to you." Charlie's beam switched down to dim. "You two stay in this room until I get back. You and Charley do not leave it for any reason. When you get hungry order something from room service."

Charlie nodded through his entire directive. "We'll be fine."

Uzmahndey tore off his robe and began rifling their bags. "Where are the Cheerios? And my passport? I'll take whatever cash we have on hand."

"One more thing. Put some pants on."

Five minutes later Uzmahndey approached a young man sitting by himself in the lobby. "I believe you might be waiting for me. Uzmahndey."

The young man stood and shook hands. "Samir." He looked beyond Uzmahndey. "It's just you?"

"Yes. How dangerous will this be?"

Samir grinned. "I do it all the time. No problem. Just don't let anyone know you are American. Can you do an Australian accent?"

"I'm black."

"Could be Aborigine." He looked Uzmahndey over. "What's in your backpack? It will be searched at the border."

"A camera. Food and water. Cheerios."

"Cheerios?"

"To snack on."

"No gun? Knife?"

"No way."

"No alcohol?"

"I don't drink."

Samir nodded. "We're good then." He took off across the lobby toward the entrance. "On the way you should work on your Crocodile Dundee."

Uzmahndey hurried after. They climbed into a sparkling new Jeep parked just outside the door. Uzmahndey was impressed. "Nice wheels."

"Oman a prosperous country. But oil running out. We diversify. Tourism big here now. Just not many people want to go to Yemen."

"You said you did this all the time."

"Give tours, yes. Take crazy American into Yemen? First time. By the way, why are you doing this?"

"It's on my bucket list."

"I hope you've taken care of everything else on your list."

Not much else was said as they drove through Salalah. Until they passed an impressive modern building. "Armed Forces Hospital. Very good, very high tech. If Houthis shoot you, I'll bring you here."

"That's not a knife." Uzmahndey said in his best Australian. He pulled out a pocket knife and brandished it. "That's a knife."

Samir laughed. "Not too good. Keep practicing." He stopped laughing. "You should leave that knife in the Jeep."

"It's a pocketknife."

"I'll say it's mine."

After leaving Salalah they ascended from the coast onto a wide barren desert plateau. The first structure they passed in the wilderness was a mosque. Not until they climbed into hills did the countryside become more scenic. At the first town they entered Samir pointed out a lush green park. "Quairoon Hairiti Garden. Good place to stretch our legs."

"Keep going. I want to get this over with and get back to my family." After that it was back to desolate sands.

Nothing much else was said until, hours later, they approached the border. Samir grew tense. "Forget the Crocodile Dundee. Say you're British."

"I've got an American passport. Besides, why is it so bad being an American?"

"America has too many enemies in the world. No one likes Americans."

They pulled up to the booth at the Shihen Customs Station. The official spoke with Samir in Arabic. He leaned in to look Uzmahndey over, then took his papers and studied them. He handed them back. And that was that.

Uzmahndey released a deep breath as Samir drove into Yemen. "That wasn't so bad. He didn't even search my backpack."

"Getting into Yemen is easy. Getting back out is the hard part."

Now that he was actually in Yemen, Uzmahndey was on a razor's edge, swiveling his eyes and ears in all directions. "Have you guys got my back?"

<u>Of course.</u>

<u>We're on high alert.</u>

<u>If you die, we die. Of course we've got your back. It's our back, too.</u>

Samir stared at him. "I don't have your back. I'm just driving."

"I wasn't talking to you."

Samir peered into Uzmahndey's ear searching for a device. "You're not communicating with someone else, are you? You're not some kind of special ops? Working for the Saudis?"

"I'm just talking with the voices in my head."

You notice how readily he accepted that? He thinks you're insane.

Uzmahndey bit his tongue, determined not to freak out his guide any more by conversing further with the xenobots. They passed through a small town. "Do the Houthis control this part of Yemen?"

Samir glanced at him. "Are you talking to me now?"

"Yes."

"The Houthis are in the west. Besides, they have no reason to bother us." He glanced sideways again with a worried expression. "Unless you give them one. Don't go around talking to yourself. If they hear you they might think you are demon possessed and toss you down into Hell." Seeing Uzmahndey's questioning look, he explained. "Well of Barhout also known as Well of Hell." Samir grimaced. "We shouldn't talk about it. Bad luck."

He sighed. "But if you insist. For centuries it's been considered a gateway to Hell. A prison for uncontrollable Jinn, where evil people go in the afterlife. It has a terrible stink. A hadith from the prophet Mohammad says, 'the worst water on the face of the Earth is the water at Wadi Barhout'."

Samir's grim expression relaxed. "But we no longer believe that. A team of Omanis repelled to the bottom, and survived. They even drank the water down there, and lived. They measured the Well at 367 feet deep. The opening at top is 98 feet across, but it widens to 380 feet at the bottom."

"Where does the water come from?"

"Underground waterfalls. There are several." His customary grin cracked back to the surface of his face. "But there are other things to worry about. They say if you get too close to the edge you can be sucked in and fall to your death."

"You just said Omani's made it in."

"They were experienced cavers. They don't fall in anywhere. Besides testing the water, they tried the air, too. They said it's breathable. But they saw a lot of snakes down there. They were afraid they'd find worse."

Recalling the pit of snakes scene from the first Indiana Jones movie, Uzmahndey shivered. "What could be worse?"

"Unexploded ordinance. The Houthis drop bombs into caves, just in case people are hiding in them. But they didn't find any undetonated bombs."

After passing a small inn in the hills, they were in barren desert beyond all signs of civilization. Not long after, Samir turned off the paved road onto a dirt track. Uzmahndey saw no signs or landmarks, but at one unremarkable point Samir abruptly turned off the track and drove onto unmarked desert sand.

Maneuvering around several football field lengths of rock outcrops, they came to the large sinkhole. Samir parked a safe distance back. "Since you don't have any equipment I don't suppose you are climbing down into it."

"I just want a picture." He got out of the Jeep and extracted his camera and the Tupperware containing the Cheerios from his backpack.

Samir couldn't tamp down his curiosity. "What are you doing with those?"

"I'm hungry." He started to walk towards the Well, but glanced back when he realized Samir hadn't left the Jeep. "Coming?"

"I'll wait here. I'm a scientific person, but still, why chance to antagonize a Jinn?"

Uzmahndey tiptoed toward the edge. He didn't feel anything pulling on him, trying to suck him in.

Watch out!

He jumped back.

"What?"

Bad couldn't answer because he was laughing too hard.

Nothing is wrong. Go ahead.

"Red card, Bad. You will be ejected if you get another." Uzmahndey reached the wire fence erected around the opening. He couldn't see far down into the Well of Barhout, there were nothing but shadows. Was there a demon lurking down there? Not the evil Jinn Samir was frightened of, but a monstrous alien? Would it rise out of the well and drag him down to Hell? He opened the Tupperware and extracted a Cheerio. Now what?

Climb down to the bottom and place it in the middle of the snakes.

"You're kidding."

He is. Just toss it in.

"Second red card, Bad. You are out of the game. Now shut up." With an underhand toss Uzmahndey sent it sailing into the pit. The little cereal ring disappeared into the void. "That's all?"

Yes. We are finished here.

Except for Bad. He wishes to speak.

"He's been ejected."

Then I'll speak for him. He has a valid point.

Uzmahndey sighed. "Go ahead, Ugly."

Why are none of Gaia's children or siblings here?

"Because the kids aren't here."

Could be. But they haven't just been attacking the kids. They've also been trying to dissuade you from helping. With Angela not present this would seem like a perfect opportunity to try again.

"Maybe they've given up on that."

Maybe.

The xenobots were really getting paranoid. He snapped a picture, so Samir wouldn't get any more paranoid than he already was. Keeping a close eye on the foul-smelling hole, he put the camera away and backed off. He'd done it. Placed the xenobot in a portal, by himself, just like Angela would have done. Without being attacked. He wondered why? Not waiting for an answer, he rushed back to the Jeep.

The two remained tense while they backtracked to the border. Despite Samir's apprehension, they had no difficulty crossing back into Oman. "They must be in a good mood today."

"I'm sure he is, since he kept the forty rials I slipped him with my passport when we got here."

Samir grinned. "So, Crocodile, maybe you are as wily as your namesake."

The rest of the long drive back to Salalah was much more relaxed. So much so that when they stopped at a gas station Uzmahndey sprang for two bags of chili flavored chips.

Chapter 20

Interlude Three

Back at the Atana Stay Salalah, Uzmahndey sent Samir off with what was left of the chili-flavored chips and a good tip. He knocked on their room door, expecting the chain and bolt to be on. No answer. He listened, since maybe the TV was up too loud for them to hear. Silence. Maybe they were asleep. He knocked harder. Still nothing. Starting to panic, he yanked out his card key and swiped it. The chain and bolt were not on. He flung the door wide. The room was empty.

He saw their clothes on the bed. Damn, they'd gone down to the pool. After he'd ordered them to stay in the room. Uzmahndey rushed out to the pool. He scanned the poolsiders in a frenzy.

I see Snugglesaurus.

Uzmahndey ran over to snatch up the stuffed animal from where it lay on the cement next to a lounge chair. He turned to a nearby couple, who were watching his frantic scampering.

"Did you see the child who had this?" He waved the stuffed dinosaur. "It belongs to my son."

The man shook his head. "We just got here."

Bad is asking...

"Yes he can! But it better not be a joke! This is serious!"

Charlie would never leave Snugglesaurus behind willingly. They were taken. This is why you weren't confronted at the Well of Barhout. Gaia was counting on her followers to snatch them.

Snugglesaurus is contacting us.

Uzmahndey stared at the stuffed dinosaur he held. "And?"

He says he can track Charley and Charlie. As long as they don't get too distant.

But you need to calm down if you are going to help them.

"Did he contact the police?"

"The police haven't been here," the man said.

Uzmahndey looked to the couple. "Sorry. I'm thinking out loud. I'm a little upset." He walked away to find a quiet corner.

We don't want the police involved.

"They've been kidnapped."

We can handle this ourselves.

"How? I'm in a foreign country with no idea where they've been taken, with no way to get around."

Snugglesaurus sent a text message from your phone to Samir to get back here in a hurry if he wants to earn a lot more money. He texted back he's on his way.

Uzmahndey ran up to their room to jam all their clothes into their bags. All the while he was packing in a frenzy he talked with the xenobots. "Are they alright?"

Snugglesaurus says they are alive or he wouldn't be able to track them.

"Where are they?"

He doesn't know for sure, but they are still in the city.

"He doesn't know?! I thought he was tracking them!"

Calm down. You are no help to them if you panic.

Uzmahndey ran down to the lobby with their luggage and out the front.

Samir's Jeep idled before the hotel entrance. "Long time no see, Crocodile Dundee."

Uzmahndey tossed the bags in the back. "My family has been kidnapped." He jumped into the front passenger seat.

Samir grew somber at once. "Have you called the police?"

"I don't have time to go to the police. They could be killed while I'm filling out a missing person report. Will you help me? I'll pay you whatever you ask."

"I will surely help you save your family. Do you know where they were taken?"

"Yes."

"Where?"

"I don't know. But I can tell you how to get there."

Snugglesaurus related directions to the xenobots, and they relayed the information to Uzmahndey, and he told Samir how to go. Hearing him mutter out loud as he talked with the xenobots, Samir eyed him sideways. "Who are you talking to?"

"Myself. I do that when I get nervous."

Nerve-wracking miles later Samir pulled the Jeep to the curb before a block of apartment buildings. "This is it. What do you want me to do?"

"Just stay here. I've got this. But when we come out I want you to drive us to the airport. Will you do that?"

"I can help."

"You've helped plenty already. Just be ready to race out of here." Uzmahndey jumped out with Snugglesaurus.

"You can leave that here."

"I need it." Uzmahndey walked down the sidewalk. Apartment buildings lined one after the other on both sides of the street in this residential neighborhood.

<u>Third one on your right.</u>

Uzmahndey stepped up to the entry door. It buzzed. "Snugglesaurus?"

<u>Of course.</u>

Uzmahndey hurried in.

<u>Third floor.</u>

He bound up the stairs.

Slow down.

"Why should I slow down?"

This close Snugglesaurus can communicate with Charlie.

He has alerted Charlie you are coming. She is informing him what the situation is inside the apartment. In turn, he will tell us and we'll tell you.

"Damn, that could take all afternoon."

It won't. Charlie and Snugglesaurus are used to communicating with each other. They are doing it quickly.

Uzmahndey reached the third floor. No one was about. "So what's going on inside?"

There are four people. Three men and one woman. One man is in the bathroom. The woman is in the kitchen. The other two are in the living room with the children. They are all watching TV.

Tell him something useful. The three men are armed, but none of them have their guns out. The man in the bathroom has left his gun sitting on a table by the closed door. Charlie and Charley aren't tied up. They are sitting on the floor before the TV, and the two men are sitting in chairs behind them watching a football match.

"Is the door locked?"

Yes. Snugglesaurus has acquired the code to unlock it. He will do so as soon as you are ready to attack. The apartment is 309.

Uzmahndey stepped up to 309 and put his hand on the knob. The lock beeped. He threw the door wide and burst in.

The two seated men turned at the sudden sounds.

Uzmahndey dashed forward and punched one man so hard he was knocked out of his chair flat on his back.

The other man scrambled to his feet and pulled his gun.

Charlie sprang up and grabbed him from behind, preventing him from raising his gun.

Uzmahndey tossed Snugglesaurus down to Charley, who was still seated on the floor, then punched the man Charlie held harder than he punched the first one. Bones crunched, and the man collapsed.

The bathroom door flew open, and the man ran out and snatched up his gun.

Uzmahndey was a blur as he charged and knocked the gun out of his hand. He punched the disarmed man in the gut so hard he knocked the breath out of him. When the gasping man doubled over, Uzmahndey caught him with an uppercut that lifted him off his feet and laid him out flat.

The woman charged out of the kitchen with a huge butcher knife raised high to stab.

Uzmahndey raised his left arm to fend off the blow. The blade sliced him to the bone. Uzmahndey punched her with a right so hard she flew back to sprawl out cold on the kitchen floor.

"Let's go!" he yelled.

Charley, already up on his feet with Snugglesaurus, ran out the door. Charlie ran out behind him. Uzmahndey ran after them out into the hall. They dashed down the stairs.

Only by the time they reached the second floor landing did it register that Charlie and Charley were wearing swim suits. "I told you two to stay in the room."

Charlie cast a frantic look back as she scurried on downstairs. "You're bleeding."

<u>Just keep going.</u>

<u>We've got this.</u>

<u>Yeah, we'll patch you up like we always do.</u>

They ran outside.

"The Jeep!" he directed the other two.

Seeing them coming down the sidewalk in a mad rush, Samir started the engine. Charlie and Charley lunged into the back seat, and Uzmahndey fell into the front. "You're hurt."

"I'll pay you whatever it costs to remove blood stains."

"I don't care about that. You need to go to the hospital."

"I can't. Just take us to the airport."

"If you show up at the airport with a wound like that, security will call the police."

Uzmahndey swore.

"Allah gahfara," Samir answered his curse as he drove away. "Is anyone chasing us?"

"No." Uzmahndey smiled at him. "They should all be taking long naps."

Samir glanced between Uzmahndey and the road. "You've stopped bleeding so bad."

"It's the xenobots," Charley exclaimed.

Samir glanced into the rearview mirror. "Are you and your mother okay?"

"Yes," Charlie answered before Charley could blurt anything else he shouldn't, such as that she wasn't his mother. She leaned forward and threw her arms around Uzmahndey's shoulders. "My brave husband rescued us."

Uzmahndey shrugged her off. "Don't. I'm angry with you. You were told to stay in the room while I was gone."

"We got bored," Charley said.

Uzmahndey turned around to glare at him. "Don't think I won't give you a good spanking." He looked to Charlie. "You, too."

She smiled. "I'll look forward to it."

Samir pulled into a pharmacy parking lot. "I'll get some supplies." He hopped out and hurried inside.

Uzmahndey swiveled around to the back seat. "What were you thinking?"

Charlie pulled on the straps of Angela's one-piece. "I put on the right swim suit."

"Maybe we should call this off."

Charlie appeared stricken. "What do you mean?"

"Angela is gone. You won't listen to me. Maybe it's time we all catch a plane to Hawaii."

Charlie was aghast. "No. We have to finish this. Angela will be back. You said."

"I know. And when she does come back she'll probably kick my ass if I stop. But you put the life of my son in danger."

"I won't do that again. I promise."

"You've got to understand we have dangerous people after us. And a bunch of powerful ancient aliens."

"So the sooner we finish this the sooner Gaia will be restrained. Snugglesaurus says."

Uzmahndey glared at the stuffed dinosaur Charley clutched in his lap.

"What is our next destination?"

"Dar...va...za Gas Cra...ter," Charley stumbled over.

Samir approached with a bag of purchases. He climbed in and looked Uzmahndey's injured arm over. "The bleeding stopped." Samir's curiosity was running rampant. "That cut looks deep. You're not much of a bleeder." He poked around in the bag. "That's a good thing, because I'm not much of a doctor."

"I'll do it," Charlie said. "Come back here, husband."

Uzmahndey scowled at her. "Since when did you become a doctor?"

"I'm not. But Snugglesaurus will tell me what to do."

Uzmahndey got out, and Charley scrambled between the seats in to the front. Uzmahndey climbed in back.

Samir looked over the stuffed dinosaur Charley had brought with him. "Is that Snugglesaurus?"

"Uh-huh," Charley answered.

"And he's going to tell your mother how to tend to a knife wound."

"Uh-huh."

Samir shook his head. "You Americans are too weird."

"Check your bank account," Uzmahndey said, as Charlie got busy cleaning the wound.

Samir did on his phone. He looked up in awe. "It's too much."

"Then donate the surplus to your favorite charity."

Samir watched Charlie work. "She just cleaned that deep wound with alcohol and you didn't even flinch."

"It's the xenobots," Charley said.

"*You* be quiet," Uzmahndey directed at him. "I'm still very angry with you."

Charley turned around forward and made himself small and still.

"You'll have to tell me more about these miraculous xenobots," Samir said.

"If I told you then I'd have to kill you," Uzmahndey said, without smiling.

"Okay. I probably don't want to know anyway." Samir turned back around. "Can your wife work while I'm driving?"

"Yes," Charlie said.

Samir pulled out of the parking lot and drove toward the airport.

<u>I hope you were bluffing about not continuing the mission.</u>

"I wasn't." Uzmahndey answered. He caught Samir's eyes darting to the rearview mirror. "I told you. I talk to myself."

"When you get nervous. Am I driving too fast? While your wife works on your arm? Is that making you nervous?"

<u>Are you prepared to swim back to Hawaii?</u>

"What are you talking about?"

"Your knife wound."

"Excuse me, Samir. I can't carry on two conversations at the same time. Right now I need to talk to myself."

Charley leaned over to whisper to Samir. "It's the xenobots."

<u>Do you really think Snugglesaurus will purchase you a plane ticket to anywhere except the next destination?</u>

"Then I'll buy tickets with my own money."

Do you think he will allow you to access your own money?
"He can do that?"
Are you seriously asking that? After you've seen all it can do?
"Damn!"
"Allah gahfara," Samir recited once again.

Chapter 21

Darvaza Gas Crater

Samir pulled into a park en route to the airport for Uzmahndey to remove his blood-soaked clothes so Charlie could clean the blood off him. After donning clean clothes, which included a long-sleeve shirt that concealed the bandages on his arm, he and Samir exited the Jeep so the other two could change out of their swimsuits.

Samir dropped them off at the Salalah airport. Snugglesaurus had booked them the first flight out, which went to the capital city of Muscat. After this short jaunt they ate dinner at the airport, since the upcoming flight to Ashgabat, Turkmenistan, was going to be much longer. Also, the xenobots had been busy and were ravenous.

On this flight Charley played with Snugglesaurus, which meant he was being tutored by the AI, while Charlie watched videos. Uzmahndey tried to access his bank account. When the page was unavailable, he heard Bad *snicker.*

Uzmahndey tried calling Keanu, but there was no answer. So he called the Moon and Turtle. A voice he recognized, but couldn't put a name to, answered when he asked for Keanu. "Who is this?"

"Uzmahndey. I'm a friend of Keanu."

"I know who you are. You run that escort service three doors down."

"It's not an escort service. I'm a tour guide. Can I speak to Keanu?"

"He's not here. He hasn't been here all week."

"Is he sick?"

"He's disappeared. No one has seen him. Call the police. They might know something. I can't talk anymore. It's crazy busy, and we're short-handed."

Uzmahndey stared at his phone after the abrupt ending of the call.

The sooner you finish this, the sooner Keanu will be safe.

The entire world will be safe. Including your son.

Yeah, just keep going.

Upon disembarking at Ashgabat International, the three exhausted travelers caught a taxi to Oguzkent Hotel. Uzmahndey was impressed with the towering brilliantly-lit edifice.

"This is like something on the Vegas Strip." Walking inside didn't disappoint. The cavernous atrium was open to the twelfth floor. The lush purple and gold carpet was as garish as that of Excalibur or Orleans. "Wow. Everything but the slot machines."

They were taken to a room near the top. Charley climbed into the middle of the king-size bed with Snugglesaurus. Charlie approached Uzmahndey. "Let me take a look at your arm."

Uzmahndey removed his shirt, and Charlie removed the bandage. The deep cut was nearly healed, leaving only an ugly scar.

We can heal that, too, if you want.

We thought maybe you'd want us to leave it.

It makes you look wicked mean.

Uzmahndey probed the scar. There was no pain. He flexed his arm, moved it every which way. He seemed to have full use of it. This brought a smile. "Man, I am going to have a long football career."

Charlie led him into the bathroom, where she cleaned off the dried blood. "Am I hurting you?"

"Not at all." He kissed the top of her head. In return, she kissed him on the lips. He backed away. "What was that?"

"Nothing." She walked out, twitching her hips. "I'm still waiting for that spanking."

"Forget it. It's *supposed* to be a punishment." He followed her out of the bathroom. "I'll tell you one thing. No swimming here. Not after what happened last time."

Charlie spun on her heel. "That pool is beautiful!"

"Dad!" Charley whined from the bed.

After relaxing at the pool for several hours – Charley especially liked the waterfall feature – everyone was refreshed and rested and in a better mood when they went up to the rooftop restaurant for a late dinner. Gazing through the window they were seated beside out into the expansive dark wasteland beyond the city lights, Charlie asked Uzmahndey, "Aren't you curious what we're going to see?"

"No. I'm through being a tourist. I just want to get this over with and get back home."

Charlie turned dour. "I don't have a home."

"You were born in Hawaii. That makes you an American." He glanced at the stuffed dinosaur his son held. "I'm sure Snugglesaurus can produce birth records for you."

She brightened. "So Hawaii is my home?"

"For as long as you want it to be. I'm not about to abandon you, not after all we've been through together. As long as you behave yourself."

Charlie's mischievous grin returned. "I'm just teasing. I don't really want to be your wife. I'm pretending to be because it's the easiest way for us to travel. And I really don't want you to spank me. I've seen how hard you can hit."

"Me, too," Charley chimed in.

Uzmahndey had the shurpa soup. He had considered the dograma chorba, until Charlie informed him Snugglesaurus had informed her the lamb meat in it included the heart, kidneys and lungs. So he had shashlyck with his soup instead. Charlie and Charley, not nearly as adventuresome, both had gutap bread stuffed with beef and potatoes.

The next morning Snugglesaurus had a rental car waiting for them at the hotel entrance. Uzmahndey drove north into the Karakum Desert. Several miles outside of town he pulled over. "Charlie, get up here and drive."

"Are you serious?"

"You need to learn. In case anything ever happens to me. There is not much traffic, we're out in the middle of nowhere, and the road is straight as an arrow. You'll have sight clearance for miles."

Uzmahndey scooted over, and Charlie got out and climbed in behind the wheel. He gave her a quick rundown on the mechanics, and they lurched back onto the road. The drive was slow and weavy for a while, but she caught on quickly. She would never admit it, but he suspected she was getting help from Snugglesaurus. Charlie freaked when a semi rushed toward her heading for Ashkabat, and nearly ran off the road trying to stay out of its way. She also freaked when someone raced up behind her. Uzmahndey had her slow down and pull as far to the right as she could to allow him to pass. After those first several encounters with traffic, she calmed down. After an hour she pretty much stayed on her side of the yellow line. After the second hour he had to make her slow down.

In the southern reaches of the Karakum they passed a few small fields of cotton, and grazing cattle. But the deeper into the desert they progressed, the more desolate the sands became. They made several stops to give Charlie a break from driving. One stop, at Charley's insistence, was to see the camels at Turkmen Market. They also stopped to see one of the medieval fortresses along the ancient Silk Road caravan route this road was built upon. All this despite Uzmahndey swearing off being a tourist just the night before. He had never been this way, and he knew he may never again. He also had his son to consider; Charley was fascinated with the camels.

So the four hour drive stretched into five. At the end of it they turned off the main road onto a dirt track that led to a parking area for the Darvaza Gas Crater. Charlie parked safely away from the other vehicles. She cut the engine off, pleased with herself. Until she saw Uzmahndey frowning at her. "What?"

"You didn't shift into park." He pointed at the shift lever.

Charley pushed and pulled on it, but it wouldn't move.

"You need to turn the key on."

Charlie started the car.

"That wasn't necessary."

"You said..."

"Turn the key on, not start the engine. But go ahead."

Her frown deepened when she tried to shift and still couldn't.

"Put your foot on the break."

Charlie turned her frown on him, then put her right foot on the brake pedal and shifted. After several tries she got into park.

"You're done. Finally, *now* turn it off."

Charlie did, then smiled pleased with herself. Until she noticed the scowl on Uzmahndey. "What?"

"We need some strategy here." Uzmahndey looked out the windshield at the dozen or so people roaming about the site. "Good, how many of these people here are Gaia nut jobs?"

We can't tell.

"So let's assume some might be here. Let's also think about what we are approaching. A burning gas well. Gaia could cause it to blow up in our faces. There was only a small jet of natural gas at Eternal Flame Falls, yet it produced an explosion big enough to knock Angela off-line."

"You think Gaia will attack us here?" Charlie asked.

"Sure seems like a good opportunity. So here's what we're going to do. You and Charley stay here in the car with the doors locked. If anyone approaches the car honk the horn. I can get back here in a hurry. Meantime, I'll go toss the Cheerio in and get back here as quick as I can. Hoping I don't get blown up."

"That's why you gave me the driving lesson. You're afraid something might happen to you."

He took a Cheerio out of the Tupperware container. "You might have to drive me to an ER. Or to a morgue."

"Stop it. You're scaring Charley."

Uzmahndey looked back to see his son still as stone clutching Snugglesaurus, staring at him with bug eyes. Uzmahndey winked at him, then looked back to Charlie. "If I don't make it back to the car, drive back to the hotel. Snugglesaurus will help you get out of Turkmenistan. And I'm sure Ghost will show up to help, too." He put the Tupperware container in the glove box. "You've got the xenobots, so you can go on whenever Angela gets back."

He climbed out. "Lock the doors." He shut his, not budging until hearing all the locks click.

Uzmahndey started down the walkway toward the gas crater. None of those scattered around the rim seemed to pay any heed to him. There was a wire fence erected on the very edge. Uzmahndey stepped up to peer down over it. Fire flickered along the sides at the top, while deeper down flames blazed higher. He tossed the Cheerio in, then turned away.

"Uzmahndey."

He whirled back around.

A well-muscled bearded male with flames dancing across his swarthy skin hovered just below the rim. He looked a stereotype of a genie. "You should come here at night. The Gate of Hell is much more impressive in the dark."

Uzmahndey glanced around at the other tourists. No one else seemed to notice this manifestation, or hear anything it said.

"I am shielding myself from all others. Only you can see and hear me."

"Who are you?"

"One of the ones you are trying to subdue."

Uzmahndey remained on the precipice of fleeing. "Why haven't you blasted me with fire?"

"I am not interested in harming you. But if you had brought the children with you, I would have."

"Why do you want to kill them?"

"They are trying to kill us."

"They are only children."

"Who grow up amazingly fast. And whose flesh can't be cut with a knife. Hardly human children. Why are you helping them?"

"One of them is my son."

"That was ingenious, getting you to mate with the machine."

"That you nearly destroyed."

"That wasn't me."

"Who was it, then?"

"My sister."

"Do you people have names?"

"Yes, but they are for our worshipers." When Uzmahndey didn't reply, he went on. "The alien you call Ghost is going to enslave the Earth."

"He says he is saving it."

"Why should you believe him? Be careful which side you end up on in this conflict. You could help bring about the destruction of your world." The image started to fade.

"Wait! What happened to Keanu?"

The fiery being blazed back. "He is unharmed. My aunt is entertaining him, so I sincerely doubt he has any complaints." As his laughter echoed in the pit, his form dissolved into smoke and wafted away.

Uzmahndey walked back to the rental car. Charlie unlocked it, and he opened the driver door. "Lesson's over. I'm driving."

Charlie hopped out and got in back. "You said you were going to be quick."

"One of them showed up." He started the car and backed out.

"Gaia?"

"One of her sons. Or consort. Or both." He drove out of the parking area along the dirt track back toward the highway.

"I-ap-e-tus," Charley stuttered, from the back seat. "Snugglesaurus said."

"Yeah? Who is his aunt? Who has Keanu?"

A brief moment later, Charley stuttered again. "E-ros."

"Eros? As in erotic?"

"Uz!" Charlie protested. "He's three. Snugglesaurus isn't going to tell him what that word means."

"No wonder Keanu won't have any complaints." Uzmahndey smiled. "Maybe he *is* enjoying himself."

"He is," Charley said, smiling at his sister. "Snugglesaurus says."

Uzmahndey lost his smile as he pulled onto the pavement and sped south back towards Ashgabat. Iapetus hadn't attacked him. Uzmahndey had never been directly attacked by any of them, or by their worshippers. Like the others, Iapetus had been intent on turning him against Angela. Every attack had been directed against Angela or Charlie. But the latest attack, the kidnapping, had imperiled his son. No way was he going to help them. He had skin in the game now.

That's why it was an ingenious move.

"And not the only one."

What do you mean?

"Back at Kilauea, in retrospect, it was awfully easy for me to get my hands on the Tupperware with all the xenobots. Those are vital to the mission, and Angela is pretty strong. Why did she let me take them and swallow you three?"

Whoa, there, QAnon.

"And why is Ghost using my old college coach's voice? There are plenty of voices in my memory for him to choose from. Why choose the one I was conditioned for four years to trust and obey without question?"

You think those were ploys?

"I *think* I'm being played big time."

"Who's playing you?" Charlie called out from the back seat.

"Everyone. And I don't like it." Uzmahndey clammed up after that, refusing to converse any more with Charlie or the xenobots. He stewed in silence all the way back to Ashgabat.

Chapter 22

Sunken Forest of Lake Kaindy

With Uzmahndey driving, it took less than four hours to get back to their hotel in Ashgabat. He was in too foul of a mood over feeling manipulated to take his son and Charlie swimming that afternoon, or to enjoy their rooftop meal that evening.

Uzmahndey's mood was not improved the next morning when he awoke with Charley crowding him. He rolled over to shove his son off, but stopped when he saw why he was being crowded. A growth spurt during the night. His son was still sound asleep, but Charlie was sitting up in her bed with a bright smile. "Snugglesaurus says he's eight now."

Uzmahndey scrambled up out of bed, immediately wide awake. "That is so freaky."

Charlie shrugged. "It's what happens to us."

"He'll be a zombie all day."

"Don't call him that. It takes us a while to adjust to the new dimensions of our bodies." She looked at the stuffed dinosaur in Charley's arms. "Snugglesaurus is already working on him while he's sleeping. Uploading information he needs to function as an eight-year old boy."

"Also freaky." Uzmahndey headed for the bathroom. "We still have to travel today."

"He'll be good to travel. Just don't expect him to talk much."

Once Charley was awake enough to walk, Charlie put a tee shirt of hers on him, and they drove to a nearby store to purchase clothes that fit. The clerks weren't too upset with an eight-year old boy walking around their store barefoot in a daze wearing a tee shirt that fit him like a dress. Turkmen seemed as accommodating as Omanis.

Later that morning, the flight from Ashgabat, Turkmenistan, to Almaty, Kazakhstan, was short in comparison to most of their air travel. Charley cuddled up in his seat with Snugglesaurus and slept the entire way. Uzmahndey tried another call to Keanu, but there was still no answer.

Uzmahndey picked up the rental car Snugglesaurus had waiting for them at the airport. Charley dozed in back with the stuffed dinosaur wrapped up in his arms. Charlie, seated in back next to him, gazed out the window at the passing scenery. The skyscrapers of the business district stood in stunning contrast framed against the towering snow-capped Trans-Ili Alatau Mountains they were planted at the foot of. Yet no one was in much of a mood to discuss the scenery. They passed without a word from urban development into fertile farmland.

Turning south hours later, they left pastureland and plowed fields behind to enter an arid landscape, passing from desolate mountains down to withered flatland and back up again into more dry mountains. Eventually, they reached the Sharyn River, which led to greener terrain. They drove through a small town at the foot of forested mountains. Ascending high into ever more rugged topography, they arrived at the parking for Lake Kaindy.

"Snugglesaurus says it's a mile hike to the lake," Charlie said.

"Charles?" His son failed to respond. His eyes were open, but he was slouched back into his seat. Uzmahndey turned to Charlie. "Can he walk? If he was still three I'd carry him."

"If he was still three there wouldn't be a problem." She shook him.

"Charley!"

He sat up and looked around.

"We're going on a hike."

This high in the mountains the air was chilly. The trail was muddy and steadily downhill. With Charley in the condition he was in it was slow going. Even so, emerging from the trees onto the lake shore, the sight was startling. The small mountain lake was crystal clear. The grove of pine trees rising up out of the water were eerie ghostly white spires. Although the evergreens were dead and needleless, the trunks were intact and the bare branches had been well-preserved. Yet the trees weren't entirely dead. Above the water the evergreens were bleached stripped-bare lifeless wood spires, while below the water vi-brant live green needles adorned healthy branches coming out of the thriving brown trunks of these same trees. Kept vital by the frigid water, these astounding trees were totally alive below the waterline while above it completely dead. The water was so clear and pristine this flourishing mystical underwater forest could easily be seen, contrasting so strangely with the pale dead trunks of these same trees above the placid surface of the lake.

Charley plopped down on a rock with Snugglesaurus, while Uzmahndey took the Tupperware container with the Cheerios out of his backpack.

"I've got bad news for you," Charlie said, gazing out over the lake. "Snugglesaurus says the Cheerio has to be placed in the roots of a certain tree out in the middle of the lake."

Uzmahndey glared at her. "You're kidding me. I can't just toss it in?"

"Not this time. You need to do like Angela did in Black Lake in the Azores, and in Mono Lake in California."

"That water was warm." He dipped a finger into the lake. "This is ice." He peered out at the trees. "Which one?"

<u>We'll guide you to it.</u>

"You really expect me to swim in this freezing water?"

<u>We can maintain your body temperature.</u>

<u>For a while.</u>

Uzmahndey looked around. There were a dozen other people present. He sat next to Charley to remove his shoes.

"Are you really going in?"

Uzmahndey saw a nearby young couple watching him. He nodded yes to the man as he stood and dropped his shirt down by his shoes.

"It's too cold. You'll get hypothermia."

Uzmahndey stepped out of his pants.

"I'll be quick."

Most everyone else strung out around the lake was watching him by this time. He extracted a Cheerio from the container and, taking a deep breath, walked into the lake. His feet and legs stung. He had never been in water anywhere near this cold. "Guys, you said you'd help."

<u>We are helping.</u>

When the water reached his knees and he could no longer feel his feet, and his legs began to tremble. He dove in. His heart nearly stopped when his chest hit the water. His breathing did stop. His shivering was so violent he had to clench his teeth to keep from chipping them. Yet he could stroke; he hadn't been immobilized. And not only could he swim, he could swim faster than he ever had before. That made sense, since he could run faster than ever before. He wondered if he could leap higher than ever before, over defensive backs to catch passes they couldn't reach...

<u>Focus. We cannot maintain your body temperature in this frigid water for long.</u>

<u>You need to be in and out quick.</u>

<u>*Don't go all goofy-fried on us.*</u>

Uzmahndey saw the tree they were guiding him to. Almost there. A few more flaps. Strides. Strokes! He was so numb how could he ache like this? He wondered how many fingers and toes he would lose? How many could he lose and still play football? There'd been that kicker who played with no toes on his kicking foot. As long as he could still hit Logan Wilson. He didn't have to tackle him, just knock him on his butt. He didn't need all his fingers or toes to block downfield.

A woman emerged from out of the green trees at the bottom of the lake clad in a plain robe that billowed all about her. She wasn't exceptional. No Aphrodite on a clam shell. Not the beauty his icicle-strung mind should have hallucinated. She swam out in front of the tree he was headed for and opened her arms wide.

"Stay with me."

How was he hearing her? She was underwater, he was on the surface. "Who are you?"

"Tethys." She beckoned.

So they deigned to give him their names now. What had changed?

<u>Maybe they are growing more desperate.</u>

Her voice was entrancing. "You can stay down here. With me. And the trees. They live here, under the water. You can, too. Live here forever. With me. In this enchanted forest. Come."

Uzmahndey dove. She rose up from the bottom to meet him. He swam into her arms, then spun around out of them, just like the spin move he had done so many times on the football field. The defender thought he had you wrapped up in his arms, then you plant your right foot and spin out of his clutches, leaving him looking like a fool flat face on the ground grasping at blades of grass while you run on to score. No, not score. Reach the tree. Uzmahndey shoved the Cheerio into the soft mud at its roots.

He kicked off the bottom upward. Where Tethys floated above awaiting him. She enfolded him with her arms.

"Why are you doing this?"

Uzmahndey shrugged her off. He'd broken out of tackles from players twice her size. Just because he was slight they always misjudged him, thought he'd go down easy. No way!

Uzmahndey broke the surface. Yet he still couldn't breathe. It felt like his lungs had collapsed.

He started to go back down. In a panic, he peered down into the clear water. Tethys had his right ankle. She was pulling him back under.

"Uzmahndey!"

His cloudy eyes cleared enough to look toward the shout. Charlie stood on the shore waving her arms above her head and screaming his name, again and again.

"Uzmahndey! Uzmahndey! Uzmahndey!"

Just like the crowd had, that time he'd scored, when they'd beaten the Rams, at home. He kicked his foot free, and swam.

Once he neared the shore several people waded out to drag him in. He was stretched out on a blanket. His undershorts were cut off. Blankets were wrapped around him. A towel was used to dry his neck and chest. And his groin? Come on! He forced his eyes open to see who had hold of his stuff. Charlie's crying face shimmered above him. Okay, he closed his eyes, if someone had to do it, let it be Charlie.

At some point the blood thrumming in his ears lessened enough for him to hear the voices inside his head.

<u>We thought we were dead.</u>

THOUGHT *YOU* WERE DEAD?

<u>Hey, he's finally doing it. Talking to us without talking. We might have a ventriloquist here.</u>

<u>If you die, we die. I thought we established that.</u>

THEN YOU SHOULD DO A BETTER JOB KEEPING ME ALIVE.

<u>It took all we had.</u>

<u>I just knew you were falling for that underwater woman. And she wasn't even that hot.</u>

I JUKED HER.

<u>I was so proud of you.</u>

WAIT TILL YOU SEE-

"-what I do to Logan Wilson."

"What?"

Uzmahndey looked up. The young man he had spoken to before going into the lake was hovering above him. How was he doing that, floating in the air?

"You said something about Logan Wilson." Uzmahndey stirred, but the man pressed gently on his chest. "Don't try to get up yet. Tell me who Logan Wilson is, and what you are going to do to him, and why."

Why was the fool talking about Logan Wilson? He wasn't even there. And the man wouldn't know him if he was.

"He's a Bengal."

"A tiger?"

"No. A man."

"A Bengali?"

"No. Football player."

"Ahh. What club does he play for?"

"Not club. Team. Cincinnati."

"FC Cincinnati. I've heard of them."

"No. Not soccer. Football. NFL."

"American football. Yes. Cincinnati Bengals."

"Yes. Finally. You're kind of dense."

Charlie laughed. "He's just trying to get you to think." Her face loomed before him. "These people drug you out of the lake."

Uzmahndey looked around to find a concerned crowd gathered around.

Charlie pointed to a family of four. "These people are camping here. They provided the blankets and towels."

Uzmahndey located who she was indicating. He hoped he didn't frighten the kids with the smile he attempted. Then his eyes darted all around. "Where's Charles?"

Charley kneeled beside him. "I'm here."

They were safe. He was safe. He'd done it. He hoped he wasn't damaged too badly.

<u>You'll be okay.</u>

"I won't lose any fingers? It's hard to catch passes without all your fingers. Or toes? It's hard to run and cut without all your toes."

"You are still a deep shade of blue," the man who Uzmahndey had been talking with said. "You'll have to wait until you get to the hospital to see how much damage you've done to yourself."

Charlie stood. "Can we get him back to our car? He's got dry clothes there."

"Yes. This fellow here." The man helping him indicated another young man in the crowd. "He's already cut two saplings. We'll use them with these blankets to make a stretcher and carry him back."

"No, you won't." Uzmahndey stirred.

"You are not strong enough," the man protested.

"You have no idea how strong I am." With his help, and some others, Uzmahndey stood.

"Oops." Charlie wrapped the blankets tighter as he stood. "There are children."

"What were you doing?" another man demanded. "That was insane. Are you suicidal?"

"Something I'd sworn to do." He shifted from one numb foot to the other. Throwing his arms across two sturdy sets of shoulders, he attempted a step. His legs trembled, and stung so badly it felt like they were on fire. But he remained upright. He released the shoulders. With no feelings in his feet it was hard to keep his balance. "Let me go. See if I can stand."

All hands released him.

Uzmahndey swayed, but stayed on his feet. He nodded he was alright.

"Whatever you were doing," a young woman said, holding up her phone. "I got an amazing video."

Oh, no, Uzmahndey moaned silently. Another viral video.

"Who had hold of your foot?" she asked.

"You saw that? I thought I was hallucinating. Out of my head from the cold."

"It's on the video."

"Something is on the video," another man said. "It could be vines wrapped around his foot."

"Yes," the young man who had helped him up said. "No way is there someone else swimming in the lake."

"Divers have gone down to the bottom," another man offered. "In wet suits."

"Was there a diver down there?" the young woman asked.

Uzmahndey shook his head as he began the long slog back up the muddy slope to the parking area. He couldn't think about that now. He had to lift one foot up, move it forward, place it on the ground, shift his weight forward, lift his other foot up. And do it going uphill. It took all he had. The more steps he took, the more the stinging in his legs eased. It didn't go away, it was merely transferred to his feet, replacing the numbness with agonizing pain. With each step it felt like he was treading on broken glass. Several others trailed along. He looked around with a question on his face.

"To make sure you make it to your car," someone replied.

"Thank you all so much." Charlie stepped up alongside Uzmahndey. "I'll get my husband dressed when we get there. I can drive back."

Uzmahndey leaned heavily into her. "I can sleep in the back seat?"

"I don't know how much sleep you'll get with me driving."

Uzmahndey shut up. It was too hard to talk. And his entire body hurt too much. He tried thinking his conversation again.

CAN'T YOU GUYS DO SOMETHING.

<u>The pain you feel is a good thing.</u>

<u>It means you are still alive. Don't do anything like this again.</u>

<u>Who are you trying to kid? You know he will.</u>

Chapter 23

Lake Baikal

Charlie didn't drive for long. And Uzmahndey didn't sleep at all. Watching her navigate the twisting road coming down out of the mountains from Lake Kaindy was way too stressful. He insisted she stop at the first town they came to. Snugglesaurus directed her to a hostel in Karabulak.

She helped Uzmahndey limp inside, explaining to the manager that her husband had fallen in the lake and nearly drowned, and needed to recover. The manager placed them in one of the few single rooms. Exhausted, as he had been all day, Charley was content to climb into the top bunk with Snugglesaurus. Charlie shoved Uzmahndey into the bottom bunk with his clothes on then climbed in with him.

"What are you doing?" he stammered. He was still shivering, although by this time it no longer felt like his skeleton was dislocating at the joints.

"Helping you get warm." She snuggled up to him beneath the blanket.

"Just because you handled the family jewels…"

"They said that was your most exposed organ and was in danger of permanent damage. It needed to get dry and warm right away. I was supposed to be your wife. So who else would do it?"

"You are not my wife. Don't forget that."

Charlie welded her body to his. "I love you, Uz. I would do anything for you. Anything at all."

Uzmahndey at last relaxed in her arms. "I know you would. And I love you, too. Just not..."

"As a wife. I understand. Now hush, and rest."

Feed me, Seymore!

Uzmahndey opened his eyes. He was in bed. The bottom bunk. With Charlie.

We're starving! I feel like Venom yelling at Eddie. And I am not even asking for human brains.

Charles! Uzmahndey scrambled across Charlie out of the bottom bunk to peer up into the top bunk. His son was lying in bed with Snugglesaurus.

"Hello, Dad. Are you okay now?"

"Yes." He hugged him. "How are you doing?"

"Okay. What are we doing today?"

"I don't know. I *do* know we're not swimming in a mountain lake again."

Charlie climbed out of the bottom bunk and leaned into the top next to Uzmahndey. "How are you this morning?"

Uzmahndey stretched, twisted all about. "Okay, I guess." He wriggled his fingers and toes. "These all seem okay."

Charlie gave an impish smile. "Is everything else okay?"

Uzmahndey frowned at Charley. "I'll check later."

Food!!

"Bad is starving. Are you two hungry?"

"Yes," Charley exclaimed.

"Let's go find some breakfast."

After eating two helpings of everything available at the little hostel, Uzmahndey was fit to drive. The long trip back to Almaty was uneventful. But his mood was much improved from the preceding day. Surviving a brush with death put things in perspective. So they thought *they* were manipulating *him*? To get *him* to do what *they* wanted? *He* was manipulating *them* to get what *he* wanted. Back in the NFL. And if these aliens living at the center of the Earth couldn't stop him, then no defense in the league could stop him. He would be legendary!

At the rental office he returned their car to the agent asked if he was alright. When Uzmahndey appeared uncertain how to respond, the agent brought up on his phone the video taken the previous day of him floundering in Lake Kaindy.

"Who was in Lake Kaindy with you? It looks like someone is holding your foot."

Denying that it was him, Uzmahndey hustled them out of the office to hail a taxi. The driver asked if he was okay, and who that woman in the lake with him was? When the ticket agent at the airport terminal gate studied his face, Uzmahndey merely frowned and said he was okay.

The airline tickets Snugglesaurus had purchased landed them in Irkutsk, Russia. A taxi from the airport took them to the Irkutsk Hotel, downtown overlooking the Angara River. It was modern and comfortable, and the room Snugglesaurus had secured for them, with a double bed and one single, was suitable. The first thing Uzmahndey did upon entering the room was shave off his beard.

Charlie laughed at this. "Now you look like the guy in the Giant's Causeway video."

"But not like the guy in the Lake Kaindy video. That one is more recent." He considered his image in the mirror. "If I leave my hair long, then I won't look like the guy in either video."

They found a restaurant in the hotel.

"Is potato," Charley cracked upon opening the menu.

Uzmahndey glared at him. "Just what is the AI teaching you?"

Charlie studied the menu. "This soup looks good."

Uzmahndey saw what she was looking at. "Bukhleor. It has meat and onions." He looked to his son. "No potatoes. Good for a starter."

Charlie smiled at him. "Are the xenobots still recharging?"

"Yes. I'm so hungry I could eat a horse."

"It's on the menu," Charley said. When Uzmahndey frowned at him, he pointed it out. "Right here. See?"

"The Buryat people eat horsemeat." A waiter had appeared, unnoticed, at their table.

Uzmahndey raised sheepish eyes.

"We'll start with three bowls of bukhleor."

"And that's just for him," Charley said.

"May I also suggest kuruul. It is a local favorite, a cheese made from goat milk. It goes well with airag, which is horse milk with honey, sugar, and raisins." Seeing the questioning looks at the mention of horse milk, the waiter continued. "The Buryat people believe airag has medicinal properties, and heals many conditions. Milk is considered sacred here. To finish your meal you should try our tea. The Buryat favor green tea with milk, salt, and butter."

Uzmahndey nodded at all this.

"So five bowls of bukhleor?" the waiter asked.

Uzmahndey considered for a moment. "Six."

Charley was bouncing off the walls when they returned to their room.

"The waiter should have told us the horse milk in the airag was fermented," Charlie complained.

"You shouldn't have been drinking it, either," Uzmahndey said.

"Really?"

"It was good!" Charley said. "I'll have some for breakfast, too!"

"No you will not," Uzmahndey said.

"I am an adult now, you know," Charlie complained. "I can legally drink here, in Russia. Snugglesaurus says so."

"But I don't say so. Go put your pajamas on." She dug them out of her suitcase and stomped into the bathroom, while Charley bounced on the single bed. "Over here, buddy. That's your sister's bed. You're with me."

Early the next morning a rental car was awaiting them at the front entrance. During the long drive through open countryside Charlie and Charley took turns relating information Snugglesaurus fed them about their destination. Lake Baikal was the largest freshwater lake in the world. It held twenty percent of the world's fresh water. At over a mile deep, it was also the world's deepest lake. And it was getting deeper. It had formed at a fracture where two continental plates were pulling away from each other. Eventually, a new ocean would form there. This lake was considered the Galapagos of Russia. There were many unique species of flora and fauna there that were found nowhere else on Earth.

"And there are monsters in the lake," Charley eagerly added. "A giant dragon. They call it Lusud-Kahn."

"That's just a myth," Charlie insisted. She was in front, giving Charley the whole back seat to spread out in.

"You say that," Uzmahndey said, "after all we've seen. There very well could be a monster waiting for us in the lake."

"They've found pictures of it," Charley eagerly continued. "Carved on rock a long time ago. In the pictures it's standing upright under the water with fish swimming around it. It's a huge lizard, with a forked tongue, wicked claws, and plates of armor on its back."

"That sounds like a dinosaur," Uzmahndey said. "This area is pretty remote.

"Do you think some survived into human times?"

"That's ridiculous," Charlie said.

To stave off an argument, which were becoming more frequent between the two since Charley had turned eight, Uzmahndey changed the subject. "Tell me about Shaman Rock."

Once again the brother and sister took turns speaking. Shaman Rock was on Olkhon Island, the sacred center of shamans in the Northern Hemisphere. The island had been a refuge for Mongolian shamans hiding from persecution in the time of Genghis Khan, and later for Buryat shamans when Buddhism spread throughout the land. Traditional rites were still performed all around the shores of Lake Baikal to this day, but especially on Olkhon Island, and there especially at Shaman Rock.

Charlie insisted on being the one to relate the legend of Shaman Rock. "Baikal, a great and rich ruler, had a beautiful daughter, Angara. A handsome hero, Irkut, vied for her hand in marriage. Although he failed to win her heart, he became the favorite of her father. Another young man, Yenisei, did win her heart, but Baikal, since he preferred Irkut, did not give his consent to their marriage. So he imprisoned his willful daughter. But she escaped with the help of her brothers, and fled to her love, Yenisei. Her father became so enraged that a furious storm arose. A powerful lightning strike split a mountain. Baikal flung a fragment of this mountain, Shaman Rock, to block the path of the escaping lovers. To this day Shaman Rock is the site of mystical ceremonies. If you stare at it long enough, you will see the faces of shamans who have held sacred rites there."

At the end of a four-hour drive they arrived at the ferry to Olkhon Island. Uzmahndey grew more worried the longer he waited in line to drive onto the boat. He had nearly died in the last lake he entered, and here he was about to take a boat across another dangerous lake. Would Lusud-Kahn, or one of Gaia's creatures, rise up to swamp the ferry boat? The ferry boat arrived, at last.

As soon as Uzmahndey drove on board and parked, he suggested they get out of the car. He told them the reason was so they could see better, but truthfully he thought they had better chances of surviving the boat going down if they were out on deck. Uzmahndey led them to the railing, and placed an arm around each of them.

Charley thought nothing of this, but Charlie looked at him with concern. "Are you okay?"

Uzmahndey nodded, pulling them both close. He gazed down into the lake. The blue water was so clear he could see to a great depth. He didn't see anything moving in those depths. A quarter-hour later he herded the two back into their car, and they drove off the boat. They had made it onto Olkhon island without incident. Would they make it back off?

The other two sensed his anxiety, and fed off it. "This island is the most sacred place on Lake Baikal," Charlie said.

"And we're headed for the most sacred place on the island," Charley added.

There were numerous sacred sites on the island, but Uzmahndey made no detours on the way to Shaman Rock, speeding through the barren craggy land with eyes riveted forward. He didn't slow until they approached the small town of Khuzhir. They passed several religious sites, a campground, and many small inns. Also many coffee shops. Their fleeting aroma was tempting, yet he resisted. Uzmahndey was determined to get this over with as quickly as possible and get back off the island.

Don't lose your nerve.

We've got you.

"Yeah, like you did in Lake Kaindy."

We saved your butt there.

"Barely. I nearly died."

Charlie placed a reassuring hand on his shoulder. "Are you okay?"

He looked away from her concern. This main avenue through town was teeming with tourists, many in outlandish garb. It looked like a mash-up of a comic-con and a Ren Faire, with an Oriental slant.

Finally, Uzmahndey eased out of town and parked their car in a crowded lot. The Shaman Stone reared up before them on the lake shore. Uzmahndey looked around as he climbed out from behind the wheel. Dozens of tourists and serious pilgrims milled about the parked cars. Would it be safe to leave Charlie and Charley behind? With all these strangers around? Were any of Gaia's worshippers lurking in this crowd?

Seeming to sense what he was considering, Charlie spoke up. "No way are you leaving us behind. We're in this together."

"Yeah, Dad. Let's go." Charley started off toward the foot path leading down to the lake.

Uzmahndey yanked him back. "On one condition. You two do everything I say. And stay behind me." Realizing how on edge he was, they both readily agreed. Uzmahndey cast his gaze about the crowd one last time. "How about it, guys? See anyone suspicious?"

<u>Not yet.</u>

<u>We'll keep a lookout.</u>

<u>The only one acting suspicious is you. Calm down and don't draw attention to yourself.</u>

Uzmahndey set off toward Shaman Rock, Charlie and Charley a step behind. They approached the thirteen poles wrapped in hundreds of colorful ribbons.

"I should have brought a green one," Charlie said. "For health, for the Earth." Uzmahndey took each by the hand and drug them on without pause.

They reached a rise overlooking the lake. A narrow peninsula extended from the mainland out to the Rock. A Buryat shaman was conducting a ceremony at the base of the sacred stone. Charlie leaned in to whisper. "Snugglesaurus says you need to place the xenobot in the lake at the foot of the stone. You'll never be able to throw it accurately from this far away. We've got to go down there."

"Will I be allowed to?" Uzmahndey asked. "With a ceremony going on?"

This ceremony will be a distraction. Everyone is watching the shaman.

Go down to that rocky beach near the end of the trail. That should be close enough for you to toss it where it needs to go.

You know you could play quarterback when you get back in the league. With us helping you have a rocket arm.

Uzmahndey worked his way down the slope through the crowd of onlookers, with Charlie and Charley in tow. Nearing the front of the crowd, they moved to the side down to the lakeshore. He gazed out over the water. It was placid, clear, beautiful. With the chanting of the Shaman, set to an accompanying steady drumbeat, incense and aromatic wood smoke wafting on the gentle but biting breeze, blue sky, blue lake, the vibes of the holy place permeated his being. He had felt something like this before. The roar of seventy-thousand screaming fans, blasting rock music echoing about the stadium, teammates banging into each other, pumping up each other's adrenaline, the quarterback under center barking out nonsensical sounds like the shaman droning out prayers only his god could comprehend.

He's going into a trance.

Snap out of it, Uz.

Hike!

That did it. The age-old command he had heeded since Pee Wee league. Uzmahndey got moving. Slipping a Cheerio from its container, he prepared to throw it out into the water at the base of Shaman Rock.

Until a loud crack! The water grew brilliant. A hubbub arose from the crowd. The shaman paused. Uzmahndey's cocked arm froze.

As did the water. The portion of the lake around Shaman Rock had become coated with ice. In an instant. People swarmed down to the water's edge to better witness this miracle. Had the shaman done this? A muffled respectful murmur spread through the crowd.

Uzmahndey lowered his arm. Exactly where the xenobot needed to be inserted was frozen over. What was he supposed to do now?

Most awestruck people merely gaped in wonder. A few adventuresome souls tested the ice. It held. Some started venturing from shore.

"The lake freezes over in the winter," Charlie said. "People walk all over the lake then."

"Look at the bubbles!" Charley exclaimed. He stepped forward for a better view.

Uzmahndey yanked him back, but couldn't help looking himself. An amazing tapestry of frozen air bubbles were trapped beneath the surface in the ice. The frozen water was so clear and clean you could see these twisting columns of innumerable bubbles swirling up from out of the depths captured in this sudden miraculous ice. Every person present had phones or cameras out taking pictures or videos.

Uzmahndey knew it was no miracle. It was Gaia's doing. He had to do something. He couldn't wait until the ice melted. It should never have frozen in the first place at this time of year, so who knew how long it would be before it thawed.

"Stay right here." He ordered, pinning one then the other in place with his steely gaze. "Do not take one step."

Uzmahndey joined the adventurous ones out on the ice. It held. He made his way toward the base of Shaman Rock, where the Cheerio needed to be placed. The others out there ignored him. They were each on their own individual spiritual journey at this mystical experience.

Until he stomped his foot.

"Are you crazy?!", and other more colorful phrases in languages he didn't understand were flung at him. He stomped again. He had to get through the ice. People hurried back to solid ground. He stomped once more. He knew every phone and camera was focused on him. Just what he needed, another viral video. "Come on, guys, help me."

Help you kill us? Why should we?

You realize if we break through and fall in there is a good chance of it refreezing and trapping us in the ice.

Have you thought this through? What is your plan here?

"Break through the ice, drop the Cheerio in the lake where it needs to go, then get the hell out of Dodge."

Interesting.

We could make you a placekicker. Give you the strongest leg in the NFL.

If we live. You two are as crazy as he is.

The ice erupted five yards away.

That's curious.

That's not where we were stomping.

Who cares. Its close enough. Just toss the xenobot in and get off the ice.

Before Uzmahndey had a chance to do any of that, a body rose up out of the lake through the hole in the ice. Angela. He merely watched, stunned, as she scrambled up out of the water and lunged across the ice at him. Snatching the Cheerio from his grasp, she tossed it into the hole she had made then grabbed his hand and pulled him toward the shore.

The ice gave way, and started to dissolve as quickly as it had frozen. Angela and Uzmahndey fell through, but it was into water only up to their knees. They waded on toward the shore. The water started to refreeze, just as Ugly had feared. By this time the water they were in only just topped their ankles. Before the ice could freeze solid, they were able to stomp through it the few steps they needed to make it out onto the shore.

Charlie and Charley were at their side in a flash. Angela didn't pause for the hugs they offered. Without a word she grabbed them each by the hand and drug them up the hill. Uzmahndey scrambled up after them.

The crowd of gawkers parted before them, some bowing in supplication.

Chapter 24

Stone Forest

Uzmahndey and the two children raced with Angela all the way back to the car. Where Uzmahndey caught Angela up in his arms and hugged her.

She knocked him away. "Get us out of here."

He laughed. "I'm glad to see you, too."

"We've no time for this."

Uzmahndey acquiesced, and unlocked the doors. Angela shoved Charley into the back seat, and Charlie climbed in next to him. Uzmahndey and Angela piled into the front. He had a thousand questions to ask and a million things to say, but it all would have to wait.

Most of the crowd was still at Shaman Rock reveling in the miraculous event they had just been a part of. This was the second coming for these New Agers. He sped away back into town.

"Slow down," Angela barked. "No one is chasing after us. Yet."

Their speed-limited passage through the narrow winding lanes of Khuzhir went unnoticed. News of what had happened at Shaman Rock had not preceded them. Now there was time to find out what was going on. "How did that happen?" Uzmahndey asked.

Or maybe not. "Later." Angela's tunnel vision bored ahead.

Uzmahndey's vision was blurred. Too much had happened too sudden too unexpected. But Angela was back, that's all that mattered.

"Good to see you, Mom," Charley called out from the back.

"I'm not your mom."

That was brutal. But Uzmahndey was forced to disregard her sharp attitude when he turned a corner and came upon a mob blocking the street. He stopped the car.

"Don't stop," Angela ordered.

A dozen men and women approached. These people did not look like the local Buryat, nor were they comporting like tourists.

<u>Some of them look familiar.</u>

<u>*Yeah, these are Gaia worshippers.*</u>

"Go!" Angela yelled.

"Where? I can't run them over."

The gang halted their advance and looked up. Uzmahndey craned his head forward and looked up through the windshield to see what had caught their attention. He could see nothing in the sky.

<u>*Now would be a good time to get us out of here.*</u>

<u>Back up and take that street on your right.</u>

<u>We'll direct you. Just drive.</u>

Uzmahndey did as Good, Bad and Ugly urged. While the mob remained rooted in the middle of the street behind him, gazing skyward. Following Ugly's directions, they detoured around the blocked street and were soon on their way out of the small town.

"Now you can drive fast, Uzmahndey."

Charlie and Charley both screamed. Uzmahndey slammed on the brakes and jerked around to look into the back seat for the reason for their scream. The QAnon Shaman sat between the brother and sister, who were both clawing at their doors trying to escape. The Shaman sighed. "This is not fast."

Uzmahndey recognized the familiar voice. "Ghost?"

"Of course," Angela spat. "Drive. Fast. Go. Now!"

Uzmahndey turned back around and sped away. "What just happened?"

"I created a diversion. But it won't divert for long."

Uzmahndey was having difficulty keeping the car on the road. "What did they see?"

"Whatever their heart desired. Christ, Allah, Yahweh, Buddha, Baikal, Gaia. I left it to each of their own imaginations. But the holograms won't last much longer."

"Why do you look like that crazy guy at the Capitol Riot?"

"To show you how you looked to everyone back at Shaman Rock."

Uzmahndey ran off the road. "You made me look like that freak?"

Angela grabbed the wheel. "You're going to kill us."

"Want me to drive?" Charlie asked.

Angela steered the car back onto the road. "Charlie drives?"

Uzmahndey knocked Angela's hands off the wheel and took control of the car. "Tell me why you made me look like that loser."

"That loser is what will appear in all the photos and videos that will be flooding the Internet. Instead of your image."

Uzmahndey ran his fingers through his hair. He still had not gotten used to it being longer again.

"I thought he was in jail."

"So you were a fanboy engaging in cosplay. Relax. It was only a hologram. I lifted it as soon as you escaped the scene."

"I bet you looked cool as a shaman, Dad," Charley exclaimed.

Uzmahndey glanced in the rearview mirror at his son. "That loser isn't a real shaman. He is a deluded fool."

"If you have everything under control now." Ghost prepared to snap his finger.

"Wait," Uzmahndey exclaimed. "Is Angela okay?"

"Mostly. I was in a hurry to get her back to you. She's not as elegant as before. But she should suffice." The alien completed his finger-snap, and the QAnon Shaman disappeared from the back seat.

"Wow," Charley said. "Who was that?"

"Angela's father," Charlie answered.

"Grandpa?" Charley marveled.

Uzmahndey focused his worries on Angela.

"You look elegant to me."

"Just drive," was her inelegant reply.

Not another word was spoken until they pulled up in line to await the next ferry off the island. Uzmahndey gazed out the back window. If Gaia's people were in pursuit, they could catch up to them there. "You two keep an eye out for anyone coming up behind us who looks perturbed," he directed the two in the back seat.

He turned to Angela. She sat as stiff and motionless as a poorly-chiseled statue, peering straight ahead out the front windshield. "Can we talk now?"

"About what?"

"For starters, what just happened back there?" When she turned a blank expression his way, he grew agitated. "In the lake. At Shaman Rock."

Still, no flicker in her stony face.

She looks the same.

But she's not behaving the same.

Ghost said she wasn't as elegant as before. Try being more specific with your questions.

"How did the lake freeze over?"

"It didn't freeze over."

"It did. That wasn't a hologram. I walked on it."

"Just that section of the lake froze."

So it didn't freeze over. *Oh boy. You need to be* very *specific with your questions.*

"You guys shut up. I'll deal with this." Angela turned her face forward. "Not you. I didn't tell you to shut up, Angela."

She looked back at him. It didn't appear she would have been upset if he *had* told her to shut up.

"Did Gaia make the water freeze?"

"No. It was Tartarus."

"One of her children?"

"No."

"Tartarus was created at the same time as Gaia," Charlie said. "According to Snugglesaurus. So I guess he's like her brother. But Gaia had children with her brothers. That family is really messed up."

"Any more messed up than ours?" Charley asked. He sounded bitter.

Uzmahndey fired a dark look into the back seat. "You two be quiet, too. Let me deal with this."

Charlie sank back into her seat with an injured look and gazed out her window.

While Charley smirked. "I'm still keeping watch, Dad." He focused his attention out the back window.

Uzmahndey returned his attention to Angela. "How did you end up in the ice?"

"Father projected me there from his lab."

"Into solid ice?"

"It wasn't solid."

"She's talking about the bubbles," Charlie said in an aggrieved voice, without averting her gaze from out the side window. "They're caused by methane gas oozing up from the lake bottom. If anyone is interested."

"Did I weaken the ice by stomping on it?"

Angela didn't respond to his question. Instead, she had one of her own. "How many portals have you sealed since I left?"

"The Well of Barhout, the Darvaza Gas Crater, and Lake Kaindy."

"That's all? Three?"

Uzmahndey lost his cool at this. Her being unresponsive was one thing. But to be critical like that? After all they'd been through? "I nearly died in Lake Kaindy."

"And he rescued us, Mom," Charley blurted out. "From kidnappers."

Uzmahndey didn't tell him to shut up this time. But he should have.

Angela was aghast. "You let them get kidnapped? Both of them?"

Uzmahndey whacked the steering wheel with his open palm and looked away in disgust. That was it. He was through with her.

But she wasn't through with him. "Don't hit the wheel like that. You'll damage it. I told you before you don't realize how strong you are."

She remembered something she had said, from before the White Desert, before she was wrecked. A glimmer of hope. Before Uzmahndey could fan that spark, cars coming off the just-docked ferry began rolling by. He started their car up. Angela looked straight ahead while he pulled forward. At least she was back. There would be time to work out her kinks later. She was back.

The rest of the return drive to Irkutsk was uneventful. It was late in the afternoon when they walked into their hotel room. Uzmahndey went straight for the TV. Sure enough, video from Shaman Rock was playing. The QAnon Shaman was stomping on the ice.

"You're safe, Dad," Charley said. He and Charlie had gathered around him to watch. "No one knows it was you."

Uzmahndey turned away. Angela had pulled a chair up next to the double bed and sat to stare at it. She had already assumed her position for the night. Despair settled in as Uzmahndey looked her over. This was worse than before. She hadn't merely been knocked off-line this time. The sandstorm in the White Desert had done real damage.

He sat on the edge of the bed before her. Her eyes flicked to his face, then away. Was this how the loved ones of Alzheimer's patients felt? To look at someone so familiar, yet see no sign of recognition in their face? He had accused her once of being a mannequin; now she really was one.

"Angela?"

She looked at him with vacant eyes. He sighed.

"Nothing."

The next morning Uzmahndey awoke in the single bed to find Angela unmoved from the night before. Charlie and Charley, cuddling Snugglesaurus, slept soundly under her protective gaze. Uzmahndey studied Angela's monotone face. He swore he would not abandon her. She had saved his life numerous times. Even if she was not the biological mother of his son, she *had* given birth to him, and nursed him, and cared for him. He could not abandon the young woman in bed with his son, either. Charlie had grown up before his eyes. The four of them had become a family, if far from the Ozzie and Harriet ideal. He looked to the ragged and crudely-mended stuffed dinosaur in Charley's arms. Even that thing. He couldn't imagine not having Snugglesaurus along.

What about us?

He groaned.

"Do I have a choice?"

Angela looked at him. "I could remove them. Or deactivate them."

How did she know what he was talking about? Could she now hear the xenobots inside his head, or wherever they were in his body? She hadn't been able to do that before. Or if she had, she hadn't let on she could. Another complication to consider. His to-do list of problem solving was growing exponentially.

"No," he finally said, focusing on the problem of the moment - hanging onto his ticket back into the NFL. "That's part of the deal. My reward for doing this. I get to keep the xenobots. And they remain functional. Right?"

Angela nodded.

"Besides, they no longer feel like intruders. They feel like a part of me, merely odd corners of my mind."

"Extremely odd." Charlie raised up. "Where to now?"

"Shilin. That's in China." Charley opened his eyes. "Snugglesaurus told me last night."

The route from Irkutsk to Kunming was complicated. After two connections and over twenty-four hours, they flew from southern Siberia in Russia to the Yunan Province in southern China. Three of them were walking zombies by the time they deplaned at Shilin, the nearest large city to their destination - the Stone Forest. Only Angela was coherent as they stumbled out of the terminal, so she took the lead.

He was relieved to let her. Angela was once again posing as his wife. He was also relieved Charlie was no longer saddled with that responsibility. She had played that role with way too much enthusiasm. She was now supposed to be Angela's younger sister, and Charley, as ever, was his and Angela's son. Snugglesaurus had all the false online documents in order, so they breezed through customs.

Angela hailed a taxi to take them to the Hanggong Holiday Hotel, where Snugglesaurus had secured them a room with two double beds. Upon entering, Uzmahndey flopped across one bed, and Charlie and Charley, with the stuffed dinosaur between them, flopped across the other. Angela pulled up a chair.

Nearly twelve hours later, Uzmahndey stirred. It was dark. He looked to the other bed. Charlie and Charley were asleep. He looked to Angela's chair, but it was vacant. She was standing naked in the dark room before the window, gazing out upon the lights of Kunming. It was night, and the city was brilliant. Rising to join her, he found himself naked, also.

"I had an express laundry service do our clothes. You let them all get filthy."

Uzmahndey recalled fuzzy memories of Angela stripping his clothes off during the night. He sat back down on the edge of the bed and drew the cover across his lap then glanced at the two sleeping in the other bed. "Those two won't like the idea of sleeping together without their pajamas."

"They were too tired to argue." Angela turned away from the window to him. "Snugglesaurus purchased tickets for us to take a tour bus to the Stone Forest. Get a shower before the others wake up."

"You take good care of us, Angela."

"Better than you did."

She sounded belligerent. Was that better than indifferent? Or was he merely projecting his hopes onto her blank slate like before. Glancing back to make sure the others were still asleep, he stood and walked up behind her. "You're right. I've missed you." He slipped his arms around her waist and drew her near.

She glanced back over her shoulder. "Go take a shower."

At least she hadn't pushed him away. Was that progress? Or further folly on his part? Uzmahndey released her and turned away. Switching on the bathroom light, he glanced back and noticed the reflection flash in Charlie's open eyes. He held her gaze for a moment then closed the door.

On the tour bus en route to the Stone Forest, Uzmahndey read up on his phone about this portal. 'Covering an area of

186 square miles, the Stone Forest is a massive otherworldly landscape of karst formations over 270 million years old. Over the millennia seismic activity and water and wind erosion have carved the present-day limestone formations. The giant stalagmite-like pillars create huge arrays of labyrinths easy to become lost in. At Shilin many smaller stone forests feature caves, waterfalls, ponds, a lake with an island, and even an underground river. The Stone Forest has been designated a UNESCO World Heritage Site.'

"Did you read about the Ashimi Stone?" Charlie asked.

When he turned a blank face to her, she rushed on. "Ashimi was a beautiful Sani girl who was turned to stone when she ran into the forest after being forbidden to marry the man she loved."

"Tell him the good part," Charley butted in. Not waiting for her to, he rushed on. "They hold a festival every year where they have wrestling, bull fighting, pole climbing, dragon play-ing, lion dancing, and the A-xi Moon Dance, whatever that is."

"That is not happening now," Angela said. "It's crowded enough. We don't need a festival."

"But we *are* going to see the Ashimi Stone?" Charlie asked.

"That's not where the portal is," Angela said. So she was paying attention to their conversation, even when she didn't seem interested. That was slightly encouraging.

Despite Angela's disclaimer, they did see the Ashimi Stone. They walked right past the ancient rock monument standing in a pool of water that vaguely resembled a human form. Charlie attempted to linger to listen to a tour guide relate the legend in English to a group of Americans, but Angela tugged her along. She led them deep into the Stone Forest, weaving them down a tangled maze of paths writhing through dense majestic clusters of chaotic rock to Quifeng Cave.

The four stood at one end of a small pool before the cave at the top of steps leading down into the water.

"Are we going in the cave?" Uzmahndey asked.

"No." Angela walked onto the rocks to the side of the steps.

"Come on." Charley scampered after her.

Uzmahndey shrugged, waving an arm in their direction. "After you."

"We could at least have stopped at the Ashima Stone for a minute," Charlie hissed as she passed before him.

Uzmahndey followed. "Slow down!"

"Keep up!" Charley called back.

Rounding one large rock spire, Uzmahndey bumped into Charlie. "Why did you stop?"

"Where are they?"

He looked all around. Angela and Charley were nowhere to be seen. "Angela!"

"You should leave."

Uzmahndey and Charlie spun around. A lithe female beauty reclined across the rocks before them with only her lustrous long black tresses, draped carelessly about her bare supine alabaster form, covering her. Huge bright eyes beneath thick black brows dominated a finely-chiseled face. The young woman seemed as natural an outgrowth of the surrounding rocks as the algae that covered much of them.

Uzmahndey froze at this sudden appearance of such a perfect female form. He immediately grew as erect as a dowsing rod quivering above an underground lake. It took an elbow jab from Charlie to activate him.

"Do you like what you see?"

He slipped Charlie a guilty look then averted his gaze from the flawless sexuality splayed so invitingly before him. Still, her scent, the afterimage emblazoned in his stunned mind, even the vibrations of her caressing voice, enthralled his captive soul. He cast wild nearly-unseeing searches all about the fantastical stone creations surrounding them.

"Where are they?" he at last croaked.

"Lost in the forest." Her purr echoed off the rocks. "The boy will die of thirst before they find their way out. You should go back to Hawaii."

"That's my son. We're not going anywhere without him."

"I said you."

Uzmahndey stepped in front of Charlie and reached back to place protective hands on her, while latching his skittish eyes onto the woman's endless eyes. "I'm not going anywhere without her, either," he exclaimed, trying to sound more in control than he felt.

With a calculated shake of her head, one perfectly-sculpted bare breast emerged from the curtain of black. "She and the boy are abominations. They need to end."

That did it. A threat to his son. Uzmahndey lunged forward and grabbed the woman by the throat. She merely smiled as she relaxed back, her other bare breast appearing. Uzmahndey, still throttling her, couldn't help but admire the pair of engorged nipples inches from his face. Until both he and she toppled backward.

The two ended up with the woman flat on her back, arms and legs spread wide open, smiling up at him with sparkling perfect teeth, while he was sprawled helplessly entangled in her lush wave of black hair with his hands still around her throat.

She reached up to tangle her fingers in his hair. "I like you with long hair."

At her touch, Uzmahndey released his grip and rolled off the soft warm body onto hard jagged rocks.

Laughter followed. "Why did you let go? I was enjoying that." She reached out to stroke him. "I can see you were, too."

Uzmahndey slapped her hand away and stumbled to his feet. Looking around, trying to look at anything other than the enticing heap of perfect female flesh at his feet, he realized he was somewhere else in the stone forest. And Charlie was not. "Charlie!"

Uzmahndey jerked around and around looking for her. The rock formations here were larger, more fantastical, and so dense they nearly blocked out the sky. He didn't see Charlie anywhere.

"You've never been through a portal before." The woman flowed upright to her feet, using both hands to pull the long black strands away from the front of her body, presenting an unimpeded view. "What do you think of our realm?"

Uzmahndey found it difficult to think about anything other than the congealed eroticism before him, and the throbbing in his pants. But he had to master his body's reactions. He had more important concerns. He faced the full-frontal woman head on.

"I think I'll kill you if you don't bring Charlie back."

"She didn't go anywhere. She is where we left her." The woman turned away, offering up the most voluptuous rolling hips ever to writhe in his twenty-twenty vision. "I could leave you, and you would never find your way back. You've read how large the Stone Forest is. On this side of the portal it is many times larger."

Uzmahndey lunged forward to seize her by the wrist. "Then you're not going anywhere without me."

She smiled back over her bare shoulder. "Why should I leave? This is what I wanted. A chance to be with you." She didn't try to free the wrist from his grip as she sat on a stone, this one resembling a throne, and motioned with her free hand for Uzmahndey to sit on a lesser stone before her.

He remained standing, keeping a firm grip on her hand.

Staring at the bulging front of his pants, which was now at eye level, she tossed her head, causing the long full tresses to flow across the front of her body and conceal it, each strand moving as if it had a mind of its own. "Is that better?"

It was, but Uzmahndey wasn't about to admit it. "Who are you?"

"Eros."

The one who had Neo! "What have you done with Keanu?"

"Nothing unpleasant. In fact, quite the opposite. Would you like to see?" With her free hand she pointed to a small pool of water.

Reflected in it was an image of Keanu naked in bed writhing in agony.

"That looks extremely unpleasant."

"To you it does. Here is how it looks to your friend."

The surface of the water rippled. When it smoothed, Keanu was seen to be entangled with a pair of nubile naked young women. What had appeared to be agony on his face was now seen to be intense pleasure.

"In his mind he is making love to a pair of beauties. He is thoroughly enjoying the experience." The water rippled once again, and when it again calmed reflected no images other than the surrounding rock formations. "I have no desire to harm him. Or you, for that matter."

"Why do you want to harm the children?"

"You call them children? You've seen how fast they age."

"Why do you want to harm them?"

"They don't vibrate at the right frequency."

"Make sense."

"The resonant vibration of the Earth is 7.83 hertz. The two abominations' brains operate beyond Gamma, above 100 hertz. This cannot be tuned to the normal Alpha brain waves of humans, which is in the range of 8 to 12 hertz."

"I have no idea what you are blathering about."

"That's a shame. We need you to understand what is going on." Eros sighed as she stood. "For now, just know that if they remain on Earth to procreate, their progeny will destroy humankind. That must not happen."

The woman collapsed at Uzmahndey's feet. Angela stood with a bloody rock in hand behind the throne-like stone on which Eros had been seated.

"What are you doing?"

"Trying my best not to give in to my baser instincts. Where have you been?"

"Placing the xenobot." Angela tossed down the rock and grabbed his hand, yanking him after her.

He stumbled over Eros' limp body between two tall stone spires.

To where Charlie and Charley stood. Charlie did not appear happy to see him. Her accusing gaze was leveled at the front of his pants. "Were you really attracted to that young boy? That is wrong in so many ways."

"What young boy?"

"No time." Angela took off at a brisk pace on a narrow twisting path through the Stone Forest. "We must get out of here before Eros comes to."

Charley charged after her. "Yeah, Dad, keep up this time."

Charlie hurried after them. "I don't want to get left behind again." She shot Uzmahndey an ugly look. "With the two of them."

Uzmahndey stumbled along behind. "That was no young boy. That was a young woman."

Charlie ignored him.

Away from Eros, he felt his passion easing.

At last.

"At last what?"

We can communicate with you again. Eros blocked us somehow.

Either that, or you being so horny shuts us out.

No, that can't be it. We were totally involved when you and Angela made love.

"Don't remind me. I'll never be able to make love again if I start worrying about what you three are doing while I'm doing it."

Oh, I don't think you'll ever have that problem. Not the way you reacted to Eros.

"Eros is the personification of love," Angela called back over her shoulder. "He was one of the three who originally emerged out of chaos here on Earth."

"He? He? That was the most beautiful woman I've ever seen."

"Eros appears in whatever form you desire. To you, a female. To Charlie, a male. A very powerful creature. Whose power is sexual desire. Of course you were attracted to him."

"Her!" Uzmahndey insisted. "I've never been attracted to a 'him'."

Charlie offered a peacemaking smile over her shoulder. "I guess I can forgive you, then, for behaving so crudely."

Charley looked from face to face to face. "What are you guys talking about?"

"Ask Snugglesaurus," Charlie said with an infuriating smile.

"Snugglesaurus won't tell him," Angela responded, deadpan as ever. "Not until he is old enough to make use of the information."

Charley held the stuffed dinosaur up before his face. "Snugglesaurus, what are they talking about?" His despondent face registered the AI's failure to respond.

"See?" Charlie crowed.

"We'll have 'the talk' when we get a chance, kid." Uzmahndey caught up to Angela. "What did you do to her? Him? Eros? Did you kill it?"

Angela ignored his question and fired off one of her own. "Why did you pass through a portal?"

"I didn't mean to."

Angela stopped as she emerged at the water's edge by the pool at the entrance to Qifeng Cave. She turned to face the other three who piled up behind her. "We're safe now. We're far enough from the portal. What else do you want to see here?"

"Everything," Charley said. "This place is so cool."

Uzmahndey heaved a sigh. He had innumerable questions, but they could wait. He turned to Charlie.

"Do you want to go back and see the Ashima Stone?"

"Not anymore." She stepped onto the platform at the water's edge. "Let's just go."

"Dad!" Charley protested. He turned to Angela. "Mom!"

"I'm not your Mom." Angela followed Charlie away from the pond.

"Quit saying that." Uzmahndey took Charley's hand and pulled him along.

"I'm not his mother. I merely gave birth to him."

"That makes you his mom. You are going to warp him." Uzmahndey gazed down at Charley's troubled face. "She's your mother, Charley. She's just confused and upset now."

"I didn't pass anything down to him."

Charlie grabbed Angela and yanked her to a halt. "Stop it." When Angela looked back at her, Charlie continued. "He only has a couple weeks of childhood. Don't ruin that little bit for him."

When Angela merely stared back, as stony-expressioned as the rocks around them, Charlie pressed on.

"I know you are damaged. That you were damaged while saving our lives. I certainly appreciate that. But please, try to be gentler with Charley."

Angela turned away without responding.

Charlie threw her arms up, signifying that she had tried.

Uzmahndey placed his hands on both their backs and urged them forward. "She'll recover. She did before. This isn't how she really is."

Charley fell into step alongside Uzmahndey. "Snugglesaurus says this *is* how she really is. That how she was before was just a computer program."

"And we are alien freaks," Charlie added, shaking off Uzmahndey's hand. Uzmahndey placed a hand on each of their heads.

Charley ignored it, but Charlie looked up in irritation. "What are you doing now?"

"Just curious. Do you two ever vibrate?"

Despite Charlie's disclaimer, they paused at the Ashima Stone to listen to a tour guide tell the tale. This time it was done in Chinese, but Angela translated for them. Charlie and Charley, despite prior claims of disinterest, paid close attention.

While Uzmahndey concentrated only on Angela. They were still a family. Badly twisted, warped, only half human, partly mechanical, infected with xenobots, with a stuffed toy powerful enough to rule the Internet, yet, still, a family.

Chapter 25

Interlude Four

When Uzmahndey was rudely awakened from Eros' embrace, he found himself in bed at the hotel in Kunming. It was night, and Charlie, in her pajamas, was looming over him instead of Eros.

"Shhh," she whispered. "You need to see this." She pointed to the other bed.

Angela was cuddled up beneath the covers with Charley, asleep with Snugglesaurus hugged to his chest.

"What's she doing?"

"Soothing Charley while he goes through a growth spurt. She did the same with me."

Uzmahndey couldn't actually see Charley grow. He assumed the process took hours. But just to know this was happening to his son while he watched was disturbing. Such an inhuman process his human son was going through. His half-human son. Who would destroy the world, Gaia's people kept insisting.

"It's not painful," Charlie whispered. "You'd think it would be, your body growing so fast. Maybe Angela numbs us somehow. Or Snugglesaurus does. I slept through most of it. Every so often during the night I'd wake up. Every time Angela would be in bed with me. Holding me."

"She really does care about you two."

"Because she was programmed to."

"It's more than that. It *was* more than that. Before she was damaged."

"She cared about you, too. Before."

Had she? It was getting hard for Uzmahndey to remember how she had been. She was so mechanical now.

"Can I join you?"

That's why Charlie had awakened him. Angela had crowded her out of the other bed. "Sure." He scooted back.

Way back. He was still excited from his dreams of the young boy. No, girl. Woman. The Eros he had dreamed about was female. Hadn't she been? Charlie climbing in under the cover distracted him from unsettling thoughts. "Now go to sleep. Tomorrow is a travel day."

Charlie laughed. "You don't have to get *that* far away. You'll fall out of bed." She scooted back into him. "Oh." She hastily scooted away.

"Sorry. I was dreaming when you woke me up." Uzmahndey rolled over away from her.

It was daylight when Uzmahndey next opened his eyes. Angela was leaning over him with a firm grip on his shoulder.

"Don't wake up Charlie," she said softly.

He looked to the other bed. Charley was still asleep. His form under the covers appeared larger.

"Not him. Her."

It was only then he realized Charlie had curled up to his back with her arm around his waist. He slipped out from under and away from her, up off the bed onto his feet.

"How is my son?" he asked softly.

"He's okay," Angela replied, just as softly. "Go take a shower."

"How old is he now?"

"Twelve. Now go." Angela gave him a swat on the butt.

"I'm right here, guys."

Uzmahndey looked down to see Charlie smiling up at them. She had apparently recognized the swat as an affectionate gesture. Had it been? He looked to Angela's face. Blank as ever.

"Go." She shoved him toward the bathroom.

That hadn't felt affectionate. He checked himself as he stumbled away. He was still sound asleep down there. Good, he hadn't been dreaming of Eros when he woke up this time. That was so disturbing.

When Uzmahndey emerged from the bathroom, Angela shooed Charlie in. Charley was still sprawled across the bed. He was mostly under the cover, but a leg stuck out. There was a light frosting of hair on it.

"He can skip a shower today. I'll just get him dressed." Angela pulled the covers down.

Damn, he was big. "Can I help?"

"Go bring some breakfast up to the room."

In the lobby the TV was playing a video of the incident at Shaman Rock. A few people stood around gawking, but others weren't. Good, it was already old news. He started to turn away.

"Special effects." A young Chinese man had spoken to him in English. "I also saw half the world turn to ash in Avengers Infinity War."

"Yeah." Uzmahndey waved at the screen. "Those stupid Russians think the rest of the world will believe anything they say."

"Of course. How could the shaman hero of the Capitol Riot be there? He's locked up in an American prison. The Russians are idiots."

Shaman *hero*? Uzmahndey let it go and walked on into the restaurant. He selected steamed buns stuffed with pork and cabbage, Jianbing crepes, and scallion oil pancakes rolled in sausage.

Back at the room, Uzmahndey found everyone dressed and ready to go. Charley was wearing some of his father's clothes. Of course the shirt was baggy and hung off him like a dress, and the pants sagged off his hips with the legs rolled up to his ankles, but it was good enough to get him out the door. Uzmahndey and Charlie feasted, while Angela forced some food down Charley. Uzmahndey was sure glad to have her back to help with the kids. His son was going to be a zombie all day.

They took a taxi to a store to buy clothes for Charley. Uzmahndey selected the outfits, while Angela negotiated all the details with perfect Mandarin. After, they caught another taxi to the train station. Snugglesaurus had purchased high-speed train tickets to Guilin. During the rapid-fire trip Charley slept and Angela gazed out the window. She always gazed out the window when they traveled. Previously he had assumed she was admiring the scenery, or trying to learn about the planet. Now he wondered if she was watching out for something. What were they in danger from this far from a portal?

Trying to dispel that disquieting thought, he turned to Charlie. To find her staring at him. "What?"

"Were you dreaming about Eros last night?"

"Yes."

"Good. I don't like to think you got excited at the thought of sleeping with me."

"Stop, or I'll need an air sickness bag."

She laughed. "There aren't any air sickness bags. We're on a train." Her mirth subsided. "Does the thought of me make you sick?"

"The thought of you thinking that I think of you like that makes me think I'll get sick. I think."

That brought on a guffaw. "That was clear as mud."

"Nothing about this family is clear. Just know that I have no desire for you. Not like that."

"Good. Because now we'll be sleeping together all the time."

"I don't think so."

"Charley is twelve now. At twelve boys become horny. He will stink of hormones. I'm not sleeping with a horny teenager."

"Why not? I have been."

That Charlie took offense to. "I am not horny." She looked away to contemplate the clouds.

Uzmahndey knew Charlie was fixated on him. How could she not be, he was the only man she had ever known? She needed a boyfriend. But how could she have one? The last young man to approach her had tried to slash her throat. Uzmahndey would not have thought Angela would ever let a man get close enough to harm Charlie, but she had allowed that knife-wielding Gaia fanatic to. Why? As protective as she was about the children. Was it because Charlie needed to hone her social skills? Angela had seemed to agree with him on that. But was that worth the risk of putting her life in danger? And if it was, why was it?

Normally, if there was anything normal about his recent life, he would have consulted the xenobots about a question like this. But since returning at Lake Baikal Angela had evidenced the ability to monitor his conversations with them. He now had to be more circumspect in their talks. So he let the problem go and tried to read up online about their next destination, Reed Flute Cave.

Uzmahndey turned his phone off in frustration. He couldn't concentrate on that, either. It was just another hole in the Earth. Too many other concerns were crowding his brain. Such as how much longer was this expedition going to continue? They had headed east out of Hawaii and were now in China. Before long they could be back in Hawaii. Then what? The destruction of mankind, as Gaia claimed? Or the salvation of mankind, as Ghost claimed? He had chosen Ghost's side. Had he chosen well? Or had he been well-manipulated?

<u>Would you like some advice?</u>

"No!"

His abrupt rebuke drew Angela's gaze away from the window.

"Good's advice was going to be that you chose well."

"Says the woman who has been manipulating me."

"Says the robot who is taking care of your children."

Uzmahndey glanced around to see if anyone was paying attention to them.

"Don't worry about someone overhearing us. You hardly believed it possible I am a robot. Do you think anyone else would believe it?"

"What happens when we finish this?"

"I don't know."

Uzmahndey scowled his skepticism at her answer.

"Father hasn't told me."

"Is he evil?"

Angela shrugged then turned her gaze back out the window.

Would she tell him if he was? She had taken his side against Ghost once. Told him something Ghost hadn't wanted him to know. But that was before she had been damaged so badly in Egypt. She had been much more human then. Would she ever take his side again?

Uzmahndey turned his gaze inward. So many concerns. Such as his son. What would happen to him when this was over? Would he be allowed to stay with his father? Or did Ghost have other plans for him? There was nothing Uzmahndey could do about him now. Snugglesaurus was too powerful. If Uzmahndey were to flee with his son the AI could track them down, no doubt. Besides, would his son *want* to flee? Charlie sure seemed committed to Angela and Ghosts' agenda. Was that because Snugglesaurus had instilled a loyalty to the cause in her while she was growing at leaps and bounds? Programmed her to support the aliens? Was the AI indoctrinating Charles the same way?

Uzmahndey studied the ragged stuffed toy in his son's embrace. Uzmahndey could try to destroy the AI. That wouldn't be easily done, if it could be done at all. In Mauratania he had witnessed the T. Rex get cut open and the stuffing ripped out, and that hadn't damaged the AI. What would happen to Uzmahndey if he tried to destroy Snugglesaurus and failed? Would Ghost destroy him? Would Angela? How about the kids? Would Charlie turn against him? Would his own son? There was a powerful bond between the two and the AI. Did Uzmahndey really want to test just how strong that bond was?

When the train pulled into the Guilin station Uzmahndey thought they'd never get Charley up on his feet. Snugglesaurus got them a taxi which took them on a short drive through a modern city to a small traditional Chinese building, the Secret Courtyard Resort Hotel, where the AI had them booked. Uzmahndey once again marveled at the beauty and luxury of their accommodations. How much money was Snugglesaurus making online to afford all this travel? Had it written some amazing algorithm that produced fortunes on the stock markets? Was it manipulating bitcoin? Was it stealing the money?

Don't ask. You don't want to know.

Ugly was right. He really didn't.

Angela led them through the lobby and up to their accommodations on the third floor. They had a suite, with spiraling wooden stairs leading up to a loft bed. Angela lugged a still-comatose Charley up to it.

Uzmahndey stepped out onto a small balcony. There were few other completed buildings in the district they were in, a few more under construction. Their hotel was in a developing area surrounded by open fields and small trees, bisected by a river. In the distance were towering sharp-peaked mountains resplendent in greenery. He eyed a wicker chair on the balcony. He was tired, but too unsettled to settle down.

Stepping back into the room, he saw Angela was still up in the loft with Charley.

Charlie was pacing the downstairs. She appeared as restless as he. "Let's go for a walk."

That suited his dislocated mood. "Where are we going?"

"Let's check out their secret courtyard."

It was small and quiet, enclosed by the hotel, with banyan, golden larch and ginko trees set in carved stone tiles. Several small pools with flowering lily pads afloat. One prominent too-big bonsai set in a large planter. They paused to examine a stand of bamboo. "You're not going to dream of Eros tonight, are you?"

So that's what was bothering Charlie. "I can sleep out on the balcony."

She appeared stricken. "No."

Uzmahndey wanted to change the subject while he still had a bed. "What do *you* dream about?"

The gambit worked. "Strange places."

"Dreams are always strange."

"And strange creatures."

"I'm not in your dreams?"

"No." She smiled. "Much stranger." The smile faded. "I think I'm dreaming about other worlds."

This statement yanked Uzmahndey to attention. He remembered her recently waking up in the night screaming from a nightmare.

"Tell me about these worlds."

"In one dream I'm floating in the clouds. I can't see much, nothing but swirling clouds. And little sparkles of ice. There are strong winds. Hurricane force. And lightning."

"What kind of creatures are there?"

"There aren't any. Only lightning. A lot of lightning. It's nearly continuous."

"What happens there? In your dream?"

"I flash." Receiving nothing but a dumbfounded look, she pressed on. "I think I am a bolt of lightning. The other lightning bolts could be beings like me."

Skepticism slipped out.

"Aliens made of energy?"

Matter and energy are interchangeable.

There could be some inner core of particles in the lightning.

Don't ridicule her. She is opening up about something that is bothering her.

Uzmahndey had enough presence not to verbally respond to the xenobots. Instead, he heeded their words and clamped down on his smirk. "Are you able to talk with them?"

"In a way."

"Are you in danger?"

"Not at all. They seem welcoming." She walked away from the bamboo. "It's silly."

He walked after her. "Dreams are not silly. Wild exaggerations, maybe, but meaningful. Have there been other worlds you've dreamed about?"

"Several. In one I seemed to live underground."

"In a cave?"

"No. In the dirt. I think I was in a tree root. Or maybe I *was* a tree root."

Uzmahndey smiled, despite himself. "This is starting to sound like 'Rick and Morty'."

Do not make fun of her!

"I'm not making fun of her." Once he realized he had spoken out loud, he tried to cover. "Of you. I've had wild dreams myself."

"I know." Charlie scowled at him. "I felt one of your dreams last night."

"Sorry about that. This bed looks big enough that we can stay away from each other." Seeing the scowl ease, he pressed on. "Any other worlds?"

"On one I was in the dirt. It seemed there was little or no atmosphere."

"You were exposed to space? Like on the surface of the moon?"

"Or just below it, in the dirt, like I said. On another I was *in* space."

"Just floating around? In deep space?"

"I wasn't floating. I was moving purposefully. They told me I was riding gravity waves."

"They?"

Charlie returned a puzzled look to his question.

"That is amazing. Do you think these beings and places are real?"

"They feel real."

"Dreams always do." They grew quiet while Uzmahndey considered. "How did you learn about these places? Did Snugglesaurus tell you?"

"No. I don't know how I know. But these weird beings I dream about tell me they have dreams, too."

"What do these aliens dream about?"

"Earth."

That floored him. Was Charlie informing aliens all across the cosmos about Earth? Could they follow Charlie's dreams here? Like Ghost had homed in on Keck Observatory? Was he helping pave the way for a mass alien invasion? Like Liu Cixin had warned of in his Three Body Problem books?

Why do aliens have to be hostile?

Most people yearn for contact with other intelligent races. *This doesn't have to be like 'The Dark Forest'.*

"But it could be."

This time Charlie responded to his outburst. "It could be what?"

He saw Charlie smile. She knew what was going on. "The xenobots believe these places and beings you dream about are benign."

"Let me talk to them."

"How would you do that?"

"Through you. Like an interpreter. You can tell me what they say. And don't lie about anything." Seeing Uzmahndey's doubtful expression, she pressed on. "Can they hear me?"

Loud and clear.

"Loud and clear," Uzmahndey repeated. He tried to explain. "They have full use of my body. They can hear your words through my ears."

Charlie laughed. "That must be so weird."

"Tell me about it."

"Which one said 'loud and clear'?"

"Ugly."

She laughed louder. "How ugly is he?"

I'm not ugly at all. Uzmahndey has never seen me. He is impugning my character for no good reason.

"Ugly says he's not ugly at all. Next question."

"Are you three really going to make Uz an NFL superstar?"

Sort of.

"Sort of?" Uzmahndey objected. "What the hell? Of course you're going to."

"What did he say?"

"Hush. Me and Good have to settle something." He focused inward. "You are not reneging on the deal."

Of course we're not. But we can't have you flying around the field like Superman. Or even like Batman. We have to keep it believable. If you are too good to be true, you'll get kicked out of the league.

Yeah. We're not double-crossing you, we're trying to look out for you.

You'll be good, just not too good.

"As long as I'm good enough to make Super Bowl MVP."

We can do that.

Uzmahndey turned back to Charlie. "Now what did you ask?"

She shook her bemused head. "How can you even think straight, with all that chatter going on inside your head?"

"Is that a question for me or for the xenobots?"

"For you. I give up on talking to them. That's your problem."

"Most of the time they keep quiet. Usually they only talk to me when there is a problem I'm not aware of."

When are you ever aware of any problem?

"You three are the problem right now. Be quiet."

"You just told them to shut up?"

"Yes."

"And they will?"

"They better."

"We better check in with Angela. We've been out here a while. She'll get nervous." Charlie started toward the lobby.

"Wait. One more question. About your dreams?" When Charlie paused, he asked, "Is Charles having these dreams, too?"

"Probably not. I didn't start having them until I turned eighteen. Once I completed the growth spurts."

Later that evening Uzmahndey and Charlie went down to the restaurant to eat dinner. They shared a meal of shumai and har gow. As they ate he looked around the small room considering another problem. Were there any good boyfriend candidates here for Charlie? She needed to start developing social skills. As of now she had zilch. Only the diners were mostly families. There would be more unattached males in the lounge.

"Why are you so quiet?" Charlie asked.

"Look around." After a brief scan, she looked back to him with questions in her eyes. "See any attractive young men?"

The questioning look evaporated. "One."

Uzmahndey sighed theatrically. "I am not a boyfriend candidate."

"Is that what you're on about?"

"Don't you ever think about young men?" Her gaze was unwavering, which brought on a deeper sigh. "Your own age."

"You're not that much older than me. I was your wife while Angela was gone."

"You *posed* as my wife." He tossed his napkin down. "That settles it. Good, what is the legal drinking age in China?"

I'll check with Snugglesaurus.

A second passed.

Eighteen.

"Would you like to stop in the lounge after dinner?"

She appeared surprised. "Why?"

"Just for a drink. And there might be music."

"You like Chinese music?"

"I like the idea of a young man asking you to dance."

Charlie wilted. "I can't dance."

"Sure you can. There's nothing to it."

"No. We can't. We have to take some dinner back to Charley."

Uzmahndey didn't press her. At least he had brought up the matter. Maybe she'd start considering young men. Other than him.

Back in the room, both of them were surprised at Angela's reaction when Uzmahndey suggested taking Charlie into the lounge for a drink.

"You should teach Charlie how to dance first." Without another word, she took the food they had brought back from the restaurant for Charley upstairs to the loft.

Leaving Uzmahndey and Charlie looking everywhere but at each other. "I could put on some music," he suggested.

"No. I'm tired." She snatched up her pajamas and fled into the bathroom to change.

Chapter 26

Reed Flute Cave

"What's for breakfast?"

Charley was back to normal. His twelve year old body bolted down the stairs from the loft. Uzmahndey and Charlie both jerked upright in their bed, yanked out of a sound sleep by his blaring charge. She turned a sleep-swollen face to Uzmahndey.

"That's what I want to stay away from." When Charley's gaze lingered a little too long on the front of her pajama top, Charlie slid back down under the covers. "Leave me alone, brat."

Angela followed him down the stairs and got everyone moving. Since Charley no longer wanted to be seen carrying Snugglesaurus – after all, he was a twelve year old boy now - it was stowed away in his backpack, close enough so it could continue his education (more like data transfer) while remaining out of sight. After a full breakfast, at which Charley finished everything anyone else left on their plates, they caught a shuttle to Reed Flute Cave. Snugglesaurus had tickets waiting for them at the gate.

It only took two hours to tour the Palace of Natural Art. It easily could have taken four, with Charley and Charlie eagerly examining every karst creation – the Statue of Liberty, Lion

Rock and Sunrise, the Crystal Palace, Pines in the Snow, Sky-scraping Twins, and each of the 77 ancient inscriptions – especially as everything was displayed in fantastic light shows reflecting off the underground river and looming stalagmites and stalactites. But Angela rushed them through. Apparently, the portal wasn't inside the cave.

Exiting underground into bright daylight, they found them-selves in the field of reeds the cave was named for. These prized reeds had been used in flutes for millennia. Removing the Tupperware container from her backpack, she took out a Cheerio and tossed it into the middle of the reeds.

The Cheerio came flying back out. Instinctively, Uzmah-ndey dashed away, chasing it down like he would an errant pass, timed his leap perfectly, and at the very top of its high arc extended his body to the fullest, straining one arm its full length, and snagged the Cheerio with his fingertips. ”Yes!” he yelled, coming down and planting a pivot foot to spin out of the grasp of anyone trying to tackle him, then dashing back to the other three.

“*That* is how an elite receiver performs in the NFL.” He offered his catch to Angela.

She took the cheerio without a word and waded into the reeds.

Unfazed by his failure to impress her, Uzmahndey turned to the other two. “You'll see a lot of that when I get back in the league.”

“That's never happened before,” was Charlie's comment.

“No kidding. There's never been a receiver like me before.”

“She's gone,” was Charley's comment.

Uzmahndey was still unfazed. “What do you guys think?” he inquired within. “Was that too much?”

<u>Angela is gone.</u>

His excitement ebbing, Uzmahndey looked to see what they all were talking about. They were right. Angela was out of sight. "Where'd she go?"

To place the xenobot in the portal by hand, since her throw was rejected.

"So where is she?"

Maybe she went through the portal.

"Is she okay?"

Does she look okay?

"I don't know. I can't see her."

Exactly, Starbrain.

"Why is Dad talking to himself?"

"He's not," Charlie answered her brother. She turned to Uzmahndey. "What are they saying?"

"Nothing useful," Uzmahndey snapped.

She's had to do this before. She swam out to the middle of Mono Lake, and down to the bottom of Long Lake, to place a xenobot by hand.

It was Black Lake.

Whatever. The point is, this is not new behavior.

Uzmahndey stared out at the sea of reeds. "Should I go after her? She might need help."

She would want you to stay with the children.

Good was right. The children came first. Besides, Angela was okay, he was sure. She had stayed underwater in the Azores for a long time. He needed to give her time. She was okay. Most likely.

I know what you are thinking.

We always do, bright guy.

"Stop sniping at each other."

"I haven't said a word to her," Charley insisted, thinking Uzmahndey was referring to him and his sister.

"Not now, Charles." Uzmahndey closed his eyes. "What am I thinking, Good?"

That Angela has gone off the rails. That this is because she was damaged.

"Well? Am I right?"

We just checked with Snugglesaurus. He said the last diagnostic he ran on her showed she is not operating at peak performance, but her level of degradation is acceptable.

"That's not very encouraging. So I should wait for her?"

Normally, yes.

"What does that mean?"

Snugglesaurus has detected unusual activity in the reeds. Something is going on that we can't see.

"Then screw waiting." Uzmahndey grabbed Charlie and Charley by the hand and yanked them after him into the field of reeds.

"Where are we going?" Charlie yelled.

"To go find Angela."

The most beautiful music Uzmahndey had ever heard brought him to a halt. A syrinx, or Panpipe, filled the air with a calming melody. Uzmahndey looked all around searching for its source.

"Do you see Angela?" Charlie asked.

"No. I'm looking for where that music is coming from."

"What music?" Charley asked. The trail they had been on was gone. All that could be seen were the tall willowy reeds they were in the midst of. Charley gripped Uzmahndey's hand tight. "Where are we?"

"Good question." He closed his eyes. "Good? Bad? Ugly?" There was no response. The xenobots weren't communicating with him. That had happened before when he had crossed over through the portal at Stone Forest. He opened his eyes. "We've crossed through a portal."

"Can we cross back?" Charley asked, fear rising in his voice.

Another good question Uzmahndey didn't know the answer to.

Charlie looked across the tall reeds in all directions. "I don't see Angela here."

Uzmahndey cupped his hands to his mouth. "Angela!"

"Be quiet. You are disturbing the music." All three spun to find an elderly man draped in classical robes standing behind them.

"What music?" Charlie asked.

The old man ignored her and concentrated on Uzmahndey. "Did you know the seven reeds that fashioned Pan's pipe came from here?" He closed his eyes and smiled. "That's Pan playing, by the way. He came to my mountain once for a competition with Apollo." The old man produced a beatific smile. "Pan's pipes against Apollo's lyre. That was the most beautiful music the world has ever known. Apollo won, of course, nearly everyone agreed. Except Midas." The old man chuckled. "You don't want to know what happened to him."

"Who are you?" Uzmahndey demanded.

"Tmolus." He made calming gestures with both hands. "Enough jabbering. Just listen to the music. Look." He pointed to birds perched in a nearby shrub. "Even their songs can't compete. They are muted by this superior tune."

It did sound good, Uzmahndey thought. So sweet, so soft, so soothing. It was like the Earth itself was humming. He could actually feel the ground vibrate under his feet, up through his soles, his ankles, up his spine into his brain. So relaxing.

"What are you doing here?"

Uzmahndey opened his eyes to find himself lying on the ground flat on his back amid the tall reeds gazing up at Angela towering over him. He was too dazed to answer.

"Where are the children?"

Uzmahndey's head was filled with flowers. Blossoms and blooms of brilliant scents and aromas, a palette of colors that smelled so richly... His cheek stung from Angela's slap.

"Get up." When Uzmahndey didn't stir, she kicked him.

Uzmahndey staggered to his feet. "What happened?"

"You lost the children."

Some weeds sprang up amid the flowers in his head. "Was I asleep?"

Angela ignored him, searching all around.

The music swelled, lulling Uzmahndey like a lullaby, back toward sleep, down, down.

Angela punched him in the gut, doubling him over. "Don't listen to it."

He wheezed, gasping. "How can I not?"

"I could burst your eardrums. The xenobots could fix them later. Probably."

He reeled away from her. "Don't do that!"

"Then stay sharp." Angela charged off.

Uzmahndey stumbled after. "Where are you going?"

"I've located Snugglesaurus. Charley has it in his back-pack."

They plowed through fields of reeds. Uzmahndey felt his legs grow heavier with each lumbering step. Every contact with the ground caused vibrations to shiver up through his bones. So he sang. "Whoop! I got children now, at least one little custoMER. And I sure ain't got no money problems now, not after this TOUR."

Until he plowed into Angela, bouncing off her solid form and tumbling to the ground. "Why'd you stop?"

She held up Snugglesaurus for him to see. "They found it and left it behind." She kicked him. "Get up."

Uzmahndey scrambled to his feet. "Stop kicking me!"

"Stop falling down." She took off again, zagging away in a different direction.

Uzmahndey zigged after. "Where are you going now?"

"Snugglesaurus can track them."

Uzmahndey knew that. The AI had tracked them in Oman when they had been kidnapped. But his head echoed so with all the beautiful music he couldn't think straight, or even crookedly.

They floundered through the sea of reeds. Uzmahndey began flagging again. Vibrations in the ground rippled the dirt up to trip his toes. So he sang as he staggered on. Drake, Kayne West, Lil Nas X, anything he could remember. Dababy, Machine Gun Kelly, DDG. He rapped to the music of the reeds.

"Will you stop that."

Uzmahndey tumbled to the ground then looked up. He had run into the old man he had seen before, Tmolus. Angela had his arms pinned behind his back. Only then did Uzmahndey realize the music had stopped. So he stopped, too, with 'Moonwalking In Calabasas' dying on his lips.

"Where are they?" Angela growled.

Growled? Was she exhibiting an emotion? But this wasn't the time to speculate about Angela's humanity. Uzmahndey sprang to his feet. The music had ended, the ground had stopped vibrating. Everything was quiet and still. Which meant he could think clearly again. "Can I hit him?"

"No need for that," Tmolus said. He turned his head to look back over his shoulder at Angela. "They are unharmed. We need to negotiate."

She nearly pulled both arms out of his shoulder sockets.

He screamed. "This isn't how it's done!"

Angela threw him to the ground and kicked him, much harder than she had kicked Uzmahndey. "Is this how it's done?"

"Just leave the planet! That's all! The children will be released! If you agree to take them with you."

Angela picked up Snugglesaurus from where she had dropped it on the ground. "What good will holding the children do you? I can make more children." She kicked him again. "But I want these two back."

"Okay." All three looked to see Pan with his pipes in hand standing nearby in the reeds. "You're right. You can give birth to more. We didn't think this through. You are making us crazy."

"*You* could leave the planet."

"*We* have been here since long before humankind became human."

"May I get up now?"

Uzmahndey and Angela looked at the old man on the ground.

"Yes, Tmolus," Pan said, "it should be alright."

When he started up, Uzmahndey knocked him back down. "Is it, Angela?"

She glared at the Pan creature. "I want Charlie and Charley."

"And we want our freedom."

"I don't negotiate. Father does that. I only destroy."

"We could destroy you,"

"Father can make more of me, like I can make more children. Worse versions of me, making worse versions of Charlie and Charley. You do not want that."

Pan sighed. "So when do we negotiate?"

"Not now, not under threat. Release them."

"They have not been harmed."

Charlie and Charley ran out of the reeds into Angela's arms. She smoothed Charlie's hair, and handed Snugglesaurus to Charley.

Tmolus climbed to his feet and glowered at Uzmahndey. "I will not forget this." He motioned toward Angela. "She is a meaningless device." He pointed to Uzmahndey. "You will suffer. You think to run swiftly? To do that you must run across the ground. Where Gaia's realm is below your feet. I will reach up from there to cripple your stride." The old man smiled. "I am one of the Ourea, not to be treated as you have done." He limped away to join Pan. They walked off, disappearing into the reeds.

Angela leveled her iron gaze at Uzmahndey. "You have made an enemy."

He joined the three. "We have enemies all over the world."

"They are opponents. He is an enemy. Your enemy."

Angela had a point. Every player on the other side of the line of scrimmage of every team he ever played against was an opponent. Only Logan Wilson was his enemy. A worry for another time. "He thinks you are meaningless."

"He's right. I am." She hugged her two children. "These two are priceless. The fools do not realize." She pulled them along with her as she walked away.

"They are not very good at negotiating," Uzmahndey said, falling into step behind the three.

"They've not had to be. People have always done whatever they were told to do."

Uzmahndey followed the trio out of the reeds. Upon stepping back onto the path, they passed back through the portal out of Gaia's realm and found themselves just beyond the exit to the Reed Flute Cave. He looked all around. No one emerging from the cave seemed to notice their sudden appearance. His roving eyes settled on Angela's granite glare. "What?"

"What was all that squawking?"

"That was music. Those songs were all big hits for major artists."

"Why were you singing?" Charlie asked.

"To block out the music. Angela was threatening to burst my eardrums."

"What music?" Charley asked.

"You couldn't hear it?" He turned to Charlie. "You, either?" Both shook their heads.

"Their brains operate on a different wavelength than pure-bred human brains like yours," Angela said. "Gaia's frequency can't affect their auditory cortex."

Is it finally sinking in, Wonderwanker?

"I really missed you guys on the other side." Uzmahndey spewed out as much sarcasm as he could muster. "Especially you, Bad."

The genes Angela is introducing into the human genome through her children will spread around the world.

This new half-human half-alien breed will be immune to Gaia's influence.

Humans will be liberated from her pernicious control.

"A new day will dawn here on Earth," Angela added.

Great. So people will be trading one oppressor for another. Because of him. But Uzmahndey never had a chance to dwell on this point. Angela knocked him down. He sprawled at her feet, looking up at her angry visage. "What now?"

"Why did you let the children get taken? Again?"

"Snugglesaurus told me to go after you."

Actually, he didn't.

All he said was he couldn't see what was happening with Angela.

It was your idea to go charging in. With *the children.*

"It was taking me time to locate the portal in the reeds," Angela said. "This one was well-hidden. But I was alright. I didn't need you. You drug the children into danger for no reason." She turned away and walked toward the exit. "You are a bigger hindrance than help to them. You should go back to Hawaii."

Charlie extended a hand to help Uzmahndey up. "She's really mad at you."

"I know. And I was so glad to see her exhibiting emotions again. Just not this kind of emotion."

Uzmahndey was lost in thought as they rode the tram back to the hotel in silence. He didn't believe she would really send him away. That was just a threat. Wasn't it? Made in anger? Which was good. Anger was an improvement over how she had been. It was an emotion, if not a positive one. But anything was better than that blank shell she had become. Yet he would not just go away. He wouldn't let her take his son and daughter away from him.

Back at the hotel matters weren't any better. They went directly up to their room. Angela ordered Charley up to his bed, insisting he needed to rest. Not wanting to hear any more arguing, Charlie escaped out onto the balcony. Leaving Uzmahndey to confront Angela. "I was worried about you."

"I don't need you to worry about me. I need you to protect the children. Not endanger them."

"It won't happen again."

"How can I know that?"

"Because I'll let you crash and burn before I lift a finger again."

"Promise?" Uzmahndey turned away. "You can't promise. You'll do the same foolish thing again and again."

He spun away from her. "I'm going for a walk."

"Can I come?" Charlie stood in the open door to the balcony.

"No," Angela declared.

"You are not going to let her go anywhere with me now? Just last night you were wanting me to teach her how to dance."

"That was before you drug the two of them through a portal. Then lost them."

"Fine." Uzmahndey stormed out. He hadn't been this angry in a long while. If ever.

You sure handled that well.

"Shut up. All of you." Uzmahndey stomped down to the lobby. He paused at the door to the lounge. How long had it been since he'd had a drink? He didn't especially want one.

But he needed one. He would force it down no matter how bad it tasted, or how sick it made him. He was seeking oblivion. He walked up to the bar. "Whiskey. Neat."

"What kind, sir?"

"It doesn't matter. They'll all taste bad." He slid his room card key across the bar for his order to be put on Angela's tab. Let Snugglesaurus pay for it.

Uzmahndey sipped the whiskey with trepidation, not sure how he would react to it. It tasted sweet. He shot it down. It burned all the way down. A cleansing fire. Were the xenobots relenting since he was feeling so bad? He didn't want to chance asking them. He wasn't sure what Angela's range of hearing them was, and he was sure she wouldn't like the idea of him drinking.

"Another."

Charlie had wanted to come with him. Angela hadn't let her. The woman was maddening. He had saved the kids' lives in Oman. After he had let them be kidnapped, sure, but what was he supposed to have done? What if he had taken them with him into Yemen and they had gotten shot by the Houthis? Yemen was a war zone. He had left them where they were safe, in the motel room with orders not to leave, and Charlie had gotten bored and left. Was that his fault? He had chosen the best of two bad options. Now he wasn't to be trusted?

Several hours later Uzmahndey wobbled out of the lounge. He was surprised he had been able to do that. Perhaps the xenobots sympathized with him and had let him drink.

"Thanks, guys." No response. "Sorry I told you to shut up. You can talk now." Still no response. So they were mad at him and giving him the silent treatment. Same as Angela.

Uzmahndey froze upon entering the room. It was empty. Angela, Charlie, and Charley, and all their luggage, were gone. Yet his stuff still lay scattered about. They had abandoned him. Or rather Angela had, and had drug the children along.

"Good, Bad, Ugly, come on, tell me what's going on?" Nothing. Were they in agreement with Angela that he couldn't be trusted?

Uzmahndey pulled out his phone and checked his bank account. Wow. Not only could he access it, but the bonus Angela had promised to pay him if he completed the tour was there. He checked his pockets. He still had his passport. He would have no problem going home. Apparently, that was what Angela wanted.

But she had stolen his children! And the xenobots were not talking to him. Or had Angela turned them off somehow? But they had been part of the deal. Was she reneging on their deal? Probably not. She hadn't reneged on paying him. Maybe alcohol was affecting them. Maybe they had inhibited his drinking for a good reason. Maybe they couldn't function with alcohol in his system.

Uzmahndey collapsed upon the bed. The first thing he needed to do was sober up. Maybe then he could communicate with the xenobots. They hadn't been physically removed. They were still in him. Maybe once the alcohol worked its way out of his system they could help him locate his family.

It's not the alcohol, buddy.

Uzmahndey lurched upright in bed. "Bad! Boy is it good to hear from you."

Don't be so sure. Not until you hear what I have to say.

"I'm listening."

I'm the only one operating. I just woke up. Angela shut us all down. That's why you can drink again. We're no longer influencing you not to.

"She shut you down? Then how are you talking to me?"

Snugglesaurus just reactivated me. He wasn't able to start up all three of us. I guess he chose me because I'm the smartest.

"Or the one most likely to irritate me."

Or that. But he doesn't agree with Angela's decision to cut you free. He believes you should have a choice.

"What kind of choice?"

You saw that you've been paid in full for the tour?

"Yes."

And that you have kept us, like agreed upon.

"If you all three work like before."

We will. The other two will eventually wake up on their own. So you can go back to the U.S. and get back into football. Just like you want. You haven't been cheated out of anything.

"Except my kids."

That brings us to your other option. Angela has headed for the next portal with the kids. You could try to catch up with them .

Uzmahndey leapt to his feet. "That's not an option. It's an inevitability. Only thing is I've no idea where they've gone."

Snugglesaurus says they are headed for the Chocolate Hills in the Philippines.

Chapter 27

Chocolate Hills

Even out of practice, and with the aid of only Bad, Uzmahndey sobered up in record time. He packed while slurping down all the in-room coffee there was.

Racing down to the lobby, he encountered his first difficulty. He had lost his translator. Angela apparently knew every language spoken on Earth, or at least was fluent in the ones needed to visit the places she needed to visit. Uzmahndey, on the other hand, could not utter a single phrase of Mandarin, and whatever it was they spoke in the Philippines. "How are you at Mandarin Chinese, Bad?"

I only know what you know. And you know how little that is.

"Can you communicate with Snugglesaurus?"

No. He's out of range.

"So we're on our own."

Not totally.

"Yeah? How's that?"

Snugglesaurus wants you to catch up to Angela. Angela depends on Snugglesaurus to arrange online transactions for her. So he could intentionally slow her down.

"Wouldn't Angela know what it was doing?"

Angela is not at the top of her game right now. She might not *realize what was going on. Also, the kids are on your side, too. I bet they both hope you come after them.*

"They're not mad at me?"

Charlie knows what really happened in Oman. That she is to blame for them getting kidnapped. And she loves you. Go figure that.

"What about my son?"

He just turned twelve. He's a work in progress. But I think he likes you.

"Okay. Here goes nothing."

Luckily, the hotel clerk at the front desk knew a modicum of English. Checking out was not too difficult since the bill had already been settled.

Dealing with a taxi driver wasn't a disaster, either. Only a single word was required, airport, which Uzmahndey supplemented with soaring sound effects and exuberant hand waving. He had enough cash on hand to cover the ride.

Uzmahndey checked the route on his phone. He had a long trip ahead of him. Flying out of Guilin, he needed to make connections in Hong Kong and Manila before flying on to Panglao Island. The Chocolate Hills were located on Bohol, the next island over from Panglao. He sank in upon desolate bones when he realized it would take over a day to get there. "I never appreciated Snugglesaurus making all the travel arrangements."

Just remember, Angela has to make the same trip. And she has two disgruntled children traveling with her. And Snugglesaurus will be hindering her. You can do this.

Uzmahndey grinned. "Words of encouragement. When did you turn into such a nice guy?"

Most of the time you get plenty of encouragement from those two losers. Most of the time you need me to keep you down to earth. But now I've got to do it all.

"I appreciate it, Bad."

Yeah? Just wait until you see what I can do for you on the football field. Good and Ugly are too nice. They won't want to hurt anybody. I'll help you knock Logan Wilson's head off.

"I'm dying to do that. Only not yet. I've got a family to take care of first."

Uzmahndey checked the departure schedules. It was hours before a flight to his first connection, Hong Kong, would leave. As a trial run, he stopped into a newsstand and purchased some snacks. His credit card ran without a glitch. So he purchased a ticket, then flopped down into a seat at his gate and wolfed down his bingtang hulu, sachima, and caramel flavored sunflower seeds.

Keep feeding me. You need me charged up at peak strength.

Once Uzmahndey finished all the snacks he had just bought, he pulled out his phone.

Sure you don't want to catch a nap? I can sing you a lullaby.

"I can nap on the plane. I need to learn about where we're going."

The Chocolate Hills were a group of unusually shaped hills, Uzmahndey read, located in the interior of the island of Bohol in the Philippines. This extraordinary landscape was unique to this island. The estimated number of chocolate hills ranged from 1,268 to 1,776, spread out over 50 square kilometers. The hills weren't big. The highest was 120 meters, with most between 30 and 50 meters.

Mystery still surrounded how the peculiar conical-shaped mounds were formed. The most plausible theory was they were weathered formations of marine limestone lying on top of an impenetrable clay base. Being in their presence was a surreal experience, one of the most bizarre landscapes you could ever encounter. At the end of the dry season the hills earned their name when the grass turned from green to brown. At all times they retained a uniform look as, curiously, no trees or clumps of shrubs will grow on them. The Chocolate Hills were a candidate to become a World Heritage UNESCO site.

By the time Uzmahndey stepped off the plane at Bohol-Panglao International Airport he was ready to keel over. Sleeping on planes and in airports was never restful, especially as disturbed as he was.

You've got to remember it's only me giving you a boost now. Don't push too hard.

"I'll rest when I catch up with them."

At the airport Uzmahndey rented a Jeep. He wondered how the others were getting to the Chocolate Hills. Angela didn't drive, not without Snugglesaurus' help. Would the AI help her now? Bad doubted it. Would she want Charlie to drive? Probably not. Snugglesaurus would most likely book them a tour. Which would put them on a schedule. While he could set his own schedule.

Uzmahndey drove away from the airport across small Panglao Island and over a bridge to the much larger island of Bohol. The road he was on followed the southern coast east for a short while, then turned north out of the coastal city of Baclayon inland up into the mountains.

The interior of the island was a tropical paradise reminiscent of Hawaii. Uzmahndey had taken so many astounding journeys on this tour, one after another, they piled up into a jumbled collage. The Earth was so beautiful. No wonder aliens wanted to come here. He had been content in his little corner of paradise on the Big Island, but there was so much more to experience. But all that was for later. Now he had to focus. He had to find his family.

Uzmahndey was so weary he didn't realize he had reached the Chocolate Hills until Bad made some inappropriate reference to Beyonce. At first the uniform brown mounds were spaced well apart and not noticeable. But the further he drove into them, the denser and more pronounced they became. He pulled off at the Café Heroina in Canmano for some badly needed coffee. With pig Spanish and even more piggish hand gestures, he learned there was a park ahead that would give the best access to the depths of the Chocolate Hills region.

Climbing back into the Jeep, he wondered, what now? He had been in such a mad rush to get there he had not given much thought about what to do once he arrived. Was he ahead of them? Angela had gotten a big head start, but Snugglesaurus was probably slowing her down, and the kids probably were, too. He had sped past several tour buses. Were now they behind him on one of those buses? Or still ahead of him? The Chocolate Hills were spread out over fifty kilometers of nearly impenetrable jungle. No telling where the portal was located in that expanse. Maybe Snugglesaurus would help.

"Bad, can you contact Snugglesaurus now? We're bound to be closer than before. Maybe we're in range."

I've been trying. No can do. I'd say your best bet is to go on to that park you just learned about.

"And then what?"

Find a shady spot and take a nap. You're about to pass out behind the wheel.

"No way."

You'll do no one any good if you wrap the Jeep around a tree. You have to rest.

"I'll rest once I find my kids." Uzmahndey was about to start the Jeep when his phone sounded off. He dug it out of his pocket.

"Dad?"

"Charles?!"

"Where are you?"

"The Philippines. The Chocolate Hills. Where are you?"

"Some church. Angela said you'd gone back to Hawaii."

"No way. Not without you and your sister."

"Can you come get me?"

"Where is this church?" There was some muffled noise. "Charles?"

A heavily-accented English speaking male voice replaced Charley's.

"Is this Charles' father?"

"Yes. Is Charles okay?"

"He seems to be. He ran away from his mother."

"She's not my mother!" Uzmahndey heard Charley yell in the background.

"He is safe with me. I'm a priest."

"Where is your church located?"

"Are you near?"

"I'm at a store in Marisa."

"That's the only store in Marisa. My church is on the same highway, ten kilometers north. St. Augustine."

"I'll be right there." Uzmahndey hung up, started the Jeep and peeled out. "We drove right past it!"

It sounds like Charles really wants to see you.

"He's my son! Of course he wants to see me."

Minutes later Uzmahndey pulled into the lot before the church. Charley was waiting for him, along with a young priest. The boy ran up to the Jeep as Uzmahndey climbed out.

"What happened?"

"I got away from her. She was fooling with those stupid Cheerios. I tried to get Charlie to come with me, but she wouldn't. She tried to stop me, but I'm too strong for her."

Uzmahndey hugged him.

"You are way too strong. I'm surprised Angela didn't track you down."

"I'm not stupid. I left Snugglesaurus with Charlie."

"You don't need to have Snugglesaurus with you for the AI to track you." Uzmahndey smiled. "He must not have *wanted* to track you for Angela. How did you get here?"

"I don't know. I ran through the jungle. Came out on this road. I saw this church."

Uzmahndey held Charley back so he could look him over. He was muddy, his clothes were torn, and his hair a thicket. But there were no scars, or insect bites, or scratches, even. His thick alien skin was amazing. He ruffled his son's hair.

"You look like you've been running wild in the jungle. Are you okay?"

"I'm good. Now." He hugged Uzmahndey.

"I bet. Thanks to those tough genes you and your sister share."

"He's an abomination!"

Uzmahndey jerked around. A man stood beside the Jeep with a gun. He fired.

Charley slumped in Uzmahndey's arms.

Uzmahndey lowered his son to the ground then charged. The man got off three more shots. Each bullet hit, staggering Uzmahndey each time. And each time he staggered on forward. He knocked the gun from the amazed man's hand. Grabbed him under the arm pits. Raised him up above his head. Hurled him against the side of the church, head first. Then Uzmahndey collapsed.

<u>What's going on?</u>

<u>What happened to us?</u>

<u>Angela had Snugglesaurus turn you off. There are more pressing matters now. We've been shot three times. I've got the worst bullet wound, the one in his chest. There's a bullet in his left side and another in his left thigh.</u>

<u>I'll work on his side.</u>

<u>I've got his leg.</u>

<u>Uz buddy, we're going to put you to sleep now. Save you a lot of pain. And it will make it easier for us to work on you.</u>

"What about Charles?"

"I'm okay, Dad." Charley, supported by the priest, was hovering above him.

Uzmahndey could see blood on his shirt. "You were shot."

The bullet didn't go very deep through that Mylar skin of his. It knocked him down and probably hurt like hell, but there's not a lot of bleeding. Now tell your son goodnight.

"I love you, Charles."

"I'm so glad you came for me, Dad."

"Always." Uzmahndey closed his eyes with a smile on his face.

Chapter 28

Interlude Five

Uzmahndey opened his eyes to find Angela looming over him. "Bitch."

Her stony expression never cracked as she glared down at him from the chair beside the bed he found himself in.

"Hi, Dad."

Uzmahndey looked to see Charley stretched out on a bed across the room. "Are you okay?"

"The bullet didn't go very deep in Charley," Angela said. "I got it out. It left a small hole and a big bruise on his chest. He lost some blood, but not too much. He's otherwise okay."

"And my daughter?"

"I'm here." Charlie's smiling face popped in next to Angela's impassive one.

Uzmahndey looked around the small room. "Where is here?"

"South Palms Resort Panglao," Charlie informed him. "Next to the airport."

He glared at Angela. "So I'm allowed to stay now?"

"You saved Charley."

"You lost him."

Angela's stare never wavered, but she didn't respond.

Uzmahndey closed his eyes for introspection. Nothing was stirring, not even a mouse. He opened his eyes and managed a weak smile. "I must have worn Bad out." The smile was so weak it easily slid into a frown. "Or did you turn him off again?"

"No. All three are active. They are just exhausted."

"They saved your life," Charlie said. "Again."

Uzmahndey ignored her, still scowling at Angela. "Did you get the bullets out of me, too?"

"No. That was too difficult. I took you to a doctor."

"Won't he report my injuries to the police?"

"Not with the amount of money Snugglesaurus paid him. And my threat of what I'd do to him if he did."

Uzmahndey had survived three bullets fired point blank. How could any defensive player ever injure him? "What will you do when this is all over? Turn them off again?"

"No. The deal we made will be honored." When Uzmahndey's scowl failed to diminish, she continued. "Wasn't all the money promised you delivered?" Seeing a slight thaw in his hard face, she went on. "You get to keep the xenobots and they will continue to function as they have been. They won't be turned off. I only did that to keep them from helping you follow us."

"It didn't work."

"I know. Somehow Bad became active again."

She doesn't know it was Snugglesaurus' doing? Interesting. Uzmahndey didn't let on what he knew. He nodded his acceptance of what she said. "How did you find me and Charles?"

"Snugglesaurus was able to get a fix on you as soon as the other two xenobots woke up. It must have been the shock of you getting shot that reactivated them."

So the AI was capable of lying to Angela. Uzmahndey looked to Charlie. "How'd you and Angela get to the church? Weren't you on a tour bus?"

Charlie laughed. "We stole a car." When Uzmahndey's eyes widened in disbelief, she continued. "It was a keyless ignition. Snugglesaurus started it. We took it from a lot in Chocolate Hills Park and I drove to the church. We left it with the priest. He knew we took it in an emergency. He said he'd see the car got returned to its owner."

Uzmahndey turned his attention to Charley. "What happened to that guy who shot us?"

"He's dead. You smashed his head into a wall. I warned you about how strong you are."

"Was he a Gaia fanatic?"

"Yes."

"How did you let Charley get away from you?"

"Because you weren't there to watch him while I placed the xenobot in the portal." She rose from her seat. "Now go back to sleep. Everyone is okay. You need to recover so we can travel."

"You aren't going to leave me behind again?"

"No. I made a mistake. I need you."

Accepting that as the most of an apology he would ever get from Angela, he closed his eyes and went back to sleep.

The next morning Uzmahndey woke up starving.

Feed me, Leroy!

"Good morning, Bad. Is Good and Ugly with us?"

Yes.

We need to refuel.

"I'll call room service." Angela was seated in a chair next to the bed. "What would you like?"

"Everything on the menu." He looked to the other bed. Charlie and Charley were still asleep. "How did you get her to sleep with her brother?"

"She was afraid she'd hurt you inadvertently in her sleep if she shared a bed with you." Angela handed him a menu.

He didn't open it. "Did you really think I'd go back to Hawaii without my kids?"

"I was so angry I wasn't thinking straight."

Look at the menu! Order something! We're dying!

"We'll talk later," Angela said. "Bad is getting upset. You need to eat now."

Uzmahndey ordered double helpings of everything they offered. Charlie and Charley woke up when the feast arrived. They both sat at the foot of his bed once he sat up to eat.

"Let me see your chest."

Charlie feigned offense. "I hope you are talking to my brother."

"You know I am." When Charley pulled up his pajama top, Uzmahndey saw the bullet wound was bandaged, with a horrendous black bruise radiating out from all around the extensive dressing. "How bad does it hurt?"

"I can't hardly move."

Angela pulled the pajama top back down. "He doesn't have three xenobots taking care of him."

"That's what you get for running away. What were you thinking? In the mountains? In the jungle? In a foreign country? That was crazy."

Charley shot a dark look at Angela. "I was mad at her for ditching you."

"She told you it wasn't my idea to leave?"

"I knew it wasn't your idea," Charlie said. "You would never abandon us."

Uzmahndey smiled at her. "Damn straight." He looked to Angela. "When's our flight?"

"We're staying another day."

"We need to get out of here," Uzmahndey said. "Gaia's people are here. You stole a car. I killed somebody, for Christs' sake."

"You and Charley both need another day to rest." Angela rose from her chair, looking to the other two. "Get up and let him eat."

Thank you, Angela.

After breakfast, Uzmahndey fell back to sleep. When he awoke, Angela was seated next to him. Charlie and Charley were on the other bed engaged in a game with the stuffed dinosaur. He looked back to Angela. "What now?"

"We complete the tour."

Uzmahndey looked to the door. "I'm worried the police will come knocking."

"Snugglesaurus is covering our trail."

"Our trail is getting awfully obvious. Videos from the Giant's Causeway and Lake Kaindy and Lake Baikal. We've put on quite a show. Gaia's people seem to have no trouble finding us. What if she knows where we're at now? Her disciples could attack us here, or contact the police and send them here."

Gaia doesn't know where we are.

Her people haven't been tracking us. They been hanging around the portals waiting for us to show up.

Now we need to shut up and listen.

"Why did you say that, Bad?"

"Because we need to talk about something else." Angela leaned in closer. "I am having problems."

Uzmahndey reacted in horror. "You're not pregnant again?"

"No. How could I be?"

"Easy. You said Charlie's father was some drunk tourist you picked up in a bar in Hilo. I'm sure there are plenty of drunk tourists in the Philippines, too."

"I am bound to you. There will be no other men."

Uzmahndey sighed. "I really don't understand how a robot gets pregnant in the first place."

You really need to have The Talk with Charles.

"Stay out of this, Bad." Angela looked away. "My problems aren't physical. They are emotional."

"Your emotions haven't seemed much of a problem lately."

"They've been coming back, but not like before. I'm having a hard time dealing with them. The learning program isn't working right. Father couldn't fix me back as good as I'd been before the sandstorm in Egypt. I got so mad at you at the Reed Flute Cave I lost control. Also, I am starting to feel attracted to you again, but I can't express it. I appreciate everything you've done to help with the children, but I haven't been able to tell you. Everything is so jumbled inside."

Uzmahndey stared solemnly into her eyes. "Being jumbled inside is a very human condition. I'd say your learning program is working good enough."

"You don't hate me?"

"You've saved my life time and again, Angela. How can I hate you?"

That evening Uzmahndey was recovered enough to sit up at a table to eat a room service dinner. He watched his son settle into a comfortable upright position, too.

"Tough kid." Uzmahndey looked from him to his sister. "Both of you are. This new hybrid race of humans will be rugged."

"It will need to be," Angela said. "The way the Earth has been degraded."

Uzmahndey dug into his double portions. "Is that what Ghost means when he talks about saving the human race?"

"No. He's talking about preventing Gaia from manipulating the Schumann Resonance."

"I still don't know how that works."

"The Schumann Resonance is the Earth's heartbeat," Angela began. "Flashes of lightning strike all over the planet at a rate of fifty times a second. This results in the formation of low-frequency electromagnetic waves that engulf the entire world. These are referred to as Schumann Resonances, and they affect human behavior. They oscillate at greater and lower energy, with a base frequency of 7.83 MHz. These frequencies are linked to different kinds of brain waves. This is real-time coherence in variations in the Schumann and brain activity spectra within the 6 to 16 MHz band. There are strange and unpredictable similarities in the spectral patterns and strengths of electromagnetic fields that are generated by human brain activity and the Earth-ionospheric resonance. The Schumann Resonance of 7.83 MHz has been linked to hypnosis, meditation, and human growth hormones, and can also affect human consciousness. A global rise in stress, anxiety or tension, such as what occurred in the opening months of the Covid pandemic, affects the Schumann Resonance. Alternatively, a spike in these frequencies affect humans."

"Sounds kind of Newey-Agey," Uzmahndey said.

Angela ignored the interruption. "Gaia controls this resonance. She can raise and lower human stress and anxiety by manipulating it. Which means she can set nations at war with one another, increase or decrease suicide rates, cause crime and murder to spike or subside."

"Why does she do this?"

"Merely because she can? As an amusement? Or perhaps she thrives at this resonance? No matter, it's time for her to stop tormenting humans. That's why we're here."

"So these xenobots you are placing at portals around the world will stop her from doing this?"

"No, but it will block her access to the surface. The network of xenobots will constrain her and her kind. Also, the new crossbreed of human and alien will be immune to the ill effects she causes. Their brains operate at a much higher frequency. The Schumann Resonance does not influence them."

"But will they still be human?"

Angela waved an arm to the children. "What do you think?"

Uzmahndey studied the two solemn faces closely following their discussion. "Warmly human." He turned back to Angela. "Why is Ghost doing this?"

"My Father is readying the human race for inclusion within the galactic community. To be accepted, humans must be rid of their overlord. Gaia."

"So being rid of Gaia means war and poverty and ignorance will all cease?"

"No, but they will be much less. And human kindness will surge into the vacuum their reduction creates."

That night Charlie climbed into bed with her brother once again, without complaint. Angela appeared at Uzmahndey's bedside in her pajamas. "May I join you?"

Despite himself, Uzmahndey smiled. So this was the real reason Charlie had agreed to sleep with her brother.

"Can you ease my pain? Like I saw you doing to Charley after his last growth spurt?"

Angela slipped in beneath the cover. "You have three xenobots to do that for you."

<u>And we do a very good job of it.</u>

<u>*Without any thanks.*</u>

"Thank you. Now shut up and go to sleep."

<u>We will give you privacy.</u>

"I don't need privacy."

Angela pulled him close.

"Do I?"

Angela cuddled up to him without answering his question.

Chapter 29

Lake Hillier

The next morning Uzmahndey woke up feeling surprisingly well for a man who had been shot three times. It wasn't actually a surprise. He knew it was because of the efforts of Good, Bad, and Ugly. Sleeping in Angela's arms had helped, too.

She greeted his crusted eyes with a twisted smile. "How do you feel?"

"Like a new man in an old body."

He was glad to be back in Angela's good graces. He didn't want her to abandon him again. But her manic expression was unnerving. She had never been good at expressing emotions, once she had learned how to have them. She had also never been good at concealing emotions. Whatever she was feeling, or not feeling, was always right there on her face, as blatant as a billboard. Right now that billboard seemed to be advertising a horror movie. How much strain was she under? He needed to get over his anger at what she had done to him and help her finish this before she went completely off the rails.

Only thing was he had other worries rattling around inside his skull. One, why had Snugglesaurus helped him? If the AI hadn't reactivated Bad there was no way Uzmahndey could ever have found his children. The AI was a great facilitator, and could achieve wondrous things online, but this time it had taken the initiative. Not only that, it had made a moral decision. Previously, it had merely done what it had been tasked with. Had the situation forced it to evolve? Or had it always possessed this capability but just hadn't evidenced it? Uzmahndey assumed the AI's prime directive was to accomplish the mission. Had Snugglesaurus decided Uzmahndey's presence was vital to the mission? Obviously, the AI wasn't under Angela's complete control. So who had the final say? Ghost, probably. But was Ghost even real? Could the series of ever-changing holograms with the voice of his old LSU coach be a creation of Snugglesaurus? Was the AI ruling the Emerald City from behind the curtain, with Ghost merely a holographic great and powerful wizard? Uzmahndey certainly didn't have a handle of the dynamics of this alien invasion force he was enmeshed in.

Second, his relationship with Angela was getting more and more complicated. She was pleased with him now, but that could change in a blink of her camera lens eye. If he angered her again would he provoke the same reaction as before? Or a worse one? Or had she been sufficiently chastised by losing Charley? Uzmahndey knew she had his back in a fight. But if she believed it was either him or the children? He had no delusions about that. Angela would throw him under the bus for their sake every time. As he would her. As she would want him to. They were both secondary to the children, and they were both okay with that.

Third, what was all that Schumann Resonance stuff about? Was it for real? He had to get online first chance he got and check it out. But could he believe what he read on the Internet? That was an old joke, but in his present situation it wasn't funny. Snugglesaurus manipulated the Internet. The AI most likely could feed any information it wanted to Uzmahndey's searches. He was sure he could Google Schumann Resonance and find endless posts on it. Would any of it be on the level? Or would it be what Snugglesaurus had invented for him to read? It was time for Uzmahndey to fashion himself a tin foil hat.

Fourth, forget it. Uzmahndey could count to infinity and not resolve anything. He had committed to a path – protect his children. There was no way he could get them away from Angela and Snugglesaurus and Ghost, or Gaia's monstrosities and her fanatical followers. His only course was to finish this and see what came of it. Liberation or enslavement for the human race? Life with his son and adopted daughter, or the loss of them?

Charley bouncing up out of bed shook Uzmahndey from his bleak ruminations. His son looked as nimble as before being shot. So today was a go. While Angela checked Charley's chest out, Charlie came over to sit on the bed with Uzmahndey.

"How was last night?"

"Restful."

"Did you get enough sleep?"

"Plenty." He knew she was digging for information on the status between him and Angela. "That's all that happened last night. Sorry to disappoint you."

"Who says I'm disappointed." She walked back to her and Charley's bed, where she peeled off her pajama top. She had her back to Uzmahndey, but still.

"Charlie!" Angela barked. "Get dressed in the bathroom. You are bothering Uzmahndey."

Charlie gathered up her clothes and with a leisurely step took them into the bathroom.

Uzmahndey looked to Angela, to find her glaring at the bathroom door as it closed. Her voice had held an edge as sharp as her glare. Jealousy? Had she learned jealousy? And she was jealous of Charlie? This damaged version of Angela was an evolving mystery. Like any damaged person. And just as unpredictable.

And dangerous.

Following a hurried breakfast, they boarded a flight Snugglesaurus had booked for them from Panglao-Bohol International Airport in the Philippines to Perth, Australia.

After another wearying passage, they took a taxi from the airport to the Swan River Oasis Resort. This was a family resort – there was disc golf and a laser tag course – so Snugglesaurus had been able to find them a suite with three beds.

Despite having felt chipper that morning, by late afternoon Uzmahndey and Charley were both flagging. You don't recover so easily from being shot no matter how many xenobots or alien genes you have. They crashed for the remainder of the day then went out for a late dinner. Familiar with the Men at Work song 'Down Under', Uzmahndey had to try a Vegemite sandwich. He had the spread with avocado on toast. And when he saw kangaroo on the menu, he hopped on it.

Returning to their room after dinner, Charlie behaved herself and went into the bathroom to change into pajamas. When Angela started undressing in the middle of the room, Charley dove onto his bed and buried his face in his pillow.

"You should change in the bathroom, too," Uzmahndey advised. "You are upsetting Charley. Twelve year old boys are touchy about people getting naked."

She looked at Charley. "You're right." She patiently waited in the middle of the room until Charlie emerged from the bathroom.

Charlie looked the tableau over - Angela standing outside the bathroom door in panties and bra with the clothes she had just taken off in hand, Charley across the bed on his stomach with his face in his pillow, and Uzmahndey sitting on the double bed looking very tired. "What did I miss?"

"Nothing. I need the bathroom." Angela started across the room.

Charlie snorted in disbelief. "Since when?"

"She's changing into her pajamas," Uzmahndey explained.

"So she's modest now?"

"No." Uzmahndey nodded toward Charley. "Charles is."

Charlie set her clothes down. "How about you?"

"I've given post-game interviews to female reporters in the locker room wearing nothing but a towel." He stood and began undressing. "There is a league rule against modesty."

Angela emerged from the bathroom in her pajamas. She gave Uzmahndey an off-kilter glare as he pulled off his pants.

"Maybe you should start wearing pajamas like everyone else."

"Never." He tossed his pants down and climbed in bed.

Angela turned the light off and climbed in with him. When he cuddled up to her, she shrugged him off.

"You are still recovering, and we have a long day tomorrow. You need your rest. Go to sleep."

As usual lately, her mood was totally unpredictable. With a weary sigh, Uzmahndey rolled over away from her.

Early the following morning Angela roused everybody before dawn. On the way to the airport they snagged some bags of Tim Tams for a breakfast on the go. While waiting for their flight, three of them also gobbled down several bags of Snickers Pods. Not nutritious at all, but delightfully filling.

It was a short flight to Esperance. This city on the southwest coast of Australia was the hub for all Lake Hillier activity. A taxi took them from the inland airport to Helispirit's helipad on the bay. Snugglesaurus had booked the four of them on a Lake Hillier scenic flight.

This was nothing new for Uzmahndey. He had escorted tourists on scenic helicopter rides in Hawaii to view the islands' tropical interiors. Angela was nonplused. Charley was thrilled. His sister was a different matter. Angela had to practically drag Charlie onto the helicopter, and during take-off she practically sat in Uzmahndey's lap. But as they flew over Cape Le Grand

National Park she became engrossed with the granite peaks passing below them. The helicopter followed the coast dotted with pristine white sand beaches and isolated coves. After flying above Cape Arid National Park, they turned south over the Indian Ocean. Flying over Goose Island, they continued on to Middle Island, where Lake Hillier was located.

Uzmahndey spotted the pink water from a mile away, even though it wasn't that large a body of water, 2,000 feet by 820 feet their guide informed them. The bubblegum pink lake was in such stark contrast to the green of the surrounding trees and the deep blue of the Indian Ocean that it seemed to glow. Only a narrow strip of land separated the lake from the ocean, so as the helicopter neared, thin bands of green trees and white sandy beach widened between the pink lake and the blue sea. It was a fantastic palette of vivid colors. The helicopter made a slow low circuit of the lake for a good leisurely view then set down on a nearby natural rock platform.

A grazing platter was set up, and champagne and beer was served, too. Only Charlie partook of the bubbly. Charley wanted to, but Uzmahndey and Angela both nixed that. As for Uzmahndey, the xenobots were back on Carrie Nation duty and dulled his desire for alcohol. Of course, Angela ate or drank nothing. She told their guide the helicopter ride had made her stomach queasy.

After the snack and drink, they were led on a short hike to the very edge of the lake. The flat expanse of water appeared as vibrant pink as it had looked from high above.

"This is no trick of the light," their guide said. "Other oddly-colored bodies of water lose their enchanting hues when examined up close."

She dipped a glass into the lake and raised it up to the sun. The water it contained was as vivid pink as ever.

"This water is truly pink." She dumped the water back into the lake. "Microorganisms living in the water are the reason for the color. There is Dunaliella salina, a red algae which causes the salt content in the lake to produce a red dye, and a red salt-loving bacterium present in the salt crusts. Despite this, the lake exhibits no known adverse effects upon humans. It is perfectly safe to swim in, or float in since the salt content is even higher than in the Dead Sea, but the Australian government prohibits swimming in an effort to preserve this natural wonder."

"Uzmahndey!"

He stared into the face of an attractive young woman. She appeared upset.

"Keep alert. I've got to see about Charlie and Charley."

Who? He looked around. It was daytime. He stood on barren rocky ground at the edge of a pink lake. Pink? Where the hell was he? In Barbie Land? The woman who had spoken to him was now with another young woman and an even younger boy. There was also a middle-aged man and another young woman. A broad body of water – which looked the right color, it wasn't pink - stretched to the horizon in one direction. He was on a coast. Looking the other way, he saw a helicopter parked on a rock slab. Had he flown in a helicopter to wherever he was?

<u>What happened?</u>

<u>Where are we?</u>

<u>Who are you all and why am I hearing your voices in my head?</u>

"It's *my* head," Uzmahndey insisted. "*I'm* the one hearing voices."

The strange woman towed the two young people to him.

"We were attacked by Mnemosyne."

"If you say so." Uzmahndey studied the faces of the two with her. They didn't look familiar, either, and appeared to be as confused as he.

"Who are you people?"

"I'm your wife Angela. These are our children Charlie and Charley."

He was married? With a son? No way. Although the woman addressing him wasn't a bad looking babe to be married to.

<u>I have the feeling she's telling the truth.</u>

<u>Or she beieves she is.</u>

<u>*Just go with it. I've got a hunch she's good in the sack.*</u>

The woman smiled at Uzmahndey. "I am."

"You can hear these voices?" He shot panicked glances all around. "I thought they were just in my head."

A quizzical expression graced her face. "It's like I can hear your thoughts." She blinked, dispelling the look. "We'll figure that out later. Right now we've got to figure out how to get off this island."

Uzmahndey looked to the helicopter. "We can't fly off it?"

She looked over to the middle-aged man and the other young woman, who were stumbling around the edge of the lake. "Not if the pilot doesn't remember how to fly." She went over to talk to them.

Uzmahndey stared at the girl and boy in front of him. "Charlie and Charley?"

They both shrugged.

"Why do you both have the same name?"

After they shrugged once again, he asked, "You don't happen to know my name, do you?"

"Uzmahndey!" Angela shouted out.

<u>*WTF? Did she just say Who's Your Mama?*</u>

Angela rejoined them and dug into the boy's backpack. She pulled out a scraggly stitched-together stuffed toy T. Rex. "Come on." She led them back to the helicopter.

Uzmahndey hung back. "I'm not getting in that thing if no one knows how to fly it."

"We're not flying. I'm calling for help over the radio."

They all six walked back to the helicopter. Neither the male pilot nor the female guide had a clue how to broadcast a message. After seeming to confer with the well-worn toy,

Angela called to HeliSpirit on the mainland to inform them the pilot was seriously ill and they needed to send someone who could fly them back from Middle Island. The person she was speaking with insisted on talking to the pilot. After a brief conversation with the addled man, they said a helicopter was on the way.

The guide and the pilot broke out the champagne and beer again. Charlie had a glass. Charley asked for some, but Angela forbade it. Uzmahndey was repulsed by the idea of drinking either champagne or beer.

Angela abstained also. "Mnemosyne's assault on my memory seems to have failed, but it still must have shook me up."

"What are you talking about?"

"I'll tell you once her attack on you wears off." She handed the stuffed T. Rex to Charley. "Snugglesaurus is working on restoring Charley's memories now."

She looked off to Charlie, who was still drinking with the pilot and guide. "It's not a bad thing for Charlie to get drunk. It will help her remain calm until Snugglesaurus finishes with her brother and can work on her."

Angela looked back to Uzmahndey. "You are a different matter."

"Why is that?"

"There is no direct link between Snugglesaurus and you. Once he is finished with Charlie, he'll have to restore Good, Bad, and Ugly's memories, and they will have to restore yours. That might take a while."

"Who is this Good, Bad, and Ugly?"

"They are the voices you've been hearing in your head. They are as confused as you are."

Yes I am.

Hell yes.

As confused as him? No way.

Angela took his hands in hers. "Try to relax. Your memories should return. To all four of you. It will just take time."

"Who is this Nemosine who attacked us?"

"I'll explain once you are able to make sense of what I say. Now I need to intervene with Charlie. I want her tipsy, not toppled."

She walked off to the happier half of the population on the island. He turned his attention to the young boy with the worn-out stuffed dinosaur. Could that really be his son?

Another helicopter soon arrived with an extra pilot. Angela explained to the two new arrivals that maybe the island should be placed off-limits until the authorities could determine if something in the lake had caused this outbreak of mass-amnesia. After interviewing the confused pilot and guide from the first helicopter, they said they would pass that suggestion along.

Angela, Uzmahndey, Charlie and Charley piled into the new helicopter, while their dazed pilot and guide boarded the original helicopter with the other new pilot. The two helicopters flew back to Esperance. The only notable event on the flight back was Charlie throwing up.

Back at the heliport, Angela herded them all away, refusing every offer of aid from the staff. She shoved the three into a taxi and directed the driver to take them to the Comfort Inn Bay of Isles.

"Our luggage is back at our hotel in Perth. But I don't think we are fit to fly any further. We'll see if you three can sleep off the effects of Mnemosyne's attack here." She booked them into a room with two double beds. Charlie curled up on one and went to sleep.

Charley objected. "Aren't you going to clean her up first? She stinks. She's covered in puke."

Angela brushed aside his complaints. "She's just got a little on her. She needs to sleep it off."

"Then I'm sleeping with Dad." Charley plopped down on the other bed.

No!

"I'm sorry, Bad." Angela pushed Uzmahndey down onto the bed with Charley. "Another time."

"Promise?" Uzmahndey asked.

Angela kissed him. "Promise."

Uzmahndey glanced at Charley. "You called me Dad."

"Of course I called you Dad."

Uzmahndey stood to undress. "His memory is back?"

"Most of it," Angela said. "As soon as Snugglesaurus is done with him, he will start with Charlie."

Uzmahndey looked to the girl out cold on the other bed. "She's passed out."

"Snugglesaurus does his best work while she and Charley are unconscious."

"Where are you sleeping?"

"She doesn't need to sleep," Charley said.

"I don't?" Angela appeared puzzled. "Why do you say that?"

"Uh-oh." Charley leaned in to whisper into his father's ear. "Mnemosyne's attack *did* do something to her. I don't think she remembers she's a robot."

"She's a robot?" Uzmahndey answered. "Yeah, right,"

<u>Actually, that kind of makes sense.</u>

Uzmahndey responded to Good as if he was a person standing in front of him. "You are still goofy. Go to sleep."

"I'm not goofy!" Charley objected. "She *is* a robot."

"He wasn't talking to you." Angela offered him Snugglesaurus.

He declined it. "I'm okay now."

"Not if you think I'm a robot."

"Give him to Charlie."

Angela stroked Charley's face then kissed Uzmahndey. "You both need to sleep. It's been a long hard day."

"Are you sleeping with Charlie?" Uzmahndey asked.

"No. Snugglesaurus is." Angela put the stuffed dinosaur in Charlie's arms.

"I told you she doesn't sleep," Charley insisted.

"That's impossible," Uzmahndey replied.

Charley grinned. "You think *that's* impossible? Boy, you haven't seen anything yet. Well, you have, but you just don't remember it."

Angela pulled a chair up between the two beds and sat.

"Go to sleep. Both of you."

"See." Charley gloated. "I told you she didn't sleep."

Uzmahndey studied Angela's stiff upright posture. "She'll get sleepy eventually." He closed his eyes. This sure was a weird lot he had fallen in with.

You got that right. I don't know who you three are or how the hell you all got in my head.

Chapter 30

Interlude Six

Uzmahndey awoke the next morning to find the same strange woman as before seated in a chair next to the bed staring down at him.

<u>That's Angela.</u>

"Good sounds okay this morning," Angela said.

<u>She's a robot.</u>

"Ugly, not so okay."

"How ugly do you need to be to be named Ugly?"

"Bad seems back to normal."

If I was normal, lady, such a good-looking chick as you would be in bed with me instead of sitting next to it.

"Maybe not. Good, you need to work on Ugly and Bad. Then you can all three work on Uzmahndey."

"Is my name really Who's Your Mama?"

Charlie sat up in the other bed, looking hung over and so dazed she didn't realize she was wearing nothing but yellow panties. Seeing the way Uzmahndey stared at her, she finally realized and snatched the sheet up to her chin. "What happened to my clothes?"

"I took them off you to wash. They had spit-up on them, and we don't have any clean clothes with us to change into."

Angela motioned toward the bathroom. "I hung them up in the shower. They should be dry by now."

Uzmahndey was distracted by the lump lying next to him. The human form under the covers was much larger than he remembered it being the night before. But then Uzmahndey was having issues with his memory. "Isn't he a lot bigger than he was last night?"

"He had a growth spurt," Angela said.

Before he could pursue that puzzle, Uzmahndey was distracted by Charlie clambering out of bed onto unsteady feet to stagger into the bathroom for her clothes. She was a beautiful young woman. But she was supposed to be his daughter. He jerked his gaze away to the slumbering giant that was supposed to be his son. "He sure is a hard sleeper."

"He'll be a lump all day," Charlie called out. "It's what happens the day after a growth spurt."

"What are these growth spurts you two keep talking about?"

"Last night he was twelve," Angela said. "This morning he is fifteen."

"That's impossible."

Charlie paused outside the bathroom. "You'll be amazed at what's *not* impossible. Once you remember what all has happened." She went on in.

"Get up," Angela ordered.

When Uzmahndey did, Angela slid in beneath the covers he had just vacated and hugged Charley's sleeping form. Uzmahndey took an alarmed step back. "What's she doing?"

"Being a mother," Charlie called out through the open bathroom door. "She helps us through our growth spurts."

He looked in to watch her struggle into jeans. "You have these growth spurts, too?"

"I did. They stop at eighteen." She slipped her bra on. "You can have my bed if you're still feeling groggy. I'm up. And in search of medication." She tugged it into place and fastened it. "My head is throbbing. I thought champagne was supposed to be fun."

Lying back down is a good idea. I have a lot of work to do.

Uzmahndey stretched out in Charlie's still-warm bed and closed his eyes.

Uzmahndey and Charley were led around the rest of the morning by a stoic Angela. They caught a taxi to the airport, where they had tickets waiting for them for a flight back to Perth. It was during the short flight that Ugly and Bad came back online.

Uz, you should be ashamed of yourself for the way you've been thinking about Charlie.

"It's not his fault," Angela said. She was seated in the middle, with Charley on one side slumped sound asleep up against the window clasping Snugglesaurus, and Uzmahndey on her other side in an aisle seat. Across the aisle Charlie was watching a video. Angela squeezed his hand. "Relax. All three xenobots will begin restoring your memories now."

Disembarking at Perth, they took a taxi to the Swan River Resort. Back in their room, Charley slumped onto a bed, while Angela and Charlie began packing all their suitcases. Uzmahndey stood in the middle of the room looking around. The place looked familiar.

"You're in the way." Angela pushed him down onto the double bed.

"Angela?"

A smile flickered. "Finally."

"Mnemosyne was in Lake Hillier."

"He's starting to remember," Charlie said.

He looked to her. "You're Angela's daughter."

Angela handed him a suitcase. "If you are feeling better how about packing yourself."

Uzmahndey began stuffing his things into his suitcase. "Mnemosyne rose up out of the lake. She was pink."

"She is the real reason the lake is truly pink," Angela said.

"Then what happened?"

"She attacked our memories. She erased the short term memories of all of you, including our pilot and guide, and blocked access to your long term ones, then scrambled the connections between the two. But her attack on my memory failed for some reason. But she did something to me. I feel different. But my memories are intact."

Now do you realize what's going on?

Uzmahndey stared at Angela with dawning awareness. "She doesn't remember she's a..."

Don't say it.

"Don't say what, Good?" Angela asked.

"...wife and mother?"

"Of course I remember."

Uzmahndey studied her. "Did you ever sleep any last night?"

"No. Bad case of insomnia, I guess."

"What ever happened with Mnemosyne?"

"When she focused her power on my memory, it was turned back against her somehow. It wrecked her mind, and she sank back into the lake."

"But you're okay?"

"I feel different. I'm not sure what all was affected. But my memories are intact." She closed the last suitcase and began rousing Charley. "I've got my hands full. You two get the suitcases."

Uzmahndey wheeled his and Angela's luggage out into the hall. Charlie followed with hers and Charley's. "I'm glad you remember who I am now."

Uzmahndey dropped his gaze. "Sorry about how I was staring at you."

"Don't be. I enjoyed it." She rolled hers and her brother's suitcases down the hall ahead of him, wriggling her tail as she went.

Uzmahndey turned to Angela coming out of the room supporting a dazed Charley. "Did Snugglesaurus teach her to do that?"

"No. She watches a lot of Tik Tok videos." She peered into his face. "You don't enjoy it?"

He scowled. "Of course not."

"How about when I do it?" She walked ahead and mimicked Charlie's strut.

The scowl faded. "That's a different matter." Angela stopped and turned back around to stare at him, awaiting further explanation. "A woman playing with her man is a good thing. A sweet thing."

"So the problem isn't what she's doing, it's who she's doing it for." Angela resumed her strut down the hall as she dragged Charley along. "I'll practice playing with *my* man."

That *is bringing back all kinds of good memories.*

"Yes it is." Uzmahndey admired Angela's hip action as he rolled his suitcase down the hall after her. He could see how Angela might forget she was a robot. He forgot at times. Maybe if they both could forget their relationship would be a lot sweeter.

By the time they touched down in Hobart on Tasmania, off the southeastern tip of Australia, Uzmahndey's memories had been fully restored.

We are finished.

You can say thank you now.

What for? Making him aware of what a nightmare he's caught up in?

"He has a family." Angela, seated next to Uzmahndey, squeezed his hand as the plane taxied to the gate. "Is that a nightmare?"

Uzmahndey studied Angela's wracked face smiling back at him in an off-kilter way. She really didn't know she was a robot. Apparently, the rest of her memories had been unaffected. She could recall everything but that. Was this permanent damage? Or could Snugglesaurus restore her memories like it had everyone else's? Repairing memory banks must be more difficult than restoring connections between synapses in human brains. Or whatever the AI had done to them. Which was yet another worry. Who's to say what he remembered now were actual memories of his, or were false memories implanted by the AI via the xenobots? So maybe Angela *wasn't* a robot? Maybe they all just *remember* her being one?

He wondered if she had remembered to seal the portal at lake Hillier? "Did you drop a Cheerio in the lake?"

"Of course. That's why we went there."

Snugglesaurus had a rental car waiting for them upon exiting the terminal.

"Are you okay to drive?" Charlie asked Uzmahndey with faux concern.

He handed the keys to her. "Go for it. You need to practice. Who knows when we might need you to drive again."

Charlie drove the short distance to Club Wyndham Seven Mile Beach Resort, where Snugglesaurus had a landominium waiting for them.

"This is huge," Charlie exclaimed, as she parked before a four-unit single story building.

"Snugglesaurus thought you'd enjoy a break from hotel rooms," Angela said. She led Charley inside while Uzmahndey and Charlie brought the suitcases in.

"Two bedrooms," Charlie marveled.

"Charley and I get the double bed," Angela lugged him into the larger bedroom.

Uzmahndey eyed Charlie uncertainly as they carried their suitcases into the smaller bedroom. He sighed in relief at the sight of two single beds.

Charlie stretched out on the one nearest the door. "Can I have your phone? I didn't get to finish watching that movie on the plane."

"Sure." Uzmahndey handed it to her. "First I want to ask you something. Have you noticed anything unusual about Angela?"

Charlie smiled up at him. "That she's forgotten she's a robot?"

"What do you think we should do?"

"Nothing. She seems to remember everything else. What can it hurt?"

"I don't know."

"Let her enjoy being a real live human for a while."

Uzmahndey backed out and closed the door. He checked in on the other bedroom. Angela had cuddled up in the double bed with Charley.

She smiled her regret at him. "Just tonight. Tomorrow he should be okay."

Uzmahndey nodded then backed out. He stepped up to a sliding glass door and gazed out upon a small patio surrounded by a privacy fence. He was too restless to settle down, having sat the entire day in airports and on airplanes. Snatching up a key card from where Angela had dropped it on the coffee table, he bound out the front door.

Blacktop lanes and cement sidewalks wound across spacious open grass lawns. He wound his way to the resort entrance then crossed Surf Road to a sandy parking lot. From there a short path led through trees to Seven Mile Beach. Uzmahndey walked along the edge of the surf on the nearly-deserted beach in the daze he had grown accustomed to. Was it winter? Summer? He had crossed the equator at some point. It felt like his brain now swirled in the opposite direction. He had crossed so many time zones he had no idea what day of the week it was. It was daytime, the bright sun insisted on that. Other than that he had no idea when he was.

Uzmahndey had worse concerns than his temporal confusion. Angela was an incredible piece of alien tech that had been knocked off-line by a fireball, sandblasted nearly to destruction by a sandstorm and hurriedly rebuilt in a haphazard way, then had her memory banks so rattled by Mnemosyne she believed she was a real woman. It was a wonder she could still function at all. Could he rely on her? He had no choice. They had nearly gone all the way around the world. Tasmania wasn't that far from Hawaii. He needed to hang on for just a little longer.

Then what? Would Angela relinquish Charlie and Charley to him once the mission was complete? Or did she have further plans for them? Did she have further plans for him? That depended on Ghost. He claimed to be liberating humans from their evil overlords who had ruled them since the dawn of prehistory so Earth could join an intergalactic community. My God, that sounded like a bad Netflix series. Ghost claimed he wasn't here to conquer the Earth, but how could Uzmahndey believe him? Or Angela? Or Snugglesaurus? Or even Good, Bad, and Ugly, for that matter?

You can believe us.

We're on your side.

Which is our *side. If you thrive, we thrive.*

"You do realize Angela hears everything you say to me."

No she doesn't.

There is a limit to her range. She has to be physically near.

Besides, you don't think we're morons, do you? We can whisper.

"Whisper? Inside my head?"

She can't hear us now.

We are far enough away and we are speaking softly.

So what do you want to know?

"How will Angela believing herself to be a real woman affect our mission?"

It shouldn't impact it at all.

She has desired to be a real woman ever since she encountered you.

So play along and reap the benefits.

"That seems awfully cold and manipulative."

Not if it's what she wants.

She's on an even keel now.

Trying to convince her otherwise could make her more unstable than ever.

"Valid point. Moving right along, what do you think will happen when this is over?"

Angela may be deluded, but she can't lie.

At least the original version couldn't.

Since Mnemosyne rattled her at Lake Hillier, I'm not sure what she's capable of.

Let's assume she still can't lie.

Always Mister Brightside.

No matter, her primary concerns haven't changed. Completing the mission and protecting the children.

She will always do what's best for them.

But is that leaving them with this dimwit once everything is over?

"Who says I want them?"

Are you kidding me? Have you taken a good look at your boy lately?

With every growth spurt your son looks more and more like you.

And then there's Charlie.

You are crazy about her.

Just in what way is the question.

"Strictly as a father."

Uh-huh.

Before Uzmahndey could further defend his mixed-up feelings for Charlie, he saw someone walking up the beach toward him. He had to stop talking. He had left his phone with Charlie, so he couldn't fake a conversation over it.

Uzmahndey stopped worrying about how weird he would look talking to himself when he saw how weird this person approaching him looked. The man was cartoonishly disheveled. The wrinkles beneath the caked-on dirt made his face look like fractured darkly-tinted glass, his hair a wild mop, his beard nearing ZZ Top proportions. Was he homeless, living on the beach? Uzmahndey began a wide detour around him. He certainly didn't want to get close enough to smell him.

Uzmahndey froze. The beach bum looked familiar. "Keanu?"

Keanu stared back at him with glazed eyes. What had Eros done to him?

Uzmahndey rushed up. "What happened to you?"

Keanu focused dim eyes on Uzmahndey. "Who's Your Mama?"

"How did you get to Australia?"

Keanu shrugged.

"Have they hurt you?"

Keanu's vague face blossomed. "I've been with these two babes. They've worn me out."

"That was only a fantasy. It was all just in your mind."

Keanu's grin nearly shattered his fractured face. "If that was fantasy then you can have reality. It's been incredible."

Uzmahndey took his arm. "You're coming with me."

Keanu didn't resist as he was led back up the beach.

"Why did Eros bring you here?"

Keanu shrugged. "We were making love in the surf. On the beach. In the trees. On the back of an out." This isn't a typo.

'On the back of an out' is a play on outback. They are in Australia.

"You're not making sense."

"Then I woke up on the beach back there and they were gone."

Uzmahndey escorted Keanu to their condo. He expected stiff resistance from Angela.

She surprised him. "He needs to take a shower. I'll wash his clothes."

"You're okay with him staying with us?"

"He's your friend? The one you were worried about Gaia taking?"

"Yes. Why do you think she let him go? And delivered him to us?"

"I don't know. It's a curious development. I'll keep an eye on him."

Uzmahndey gave up trying to figure out Angela. Had the assault on her memory banks rattled her judgment?

"Go take a shower. You can use my shaving kit." He produced it then shoved Keanu toward the bathroom. "Hand your clothes out so Angela can wash them."

Keanu looked all around the room, then back to Angela.

"Where's the baby?"

"In the other room. And she's not a baby anymore. It's a long story."

Before Keanu could ask any more questions that would take way too long to answer, Uzmahndey shut the bathroom door in his face. He turned to Angela. "Can Snugglesaurus send him back home?"

"To be caught again after just escaping?"

"You really think he escaped? Maybe he was released."

"Then we should find out why."

"So he is just going to tag along? What if he's a plant? What if he's been turned? He could murder the kids in the middle of the night."

"How will he do that? I'm not sleeping much now anyway. I'll watch him all night."

Uzmahndey threw his arms up. "I give up. I do not understand you."

"If Gaia thinks to use your friend against us, I want to learn how she intends to do it. Maybe we can turn him against her."

<u>Angela has the right idea. Keep your friends close.</u>

<u>Your enemies closer.</u>

<u>*And your friends who may actually be your enemies closest.*</u>

Angela picked up the clothes Keanu had dropped outside the bathroom door. "Besides, Charlie needs a man she can play with."

So that was it. Angela was playing matchmaker. "No way. He's way older than her."

"You are older than Charlie and she's attracted to you." Angela passed him on the way to the laundry nook. "He looks to be about the same age as you."

"He is. But that's beside the point."

Once Keanu had shaved and showered and was wearing laundered clothes, he looked much improved. He really didn't appear to have been harmed in any way. He wasn't injured or malnourished. Merely exhausted. Sexually depleted, if he was to be believed.

When Charlie emerged from her bedroom after finishing her movie she seemed intrigued by the newcomer. "You're Hawaiian?"

"One-hundred per cent." Keanu's eyes feasted on her.

Uzmahndey flared. "Hey, Keanu, that's my daughter you are drooling over."

Charlie frowned over herself. "I look terrible." She turned apologetic eyes to Keanu. "I've been feeling bad. Too much champagne." She rushed back into the bedroom she had just emerged from.

Uzmahndey followed her in, slamming the door. "What do you think you are doing?"

Charlie gathered up a clean outfit. "I just told you. Taking a shower."

Uzmahndey blocked the door. "He's too old for you."

"*You* brought him here." She walked around him and out the door.

Since Charley was still in no condition to go out, Snuggle-saurus had dinner delivered from the resort restaurant. Keanu stared at fifteen-year old Charley sitting slack-faced at the table with the stuffed dinosaur in his lap. "Isn't he a little old for that?"

Uzmahndey ignored the question. This was Angela's party, she could deal with the intruder. His friend. Possible saboteur. Sexual hedonist. Who was in danger of becoming the focus of Charlie's naïve but lustful attention. Yet his friend had been kidnapped because of him. Uzmahndey's mind was in such turmoil he couldn't eat, no matter how much Good, Bad, and Ugly demanded.

Keanu cornered Uzmahndey after dinner. "I don't know what happened to me, buddy, or how I ended up on Tasmania, but I am clearly intruding here. Loan me money for a plane ticket and I'll pay you back when you get back to Hawaii."

Uzmahndey slumped. "No way. If you were intruding Angela would let you know." He chuckled. "She doesn't hold much back." He scratched at where his short-lived beard had been. "I don't know how you are here, either, or why, but until this is over you're safer with us than back in Hawaii where they kidnapped you in the first place."

"Who kidnapped me? Until what is over?"

"It's a long unbelievable story. I promise to tell you all about it when we're both back safe in Hawaii. There is just too much going on right now."

"Okay. But I promise not to bother your daughter."

"Don't bet on it. Angela has plans."

Keanu had no reply to that. But he did have a question. "What's wrong with your son?"

"Moody teenager. He should be okay in the morning."

That night the mattress was pulled off one single bed and placed on the floor in the other bedroom for Keanu to sleep on. Angela wanted him sleeping in her room so she could keep an eye on him from the double bed she shared with Charley. That meant Uzmahndey and Charlie were to share the other single bed.

Or so he thought. When she came in from changing into her pajamas, she frowned at the sight of Uzmahndey under the covers. "Really?"

"We've shared a bed before. What's the big deal?"

"Now we've got company."

"And you don't want Keanu to know you're still sleeping with daddy." Her frown never lessened. "Fine."

Uzmahndey jumped out of bed, snatched up his clothes, and bolted out the door.

"The couch doesn't look too uncomfortable." Uzmahndey looked back to see Charlie smiling as she shut the bedroom door in his face.

He slung his clothes to the floor and flung himself down on the couch. It was a damn couch. Of course it was uncomfortable.

Chapter 31

Tessellated Pavement

The next morning Uzmahndey woke up creaky and cranky. The door to Charlie's bedroom was closed. He peeked into the other bedroom to find Angela in bed with Charley, who was still asleep and in possession of Snugglesaurus, while Keanu slept on the mattress on the floor. Angela's open eyes tracked him.

"How is Charles this morning?" Uzmahndey asked quietly.

"He should be okay." Angela climbed out of bed and began taking off her pajamas.

Uzmahndey looked to Keanu. His now wide open eyes tracked her.

"We'd appreciate some privacy."

"I appreciate what I'm seeing."

Uzmahndey kicked the mattress. "I don't appreciate you drooling over Angela."

Keanu at last averted his leer. "Sure, buddy."

"Stop behaving like a jerk, Uzmahndey." Angela was now naked, and seemed to be in no hurry to get dressed. Which caused Keanu's leer to renew.

Uzmahndey kicked *him* this time instead of the mattress.

"Uzmahndey!" Angela barked. "I've warned you. You don't realize how strong you are."

Uzmahndey snatched up Keanu's clothes and threw them in his face. "Get dressed." He gathered up Angela's clothes and tossed them to her. "You, too."

She let the clothes fall to the floor without attempting to catch them. "Get out of here and get dressed yourself."

The rest of the morning didn't go any better. Uzmahndey walked to the restaurant and brought back doughnuts and coffee and juice. Everyone was up and dressed except Charlie, who was up but still in pajamas.

Charley was bursting with energy. Despite Uzmahndey's foul mood, he couldn't help but smile at his son. "It's good to have you back among the living."

"I'm starving."

"That's why I bought *three* dozen doughnuts." Uzmahndey set everything down on the kitchen counter. "*One* dozen is for you."

Charley tore open the box and feasted.

"There's something I need to tell you. About Angela. There's been a development."

Charley smiled with a mouthful of Bavarian. "Charlie already told me."

"And you're okay with it?"

He shrugged. "Don't know what we can do about it." He stuffed in half a glazed.

"How did you sleep?" Charlie hinted at remorse as she sipped an orange juice.

"As good as I've ever slept on a couch."

Keanu ignored the doughnuts. "You can drop me off at the airport."

"No." Angela directed an unsmiling look at Uzmahndey. "If he kicks you again, *I'll* kick *him*."

Charlie was aghast. "You kicked Keanu?"

"Are you guys going to finish those?" Charley had devoured his dozen.

Keanu's stoicism broke. He snatched up a doughnut before Charley could get to it, and a cup of coffee. Which he sipped. "It's good."

"It's how you like it, Neo." Uzmahndey replied.

Keanu looked to Angela. "You better get one." He glanced at Charley still gobbling them up. "They're going fast."

Uzmahndey picked up a doughnut. "She doesn't eat much."

Angela concurred. "My appetite's been down lately."

"Mine's been up. " Charlie licked sugar glaze from her lips. Slowly, the way she'd seen it done in online videos. Uzmahndey tensed. Was she trying to flirt with Keanu?

Angela noticed his expression darken. "I mean it, Uz. Don't kick Keanu again. You'll lame him."

Charley looked all around as he chewed. "Can't we all just get along?"

Uzmahndey drove. Keanu sat up front with him. In back, Angela sat in the middle, with Charley on one side involved with Snugglesaurus and Charlie on the other side reading from Uzmahndey's phone.

"Tessellated pavement is relatively flat rock that is subdivided into more or less regular rectangular blocks resembling tiles on a mosaic floor. The most well-known example of this is in Australia on Tasmania Island. The tessellated pavement consists of a marine platform on the shore of Pirate's Bay at Eaglehawk Neck on the Tasmin Peninsula. The rock is mostly siltstone that formed during the Permian. Millennia of erosion by wave action washing sea water carrying sand over the siltstone and depositing salts in the cracks have created this distinct geologic feature."

After leaving the resort, they drove east on the Tasmin Highway and crossed the bridge over the estuary of Tiger Head Bay and Orielton Lagoon onto Arthur Highway. This took them out of the city through sparse farmland, snaking back to the coast. At Dunalley they crossed the Denison Canal and followed the coast south to Eaglehawk Neck. There they turned off Arthur Highway onto a narrow road that led them to a dirt lot overlooking the ocean.

Uzmahndey parked, and everyone piled out. A short tree-lined dirt path brought them to a set of wooden steps leading down to the water's edge.

"Now be careful," Uzmahndey cautioned Keanu. "We're near a portal. This is when a mythological god is likely to attack us."

Keanu snorted his disbelief, but stopped in mid-snort when he witnessed how Angela grew vigilant in the lead, while Charlie and Charley both huddled around Uzmahndey.

Charlie shot Keanu a nervous look. "He's not kidding."

"Yeah, buddy. Like that sea monster on top of that one-hundred foot wave at Giant's Causeway in Northern Ireland. Remember? You're the one who sent me a link to the video."

Keanu made a hurried worried scan of the open sea then rushed to catch up to the others.

Angela stepped onto the tessellated pavement. The flat rectangles of dark rock of all sizes looked like paving stones. "Stay here." She proceeded across the regular arrangement of irregular flat rocks toward the water.

Uzmahndey drew Charlie and Charley nearer. Neither objected, huddling close.

Keanu peered over their shoulders, safely behind the trio. "What's she doing?"

"Placing a Cheerio," Charley answered.

"What?"

"A xenobot," Charlie said.

"What?"

"Just shut up and watch," Uzmahndey said.

At the water's edge, Angela inserted a Cheerio into a fissure at the juncture of four of the larger stones. She rose and walked back.

"That was easy," Uzmahndey commented. Angela nodded as she approached the staircase leading down to the beach. "Why was that easy?"

"Their attack at Lake Hillier failed." Angela stepped up off the rocks. "So maybe they are more cautious now."

Uzmahndey glanced at Keanu. "Or maybe they are counting on someone else doing their dirty work."

"If I believed that I would toss him out into the ocean." The group parted to let Angela pass by, with a startled Keanu taking a half-dozen steps back. She smiled at him with a smile not the least reassuring. "After bashing his head open on the rocks."

Charley fell into step behind her.

Uzmahndey slapped Keanu on the shoulder. "She must not believe you're a threat to the kids. Looks like it's your lucky day."

He didn't appear to feel lucky.

Until Charlie took his hand. "You'll be okay."

Angela insisted Charlie drive back to the resort. Uzmahndey was okay with that; Charlie needed more experience driving. What he didn't like was Angela insisting Keanu sit up front with Charlie. Which left him squeezed into the back to one side of Angela.

"We need to encourage this," she whispered.

"No, we don't."

"Charlie has not been with any grown man but you."

"So?"

"She needs to mate. The genes need to propagate."

"That's what this is about?" Uzmahndey nodded toward the front seat. "Advancing the new hybrid race that will take over the Earth?"

"Do I get to mate, too?" Charley asked. He had set Snuggle-saurus aside to listen.

"When you are an adult," Angela said.

"Don't worry, Charley," Uzmahndey said. "That's only a couple days from now."

"What's all the buzzing in the back seat?" Charlie called back.

"Keep your eyes on the road!" Uzmahndey barked. Seeing the grin on Keanu's face, he added, "You, too, Keanu."

Back at the resort, Angela suggested they all go swimming. To keep the peace Keanu averted his eyes when Angela emerged from her bedroom wearing her one piece. But when Charlie emerged from the other bedroom in her bikini he couldn't help himself. Angela offered a pair of Uzmahndey's trunks to Keanu.

When Charley complained his trunks were too tight, Uzmahndey tossed his other pair to him. "Take these. I don't feel like swimming."

"Suit yourself." Angela led the rest of them out the door. Keanu gave him an apologetic look then turned his eyes forward to admire Charlie walking in front of him. She was using the strut she had learned on Tik Tok to good effect.

Once they were all gone, Uzmahndey settled down on the patio. "Is Angela far enough away that we can hold a private conversation?"

Yes. Especially since she is concentrating on Charlie and Keanu.

That's her primary concern now.

So we're on our own. What do you want to know?

"What do you three think about Keanu?"

Is it really him? Yes.

"How can you be sure?"

Snugglesaurus ran his DNA. It's him.

"How did a stuffed toy get a DNA sample?"

Angela got it.

"How?"

A strand of hair, most likely.

Not the way you're thinking. Are you really jealous of a robot?

Uzmahndey let that slide. "So Angela is convinced he is what he says he is, with no memory of what happened to him except believing he was engaged in a non-stop orgy."

Just because it really is Keanu and he really doesn't know what really happened to him doesn't mean she really trusts him.

Snugglesaurus located a bug planted under his skin.

"So Gaia could track us away from the portals?"

Not anymore. Snugglesaurus deactivated it.

But that was way too obvious.

"What do you mean?"

Most likely it was intended to be found. To throw us off. Make it seem like we had located the threat and neutralized it. While a more devious weapon has been concealed in Keanu.

"Surely Angela realizes this."

Angela is not playing with a full deck right now, as you well know. But Snugglesaurus remains vigilant concerning your friend.

"Is Snugglesaurus okay with Angela's plan to get Keanu and Charlie together?"

Yes. Their ultimate goal is to spread the alien genes throughout the human race.

"That will take centuries."

So? Who says the aliens' time frame is the same as ours?

Perhaps what passes as centuries for us is only weeks or months for Ghost.

Precisely. Ever wonder why Ghost is so hands-off, as you say? Maybe to him his approach doesn't seem hand's off. Maybe he has a different frame of reference when it comes to time. Perhaps only seconds or minutes pass for him while we go through days or weeks.

There is a more frightening thought to consider. Should we tell him?

"Hey! Talk to me. Not to each other."

Who's to say this is the only Angela?

Our Angela could be the one tasked with securing all the portals. But there could be dozens of others, maybe hundreds, seducing humans and propagating the new hybrid race.

"No way."

Why not? With a one-day pregnancy a host of Angelas could produce a lot of hybrid children in a short time.

Who with a months-long childhood would quickly grow up to reproduce.

Uzmahndey jumped to his feet.

"Enough. You've given me enough new shit to worry about."

Just one more thing.

Uzmahndey moaned, but didn't order Good to shut up.

There aren't many portals remaining to be sealed.

Which means Gaia must know where we are headed.

We're talking football now, superstar. You should be able to grasp this.

"You've lost me, Bad."

When you've got the ball in front of your own goal post the entire field is open. You can strike anywhere. But once you advance into the opponent's red zone your options are limited. It's much easier for the other team to defend twenty yards than the entire field. Right now we are on their ten yard line. Gaia knows where we are headed. The end zone. Don't you think she'll be making a goal line stand at these last few portals?

"How does Keanu fit in to their defense?"

Perhaps he's a blitzing linebacker.

It was nearly dark by the time everyone came in from the pool. Charlie and Keanu seemed totally at ease with each other. Angela seemed almost apologetic. "Did we leave you alone too long?"

"I wasn't alone. Good, Bad, and Ugly are good company."

Keanu looked all around. "Who?"

"His xenobots," Charlie said.

"Hey, Dad, there was this amazing girl at the pool. She was beautiful." Charley turned to Angela. "How long are we staying here?"

"We leave tomorrow morning," Uzmahndey insisted. "Early."

Dejected, Charley flopped down into a chair. "We always leave way early."

"So we need to get dressed and go to dinner," Angela said. "Charlie and Charley, go get changed."

"Together?" Charlie squealed. "No way."

"Then change in the bathroom." Angela started toward the other bedroom. "Keanu, come on."

"Together?" Uzmahndey objected. "No way."

Angela went into the bedroom then came back out with her clothes.

"Go on, Keanu. And be quick." After everyone went to their appointed rooms, she took her swim suit off. "What is your problem?"

"You are acting like Keanu is a member of the family."

"He will be." She walked out to the patio to drape the damp suit across the back of a chair.

"So it's settled. Keanu and Charlie."

Angela walked back in to begin dressing.

"They seem to like each other."

"I don't like it."

"I'm sorry, but that doesn't matter."

"Charley is starting to take an interest in girls. Will you find a mate for him, too?"

"When the time comes."

"I'm his father. So that *will* matter."

Angela sat to slip on sandals. "Okay. You will have input on selecting his mate. Is that better?"

"In our culture people select their own mates."

"And how has that worked out? Snugglesaurus, can you give us some statistics on divorce and domestic violence?"

"Leave Snugglesaurus out of it."

Keanu emerged dressed, with wet swim trunks in hand.

"I *can* pass block," Uzmahndey warned him as he went by on the way out to the patio. "I can take out a blitzing line-backer."

"You mystify me sometimes." Keanu draped the trunks over a chair then walked back inside.

Charlie emerged in a fetching halter top and short skirt, beaming. "Are we ready to go eat?"

Uzmahndey remained sullen throughout the meal. Charlie and Keanu chattered happily. Charley sized up the attractive teenage girls in the restaurant. While Angela kept a close watch on Uzmahndey.

Back at the condo, sleeping arrangements were decided. "Put the mattress back on your bed," Angela instructed Charley.

"Where's Keanu going to sleep?" Uzmahndey asked.

"In the double bed."

"With you?" Uzmahndey asked, hackles rising.

"No, with you. I'll sit up."

"You'll sit up all night?" Keanu asked. "Again? Why?"

"I'm suffering from a bad case of insomnia."

"*I'm* not sleeping with him," Uzmahndey announced.

"Then you can have the couch again."

"Fine." Uzmahndey pulled out the covers he had used the night before.

Angela, Keanu, and Charley disappeared behind closed doors. Charlie sat next to Uzmahndey on the couch. He glared at her. "What are you doing?"

"Waiting for Charley to change into his pajamas." She took his hand. "You could sleep with me."

Uzmahndey smiled, relaxing for the first time since they had gotten back from the Tessellated Pavement. "Thanks. But Angela wouldn't like it. She's planning on you and Keanu eventually sharing a bed. Once she can trust him not to kill you."

Charlie leaned away. "Why would he want to kill me?"

"It's a dangerous world, Charlie. You need to be careful who you let near you."

Charley emerged in pajamas. "Your turn."

Charlie stood with a dark expression, and went into the bedroom and closed the door without another word.

Charley bounced about the room. "Dad, you should have seen Mia. She was beautiful. And she was wearing this little bikini smaller than Charlie's."

Uzmahndey smiled at his son's enthusiasm. "We'll have to see who Gaia sends your way."

Charley froze. "What does that mean?"

"It means you need to be careful who you let near you. It could be a mythological god in the disguise of a close friend."

"Oh, that." Charley was dismissive. "Angela says they won't be a problem once we seal all the portals." He bounded over to the bedroom door and knocked. "You almost done?"

"No," Charlie barked back.

Charley burst in anyway.

"Charley! I swear!"

"Swear all you want." He closed the door behind him. "I'm tired."

Uzmahndey stretched out on the couch with a grin. Those two might be half alien, but they behaved like typical human brother and sister.

Chapter 32

Moeraki Boulders

Uzmahndey awoke from his second night sleeping on the couch just as creaky but a little less cranky than the morning before. He saw Charley was the first to emerge from a bedroom. "You're up early."

"She kicked me out."

"What did you do to your sister this time?"

"Nothing. She's getting dressed."

Already? Not like Charlie. Uzmahndey wondered if she was trying not to antagonize him by not going around in her pajamas in front of Keanu?

The other bedroom door opening diverted Uzmahndey's attention from his son. Keanu staggered out wearing only the pants he had worn the day before. He appeared nearly as frazzled as when Uzmahndey had found him on the beach.

"Come out here," Keanu directed, heading for the patio.

Uzmahndey rose from the couch and followed. "How did you sleep last night?"

"Terrible." Keanu collapsed into a chair. "Do you know how freaky it is to try to sleep with someone sitting up staring at you all night long?"

"Yes."

"She followed me to the bathroom."

Uzmahndey couldn't help but chuckle.

"I got up in the middle of the night to go, and she was right on my tail."

"Wasn't it crowded in there?"

"She didn't follow me in, thank God. But she was waiting outside the door when I came out. Am I a prisoner?"

"No. You can leave whenever you want." Uzmahndey stared hard at Keanu. "You don't want to leave anymore, do you? Because of Charlie." When Keanu shrugged and looked away, he pressed on. "You are the first man she has met outside of the family. She is extremely inexperienced. She has all these feelings and biology, and nowhere to go with them. Be gentle with her."

Keanu met his gaze. "I would never hurt Charlie."

The sliding glass door opened and Angela stuck her head out. Unlike the men, she was fully dressed. "We need to get going."

When Keanu leaped to his feet, Uzmahndey laughed. "Boy, she sure has you hopping."

"She is freaking me out."

"I understand, Neo. I've spent a lot more time with her than you have." Uzmahndey clapped him on the shoulder. "Let's go find out what's in store for us today." They walked back inside.

Charlie was modestly dressed in jeans and a baggy shirt. She frowned between the two coming in from the patio and her brother seated at the kitchen table eating stale doughnuts. "You men need to get dressed."

After turning in the rental car at the airport, they boarded their flight to Denedin, New Zealand. Snugglesaurus had created some online travel documents for Keanu, so he wasn't a problem. Having to make connections at Melbourne and Auckland, the trip turned into a full day of air travel. While in the air, Charley was involved with Snugglesaurus, Charlie and

Keanu chatted nearly the entire time, while Angela watched over the two.

Leaving Uzmahndey on his own. He couldn't even consult with Good, Bad, and Ugly, since Angela sat right next to him and would overhear everything they said. With nothing else to do, he looked up where they were headed on his phone. 'The Moeraki Boulders, also known as the Stonehenge of New Zealand, lie on the beach in Otago, on the east coast of South Island. They are remarkable for their size, up to two meters in diameter and weighing several tons, and their nearly spherical shape. They are calcite concretions formed in ancient sea floor sediments around 60 million years ago. The largest are estimated to have taken 4 million years to reach their current size. Over the millennia the sea floor rose to form the cliffs now above the beach. The boulders littering this beach emerged from the eroding cliffs of soft mudstone in which they formed. As the cliff eroded, the stones fell out and rolled across the beach. Even today there are boulders remaining in the mudstone that will eventually fall onto the beach as they come loose. Currently there are 50 or so stones. Originally there were many more, but many were taken away. The remaining stones have been declared a national treasure by the New Zealand government in order to protect them.

While at the Auckland Airport awaiting their connection, Uzmahndey interrupted Charlie and Keanu's private conversation. "Hey, Charlie, did you read up on the Moeraki Boulders?"

Both looked blankly at him.

"I know you like to hear about legends. A Maori story goes that long ago the Kahul Tipua people sailed out on an expedition to the mythical land of Hawaiiki."

He interrupted his own tale. "That sounds like Hawaii. Do you think the Maoris canoed to Hawaii? That would have been some trick."

Getting no response, he continued. "They were in a double-hulled waka – that's a canoe – called Arai Te Uru. They were attempting to transport sweet potato plants to grow back home. A storm hit and they wrecked off the Otago Coast at Shag Point. The hull of the canoe magically became a reef near the mouth of the Waihemo River. Calabashas, kumaras, and eel baskets washed ashore to form these boulders."

He smiled. "That's why some people call them eel pots. They also call them hooligan's gallstones, giant gobstoppers, alien's brains, and the bowling balls of giants."

"That's nice," was Charlie's only response. While Keanu rolled his eyes.

When they stepped off the plane in Dunedin, Angela pressed them on to the car rental desk. Uzmahndey drove, with Charley seated up front with him. In back, Angela positioned Charlie in the middle, while she took one side and Keanu the other.

Nearly as soon as Uzmahndey drove away from Denedin Airport he saw in the rearview mirror Charlie had cuddled up in Keanu's arms, and both were dozing. So Angela had them sleeping together already, Uzmahndey fumed. Even if it was just in the back seat of a car. Bad things happen in the back seats of cars.

Coming in to Dunedin from the west on Highway 1, he skirted the waterfront at the head of Macandrew Bay and emerged from the city into open countryside. This turned into yet another scenic drive, bucolic rolling hills of small farms and expansive pastures interspersed with dense forests. The road passed through the small town of Waitati and around Buckskin Bay, on through more farmland and past Hawksbury on the Waikouaiti River. The highway they were on followed this river for a short while then crossed it into the city of Waikouaiti. After that more of the same bucolicity, pictur-esque small farms and small towns set upon gentle verdant hills, until they came to Palmerston, where the highway made a sharp bend to the east. Arriving on the coast at Shag Point, they turned north and embarked on a picturesque drive along the rugged shoreline.

We are being followed.

Uzmahndey adjusted the rearview mirror away from his view of Charlie and Keanu so he could look out the back windshield.

"I don't see anyone."

They are hanging back now. They've been following us since Shag Point.

"How can you know this when I don't?"

You see everything always, but most times you see nothing.

He glanced into the back seat at Angela.

"Bad is getting cryptic on me. Have you seen anyone?"

Angela was already turned around looking out the back window.

"No."

I'm not being cryptic. Your sharp eyes see every detail. But these myriad details don't always register in your little brain.

"Bullshit. I have great situational awareness. I can scan a playing field and plot out the course of every opposing defensive player who might try to cover me."

"You are not playing football now," Angela said. "You are playing with our lives. Stay vigilant."

The road turned inland at Katiki Point. Just beyond the small town of Moeraki they arrived at the turnoff for the Boulders. Neither Uzmahndey nor Angela had spied a vehicle following them.

Dusk was approaching when Uzmahndey pulled into the parking lot. That late in the day no other parked cars were present.

"We're here," he announced to Charley, still engaged with Snugglesaurus. Angela nudged Charlie into awareness, and she raised a sleepy head from Keanu's shoulder.

Uzmahndey hopped out and watched the entrance. Several cars passed by on Highway 1, but none turned in. He joined Charley, who was studying the info board at the head of a foot trail leading down to the beach.

"Did you see something?" his son asked.

"I didn't, but Good, Bad, and Ugly did."

Angela passed by them onto the trail. "Let's do this and get out of here."

Charley followed her.

Charlie and Keanu lingered by the car.

"Come on!" Uzmahndey called out.

They joined him. "Is someone following us?" Charlie asked.

"Could be." He placed his hands on their shoulders and urged both ahead of him onto the trail.

The short trail took them down a hill to the beach. Huge stone orbs were strewn across the sand. Some were misshapen, some riven with cracks, some cracked open, but most were intact and symmetrically spherical.

Angela approached a fractured boulder split into four nearly equal sections. Charley ran along the surf, hopping from boulder to boulder when he could, when he couldn't from boulder down to sand up to boulder. Charlie walked off to look over the boulders, too.

Uzmahndey kept a close watch on Keanu. If he was under Gaia's influence this would be the time for him to attempt something, while he was near a portal and could expect help from the monsters. Keanu merely looked around, as engaged with the unusual scenery as any tourist.

"Look, Dad!" Charley ran up to the mud cliff where several stone boulders were embedded. "They're still being born."

Uzmahndey ignored him, approaching Keanu. "How are you feeling?"

Keanu tore his eyes from the boulders. "Tired, but okay."

"Did you and Charlie get a good nap?"

"We just slept. Are you mad at me for falling asleep?"

Angela finished placing the Cheerio. "Come on, Charley!"

"We just got here,"Charley answered, running up to her. "Do we have to drive all the way back now?"

"No. Snugglesaurus got us a room here at The Mill House."

Charlie joined them. "A bed sounds wonderful."

"After we eat," Charley insisted.

Angela started up the trail, with Charley behind, then Charlie and Keanu, with Uzmahndey bringing up the rear.

Angela stopped at the top of the hill, and the others ganged up behind her. Uzmahndey leaned around to see what was going on. The parking lot was full. A mob of sullen people, perhaps three dozen or more, were massed before them. Many held knives, clubs, and large rocks.

Charlie cringed. "Gaia worshippers."

"At least they don't have guns," her brother said.

"We're in New Zealand," Uzmahndey answered. "Guns aren't easy to come by here."

"Then why challenge us here?"

"Gaia is getting desperate," Angela answered. "There aren't many portals still open."

A man wielding a machete advanced. "We want the children. The rest can go."

Keanu slipped his arms around Charlie and pulled her close.

Uzmahndey knocked him back.

"What are you doing?" Charlie exclaimed.

Uzmahndey ignored her, glaring at Keanu. "Stay away from her."

Keanu raised his hands in surrender. "I was just trying to protect her."

"Stay with the children," Angela directed Uzmahndey. She walked toward the machete-wielding man. She easily dodged his wild swing with the weapon. A punch to the chest sent him flying back into the crowd. He didn't get up. Most of the others stepped back at her show of strength.

Six attacked, swarming her.

"Do something!" Charley yelled. He moved to help Angela.

Uzmahndey pulled him back. "I'm doing what she wants. Guarding you two."

Five men and two women peeled off from the mob and charged their position at the trailhead. A woman hurled a rock. Uzmahndey deflected it with his left arm then lunged forward. The largest of the men swung a heavy pipe wrench. Uzmahndey dodged it then crunched his jaw with a solid punch. Two other men tackled Uzmahndey, one stabbing a knife into his midsection. Uzmahndey cracked their heads together so hard they fell away unconscious. As Uzmahndey scrambled to his feet another man stabbed him in the back. Uzmahndey yanked the first knife from out of his stomach and slashed the man across the chest with it. As he staggered away, Uzmahndey slashed again, his throat this time, and the man collapsed in a spewing fountain of blood.

The other man and woman ran at the other three. When Charley stepped in front of his sister, the man swung a crowbar at his head. Charley deflected it with his left arm then punched him with a roundhouse right. The man stumbled back, and Charley tackled him.

The woman ran at Charlie with a knife. Keanu tried to get between them, but Charlie shoved him out of the way. The woman stabbed Charlie in the midsection. The blade sliced through her shirt, then glanced off her side. Charlie winced briefly, then smiled. "That's been tried before."

Uzmahndey snatched up the pipe wrench and cracked the back of the woman's head. He then turned on the man wrestling on the ground with Charley and bashed him, too. He kicked the unconscious body off his son. "You okay?"

Charley sprang to his feet. "Yeah." Despite what he claimed, the left arm he had deflected the crowbar with hung limp at his side.

Uzmahndey, bloody pipe wrench in hand, turned to see if any more attackers were coming. None were. Twenty additional bodies were strewn across the parking lot. Angela stood in the midst of them. Her clothes were in shreds, her skin gashed and slashed, hanks of hair gone from her head, and bits of exposed wiring sparked within the deepest cuts, but she snarled defiantly at those still on their feet. A man hurled a rock at her. She swatted it away with her bare hand as if it were a fly.

"Uzmahndey!" she yelled, never taking her eyes off those who remained upright.

"Yeah!"

"Are the kids okay?"

"You bet."

"Get their tires. I don't want any of them following us when we leave."

Uzmahndey picked up a knife from an attacker he had felled.

Charley snatched up another with the hand of his uninjured right arm. "I'll help."

Uzmahndey plunged a knife into tire after tire, as did Charley, while Angela held those who were still able to move at bay with her glare.

Charlie ran up to Uzmahndey. "You're hurt."

He glanced down to see his shirt was blood-soaked.

Keep going.

We've got you.

Yeah, man, don't stop! Slashing tires is fun!

"I can help," Keanu offered.

Uzmahndey wheeled on him with the knife. "No! You stay back!"

Keanu stumbled back.

Charlie was torn between going to him or going to Uzmahndey.

Uzmahndey resumed slashing. Soon, every tire in the lot except those on their vehicle was flat.

Angela kicked one felled attacker who was moaning.

"I don't know how many of you are still alive, but if you try to follow us I will stop and kill every last one of you." She lifted one limp body from the ground and hurled it into the middle of those still standing. They all scattered as it crashed into the dirt in their midst.

She turned to the other four. "Let's go."

Uzmahndey headed for the driver's door.

"No. You are in no shape to drive."

"I can drive," Keanu volunteered.

"Charlie drives," Angela ordered. "Uzmahndey, get in front with her. And try not to bleed all over the upholstery. We have to turn this car back in."

Uzmahndey happily complied. He did not feel like driving. He was feeling light-headed. He climbed in front. Angela, Charley, and Keanu piled in back.

Charlie turned to Angela. "We need to get him to a hospital. He's lost a lot of blood."

"No. The xenobots can take care of him. Just get us out of here." A rock hit the side of the car. "Now!"

Charlie peeled out across the lot. The still-upright worshippers scattered out of the way as she raced up the lane. Charlie screamed when the car jolted over a prone body.

Uzmahndey attempted to reassure her. "Don't worry about it. He was already dead." He looked back. "Most likely."

Charlie skidded to a stop at the entrance. "Which way?"

"I'm sure Snugglesaurus already has the address in there." Uzmahndey punched on the in-dash satellite navigation screen. "Go right."

"Uzmahndey!" He opened his eyes to see a frantic Charlie shaking him. "Thank god he's alive."

Thank me is more like it.

The car had stopped. It was dark. Charlie was crying. Uzmahndey felt dopey.

We are the reason you feel dopey.

Would you rather feel pain?

"No, thank you. Where are we?"

"The Mill House." Angela turned her attention to Charlie. "Go check us in. Me and Uzmahndey are in no condition to be seen."

"I'll go with her," Keanu volunteered.

Angela grabbed his arm. "You'll stay here."

Charlie climbed out and walked into the office.

"Dad?"

Uzmahndey tried to look back at his son, but his neck wouldn't work right. "Umm?"

"Stay awake." Angela slapped the back of his head. "Wake up!" Uzmahndey jerked upright.

"You three are drugging him too much. Dial it down some."

"Yeah, guys, Knock it off. I can deal with pain. This feels like I've had a concussion."Uzmahndey threw the door open and tumbled out of the car to the pavement. "Damn that hurt!"

Make up your mind!

"Good?" Uzmahndey gasped. "Ugly?"

Don't bother them. They are busy healing your wounds. They left it to me to keep you comfortable. Heh heh.

"Just do it, Bad," Angela ordered. "Don't toy with him."

The pain eased somewhat, but he couldn't get up off the ground.

Until Charlie helped him up. "What happened?"

Uzmahndey made it to unsteady feet. "Bad is having trouble adjusting my pain meds."

"I can help Charlie with Uzmahndey," Keanu offered. He had gotten out of the car with his arm still in Angela's steel grip.

She released him. "If you do something I don't like I will snap your spine. You saw what I did back there."

Keanu took Uzmahndey's other side and, with Charlie, led him toward the side entrance.

Uzmahndey looked back at the car. "Aren't you afraid they'll see our car?"

"It can't be seen from the road." Angela and Charley began pulling suitcases out of the trunk. "They have no reason to think we've stopped. We are too far from a portal for Gaia to be much help." She and Charley loaded up with all the suitcases and followed.

"I am going back to Hawaii the first chance I get," Keanu snarled. "You people don't trust me at all." He held up his right arm before Uzmahndey. "Look at that bruise she gave me."

Uzmahndey laughed. "You're complaining about a bruise? Half my blood has leaked out."

"I would have fought, too. To protect Charlie."

"Yeah, well, you can't blame us for being cautious."

"Yes I can."

The procession snuck into their room in a smaller building behind the main one.

"Take Uzmahndey into the bathroom," Angela ordered. "We've got to clean him up." Angela followed Charlie and Keanu as they lugged him in and lowered him down into the tub. "We've got him," she said to Keanu.

Keanu backed out of the bathroom. "I'm surprised you trust me alone with your son."

"Didn't you see Charley fight?" Uzmahndey called out. "He could take you easy, Neo. Even with only one good arm."

Angela and Charlie peeled the ripped clothes from Uzmahndey. "Oh god," Charlie gasped as the extent of the knife wounds became evident.

"The xenobots can heal them," Angela reassured. Once he was naked she began running water.

Uzmahndey smiled from close worried face to close stoic face. "My two favorite females."

"Bad, don't let him get goofy again," Angela ordered as she began scrubbing blood off him.

Uzmahndey focused on her. She was covered in nicks and bruises, but there were several deeper slashes that exposed circuitry. Had she even noticed? "Someone needs to take care of *you*."

"Yeah, a girl needs her make-up."

Charlie was aghast. "How can you two joke? You both were nearly killed."

"I won't let Uzmahndey die. I need him."

"In what way?" Receiving nothing but a mystified look from Angela, Uzmahndey reached up to pat a loose strip of skin on her arm back into place. "You can't go around looking like this."

"You can tend to me once I finish tending to you." Angela and Charlie dried him off. "Charlie, go get him a pillow."

"I'm sleeping in the tub?"

"Bad will make you feel like you are in a feather bed. Won't you, Bad?"

You bet.

"Thank you, Angela. For taking such good care of me."

"Thank you for protecting the children." She kissed him. "Now get a good night's sleep."

Chapter 33

Interlude Seven

"Rise and shine."

Uzmahndey opened his eyes to find himself supine in the bathtub, naked, with Angela leaning over him. He spied a palm tree tattoo on her upper left arm. "Where did that come from?"

"That's nothing." She stood and pulled up her shirt. A knife cut on her stomach had been incorporated into a beach scene at sunset. She presented her left side. Where she had been stabbed there was covered up with a hula girl in a grass skirt.

"And here." She turned around to show off an erupting volcano hiding a hideous scar on her back. She released her shirt to pull down her pants and hold up her right leg so a surfer on a monster wave masking a deep gash could be seen on her right thigh. "Keanu is good."

"With prison tattoos."

When Angela merely stared, he explained.

"He only used a needle and ballpoint pen ink. He could do much better if he had his instruments and real ink with him. And if he'd learned how to do something else besides Hawaiian-themed tats." Uzmahndey's smile faded. "So now you look like a biker girl back from a tropical cruise, instead of a victim of a gang rape."

Angela pulled her pants up. "I am no one's victim." She extended a hand and pulled him to his feet, looking over his several wounds. They were well on their way to being healed. "You should let Keanu take care of your scars like he did mine."

"No, thanks. If I ever get a tattoo it won't be something I'd be ashamed for any teammates to see on me in the locker room." He stepped out of the tub and into the undershorts from the pile of folded clothes she had brought in. "Maybe Eros. I wouldn't mind having her on my chest."

"Or under it, I bet."

"No way. She's too dangerous."

Angela concocted a wicked smile. "And I'm not?"

Uzmahndey finished dressing. "How is the rest of the family this morning?"

"Charley's left forearm is bruised. Other than that, he's okay."

"How about the happy couple?"

"I don't know. I haven't seen them yet."

That locked Uzmahndey into place. Except for his mouth. "You let them spend the night together? Unchaperoned?"

"Yes." Angela ushered him out of the bathroom.

"You trust him alone with her?"

"I think Keanu has proven himself by now. He is in love with her."

"And Charlie is in love with love."

"She's young. And fertile."

"Is that all that matters to you?" Angela returned a blank stare. "Of course it is."

Walking out of the bathroom, Uzmahndey spied Charley sitting out on the patio with Snugglesaurus. He joined him. "How is your arm doing?"

Charley held it up to present a spectacular bruise. "I can use it."

Uzmahndey smiled. "You're as tough as any safety I ever played against."

Charley tried his best not to bask in his father's compliment, but failed.

Uzmahndey asked the question he was really interested in having answered. "How'd you sleep last night? Alone?"

"No. Angela sat up with me."

Before Uzmahndey could inquire more about what transpired last night, the closed bedroom door opened. Charlie and Keanu emerged, she in pajamas and he in undershorts. Keanu darted into the bathroom. Charlie located Uzmahndey out on the patio then looked away.

He stepped back inside. "How was it?"

"Uzmahndey!" Angela yelled. "Leave her alone."

He turned on Angela. "Will she have a twenty-seven hour pregnancy? Will she be a mother tomorrow?"

"No. She is not like me."

He turned his scrutiny back to Charlie. "So when she gets pregnant will it be a normal pregnancy?"

"Not quite." Both Uzmahndey and Charlie focused their attention on Angela. "It will be much longer than a day, but not nine months. A compromise between the two genotypes she carries." Seeing both of them hanging on her words, Angela continued. "About half as long. Four to five months. That will be long enough not to arouse suspicions, to merely assume the baby premature."

"So is she?"

"Snugglesaurus says no. Conception will not be automatic. It will happen naturally."

Charlie erupted like the volcano tattooed on Angela's back. "Tell Snugglesaurus to keep his filthy digital probes out of my body!" She spun from Angela to Uzmahndey. "I hate you!" She careened from him back into the bedroom and slammed the door.

Keanu emerged from the bathroom to the door's echoes. "What's wrong with Charlie?"

"Nothing!" Uzmahndey gave such a dark scowl that Keanu took a step back into the bathroom. "Put some damn pants on!"

Following a muted breakfast, a worried Keanu drug Uzmahndey out onto the patio. "Does Angela have a prosthetic right arm?"

Realizing what was bothering him, Uzmahndey grinned. "Yes."

"And a prosthetic left leg?"

"Yes."

"Does she have some kind of implant in her back?"

"Yes."

"What happened to her? Was she in a car wreck?"

"A gas explosion hit her point blank in the face. And she was caught out in a sandstorm in the Sahara."

"Damn. She's tough."

"No shit. You saw how she fought yesterday. I've no doubt she could beat the crap out of me." Keanu merely shook his head. "What did she say when you were doing those tattoos on her injuries? Did she mention the wires that were exposed?"

"No. She didn't say anything."

Apparently, her mental state had made her oblivious to what was right before everyone else's eyes. "I wouldn't mention it, either. She's kind of touchy about it."

Uzmahndey drove the rental car back to Dunedin. Three pairs of eyes were peeled watching out for anyone following them, while Keanu's eyes were mostly on Angela. No suspicious cars were sighted, while Keanu seemed more open to the idea of Angela being a robot.

Entering Dunedin, Uzmahndey finally demanded answers. "Now what?"

No one had been talking much on the drive that morning, and he had been too upset with personal matters tumbling around inside him to even inquire what their next destination was.

"Chimu," Angela said. "Snugglesaurus has entered the address of their offices in the satellite navigation."

Uzmahndey glanced to the map that popped up on the dashboard screen.

"What is Chimu?"

"A cruise line."

That brought Charlie out of her funk. "We're going on a cruise? Where to?"

"Antarctica."

"Whoa!" Charley perked up, too. "Will we see penguins?"

"We could."

Uzmahndey was a bit more reserved. "Why are we going to Antarctica?"

"To lock down a portal, of course."

Even Keanu joined in with the excitement. "Will we ride a dog sled to get there?"

"No. It's not that inaccessible. It's near the coast. The cruise ship makes a stop in the Ross Sea. That will get us close enough."

"This sounds great!" Charley enthused.

Uzmahndey, not so much. "How long is this cruise?"

"Twenty-two days."

"You're kidding! That's almost a month!"

Angela smiled, in her usual twisted fashion. "It will give the newlyweds a nice honeymoon."

Uzmahndey threw a withering look into the back seat. "They are not newlyweds." He turned back around. "You are just wanting to give them ample opportunity to produce off-spring."

"So? I'm looking forward to grandchildren."

"What is this portal we are headed for called?"

"Blood Falls."

"Whoa!" Charley said, with even more enthusiasm than before. "This just keeps getting better."

Blood Falls is an extremely inaccessible location. Gaia wanted one portal away from people.

This is the best way Snugglesaurus could get us there.

Chill out, Uz. Snugglesaurus got two separate berths. Charlie and Keanu will have their own. You won't have to watch.

At the Chimu office, Uzmahndey scanned a travel brochure while waiting for Angela to take care of the paperwork. 'Visit the most pristine sea on Earth as you follow in the footsteps of the heroic age of Antarctic explorers. Departing from Dunedin, this 22-day expedition will allow you to explore the highlights of the sub-Antarctic islands and Antarctica. This area is one of the most biodiverse and wildlife-rich corners of the Earth.'

He also found a brochure on the cruise ship they would be taking. 'The Soleil is an elegant chic yacht with a sleek silhouette, quality workmanship, and contemporary décor. The 132 comfortable suites and staterooms ranging from superior, deluxe, and prestige, can accommodate up to 264 passengers.'

When Angela rejoined them after signing everything, he snapped at her. "I suppose the honeymooners are getting a superior suite?" Getting no response, he continued. "Where are we staying? In a mop closet?"

That afternoon they checked into the Distinction Dunedin Hotel, several blocks from the inner city wharf where the Soleil was docked. Upon entering their suite, Charlie took Keanu by the hand and led him into a bedroom, slamming the door behind them.

Angela parked herself in a chair just outside the still reverberating door where she could ensure the couple remained undisturbed.

Uzmahndey and Charley retreated to the suite's other bedroom. The teenage boy was puzzled. "I thought Keanu was your friend?"

Uzmahndey flopped onto his back on the double bed. "He once was."

Charley flopped beside him. "Charlie likes him."

"He is the only man she has ever met. Keanu is taking advantage of her."

"He seems to like her, too."

"She'll come to hate him, once she realizes how Angela has manipulated her." Uzmahndey turned his glare from the ceiling to Charley's wide-open face. "Help me keep an eye on Keanu. I don't trust him. He is here for a reason."

Charley looked down at the stuffed dinosaur in his arms. "But Snugglesaurus says…"

"I don't care what it says. I don't trust it, either. It could be manipulating us all, including your mother, for some evil grand scheme."

"Like what?"

"I don't know what its game plan is." Uzmahndey looked back up to the ceiling. "But I don't always run the routes I'm assigned. I can adjust my routes according to the coverage I encounter. I'm good at improvising on my feet."

The next morning the situation hadn't mellowed. Charlie still avoided him like the plague, while Keanu kept giving him weird looks. Had she filled him in about Angela? Finally convinced him that her mother was a robot? Who wasn't aware she was a robot? Uzmahndey couldn't ask Keanu about it since Angela remained determined to keep him away from the couple. He *did* notice a welcome change in Charley. His son eyed Keanu with a little more distrust than before.

After breakfast they checked out and took a taxi to the inner city wharf. Despite everything, Uzmahndey was impressed. The Soleil looked more like a massive yacht than a cruise ship. They boarded and went straight up to Charlie and Keanu's room on the next to top floor, Deck Six, the Solstice Deck. It was a superior stateroom, which featured a private balcony. Uzmahndey stepped out onto it and surveyed the harbor. "Wow. I suppose this makes your room super romantic."

"Knock it off, Uz." Angela glared at him from inside. With her prison tattoos and scars, she appeared more intimidating than ever.

Without another word, he walked back in and breezed past everyone out to the passageway. He took the elevator down to Deck Three, the Andromede Deck, where the deluxe stateroom he was to share with Angela and Charley was located. Not bad, either, he had to admit. Far from a mop closet.

Uzmahndey was too agitated to remain in the cramped quarters. He set off to explore the ship. Which didn't take long since it wasn't all that big. He found two zodiacs lashed down on the main deck. In the lobby was an interesting sculpture of a swirling school of fish. The main lounge on Deck Three seemed spacious for a ship. It was nearly all windows. He assumed when the weather wasn't fit to be outside passengers could still enjoy the view from there, and from the smaller Panoramic Lounge he found up on Deck Six. Continuing the walkabout, he discovered two restaurants - a formal dining gastronomic on Deck Six and a small open air bar and grill on Deck Seven. On Deck Four he discovered a theater.

On Deck Five he came upon what he had been longing for, a fitness room. It was deserted, which suited him. Uzmahndey started up a treadmill and a playlist on his phone and went to work relieving all his accumulated stress.

An hour later Charley walked in to discover Uzmahndey furiously pumping away on a step machine. "I thought I'd find you here."

He answered without slowing. "Where else would I be? Not the lounge. I'm not allowed to drink alcohol."

"Mom says its time to eat lunch."

Uzmahndey slowed. "Do I need to get cleaned up?"

"I don't think so. We're eating at the grill."

Uzmahndey stopped. "Okay." He stepped down from the machine. "I feel better."

"I feel great." Charley's grin was infectious. "This is going to be so much fun."

They headed for the door. "If you say so."

"Snugglesaurus says there are southern blue whales here. They are the largest animals to ever live on earth. Bigger than dinosaurs."

The two found Angela seated at a table by herself. "Where are the sweethearts?" Uzmahndey asked as he and Charley sat.

Angela appeared no happier than before. "This is going to be a very unpleasant week if you keep this up."

"Week? I thought the cruise is for twenty-two days."

"We reach our destination on day seven."

Uzmahndey grew concerned.

"It's too remote for any worshippers to attack us there."

"Unless they are already booked on the ship," Uzmahndey said. "Or more of Gaia's children are waiting for us at Blood Falls. We have nearly completed our tasks. They will start massing in force at these final portals."

The rest of the first day was uneventful. Following lunch at the grill, Uzmahndey returned to the fitness room and worked himself to exhaustion. He limped down to his deluxe stateroom to clean up then stretch out on a bunk.

Angela and Charley returned to the stateroom late that afternoon. She had taken Charley on an excursion off the boat to the Otega Peninsula to see a colony of albatross. The teenage boy hurried into the shower as soon as Angela began undressing.

"You are embarrassing our son," Uzmahndey, watching from the bed, commented. When she stepped out of her panties, a tattoo of a tropical waterfall came into view on her butt. "You let Keanu put a tattoo there!"

"Why not? We're family."

Uzmahndey watched as she donned panties and bra. "Your taste in underwear has improved."

"Snugglesaurus helped me select these." She struck a pose. "Do you approve?"

Uzmahndey smiled, in spite of himself. "Of course. I never realized Snugglesaurus had such interests."

"He scans the Internet for the latest fashions." Angela began donning an evening dress. "I hope you plan on cleaning up. Dinner in the restaurant is semi-formal."

"What does Snugglesaurus suggest I wear?"

"A tie and dinner jacket would be nice." Seeing Uzmahndey frown, she continued. "But not required. Long pants, button-up shirt, and dress shoes will do."

Seeing Angela have difficulty with the zipper, he sat up. "Come here." She backed up to him, and he zipped.

Angela smiled over her shoulder at him. "This trip doesn't have to be so unpleasant. It could be a honeymoon for us, too."

"No. I don't want another child right now. It's too crazy."

"I've got protection. Father sent me back with some."

Uzmahndey glanced to the closed bathroom door. "Charley is staying with us."

"He won't be with us all the time."

"Are you suggesting we slip some quickies in?"

Charley called out from behind the bathroom door. "I can hear every word you guys are saying!"

Uzmahndey laughed. "If you have any questions, just ask Snugglesaurus."

"Is Mom dressed yet?" The bathroom door didn't open until he got an affirmative reply. He emerged with a towel wrapped around him, refusing to meet Angela's eyes. "Good. You're dressed. Get out and let me get dressed."

"You should leave." Uzmahndey backed his son up. "Check with Snugglesaurus."

Apparently Angela did, because a beat later she slipped on shoes. "I'll wait for you two in the main lounge." She walked out.

Uzmahndey rose from the bed. "Any hot water left?"

Following his shower and donning of semi semi-formal attire, he and Charley found Angela seated at the bar. "I'm surprised you're alone. You look ravishing. No men hit on you?"

"I hit back."

"Mom! You didn't."

Uzmahndey did a quick scan. No men were within ten feet of her. "I don't think she's kidding."

In the restaurant they were seated by themselves. If Charlie and Keanu were dining, it was most likely a late-night meal.

After dinner, Angela went to check on the couple, while Uzmahndey and Charley returned to the stateroom. They crawled each into their own bunk. They were both so tired from the stress of the day they fell asleep right away.

Sometime that night Uzmahndey awakened to Angela standing next to the bed in her underwear. At her urging, he slipped out of bed and followed her into the bathroom.

"Is anything wrong?" Uzmahndey asked.

"Yes." Angela removed her bra. "Charley."

They both squirmed out of their underpants.

Uzmahndey smiled as they bumped into each other in the tight space. "It's been a long time since I made love in a bathroom. And bathrooms on boats are really tight."

"Why would you ever want to? It can't be comfortable for you."

"Sex isn't supposed to be comfortable. Adventurous is more desirable."

"Is our sex adventurous?"

"I have never met any woman as adventurous as you."

"No other man interests me. You have made me a woman."

There was a knock.

"Are you guys almost done? I can't hold it any longer."

The second day was spent at sea. Uzmahndey spent most of it in the fitness room and the spa, which were both on Deck Five. He went up to Deck Six once to check out the heated pool. He never went out to it. From inside the dining room he could see Charlie and Keanu lounging in the steam rising off it. So he went back to exercising.

On the third day they stopped at Campbell Island. Uzmahndey and Charley opted for the guided walk on the boardwalk, while Angela, Charlie and Keanu went on the zodiac boat tour around the coast of Perseverance Island.

The following three days were spent on the open sea. Charley disappeared at appropriate times. Uzmahndey suspected this was being choreographed by Snugglesaurus so he and Angela could have use of the bed instead of being restricted to the cramped nautical bathroom. He never encountered Charlie and Keanu, merely caught glimpses of them at the pool, in the lounge, at the grill, or out on the sun deck. He really wasn't keeping tabs on them; it was a small ship. Charley spent most of his time at organized activities, such as nature programs and games and movies.

Uzmahndey appreciated the attention from Angela. He knew what she was up to, trying to keep him so occupied and satisfied that his anger with Keanu did not boil over. Her strategy worked. He was happy. This was the best relations had been between him and Angela since before her near-destruction in the White Desert. Between all the exercise, the massages in the spa, and his trysts with Angela, he had never felt so well since he had been forced out of football by his bum knee. So he had no intention of correcting her self-deception. Let her think herself human if that made her feel better.

Strangely enough, it was also making *him* feel better. Her believing herself to be a real human made their relationship more authentic for him. Illogical, he knew, but yet true.

On the afternoon of day six, upon leaving the stateroom, and a warm naked Angela, who had been alerted of Charley's imminent return by Snugglesaurus, Uzmahndey poked his head around the corner on the seventh and top deck to scout out the Sun Deck. Charlie and Keanu were not there. So he found a chair off by itself and settled in. "You guys have been awfully quiet on this trip."

We didn't want to upset you.

You needed time to relax and recover from your injuries.

And for us to spend quality time with Angela.

Uzmahndey snorted at Bad's 'us' remark, but let it pass. "What's your take on her?"

She seems to be functioning well.

Her delusion isn't adversely affecting her.

Just like your delusion that you were a good NFL receiver hasn't adversely affected you.

Uzmahndey ignored Bad, as he tried to do much of the time. "Why couldn't Snugglesaurus fully restore her memories?"

We don't know.

But why wouldn't he if he could?

You ask that of a man who sees a conspiracy around every corner?

Uzmahndey ignored Bad once again. He had spent so little time talking with the xenobots he didn't want this to devolve into an argument. "What's your take on Keanu?"

<u>He has shown nothing but love and care for Charlie.</u>

He has exhibited no threat whatsoever.

So get over your guilt for introducing him to Charlie.

"That wasn't my doing. Gaia arranged that. Why?"

<u>Whatever the plan was, it seems to have backfired.</u>

"I'm not convinced. This could be a long con."

Rest assured, we're keeping your eyes peeled.

"Are you peeling my eyes while I'm in bed with Angela?"

Hey, buddy, that's hard to ignore.

"Enough. I don't want to think about you three with Angela."

Angela is aware of us enjoying her body. Any complaints from her?

Uzmahndey leaned back and closed his eyes, and his mouth. If Angela wasn't bothered by the three of them, he shouldn't let them get under his skin. Which brought a chuckle. They *were* under his skin, somewhere. And starting to seem as much a part of him as a layer of epidermis.

Later that night when he and Charley walked into the restaurant on Deck Two for dinner he was surprised to find Angela seated at a table with Charlie and Keanu. Uzmahndey produced an insincere smile. "A family gathering. What's the occasion?"

Angela's smile looked even less sincere. "Please sit down and be nice."

Charley immediately sat, Uzmahndey a bit more reluctantly. "How is the honeymoon going?"

"Successfully," Angela informed him.

That took Uzmahndey's breath. He dropped the insincerity for honest compassion as he gazed upon Charlie. "Are you pregnant?"

"Snugglesaurus says she is," Angela said.

"I'm going to be an uncle!" Charley proclaimed.

Uzmahndey turned to Angela with quite a bit less compassion. "She's got four to five months?"

"Yes. Plenty of time."

"For what?"

"For us to finish dealing with Gaia and her people. We'll be done long before the baby is due." Angela spread her gaze around the table. "That's why I gathered us all together tonight. Tomorrow we go to Blood Falls."

Chapter 34

Blood Falls

Early the next morning Uzmahndey and Charley were rousted out of bed by Angela. She hurried them into the cold weather gear she had purchased in the ship's stores on Deck Three. They met up with Charlie and Keanu, also appropriately dressed for Antarctic weather, in the grill on Deck Six for breakfast.

"It might be a while before your next meal," Angela said. "Eat hearty."

Charlie's attitude toward Uzmahndey seemed to have softened, while Keanu seemed absolutely apologetic. 'Be happy for me,' she seemed to say to him without moving her lips. While Keanu's demeanor seemed to say, 'Please don't beat the shit out of me.'

Uzmahndey smiled at Charlie. "You have my blessing." Then scowled at Keanu. "You better be serious about this."

"I'm going to be a father. How much more serious can it get?"

"Do anything to hurt Charlie or the baby and I'll show you."

Following breakfast, they trooped down to the first deck. A zodiac was prepared for their use, including a person to captain it. He zipped them across the Ross Sea. The icy water was calm, which was a good thing since Keanu evidenced regret for having eaten such a large breakfast. Uzmahndey shoved him to the edge of the zodiac so he could lean over it.

They made it to the southwestern tip of Ross Island without Keanu tossing his breakfast and were dropped off at McMurdro Station. Noticing how green Keanu still was, Uzmahndey prodded. "Do not throw up. If you do, you'll have to pick it up and put it in your pocket. Everything gets carried out here."

Uzmahndey surveyed the community from the dock. There was a substantial sprawl of one and two story metal warehouse structures. "How big is this place?"

"Nearly a thousand people are here now," the zodiac captain answered. "The population reaches its peak in the summer. Only a couple hundred remain during the winter."

As soon as Keanu was recovered enough, they walked away from the dock through a brisk wind flapping everything not securely fastened down. Uzmahndey experienced the cold even through the layers of gear, but it didn't register as uncomfortable.

A thank you for that is in order.

Uzmahndey ignored Bad, as usual, as they approached the waiting Jeep. He stepped up alongside Angela. "Snugglesaurus arranged all this?"

"Of course."

"How much does it cost for tourists to come here?"

"There are no tourists. Only scientists and support staff."

"Then it must have cost a fortune."

Angela made no response. She had no concept of money. She left the economics of their endeavor entirely up to the AI.

"How much did Snugglesaurus have to bribe people for us to be here?"

"Nothing. We are a science team come to collect samples of the iron-rich nanospheres discovered in the frozen lake beneath Taylor Glacier at Blood Falls. Snugglesaurus arranged all our necessary documentation online." She smiled at him. "So act scientific."

Uzmahndey glanced at Charley. "Kind of young for a scientist."

"We require support personnel."

They piled into the Jeep and were driven through the station. The plowed tracks took them past rows of barracks, labs, a medical center, a supply depot, water treatment, a power plant, a clubhouse, a coffeehouse, even a church – Chapel of the Ice. Driving from out of the tightly organized cluster of metal warehouses, they arrived at Pegasus Field, which consisted of three cleared runways of ice on the adjacent permanent shelf.

Squinting from the sun's glare off the wilderness of white, Uzmahndey spied a helicopter prepared to take off. "I hope this goes better than our last helicopter ride."

The five climbed in.

"Not much gear," their pilot noted.

"This is an exploratory run," Angela said.

The pilot shrugged, and they lifted off. During the short flight over a blinding snowy expanse into the bare rocky domain of the Dry Valleys, where Blood Falls was located, their pilot kept a spiel going.

"Ross Island, where McMurdro Station is situated, was formed by the activity of four volcanoes. The land all around us may be frozen, but just beneath a thin layer of ice is flowing magma. Only one of the four is still active." He pointed to the tallest peak. "Mount Erebus, the southernmost active volcano in the world."

Uzmahndey spied three colorful tents set up on rocks at the edge of Taylor Glacier. "Who are they?"

Good answered before the pilot could.

A science team.

A real one.

So don't give us away by asking stupid questions. Keep your mouth shut.

The helicopter set down on solid rock far enough distant so as not to disturb the pitched nylon. Once they all climbed out, the helicopter took off.

"He's abandoning us here?" Charlie asked.

Angela held up a radio. "He'll remain on standby at McMurdro Station." She stuck the radio into her backpack then turned to everyone else. "Stay close. We could have company here."

Keanu pointed to the tents. "We already do."

"They don't concern us." She walked across the rocks toward the tongue of Taylor Glacier, where the dull red of Blood Falls discolored the white ice it flowed out onto.

"Is that really blood?" Charley asked.

"Not very scientific," Charlie scoffed. "The red color is caused by iron oxide. Rust. The water is so briny it doesn't freeze easily."

Angela arrived at the edge of the discolored rock at the base of the falls. "Stay here. I have to insert the xenobot into a crack in the glacier where the water from the underground lake is escaping through." She removed a Cheerio from her Tupperware container and strode across the red ice.

Darkness descended.

"What happened?!" Keanu screamed.

Uzmahndey swung his arms about the pitch black. One struck another arm. He grabbed it. "Who have I got?"

"Me!" Charlie yelled.

"Charles!" Uzmahndey yelled.

"I'm right here," Charley responded. "Calm down."

"Calm down!" Keanu screamed. "Are you crazy, kid?! I can't see anything!"

"Angela!" Uzmahndey called out repeatedly. No response.

"She's gone," Charley said. "She must still be back at Blood Falls."

"So where are we?" Keanu gathered his wits enough to ask.

"We've obviously passed through a portal."

"Good?" Uzmahndey called out. "Bad? Ugly?" No response from his xenobots. They had definitely passed through a portal.

Uzmahndey reached all around the total darkness. His probing hand encountered someone else. "Who have I got?"

"Me!" Keanu answered.

Uzmahndey flung his arm away. "Charles!"

"I'm okay." Uzmahndey felt a hand on his shoulder. "Sheesh. Is everyone afraid of the dark?"

"If you are not you should be." The rumbling deep voice sounded ominous.

"Where is Angela?" Uzmahndey attempted to sound just as ominous.

"She is not here to save you this time."

"Who are you?" Charley asked.

"Erebus, young child. The namesake of the nearby volcano." The darkness lightened a bit. A humanoid outline could be seen standing before them. "Is this better?"

Charlie slung Uzmahndey's hand off and threw herself into Keanu's arms.

Her brother broke free from his father's grasp to step forward. "What have you done with my mother!?"

"The machine is undamaged. For now."

Uzmahndey lunged at the shifting shadow before them. He passed through it and went sprawling upon the rocks.

A bass laugh echoed.

"Do you hope to grasp darkness?"

"No." Charley raised Snugglesaurus high. "But we can get rid of it."

Brilliant white light blazed from the stuffed dinosaur's glass eyes. The shadows disappeared, including Erebus. The brilliant illumination revealed they were enclosed within bare rock, with no sign of Blood Falls or Taylor Glacier, or any aspect of Antarctica.

"Are we in a cave?" Charlie asked, easing her bruising clutch on Keanu and looking all around.

"How'd that happen?!" Keanu, still panicked, hadn't even noticed Charlie had been crushing his arm.

"Erebus is the ancient god of darkness." Charley revolved, shining the light into all recesses of the vast chamber they were in.

"And nothing on Earth is darker than a cave." Uzmahndey picked himself up off the rocks he'd fallen upon. "Ever been deep in a cave when all the lights were turned off? It's totally black. Not a speck of light. Like this place."

Charley, holding Snugglesaurus high to illuminate the way, walked off.

"Where are you going?" Charlie asked.

"To find Mom."

Uzmahndey fell into step behind him.

Charlie, leading Keanu by the hand, hurried to catch up. "How long can Snugglesaurus keep doing that?"

"Yeah," Keanu said, no longer paralyzed with fear. "Won't his batteries run down?"

"He doesn't have batteries," Charley said. "He's powered by a small cold fusion reactor."

Up ahead, Uzmahndey saw stars. "Night sky. You're leading us in the right direction. Toward an entrance."

Ten minutes later the four scrambled up out through a small fissure.

"Now what?" Charlie demanded.

A young man in classical robes dropped down from behind a star. "Your AI is an interesting toy, but it's not omnipotent."

Charley never wavered. "Neither are you, Uranus."

"Don't be so sure of yourself, child. You are dealing with Primordials now."

The dark sky turned blood red with the eruption of Mount Erebus, which seemed much larger and nearer than before. The brilliant fire washed out the light from Snugglesaurus.

"Behold my daughter, Aetna." A huge fiery female form emerged from out of the booming caldera to hover above the blazing cataclysm. "You encountered her once before. At Kilauea."

"Volcanoes don't bother me." Uzmahndey rose to his feet. "I live next to the most active volcano on the planet."

Uranus was unimpressed by the bravado. "Does your volcano have the likes of my three sons?"

Three giant beings appeared below Uranus, each with fifty heads and a hundred arms.

Uzmahndey picked up a football-sized rock. "We ran a play at LSU where I took a lateral and threw a pass." He hurled the rock at the nearest of the three. It struck one head between the eyes. The head lolled back, out cold. "I threw a lot of touchdowns."

"No matter. Cottus has forty-nine more." The monster advanced, all one-hundred arms reaching for Uzmahndey.

Charley moved to Uzmahndey's side. "We can't fight them here in the open." He pulled his father back toward the fissure they had emerged from.

Charlie and Keanu scrambled after them as the three giants advanced.

Charley guarded the entrance until the other three passed by, then retreated himself. "Those big things can't follow us in. The entrance is too small."

The fissure glowed redly. Lava poured over the edge into the chamber.

"The entrance is not too small for lava from that volcano!" Keanu yelled. "Now what?!"

Charley fell silent, obviously communing with the AI. Uzmahndey pulled him further back into the cavern, and Charlie and Keanu stumbled back, too.

Deep wicked laughter greeted them as they retreated before the slow but relentless advance of the blistering lava flow. "I see you have returned to my realm. Was Uranus not as welcoming as I?"

Uzmahndey saw Charley was still involved with Snuggle-saurus, so he attempted to buy his son some time. "You cannot hope to stand against what's coming. Ghost is only one being of his race. When his army arrives you will be destroyed."

"So you say. But perhaps there is no army. Perhaps he is all that remains of his race."

"Even if that's true, it seems like one of him is enough to dispatch all of you. We've locked up nearly all the portals."

"It means nothing so long as one remains open. After we have destroyed you we can re-enter your realm through that one and re-open all the others."

"If you could stop us so easily you would have done so by now."

"You've been a minor irritation. So far we've let the children play with you. And our followers. Now it's time for the primordials to step in. Such as my sister and consort, Nyx."

A dark female form emerged from the swirling smoke as she strode through the blazing lava without harm.

"You met Nyx once before. In the night sky above the desert of the sailing stones. She was merely curious then. And she was alone. This time she has brought some of our children with her."

Three black bat-like winged demons flew through the fissure above the flowing lava.

Uranus chuckled. "Nyx is the goddess of night. Her night and my shadows together are too much for your little toy. Our combined dark can overwhelm its dim glimmer."

The chamber returned to pitch black.

Although Uzmahndey could no longer see the flying demons, he could still hear their beating wings, and feel the breeze as they swooped down low. He swung wildly up into the air at them. His fists struck nothing.

"But I will allow you to see this warrior."

Logan Wilson appeared before Uzmahndey. His glowing form was bursting out of his pads, his orange and black Bengals uniform hanging in shreds off his immense muscular frame. He glowered down at Uzmahndey, who cowered at his feet.

"Whatever you are seeing, Dad," Charley called out. "it's not really there."

"I'm dreaming?"

"Snugglesaurus says Morpheus is making you dream and Phobetor is turning it into a nightmare."

Uzmahndey heard more screams in the dark. "What's going on?"

"Morpheus and Phobetor are fashioning nightmares for the others, too."

"How can I help them? It's pitch black. I can't fight what I can't see."

"You can see Logan Wilson."

Uzmahndey turned back to confront his nemesis. He looked even bigger than before. And angrier. "He's too big."

"And that's why he's still in the NFL knocking heads and you are hiding out in Hawaii running your pathetic little tour business."

His own son was mocking him? Uzmahndey launched himself forward. He tackled Logan Wilson around the knees. The huge linebacker went down with a grunt.

"This way! Now!"

Uzmahndey looked up. A beam of light was focused on a door. Snugglesaurus hadn't been able to light up the entire cavern as before, so it had focused its light in a tight beam bright enough to illuminate where they needed to go. Uzmahndey looked all around. He couldn't see Charlie or Keanu.

"Charlie! Where are you?!"

"I've got them!" Charley cried out. "Come on, Dad!"

Uzmahndey scrambled to his feet.

The darkness faded away, and the chamber was filled with the hellish glow of lava. In the dark it had advanced unseen and had nearly reached Uzmahndey, but by its light he could see the other three standing before a door.

"Nyx!" Uranus called out. "Bring the Keres."

Three full-sized winged females in flowing black robes flew into the cavern through the fissure.

Uzmahndey sprinted toward where his son waited. A wall of rock rose up before him twenty feet high. Uzmahndey dodged to the right, but the wall extended in the direction he ran and continued to block him.

"That wall's not real. Phantasos is tricking you. In dreams he can assume the shape of inanimate things. He's slowing you down so the Keres can catch you."

Uranus' voice boomed. "Your death will be horrible. The Keres delight in horrible deaths."

Uzmahndey glanced up. One of the Keres was stretching out its bloody talons down toward him. Strips of decaying flesh clung to them. He looked back to the wall as he took off running parallel to it.

"That wall sure looks real."

Uranus' laughter filled the cavern. "It's as real as your intestines will look once the Keres pull them out of you."

"He's lying, Dad. It's Phantasos."

Uzmahndey cut to the left and leaped. He sailed over the twenty-foot high wall. Landing on the other side, he saw

Charley holding the door open and waving him on. He didn't see the other two. He assumed they must have already passed through. Hearing a sizzle, he looked to see the wall collapsing before the oncoming lava, which seemed to have picked up pace.

Uzmahndey sprinted for the door. Until he didn't. He slowed. Grew lethargic. "What's going on now?"

"It's Hypnos," Charley cried out. "Another child of Nyx. He's trying to put you to sleep."

Uzmahndey was nearly knocked off his feet as he felt the familiar surge of adrenaline hit his bloodstream. Good? Bad? Ugly? They were there? With him? In Gaia's realm? Apparently they could still function, they just couldn't communicate with him.

He stumbled forward. The door was ten yards away. A first down. He'd run after the catch for many first downs. He was always aware of where the first down marker was. He could make a catch and contort his body every which way to reach the marker. He'd done it countless times. He was really good at it.

Uzmahndey staggered forward. Five yards to go. Four. Three.

His legs buckled.

"What now?!"

He crashed down onto jagged rock. He felt his knees shatter as he collapsed. He nearly passed out from the sudden agony.

"Geras. Old age. Another child of Nyx. The monster has made you think you are an old man. Too old to run."

"*Think* I'm too old? I broke both my knees!"

"You only think they are broken. Your bones are not really that brittle."

"Get up, Uz!"

That was Charlie. Cheering for him.

He *had* to get up.

Before Uzmahndey could, one of the Keres swooped down and sank its claws deep into his back. He swooned from the sudden pain so intense even the three silent xenobots could not block it as the winged creature lifted his limp body up into the air.

Chapter 35

Marble Caves

Uzmahndey gazed up into the silver and black figures gathered all around him. The pain in his back was unbearable. Why didn't the team doc help him with that?

"Don't try to move."

Concerned faces hovered above. Mostly Raiders teammates, with a couple coaches sprinkled in.

"What happened?"

"You don't remember?" Jon Gruden asked. He turned to look at the team doctor. "He might have taken a shot to the head, too."

The doctor concurred. "He'll need to go through concussion protocol."

A teammate kneeled beside him. "Logan Wilson nailed you."

Another teammate chimed in. "He was flagged for hitting a defenseless player."

"We're playing Cincinnati?"

The player looked up to the doctor. "He doesn't know where he is. He *did* take a knock on the head."

"Everyone back up." Gruden stood. "The cart is here."

The huddle around him parted to allow the cart to pull up close. Uzmahndey could now see all around. Broad daylight. Inside a stadium. Flat on his back on the playing field. Damn, his back felt like it was on fire! The stretcher was slipped under his prone body, every jostle agonizing! They raised him up off the ground onto the cart, every jolt agonizing! Uzmahndey screamed!

"Uz!"

That wasn't a player. It sounded female. Uzmahndey pried his eyes open. She wasn't wearing a cheerleader outfit, or holding a microphone. Who?

"Charlie." Tears streamed down her face.

Had he said that last out loud? Uzmahndey closed his eyes. Why hadn't the doctor given him anything for the pain?

<u>We did.</u>

<u>*And we still are. It's just a lot of pain.*</u>

Two Raider players were beside him at the cart. They removed their helmets.

"Good? Bad?" Uzmahndey looked all around. "Where's Ugly?"

"He's gone."

"Good? What do you mean? Bad?"

"I said that."

Uzmahndey focused on a face inches from his. Charlie's. "I never got injured playing Cincinnati."

"You aren't playing anywhere. You are talking out of your head."

Uzmahndey closed his eyes. He *was* talking out of his head. It wasn't a back injury that knocked him out of the NFL. It was his right knee. Logan Wilson never gave him a cheap shot. Logan Wilson didn't take cheap shots.

When Uzmahndey opened his eyes again it was dark. He couldn't see anything. "Charlie!"

"I'm right here." Her creased face appeared above him.

"What happened?"

"You were hurt really bad."

"Can't my buddies fix me up?"

"Good and Bad are trying to."

"Why isn't Ugly helping?"

"He's not in you any more."

"What are you talking about? Where'd he go?"

"Charley took him out of you."

"Why would he do that?"

"To save us."

His own son! Had robbed him of a xenobot! His ticket back into football! How could he?!

Uzmahndey opened his eyes. It was light. Less pain, but still intense.

On a scale of one to ten.

"Nine point nine," he muttered through papery lips.

I'm sure it's less than that. Don't be a wimp.

"Why'd you guys abandon me?"

In Gaia's realm we can't communicate with you.

And we didn't abandon you. We were doing all we could.

"You sure aren't doing much now."

Ugly is gone.

We had to learn to work without him.

It took a while.

It was like starting from scratch. I never realized the ugly thing pulled so much weight.

"That's just a name. He isn't really ugly. I have no idea what any of you look like. The only time I ever saw *you* two you both had Raider helmets on."

Whoa, if you are seeing us as football players then you are hurt worse than we thought.

Uzmahndey looked around. Charlie and Charley were both curled up asleep on the grass amid a grove of trees. He could see nothing else. He closed his eyes so he could concentrate on conversing with his remaining two xenobots.

"Why did Charles steal Ugly?"

We escaped out of Gaia's realm through a portal.

Then we had to seal the portal to keep them from coming after us.

"Angela?"

We don't know where she is.

And she has all the Cheerios.

One of us had to be sacrificed.

A xenobot was needed. In a hurry. We drew straws. Ugly picked the short vein.

"How did Charley get Ugly out of me?"

Through your wounds. The Keres ripped your back wide open.

That's why you hurt so bad. The wounds were extensive to start with. What Charley did made them worse. You lost a lot of blood. We had to focus on saving your life instead of relieving your pain. And there were only two of us. And we had to learn to work together without Ugly.

It was challenging.

"So Charles took Ugly to seal the portal we escaped through?"

Yeah.

"Which portal is this?"

We don't know. It was the closest one Snugglesaurus could find.

We couldn't be choosy. It was a mad scramble to get out of there.

"So why not ask the AI now? Since we've stopped scrambling?"

He's not here.

Good! I thought we were holding back on telling him anything disturbing.

What they had told him *already* wasn't disturbing? What could they possibly be withholding that was worse? "Where the hell is he?"

Bad, I can't lie. Keanu ran off with Snugglesaurus.

"I knew it! I knew Keanu was up to something!"

I guess he was scared after all that happened. And he'd seen how much money Snugglesaurus could manipulate. It was too much of a temptation for him.

"Couldn't Charles stop him? My kid was impressive in Gaia's world. It must have been him that saved me from that demon bird."

It was. But Charles is out of commission.

"Was he injured, too?"

No. The strain of all this has brought on a growth spurt, and neither Snugglesaurus nor Angela is here to help him through it. He's completely out of it.

"How is Charlie? And her baby?"

She seems okay.

The baby we don't know about. It's Snugglesaurus that was following the progress of her baby.

"And Snugglesaurus is gone. Damn Keanu. I will skin him alive when I get my hands on him." Uzmahndey started to sit up, but never got past fifteen degrees from horizontal. He collapsed with a moan.

Uzmahndey opened his eyes. It was either still light, or it was light again. He looked around. Charley was sprawled on the ground – still, or again? - but Charlie was gone.

"Charlie?" No response to his croak. "Charlie?!"

She stumbled out of the trees and landed on her knees beside him. "What's wrong?"

"Are you okay?"

"Yes."

"And your baby?"

"I think so."

"Where are we?"

"I've been looking around. We're in a forest on a coast. And it's cold. But not as cold as Antarctica."

"How did we get here?"

"That thing Erebus called a Keres sank its claws into your back and started to fly away with you. Charley jumped up and ripped you free. That tore up your back really bad. Then he dragged you through the portal back into our world."

"But you don't know which portal."

"No. We ended up in the water. The portal was in a sea cave. We drug you out of the water up onto rocks. Then we had to seal the portal we'd just come through right away, before all of them could come after us. But Angela wasn't here with the Cheerios. So Snugglesaurus told Charley how to extract one of the xenobots through the open wounds on your back. That tore your back up even worse. But Charley was able to seal the portal with Ugly. He was really sorry about all the pain he caused you and all the damage he did, but we were in a hurry. Those monsters could have come through at any minute."

"Then he had a growth spurt."

"Yes."

"And Keanu ran off with Snugglesaurus."

Charlie burst out crying. "It was crazy. I didn't know what to do."

"Hey, it's not your fault. I'm sure you did everything you could." He reached up to stroke her hair. "The only thing you are guilty of is bad judgment."

"He's *your* friend."

"He's under Gaia's influence. Angela never should have trusted him. Your mother was so determined to get you pregnant. Let's blame her."

The tears slowed. Charlie took a deep breath.

"I'm healing, and Charley just needs to sleep."

"He needs a lot more than just sleep. Snugglesaurus isn't here to help him bridge the three years he skipped. And Angela's not here to soothe him, either. I don't know what will happen to him." Charlie stroked Uzmahndey's face. "Are you really getting better?"

"I'm feeling better. I've still got two xenobots who are working on me."

That brought a glimmer. She rose to her feet. "I'm going to look around some more. Try to find out where we are. I won't go too far. Yell if you need me."

"I will. I'm good at yelling."

Charlie presented a tentative smile. "You are. But you're getting hoarse."

Uzmahndey closed his eyes once more.

"Who's Your Mama!"

Uzmahndey opened his eyes. Logan Wilson towered above him. "Did you really think you'd play football again?"

"I'm coming for you, Logan Wilson."

"No you're not. You can't even stand up. You're going back to Hawaii to your sad little office. To skip rope every day and get drunk every night. You're not even a good tour guide. Look where you've led *this* group."

"I'm not leading it."

"Exactly."

Uzmahndey closed his eyes. "Leave me alone, Logan Wilson."

Uzmahndey opened his eyes. It was dark. "Charlie?"

"I'm right here." A moment later she was at his side. "Drink this."

Uzmahndey raised his head enough to sip from a bottle. Water. Wet and wonderful. He gulped several times then leaned back. "Where did you get a bottle of water?"

"Keanu brought it."

Uzmahndey looked to see Keanu standing behind her.

"You rat. Why did you come back?"

"I'm no rat. Of course I came back."

"Your conscious get to bothering you, rat?"

"No!"

"He never intended to abandon us." Charlie leaned back to hug Keanu's legs.

Keanu placed his hand on her head. "I wasn't doing any good here. You were more dead than alive, Charley had passed out. So I grabbed Snugglesaurus and went to look for supplies. He directed me to a shack ten miles or so down the coast. It took me a while to get there and back. I'm not in the best of shape to start with, and I'm running on fumes. But with Snugglesaurus' help I bought some food and water and medicine."

Charlie mock-punched Keanu in the leg. "You could have told me what you were doing."

"It was a madhouse. I just went."

"Thanks for coming back, buddy," Uzmahndey said.

"Of course I came back." He kneeled down beside Charlie and stroked her stomach. "I'm not about to abandon my son."

Uzmahndey looked to Charles. He was still unconscious and prone on the ground, but now had his arms wrapped around the stuffed T. Rex. "Snugglesaurus doesn't know where Angela is?"

"No," Charlie replied.

"Can it get us out of here?"

"I'm sure he can. Snugglesaurus has taken us around the world this far."

"What can we do without Angela? She has all the xenobots."

"Not all of them."

Uzmahndey didn't like the sound of that. "What do you mean?"

"Snugglesaurus says only two portals remain."

"How can we seal them without Angela?"

"You've got two more xenobots."

"No!"

Charlie and Keanu both shrank back from the vehemence of his denial.

"This was to be my reward. Those xenobots are getting me back in the NFL. This is why I'm going through all this. To get back into football. One might be gone, but two of them should still be enough. No way. I'm keeping these two." Uzmahndey closed his eyes and rolled away from them. He was so angry the pain didn't register at all.

In the morning Uzmahndey felt strong enough to stand. There was still pain in his back, but not agony. He could move without passing out. Which was good. He had to get started back to Hawaii.

"How are you doing, Dad?"

Uzmahndey looked to see Charley was still prone on the ground, but awake.

"Better. You?"

"Better." He stretched. "That was the last one. I'm eighteen now."

"You were amazing on the other side. You saved my life." Uzmahndey looked around. They were alone. "Where are they?"

"Charlie swam out to the Marble Caves to make sure the portal is still sealed."

"Keanu?"

"He went with her down to the beach. But I don't think he's swimming." Charley smiled. "The water is really cold. And he's not too athletic. But he's proven he's trustworthy."

"If you say so."

"We'd be in bad shape if he hadn't come back with Snug-glesaurus."

"Would the AI have allowed itself to be taken? That thing is pretty powerful." Uzmahndey was pleased with the doubt that crossed his son's face. The two of them had to stay vigilant with Keanu. He had been sent to them for a reason. "Any idea where we are?"

"Snugglesaurus says Patagonia." Drawing a blank stare, Charley continued. "On the southern tip of South America, not too far from Antarctica. It's part of Chile."

"Too bad we didn't emerge closer to Hawaii."

"Why's that?"

"So we can go home."

"That's not my home."

"It will be. You'll love it. It's beautiful there."

Charley climbed to his feet. "Maybe someday. But we still have work to do."

"Not without Angela."

"Why not. We've sealed four portals without her."

"We had the Cheerios for three of them."

"We've still got what we need."

Uzmahndey took a step back. "You are not getting Good and Bad."

Keanu and Charlie emerged from out of the trees, with Charlie in her underwear dripping water and Keanu, who was dry, carrying the rest of her clothes. Her smile was sparkling. "Ugly is holding the portal. Snugglesaurus says the sea cave the portal was located in is called The Cathedral. It's beautiful. I didn't have the chance to appreciate it before, everything was too crazy. All the Marble Caves are beautiful."

Keanu wasn't smiling.

"She swam around to see the other ones." In fact, he appeared ragged out. "Where does she get all that energy? I'm exhausted just watching her."

"It's my alien blood. And my tough hide protects me from the cold water. If a knife can't slice through it, hypothermia isn't going to do much damage. Not like it did Uz in Lake Kaindy." Charlie stopped upon finally noticing Uzmahndey and her brother's dark faces. "What's wrong?"

"My father is ready to go back to Hawaii."

"We're not done." Charlie turned to Uzmahndey. "And you accused *Keanu* of abandoning us!"

Uzmahndey plopped back down. "Damn, I'm not strong enough for this." He looked up to find all three glaring at him. Even Snugglesaurus seemed to glare. He imagined lasers shooting out of those glass eyes and frying him. But that would kill Good and Bad. They claimed they couldn't live without him. So Snugglesaurus probably wouldn't do that.

He dropped his head. "Okay. I'll go with you to the next portal. Maybe Angela will show up by then." His eyes shot up defiantly. "But I am not giving up my last two xenobots. No way."

Chapter 36

Salar de Uyuni

After another day of rest, and the depletion of provisions Keanu had brought back, the party set out on foot through the Patagonian wilderness. Snugglesaurus guided them toward the shack it had led Keanu to. It was slow going through the untracked scrubland and boreal forest along the rocky coast, from which they could see snow-topped peaks, and a glacier snaking down out between two of them to slide into the icy bay. The trek was difficult not only because Uzmahndey's ripped-open back hadn't been completely healed by the overworked and understaffed xenobots, or because of Keanu's near physical collapse. A frigid hurricane-force wind had sprung up and threatened to blow every one of them off their feet. It succeeded several times with Keanu. His meager reserves were nearly used up.

Uzmahndey slogged along on his own. His back throbbed with every trembling step, but he could endure it with the help of the endorphins Good and Bad flooded his system with. What Uzmahndey couldn't endure was the thought of losing those two remaining xenobots. They weren't eager to leave him, either. Both liked the symbiotic relationship they had forged with their host. So the laborious hike through the wild Antarctic-wind lashed Patagonian wilderness proceeded in silence.

At the end of the second endless day they reached the shack. The owner allowed them to shelter there overnight once he realized Keanu's condition. This was a departure point for boat tours to the Marble Caves, so the next day they caught a ride back on a bus that dropped off a group of tourists. It took them north to the small village of Puerto Rio Tranquilo, where they located a store to restock food and drink. They then checked into a cabin in Cabana Valle Exploradores. Rustic and tight, but heated, with its own bathroom. Most importantly, it provided shelter from the merciless Patagonian howl. Charlie cleaned Keanu up and tucked him under heavy blankets into the double bed in one of the two closet-sized bedrooms, then joined the others in the kitchen.

Uzmahndey sat at a rickety wooden table gobbling down a peanut butter sandwich.

"Good and Bad are starving. I've been overworking them."

"Is he okay?" Charley asked his sister.

"Yes. He just needs to rest."

"How about you? And the baby?"

"We're good."

"You can clean up next."

"In a minute. I want to talk about what we are doing."

"Heading for the next portal. Salar de Uyuni. In Bolivia."

"What are we doing once we get there?" Charlie turned accusing eyes upon Uzmahndey.

"We'll find out when we get there," her brother answered.

Uzmahndey swallowed the last of his sandwich then slathered peanut butter on another slice of bread. "What is Salar de Uyuni?"

"The largest salt flat in the world," Charley replied without a trace of accusation in his voice. "Possibly the driest, flattest, place on Earth. Scorching by day, freezing by night."

"We go to the funnest places." Uzmahndey stuffed the sandwich in and chewed, impeding his participation in any further conversation.

Keanu never emerged from the bedroom the rest of the day. Charlie joined him that night. Uzmahndey and his son retired to bunk beds in the other bedroom. As they both stripped down to undershorts, he studied his son. At eighteen, Charley had completed his inhuman growth. He appeared muscular and trim. The alien half of his genes had sculpted him into a powerful specimen.

And he has bigger balls than you.

"Of course he does. One of them is alien." Yet Uzmahndey was convinced the genes Charley had inherited from him had helped, too. "You don't seem upset with me. Like your sister is."

Charley climbed into the top bunk. "You'll come through for us."

"If that involves giving up my xenobots don't be so sure."

Charley rolled away without responding.

The next day they caught a bus heading north. It was a jarring trip along the coast to the slightly larger town of Puerto Murta over roads that ranged from nearly paved to nearly impassable. Their bus bumped across rocks the size of bricks packed high in barely-discernible tracks, across packed dirt and smaller rocks, across loose pebbles, across coarse gravel, across broken cobbles, even across sections of actual surviving pavement. Spine-fusing jolts tossed soft bodies about the insubstantial seats.

But the scenery was astonishing. Patagonia was second only to Antarctica as the wildest most primitive landscape Uzmahndey had laid eyes on during this entire world-spanning odyssey. Their bus continued north up the Rio Murta into towering snow-capped mountains. They turned away from the river and continued up another valley through mountains not as high but just as wild. The road continued writhing its way north past snow-capped peaks, taking them through one national park after another. Uzmahndey hardly dozed, he was so intent on the amazing scenery framed by the filthy window he pressed his face against.

The road led them back to an inlet, and northward up it. After traveling through yet two more national parks, at Puerto Montt on the Pacific coast the bus continued north on a much better highway. This took them away from the coast and out of the wilds of Patagonia into the tame agricultural heartland of Chile. After several transfers and over a day and a half of cramped jarring bus travel, they pulled into Santiago, a sprawling modern city of five and a half million.

They took a taxi to a hotel near the airport, the Hilton Garden Inn. Charlie practically lugged Keanu up to the Evolution Room Snugglesaurus had secured for them. She stretched him out on the double bed nearest the bathroom. Besides two double beds, there was a desk, flat screen TV on the wall, refrigerator, a gleaming bathroom with walk-in shower, and air conditioning.

"This is nice," Uzmahndey said. "Let's just wait here for Angela to show up."

Charlie scowled in reply, but Charley nodded. "Keanu needs a day or two to recover."

"How about a month?" Keanu mumbled from flat on his back.

The next two days flew by. Charlie tended to Keanu. Charley attempted to track down Angela through Snugglesaurus, to no avail.

"Hopefully, she will show up on Snugglesaurus' radar as we get closer to the next portal. She has to be headed there, too."

"If she escaped from the other side," Uzmahndey said.

No one will ever accuse you of being Mr. Brightside.

I'm proud of you, Good. That's the darkest thing you've ever said.

Uzmahndey spent the two days wisely by eating a lot. His favorite dish served at the hotel restaurant turned out to be chorrillana, which was a large plate of sliced beef and French fries smothered in scrambled eggs and fried onions. He sampled some of their other offerings, such as pebre, a Chilean salsa that tasted nothing like the Mexican variety and was served with warm bread; porotos Granados, a bean stew with mashed corn, onions, and pumpkins; and chacarero, a steak sandwich topped with green beans, tomato, and green pepper. By the second day he was restless enough to get out and try some Santiago street food, such as completo, a huge hot dog topped with everything you could imagine; empanada de pino, a large baked pie stuffed with minced meat, onions, raisins, black olives and hard boiled eggs; and pumpkin fritters called sopapillas. After two days of this Good and Bad begged for mercy.

Although Uzmahndey's back no longer hurt, it was criss-crossed with scars.

"Keanu could make those scars look better," Charley suggested one night as they undressed for bed.

"With a volcano? A hula girl? No thanks. Besides, he's in no mood to do anything but moan."

Uzmahndey had taken notice of how irritable Keanu had become. He had every right to be irritable. They had pushed him beyond human endurance. They couldn't expect him to keep up, but had forced him to. So Uzmahndey let it slide.

What produced too much friction to slide was the attitude of the hotel staff, especially the servers in the restaurant where Uzmahndey spent so much time. He had ample opportunity to witness how rude they were. Perhaps these Chileans had encountered too many ugly Americans.

When he ventured outside to sample the street food he saw that it wasn't only him. Other tourists from the hotel, be they European or Asian, were treated just as badly. Even other Chileans. What was going on?

Uzmahndey mentioned this to his son.

"I don't know. I haven't been out as much as you." Charley smiled. "I haven't been as hungry as you."

"Let's take a walk." Uzmahndey led Charley on a stroll through the neighborhood. Sure enough, tempers flared on the left and the right. "If this was America, people would be pulling out guns and shooting each other."

"The Chileans we met in Patagonia weren't like this. They were friendly and helpful."

"I've not met people this bad-tempered anywhere else around the world," Uzmahndey said.

"We'll see tomorrow how the Bolivians are behaving."

"Tomorrow? Have you heard from Angela?"

"No."

"Then why press on until we do?"

"We can't give up. We'll do what we can without her."

The next day they caught a taxi to the airport. Where the ticket taker yelled at them for their poor Spanish. Uzmahndey nearly yelled back at her, until Charley restrained him. He was angry enough to go off on airline personnel like passengers in the states had been doing ever since the Covid lockdown began. He felt a strong urge to punch the flight attendant who spilled a drink on him. It wasn't her fault, there had been turbulence, but he had seen red. Whatever was happening was affecting him, too.

During the flight Uzmahndey closed his eyes and took stock with his two remaining xenobots.

"What's going on, guys?"

You expect us to figure out you stupid people?!

He's joking.

"I don't think it's funny, Bad. I nearly punched that street vendor who tried to short change me."

<u>You would have if not for us.</u>

<u>*Yeah, we've been keeping your cool for you! On top of every-thing else we've had to do!! With only two of us now!!!*</u>

"Are you still trying to be funny?"

<u>*Yeah. Why aren't you laughing?*</u>

"No serious thoughts from either of you?"

<u>We have been kind of busy.</u>

<u>*You bet we have!!!*</u>

When they touched down in La Paz the situation in Bolivia seemed worse. By then even Charlie, who had been so involved caring for Keanu to be oblivious to the slights piled on her, noticed. "What's wrong with these people?" she asked her brother, still not talking to Uzmahndey.

He had been keeping his distance from her, anyway. He was afraid once they got to the portal she might try to tear him open and snatch a xenobot out.

Snugglesaurus paid an enormous sum for a connecting flight to Joya Adina Airport, on the edge of Salar de Uyuni.

"He ripped us off," Uzmahndey complained to Charley. "You should have let me haggle the thief down."

"How could you haggle? You barely know any Spanish. Besides, our funds seem to be limitless."

"That's no reason to let everybody cheat us!"

Charley studied Uzmahndey's reddened face. "Calm down, Dad."

Uzmahndey took a deep breath. Why was he so upset?

During the connecting flight, Uzmahndey sat back, closed his eyes, and tried to relax.

"Any insights on why everyone is so disturbed? Including me?"

<u>I detect a change in the Schumann Resonance. The heart-beat of Mother Earth.</u>

"Which is Gaia."

Yes. Every second in the atmospheric cavity between the surface of the earth and the ionosphere about one-thousand lightning flashes around the globe travel this pocket, sending electromagnetic energy signals to all the microorganisms below. These signals couple us to the Earth's magnetic field, and are also thought to be inversely influenced by our mass emotions, and the sum of human consciousness.

"Gaia manipulates this?"

Yes. Humans are tuned to the resonant vibration of the Earth. This is why nature is so healing to people, why getting outside in the woods and other natural settings can be so restorative. It helps people match the Earth frequency of 7.83hz, which boosts the body's natural ability to heal and regulate itself. Studies have shown that Schumann Resonance frequencies have particular effects on the human brain and nervous system, the cardiovascular system, circadian rhythms, immune function, DNA, and more. Schumann Resonance Extremely Low Frequency waves in the Earth's magnetic field overlap with human brainwaves, corresponding to the high theta of the human range.

"High Theta? You're losing me, Good. Just give me the Cliff Notes."

Entrainment is the process whereby two oscillating systems, which have different periods when they function independently, assume a common period when they interact. These two oscillators fall into synchrony. This creates kindling, the matching of neurons across the brain. Many cultures implement vibrational techniques in hopes of synchronizing with the frequencies of the Schumann Resonance. They believe these frequencies can heal body and mind. In the ebb and flow of these energies high blood pressure is reduced and depression is alleviated. By the syntonization of brain waves to the Schumann Resonance of

<u>7.83 hz, accomplished through music or meditation, people benefit from a huge energy intake from the Earth's own energy field.</u>

"This is all fascinating, Good, but what does it have to do with us?"

<u>The intensity of the Schumann Resonance is affected by lightning strikes, cloud-to-cloud lightning, intense thunderstorms, solar activity directed at the Earth such as solar winds and solar flares, geomagnetic disturbances, scalar weapons, and energy bursts of unknown origin.</u>

Except we know what the 'unknown' origin is.

"Gaia?"

Bazinga.

From the airport, a short taxi ride took them to the small salt-mining town of Colchina, where the Palacio de Sal – the Salt Palace – perched on the edge of the Salar de Uyuni.

"Is it really built out of salt?" Uzmahndey wondered aloud.

<u>Yes. Our room is an igloo fashioned out of blocks of salt.</u>

Once ensconced in their salt igloo, Keanu flopped onto one bed and Charlie sat beside him.

Watching those two felt like Uzmahndey was listening to someone scrape their fingernails across a blackboard. "Now what? We wait for Angela to show up?"

"No," Charley answered. "Snugglesaurus has booked us a 4-wheel tour into the salt flats for tomorrow morning. So rest up."

"I'm too restless to rest. I saw in the lobby they have a spa."

Uzmahndey found his trunks and went into the bathroom to put them on, then donned his clothes over them. He bolted out of their room and down the narrow salt-block hall to the lobby. Where he found several intriguing salt sculptures. Which intrigued him enough to make him want to see the real thing.

Uzmahndey stepped outside to gaze across the salt flats. The dazzling tabletop-flat white vista was blinding. The surface salt at his feet had dried into a mosaic of hexagonal squares. At the distance of several first-downs water covered the salt, creating an incredibly flat reflective surface. In the far distance he could see mountains.

He walked to the water's edge. It was like peering into a mirror. The sky was reflected so precisely it was difficult to determine which way was up. He kicked off shoes and socks, rolled up his pants legs, and waded in. The warm water came up only to his ankles.

"What do you think, guys? Any volunteers?" Silence within. "This looks like an interesting place. Either of you want to stay here to seal the portal?"

No.

No.

"I can't blame you. I like being mobile myself."

Uzmahndey splashed back out, picked up his shoes and socks, and walked back into the lobby. The desk clerk directed him to the spa. He chose the JAYU experience. After stripping down to his swim trunks, it began with him entering their indoor swimming pool for a hydro massage circuit conducted by a young female masseuse. Next he was immersed in a water-filled bathtub with a high salt content. After that, he reclined on a hard pallet to be completely covered in salt granules. He then rolled over for his back to be covered by mineral mud extracted from nearby Thanupa volcano. The course ended with a gentle foot massage.

Uzmahndey returned to their salt igloo limp as a rag. The chalkboard scratching had lessened in intensity, though he could still hear it in the background. He found Charlie and Keanu in bed under covers, and Charley perched on the edge of the other bed with Snugglesaurus.

"Still learning how to be eighteen?"

Charley smiled up at him. "Snugglesaurus is searching for Angela."

"Any luck?"

Charley shook his head no.

"Could she be trapped in Gaia's realm?"

"We got out."

"But we had the AI. It was Snugglesaurus that found a way out, right?"

Charley nodded.

"So she could still be stuck there. That's probably why the AI can't locate her. The Internet doesn't extend into Gaia's realm. Or there could be another reason."

"Mom could be dead."

"I was going to say destroyed. There were some wicked monsters at Blood Falls. And she was on her own."

"In either case, we keep going."

"If you're going on, then I am, too."

Charley smiled his appreciation at Uzmahndey.

"This salt flat is huge. Do you know where the portal is?"

"Snugglesaurus says it's on Isla Inkawasi."

Uzmahndey sat next to his son. "How difficult will it be to take another xenobot out? Will it hurt much?"

"It's bound to. But maybe the remaining xenobot can numb the pain."

"Maybe?"

"You were suffering much worse pain last time with your torn up back. You didn't notice how painful it was for me to get the xenobot out. This time won't be like that."

"Just wait until the last possible moment to do it."

"We will." Charlie had rolled over from Keanu, who was asleep, to gaze upon Uzmahndey with teary eyes. "We'll be as gentle as we can."

Late that night Uzmahndey awakened from a nightmare in a cold sweat. Charlie had been ripping his back open so Charley could get at the xenobot, digging his fingers around Uzmahndey's spine and between his ribs searching for it.

Uzmahndey crawled out of bed. It seemed like Phobetor still had hold of his psyche. The flames searing across his back, which had ebbed days ago, flared anew. His mind raging, there was no chance of him going back to sleep. He stepped into his pants.

"Are you okay?"

Uzmahndey looked to see Charlie awake and staring at him from the other bed.

"Yeah. I just can't sleep. I'm going for a walk in the salt flats." Seeing that she continued to watch him as he slipped on his shirt, he forced a grim smile. "Don't worry. I'm not running off with my xenobots."

It was very late, or very early, however you wanted to look at it. The halls were empty. Only the night clerk behind the desk in the lobby acknowledged him before he walked outside.

To the most astounding sight he had ever witnessed. The clear and cloudless night sky presented the heavens in all its bare unadorned glory. The myriad stars reflected in the vast flat plane of the salt flats covered in shallow still water seemed to accomplish an impossibility – it doubled infinity. He gazed upon two worlds, two dimensions, mirror images of one another, above and below, an endless reality of depthless sparkling wonder.

"How are you, Uzmahndey?"

He spun around to find Angela standing behind him. "Angela? How?"

"It's a long story."

He embraced her. "I've got all night."

She returned the hug with care, then released him. "Let me see your back."

Uzmahndey peeled off his shirt and turned around.

She traced his tangle of scars with gentle fingers. "Does it hurt?"

"Not much. Good and Bad fixed me up." He turned back around to face her. "Now tell me what happened to you."

"Let's walk." She took his hand and led him along the edge of the water. "In Antarctica I planted a Cheerio in the crack in the ice where the red iron-rich water was flowing out of Blood Falls. After sealing the portal I turned back around, but you all were gone."

"Gaia's children Erebus and Uranus pulled us through the portal into their realm. Nyx and a bunch others showed up, too."

She nodded primly, irritated at the interruption but determined not to show it. Much. "I assumed you had been drawn into Gaia's realm before I sealed it. But then it was sealed, so I couldn't go in after you. You were on your own."

"We got out through a portal Snugglesaurus located that led to the Marble Caves in Patagonia. In Chile. Which we then sealed. With Ugly."

Angela sighed. "This will take all night if you keep interrupting."

"Okay. I just want to know one more thing." After she sighed again, he asked, "Why didn't you contact us? The kids have been worried sick about you."

"At first I couldn't. I reached out for Snugglesaurus but couldn't make contact. I assumed it was because he was in Gaia's realm with you. As soon as all of you emerged in Marble Caves he established contact."

"Why didn't he tell us?" Following a silent glare from Angela, Uzmahndey dropped his head. "Sorry."

"I instructed him not to. He informed me all four of you had survived, although you were badly injured. He assessed the two remaining xenobots could heal you. And the portal at Marble Caves was sealed, so nothing could pursue you."

She raised a hand to forestall Uzmahndey from asking the question she knew was coming. "I wanted to see what Keanu would do. You seem to think I blindly trust him. I don't. But he was your friend. If he was of good enough character for you to approve of, I judged him worthy of Charlie. But Gaia delivered him to us for a reason. He was bound to strike against us at some point. And he did, when we were at our weakest. I was gone, you were incapacitated, Charley was laid low with a growth spurt, and Charlie was blinded by love. So Keanu snatched Snugglesaurus and ran."

"You're wrong." Uzmahndey defied her glare. "He went to get food and water and medicine, and he needed Snugglesaurus to guide him."

"That's what he told you. He intended to run off with Snugglesaurus. Keanu saw him as a source of unlimited wealth and power."

"Then why did he come back?"

"Because I was right to trust him and you were right to befriend him. He couldn't abandon his wife and child. He is too good a person for that."

"What if he *had* run off with the AI?"

"Where could he have gone? I knew where Snugglesaurus was. I would have tracked Keanu down and destroyed him."

"Okay. So he's half a rat."

"The good half prevailed. Gaia didn't expect that. For as long as she has existed with humans, she has little understanding of their make-up. That shows her arrogance. She expected Keanu to act in his personal best interest."

"So why didn't you contact us *after* Keanu returned with the AI?"

"I still wanted to keep an eye on him. And you were doing okay without me."

"How did you get out of Antarctica?"

"I'll tell you if you quit interrupting." Following a reluctant nod from Uzmahndey, she continued. "I called on the radio for the helicopter to come pick me up. I told him you four had wandered off and gotten lost in the dry valleys. A rescue party searched for you, but of course there was no trace, not even footprints. You had simply vanished."

A pause, for Uzmahndey to interrupt. When he didn't, she continued. "I was taken back to the cruise ship on the Zodiac we'd arrived in. The cruise was cut short, and the boat headed straight back for Dunedin. I pretended to be in shock at the death of my four companions, so serious questioning was postponed until the crew could turn me over to the New Zealand authorities. The night before we reached port I jumped ship and swam to shore. When they couldn't find my body, they assumed I was dead. The water was frigid. Any person would have died of exposure before they could reach the shore. With the mental state I had pretended to be in, they assumed I had committed suicide."

"Wait a minute." Uzmahndey braved her irritation at the interruption, but he couldn't help himself. "*Were* you trying to commit suicide?"

"Of course not."

"Then you knew the freezing water wouldn't kill you?"

"Are you asking if I am aware I am a robot?"

"When did you remember?"

"Snugglesaurus informed me the night before we left the cruise ship for McMurdo Station. He anticipated we were heading into danger and believed the information was critical."

"You mean he could have fixed you at any time?"

Angela nodded yes.

"Then why did he wait so long to do it?"

"This was the completion of my learning program. To fully immerse me in being human."

"You mean it was going to happen all along?"

"Yes. Mnemosyne's attack merely activated this final stage of the learning program early."

Had it made her different? More human, after fully believing she was? Even Pinocchio had never forgotten he was a puppet.

"Can I finish my story now?"

"By all means."

"By the time I reached the New Zealand coast, Snugglesaurus had already created a new online identity for me. He told me that after sealing the portal in Marble Caves, you four were en route to seal the one here. So he arranged a flight for me from Dunedin to La Paz. Then I took a bus here. Snugglesaurus bought a ticket for me to join your tour tomorrow."

She stopped to pull Uzmahndey around to face her. "Were you worried about me?"

"I was worried about having to give up another xenobot."

Angela laughed. "About that." She pulled out her Tupperware. "Open your mouth."

Uzmahndey was stunned. "You are replacing it?"

She popped a Cheerio into his gaping mouth before he could utter another word. "This one is special. And it shouldn't knock you out like before. It's only one xenobot this time shocking your system, not three at once. And the other two already in you will cushion the blow. You should be fine by morning."

"Why are you doing this, Angela?"

"I'm impressed by what you did. Giving up one of your xenobots."

"I didn't do it willingly. I was out of it when Charley took it."

"But you were willing to donate another precious one."

"I was considering it. I hadn't made up my mind."

Yes you had.

One of us was going to be stuck here.

Angela laughed. "I wonder which one it would have been."

It would have been Good. No way can Uz do without me.

Uzmahndey wavered on his feet. "Maybe this new xenobot will hit me harder than you think."

Angela took hold of him. "I better get you inside."

Wake up, Uzmahndey.

That voice was different. "Are you the new xenobot?"

Yes.

It sounded very different. "Why don't you sound like the others?"

Because I'm female.

"Female! I didn't know the xenobots even *had* a gender."

I am definitely male.

Yeah, Uz, no confusion here about my *gender. I'm male.*

Uzmahndey's eyes popped open. Angela, Charley, Charlie, and Keanu were gathered around his bed, all appearing quite amused. He directed his ire at Angela. "Why did you put a female inside of me?"

"To give you a broader insight into the human condition. Half your fellow humans are female."

Uzmahndey's eyes narrowed on Keanu.

Do not say anything bad about Keanu.

Angela doesn't want to cause trouble between him and Charlie. He ultimately made the right decision. So leave him alone.

Uzmahndey returned his gaze to Angela. "I bet you think this is funny."

Her smile informed him she did. "What are you going to name her?"

"How about Angel? Since she came from you, Angela, and you seem to stick with a name you like."

Angela nodded her approval. "Angel it is."

Just don't think that's what I am. I am nobody's angel.

She sounds like bad news.

I like her.

Uzmahndey rose. He was steady on his feet. Ingesting Angel had gone more smoothly than the last time he had eaten Cheerios.

After breakfast, a hearty one for Uzmahndey since Angel's appetite did not seem at all feminine, they trooped out to the four-wheel transports awaiting them. Other guests joined them, and a caravan of five vehicles took off across the salt flats.

The train graveyard was their first stop. There were over a hundred ruins of train cars rusting in the salty environment. Most were well on the way to dissolving back into the elements. Graffiti of all sorts, some quite striking, adorned the decaying hulks. Other tour groups were present, which made for a considerable tense and testy crowd. A fistfight erupted, promptly broken up by the tour operators.

Uzmahndey pulled Angela aside. "Have you noticed how badly people are behaving?"

"Snugglesaurus tells me Gaia has jacked up everyone's gamma brain waves to higher frequencies. No one is dropping down anywhere near the delta brain wave frequency of 4.11hz, what is required to achieve deep dreamless sleep. She is driving humanity to a nervous breakdown. If she keeps this up wars are bound to break out. Perhaps even nuclear war."

"Why is she doing this?"

"It's a scorched earth strategy. If she can't have the Earth, then she will leave nothing for us, either."

"So Gaia has given up?"

"No, just a different strategy. She hopes if humanity is nearly wiped out by nuclear war and the resulting nuclear winter, then the ruined world that remains won't be so attractive to my father."

The next stop on the tour was Colchani, a small town on the edge of the salt flats. The Salar de Uyuni contained an estimated ten billion tons of salt, of which 25,000 tons were excavated and processed annually. Artifacts crafted of salt, and textile art fashioned from llama and alpaca, were displayed for sale throughout the small town. The tour led them to a traditional salt factory to show how the element was refined. After, they visited the Salt Museum, where they could see the kind of salt bricks their hotel was constructed of.

Once they finished at the museum, their tour group set off into the interior of the salt flats. A magnificent hour and a half was spent splashing through shallow water, distorting the reflective image of the sky. The brilliant salt flats were ethereally beautiful in their exotic desolation, with the universe shimmering above and rippling below. The vehicles stopped several times for people to get out and explore the wet white wonderland. And, of course, to pose for photographs.

During one of these stops Angel spoke up.

Look to the west.

Uzmahndey scanned the horizon.

To your other west, dummy.

Uzmahndey looked the other way and saw another tour caravan approaching. "So what? More tourists. I've seen several of these four-wheel drive caravans today."

Keep an eye on this one.

Uzmahndey did. When they boarded their vehicles and continued across the salt flats, he saw the distant caravan was headed the same way. He nudged Angela. "We're being followed."

"Not necessarily. There are a lot of tour groups out."

"This is a big place to explore. Why would they get so close?"

"Because they're headed for the same destination we are. Incahuasi Island is a major attraction. Nearly everyone who visits the salt flats comes to see it."

"Is that where the portal is?"

"Yes. We'll get there first. Let's see what happens when they get there."

Approaching Incahuasi Island was like approaching a sandy atoll in the South Pacific. In the far distance it appeared as a dot on the horizon. The nearer they came, the larger it grew. On the final approach Uzmahndey could see a dozen four-wheel drives were already parked before it. Tourists scrambled all over the rocky isle dominated by huge cacti. Their five vehicles joined the parked throng and everyone hopped out.

Uzmahndey noticed the four vehicles following them had cut the distance considerably. "They're moving fast," he noted to Angela.

"Snugglesaurus is keeping an eye on them."

So will I. If you will.

She wants you to look at them so she can see what they are doing.

"Don't mansplain, Bad. I know what she means."

But when their tour guide announced llama steaks were available at the cook shack, Uzmahndey averted his gaze to put his order in. He then ascended to the highest point on the small rise for a better view. The vista was mind-boggling. A flat surface of reflected sky stretched out to all horizons. Other islands rose up out of the reflected clouds. Distant mountains bordered the expansive salt flats. And the four worrisome vehicles drew ever nearer.

"Uz!"

Uzmahndey looked to see Keanu step behind one of the large cacti, putting his hat on top of it, sunglasses on spines below his hat, then sticking his arms out.

"Saguaro Man!"

"That's not a saguaro, Neo."

The spray of automatic weapon fire sent all the American tourists ducking for cover. They were used to this. Mass shootings were a bi-weekly occurrence back home. Most of the other tourists and their guides merely stood around searching the sky for fireworks. As Uzmahndey ducked down he located the shooters. The four vehicles that had been following them had arrived, and a couple dozen well-armed men and women had jumped out and begun firing. The stupefied starers began falling. At last, the rest joined the Americans in sheltering among the larger rocks.

Uzmahndey checked on his group. Charlie and Keanu had ducked behind a large rock. Angela and Charley had found cover farther down behind the cook shack. Uzmahndey utilized his receiver agility, speed, and sure footwork, augmented by the three xenobots, to run an evasive route down to Charlie and Keanu. "Gaia worshippers?"

Stoked to a frenzy by the increase of the Schumann Resonance.

This isn't New Zealand. They've got serious firepower this time.

You must stop them. They will kill everyone here just to get us.

Half of the attackers advanced up onto the island, while the other half remained by their vehicles to cover them.

"I don't have a weapon. What can I do?"

Nothing. Stay down.

"What kind of strategy is that? They are coming right at us!"

It's Snugglesaurus' strategy.

"Really? Do you care to share his plan?"

Yes! The plan is for you to keep your stupid head down.

Angel had been with him for less than a day and she was already getting on his nerves even worse than Bad. What did the little stuffed dinosaur think it could do against automatic rifles?

Two rockets blasted the attackers' parked vehicles, obliterating the dozen worshippers who had remained behind. As salty earth and demolished metal and bloody body pieces rained down on the cowering tourists, the dozen who had approached the island firing froze and looked up. The drone that had just delivered the two missiles banked up for higher altitude.

That was an MQ-9 Reaper.

Wasn't that beautiful?

Enthusiastically bloodthirsty. I really *like her.*

Uzmahndey leaped to his feet and sprinted down the hill.

Snugglesaurus said to stay down.

Screw the toy dinosaur. Go for a gun.

Uzmahndey ignored Good and heeded Angel. While the attackers were freaked out and looking up for more drones, he snatched up an Uzi that still had a hand attached to it. He knocked the bloody thing off and opened fire. The three nearest Gaia fanatics collapsed. The remaining nine ducked down, searching frantically for where the shooting was coming from.

Uzmahndey dropped flat on the ground. Still searching for a target, he saw Angela dash out from behind a large rock to tackle one attacker and take his gun away. She opened fire with it, killing him and one other. The surviving seven trained their weapons on Angela. She was riddled, fell, shrugged, raised to a knee, and killed two more.

While all their attention was focused on her, Uzmahndey picked off another. The remaining four broke and fled. He and Angela both stood upright to fire after them. Uzmahndey got one, while Angela got two.

The lone survivor jumped into a four-wheel drive that hadn't been blown up and sped away.

Uzmahndey sprinted down off the island and leaped into another intact vehicle with the key in.

He's harmless now.

Yeah, Uz, you don't have to chase him.

Go gut the bastard.

Uzmahndey sped across the salt flat, drawing inexorably closer.

He doesn't know how to drive that vehicle.

And Uz does?

Snugglesaurus is telling me how. I'm telling Uzmahndey.

Uzmahndey pulled within twenty feet.

Veer!

Uzmahndey did, just as the worshipper turned around with Uzi in hand and fired off the remaining shots in his weapon. Uzmahndey swerved out of his sharp turn, smiling like an idiot.

"Thanks for the warning, Angel!"

He's out of ammo. You got him now.

Uzmahndey rammed the vehicle from behind. It flipped, sending the driver air born. Uzmahndey pulled up close to the body splayed on the ground, and hopped out.

He looks dead.

Don't trust it. Make sure.

Cut his head off and put it on a spike.

"I don't have a knife."

Do it with the Uzi. You've got enough bullets left.

Damn, girl.

You don't need to do that.

Uzmahndey kicked the body over. Dead for sure.

He drove back to the island. Six people were dead, another dozen or more wounded, some seriously. He saw Angela and two tourists, apparently with medical capabilities, helping the tour guides tend to the wounded. Uzmahndey could see she had been riddled with bullets, but appeared uninjured. Several people standing a safe distance away seemed to have noticed this, also, and were keeping a keen eye on her. They couldn't understand how she could have been shot so many times and not even bleed. Charley, apparently under Snugglesaurus' direction, was treating bullet wounds, also. Charlie, holding the stuffed dinosaur, and Keanu stood off to the side watching.

Uzmahndey joined the couple.

"Did you get him?" Keanu asked.

"Yeah." He looked to Snugglesaurus. "Did he call in a drone strike?"

"Yes," Charlie answered.

That was so cool.

Foolhardy, if you ask me.

Nobody did, wimp.

Angela and Charley joined them. "Does that Jeep you took still have enough gas in it?" she asked Uzmahndey.

"Yeah. Ready to get out of here?"

"Yes. I placed the Cheerio. This portal is locked down." The five trooped down to the Jeep.

One of the tour guides intercepted them. "You can't leave. This is a crime scene. The police will want to interview you."

"Why?" Angela demanded. "All we did was defend ourselves. We saved a lot of lives."

"What do you know about that drone?"

Charley spread his arms wide. "We're tourists. Attacked by terrorists. In *your* country. How can we know anything about anything."

"You Americans sure know a lot about guns," the tour guide sneered. "Bloody Americans."

Charlie climbed into his face. "And it's a good thing we do! We'd all be dead!"

Angela pulled Charlie into her arms. "My sister is pregnant. I need to get her and her baby checked out."

The tour guide didn't back off. "You are Americans. That had to be an American drone. You know something about that drone attack."

"There are other Americans here," Uzmahndey said. "The people who were smart enough to take cover. Ask them."

He climbed in behind the wheel, and the other four piled in. Uzmahndey raced away.

"We're not going back to the salt hotel," Angela said. "Bolivian officials will be waiting for us there. Snugglesaurus will plot a new route."

The GPS screen on the dash came to life.

Uzmahndey adjusted the direction of the Jeep to what he saw on the screen. "That was amazing what he did. How could he locate a drone and gain control of it and direct it here so quickly?"

"You don't appreciate Snugglesaurus," Angela replied. "Time is practically inconsequential to an AI of his power. What would take hours, days, for a human mind to accomplish, he can accomplish in picoseconds."

Uzmahndey shot a sneer over his shoulder at Keanu, seated in back with Charlie and Charley.

"You were playing with fire, Neo, when you snatched Snugglesaurus. He could have brought a missile down on your ass."

Charlie looked in confusion from Uzmahndey's mocking face to Keanu's guilty one. "He didn't snatch Snugglesaurus. He was going for food and water." She looked accusingly at Uzmahndey. "And medicine, for your back."

Way to go.

The old silver-tongued devil let it slip.

Why not? You should kill the son of a bitch.

The rest of the drive passed in silence as Uzmahndey followed the route plotted on the GPS screen. Angela glared at him. Charley shook his head in bemusement. Charlie scooted out from Keanu's embrace. Keanu's guilty eyes stared off into the distance.

Did you really actually graduate from LSU?

Chapter 37

Interlude Eight

Uzmahndey drove the stolen Jeep northwest across the salt flats. The other four remained vigilant for pursuers, either Gaia worshipers or Bolivian officials, but spotted neither. No longer interested in the scenery, Uzmahndey kept his gaze locked on the horizon. The Salar de Uyuni had lost its charm. Blood had been mixed with its salt.

<u>Are you okay?</u>

"I've killed a lot of people."

Angela, seated beside him, looked on with concern. She had apparently gotten over her anger at his gaffe about Keanu. But she remained silent.

<u>It was necessary.</u>

<u>*They were trying to kill you and your family.*</u>

<u>*They deserved to die. They were cold-blooded murderers.*</u>

"I've hurt people. You can't play football without hurting people. But never viciously. Never intentionally. I've never injured anyone so badly they were carted off the field."

<u>That's a part of football.</u>

<u>*All players accept the risk. Look what happened to you?*</u>

<u>*What happened to him? What did I miss?*</u>

"Be quiet, Angel," Angela said.

Uzmahndey glanced at her. "Leave her be. I like her fire."

"I've got something to show you. Give me your phone."

Uzmahndey realized she was trying to distract him from his morbid thoughts. It was amazing how human she had become by this point. He imagined believing herself to be human, even for only a short spell, had humanized her even more. She could empathize enough to sense what he was feeling, understand it, and respond. The concern Angela evidenced for him went way beyond algorithms. He dug out his phone. "I doubt there's service out here."

"Snugglesaurus has access to the Internet from anywhere on the planet." She turned the phone on. "He's downloaded some news stories I want you to see."

Since there was nothing but uninterrupted salt flats ahead for as far as he could see, Uzmahndey could follow the video on his phone while driving. The first concerned the disappearance of four cruise passengers posing as a science team in the Antarctic near McMurdo Station, and the subsequent apparent suicide of the fifth surviving member, who was thought to have thrown herself off the cruise ship into the ocean.

The next video detailed the developing story of the terrorist attack on a group of tourists in Salar de Uyuni. It included cell phone footage of Angela and Uzmahndey firing upon the terrorists. These clear images were transposed against security camera images of the two on board the cruise ship Le Soleal. The mysterious female survivor of the fake science team that had disappeared in Antarctica and who was thought to have committed suicide was still alive. She and an associate supposedly lost in Antarctica had made their way to Bolivia and were involved in the terrorist attack there.

Angela cut the phone off. "We are becoming too well-known. We need to finish this quickly."

"What is our next destination?"

"Our final destination. Canyo Cristales."

"Where is that?"

"Columbia."

"What airport are we headed for?"

"We're driving."

"I thought we were in a hurry to finish this."

"You saw those news stories. Snugglesaurus can confound facial recognition programs to keep us from being tracked down digitally, but he can do nothing to prevent us from being recognized in person. We would never make it through airport security."

"How long of a drive are you talking about?"

"About three-thousand miles."

"That will take a week."

"Not if we don't stop."

"I can't drive three-thousand miles without stopping."

"You won't have to. Charlie can drive. Does Keanu drive?"

"He lost his license. Over a DUI. And Charlie doesn't have one."

"Yes they do."

Uzmahndey grinned. "Snugglesaurus?" The grin didn't last long. "That was some stunt he pulled with the UAV. I thought he was smarter than that."

"He saved our lives."

"Did he have to do it in such a spectacular fashion? You know that drone was probably American. Don't you think the U.S. military will storm heaven and hell to find out who hacked one of their armed UAV's? And how they did it? So now we have the most powerful military on the planet after us."

"Another reason we must hurry."

"By driving three-thousand miles through the Andes Mountains on dirt roads?"

"All the roads won't be dirt, and we won't always be in the mountains. Snugglesaurus will alter whatever alerts go out about us. Like the make of our vehicle, and its license plates."

"Yeah, Dad," Charley leaned forward from the back seat. "Snugglesaurus has taken good care of us so far."

"Sure he has." Uzmahndey whacked the steering wheel. "You know, it's not even the Bolivian prison cell I'm worried about. It's the black site secret prison the CIA will stick us in. You know, the kind where they do all the torture? That's what I'm concerned about."

"It will never happen." Angela turned off his phone and set it aside.

Shortly after, they drove off the salt flats onto a mere trace of a road.

"We sure won't make much progress on roads like this."

"We're meeting some people." This track led to the little village of Bella Vista. Angela pointed to a small shabby café with three rickety tables set up outside.

"Who are they?"

"Smugglers."

"You mean human traffickers?" Uzmahndey burst out laughing. "Of course they are!"

"We have to get across the border. Chilean soldiers are there. They'll be on high alert because of what happened today."

Uzmahndey parked.

"So we are abandoning the Jeep?"

"No. The smugglers know a route through the mountains."

"A route the border guards aren't aware of?"

"Chile has been having trouble with Venezuelan migrants. Normally, they don't care about Americans."

"And we're supposed to trust human traffickers?"

"Snugglesaurus has set it up." Angela climbed out of the Jeep.

"That's supposed to make me feel better about this? If something goes wrong is he going to call in another drone strike?"

Charley roused his sister and Keanu. Charlie looked around in a daze. "What's going on?"

"Look sexy," Uzmahndey said. "We're going to traffic you."

Uzmahndey followed Angela into the café. Three men lounged around a table in a corner. Since Angela conversed with them in Spanish, Uzmahndey had no idea what was said. But they stood and walked out to look the Jeep over. The oldest of the trio said something to Angela, then the two younger ones climbed onto an ATV. Angela shooed Uzmahndey back into the Jeep.

"I'm supposed to keep up with that?"

The ATV sped away down the dirt road.

"He won't lose you. If we don't make it across the border they don't get their bonus."

Uzmahndey started the Jeep and followed. "So now we are supporting human trafficking. I thought you benign aliens were to be an improvement over our current overlords?"

<u>Snugglesaurus will turn these people in once we are across.</u>

<u>The Bolivian police will be here in less than a week.</u>

<u>Why can't we just kill them once they get us across?</u>

Uzmahndey ignored Angel's bad advice. "Why wait so long to turn them in?"

"That will give us time to be far away from here," Angela said.

Uzmahndey followed the ATV out of town. The track through the mountains was treacherous, but doable. After a jostling hour over rocky terrain, they descended from the mountains into the even smaller village of Cancosa.

"We're in Chile?"

"Yes."

Angela climbed out to converse with the two. One of them talked on his phone for a moment. Apparently, he was conferring with the older one back in Bolivia to see if the money transfer had gone through. A moment later he put the phone away, and the two climbed back onto the ATV and drove back the way they had come.

Angela climbed back into the Jeep.

"Snugglesaurus paid them?" Uzmahndey asked.

"Yes. But they won't have long to enjoy their money. Let's go." As Uzmahndey drove through Cancosa to get back on their route, she said, "Snugglesaurus doesn't make moral choices. He merely does what is expedient."

"So why did he agree to turn them in?"

"To please you. Keeping you engaged in this endeavor is the expedient thing to do."

Uzmahndey heaved a world-weary sigh. "Tell him I appreciate the effort."

"He knows."

Uzmahndey studied her calm face. "I'm glad you're not like that."

She smiled at him. "Because my programming has evolved to make moral choices? It's merely mathematics."

"It's all just numbers. So what?"

That snagged Charley's attention. He had been following their conversation from the back seat. "What do you mean, Dad?"

"Football, for example. It has been reduced to mere numbers. There are stats on stats of the stats. Pretty soon they'll do away with actual athletes and play the game virtually. By the time Madden 99 comes out there won't be any flesh and blood teams left."

They continued southwest out of the desolate arid mountains into the even bleaker terrain of the high Andean desert. Which changed so drastically as they drove into the Salar de Huasco that Uzmahndey pulled over. He gazed out across an expansive blue-water lake populated with pink flamingos. Other exotic birds waded about, and flew about, while llamas grazed on the sparse growth of the scrubland all around.

Barren snow-peaked mountains rose up on the distant side of the lake.

"This is beautiful," Charlie exclaimed. She opened the back door.

"What are you doing?" Angela asked.

"Keanu needs to stretch his legs."

Charlie seemed to have gotten over her anger at Keanu over what he had nearly done. She helped him out then escorted him down toward the lake.

"Not a bad idea." Uzmahndey climbed out and joined them. "How are you doing, Neo?"

"Okay now. Back on the salt flats I thought I was going to die."

"Yeah, that thought crossed my mind, too." A pair of strolling rheas caught Uzmahndey's eye. "Are those ostriches?"

Rheas.

"Are they dangerous?"

Only if you try to mate with one.

Uzmahndey burst out laughing.

Charlie reacted as if such behavior was normal. "What did Bad say?"

"That I'm safe. How did you know it was Bad?"

"He's the funny one."

Keanu presented him an off-kilter stare. "That must be so weird. Having people in your head."

"I've gotten used to it. It's sort of like being mic'd up during a game." He spied Angela waving them back over to the car. "She's getting impatient."

They turned back toward the road.

"I'm glad there's only one more portal," Keanu said. "This has been too scary."

"You think this is scary? You should try facing Logan Wilson."

When they joined Angela and Charley at the car, she made a suggestion. "Take a break, Uz. Charlie can drive for a while. This is a good road."

"Yeah, this one's even paved. She's welcome to it."

Keanu joined Charlie in front, while Angela took the middle in back. Uzmahndey climbed in and settled into her. "You're nice and soft for a robot."

She pulled his head down to her bosom. "Just relax."

BANG!

Uzmahndey woke up with a start! He jerked upright from Angela's embrace. It was dark. He was in the back seat. Charlie was driving. "What happened?!"

"Road rage," Charley, seated in back on the other side of Angela, said. "One car just side-swiped another, knocking it into oncoming traffic and a head-on collision. It looked intentional."

"Gaia is still amping up the Schumann Resonance." Angela helped Uzmahndey sit up straight. "How are *you* feeling?"

Uzmahndey paused to consider. "Okay."

We are moderating the Schumann Resonance's effect on you.

Now that we know what's going on.

I really feel like clocking somebody out. But I got it under control.

"Where are we?" Uzmahndey asked.

"Outside of Inique. We just turned north onto the Trans American Highway."

"You doing okay, Charlie?"

"She's doing fine." Angela pulled Uzmahndey's head back down to her breast. "Settle back down, Uz."

Later that night Uzmahndey awoke again. He was nestled in Angela's softness. What a pleasant way to wake up. He gently squeezed.

Angela laughed. "Why are you groping Charlie?"

Uzmahndey shot straight up. Angela was in the middle of the back seat, as before, and Charlie was relaxed into her other side. Charley now sat up front with Keanu, who was driving.

Charlie rose sleep-addled from Angela's other shoulder. "What's going on?"

"Nothing," Uzmahndey growled. "I'm just confused." He looked out the window. The darkness of the vast Pacific Ocean filled his view. "When did you stop driving?"

"Right after that wreck. That shook me up." She scooted as far away up against the door on her side as she could get. "Seeing that was nearly as bad as waking up with you pawing at me."

"I thought you were Angela."

"Hold that thought, honey." Angela turned her attention to the front. "Pull over, Keanu."

"Gladly." He eased onto the shoulder. "These crazy drivers are driving me crazy." His hands were trembling as he released the wheel.

"Don't worry," Charley said. "I've kept an eye on him. He hasn't gone off on any of them."

Angela looked to Uzmahndey. "I'd rather you drive us through the border crossing."

"We're at the border?" Uzmahndey looked around. "Which border?"

"We're crossing into Peru," Charley said.

"We're just going to drive across? No human smugglers?"

"We're on the Trans American Highway now. Droves of Americans drive up and down it. We won't stand out here. Snugglesaurus can get us across undetected. He says this border crossing is one of the fastest on the Highway."

Uzmahndey climbed out of the back, coming face to face with Keanu, who had just climbed out from behind the wheel.

His twitching face was beaded with sweat. "I don't appreciate you fondling my wife."

Uzmahndey let it pass as he started to climb in front. Until Keanu shoved him in. Uzmahndey sprang back out and grabbed Keanu by the shirt collar.

"Stop it, Uz!" Angela yelled. "Don't cause a scene. We're trying to be inconspicuous. Snugglesaurus can't protect us from stupidity."

Uzmahndey released Keanu. "Get in the car before I drive off and leave you standing here." He climbed in behind the wheel. Charlie drug Keanu into the back.

The border crossing was as easy as advertised. All of their online documents were in order. They breezed through in fifteen minutes, speeding away from the bright lights and continuing north on the Trans American.

Soon the road turned west, and they were back on the Pacific coast. Once north of Ite the coast became more undeveloped, more natural, more incredible. At Ilo they passed an airstrip.

Uzmahndey sighed. "It sure would be nice to fly to where we're going."

"We don't want to press our luck," Angela answered from the back seat.

Uzmahndey glanced into the rearview. She and Charlie had changed places. Charlie was now in the middle, cuddled up with Keanu, with Angela on her other side. Despite Charlie's ministrations, Keanu continued to jerk and twitch.

"Is he going to be okay?"

"Yes," Charlie affirmed.

Uzmahndey looked to Charley, seated next to him. "How much farther?"

Charley closed his eyes to check with Snugglesaurus. "At this pace, two more days."

Uzmahndey glanced into the side view mirror at the airport receding behind him. "We could be there in hours if we flew. If Snugglesaurus can get us through a border crossing..."

Angela cut him off. "It's not worth the risk."

Ten hours later the highway turned inland away from the coast. Uzmahndey rubbed his bleary eyes. "Where's it taking us now?"

"Nazca," Charley answered.

Uzmahndey perked up. "Nazca? Where the Lines are?"

"We have no time for sight-seeing," Angela barked from the back seat.

"The hell we don't," Uzmahndey barked back. "If we can waste days driving instead of flying, we can spare an hour here. I need to get out of the Jeep for a while, anyway."

"Mom, the highway goes right through the Nazca Lines." Charley was becoming adept at refereeing between his parents. "It won't take much time to see some of them."

Uzmahndey pulled over at the enigmatic lines of one geometric design. He got out and scanned the indecipherable flat figure. "What is this one supposed to be?"

The other four piled out.

"Snugglesaurus says it's some fantastical winged bird," Charley answered. "When seen from the air."

Uzmahndey walked along the side of the road, flexing his stiff legs. "This would have been a good site for a portal."

"The portals are all geological formations." Angela stepped up alongside him. "This is man-made."

"Or alien-made," Keanu added.

"The Darvaza Gas Crater in Turkmenistan was man-made," Uzmahndey noted.

Charley joined his parents. "The pocket of gas beneath it wasn't."

Angela began herding them all back toward the Jeep. "Are you ready for a break, Uz?"

"I can drive," Charlie volunteered. "As long as no one tries to run me off the road."

When Keanu started to climb in the front passenger side, Angela grabbed his arm.

"No you don't." He turned an irritated eye on her when she tugged him back. "It's not that I don't trust you, Keanu. You're becoming too unstable. You're sitting in back with me where I can watch you."

Charley climbed in front with his sister. Angela scooted into the middle, dragging Keanu in on one side while Uzmahndey climbed in on the other.

As they all settled in, Keanu snarled at Uzmahndey. "Don't fondle me in your sleep."

Punch him, Uz. He's asking for it.

You are not helping, Angel.

It might help.

"Don't do it," Angela warned. She pulled Uzmahndey's head down to her bosom, as before. "Settle down and take a nap, so you can drive some more later. You can fondle me all you want."

Uzmahndey next opened his eyes to Angela shaking him. "What's going on?"

"Charlie just dozed off at the wheel." It was dark again, and they were on the side of the road.

"Can't Keanu drive?"

"Look at him."

Uzmahndey looked. Keanu appeared to be a quivering bowl of enraged Jell-O.

"Do you want him driving?"

Without another word, Uzmahndey climbed out and looked around. Charlie had pulled into the parking lot of a small restaurant.

"Where are we?"

"Outside of Buena Vista, Peru. Get back in the car."

Uzmahndey turned incredulous eyes from the restaurant to Angela.

"We're not going in to eat? I'm starving."

"Me and you are too well known to risk going in anywhere we don't have to. And Keanu is in no shape to go inside."

"Then Charles and Charlie can go in and bring out food."

The brother and sister walked into the restaurant.

Uzmahndey climbed in behind the wheel. "Did Charlie run off the road?"

"Nearly," Angela answered. "Her brother stopped her."

"Has *he* slept at all?"

"He dozes."

Uzmahndey rubbed his eyes. "I feel like I could sleep for a week."

"They are bringing you some coffee."

Once they finished eating and were back on the road, the Trans American Highway veered back to the coast.

Three hours later they drove into Lima.

"Be careful here, Uz," Angela cautioned. "I'm sure there are a lot of crazed people here. Keanu keeps getting worse, so everybody else must be getting worse, too."

Uzmahndey drove defensively, keeping a wary eye out in all directions. Nothing untoward occurred, until they drove into the Plaza Ramon Castilla traffic circle in the downtown district. A shot rang out, fracturing the back driver side glass. Uzmahndey sped out of the circle.

Charlie, who had been asleep in back cuddled up to Angela, jerked upright. "What was that?"

"Someone shot at us," Uzmahndey remarked casually.

"They might not have been aiming at us," Charley noted. "It could have been incidental."

"If it's like this here in Peru," Uzmahndey said, "imagine what it's like in the States. It must be a bloody war zone."

Angela lowered the damaged glass. "We don't want people to see we've got a shot-out window."

"Why not?" Uzmahndey asked. "There's probably a lot of them. We're likely to start seeing dead bodies piled up on the street corners."

Charley's head swiveled back and forth. "I'll be glad when we're out of this city and back out in the country."

North of Lima, they were soon back on the coast. At Trujillo, Angela told Uzmahndey to pull over.

"Why? I'm still good."

"You need to rest. I want you fresh when we cross over into Ecuador."

Uzmahndey pulled onto the shoulder, and he and Charlie switched.

"Nobody has tried to run you off the road, have they?" she asked. "Or shot at you?"

"An alpaca ran out in front of me." Charlie stared in disbelief. "It did. Gaia is probably driving animals as crazy as she is people. Did you ever see that old Hitchcock movie, 'The Birds'?"

She shook her head no as she climbed in behind the wheel.

"Of course not. I forget you've only been alive for a couple of months. You should watch it when you get a chance."

Uzmahndey nestled into Angela once again. He was so exhausted he fell asleep as soon as Charlie pulled out.

It seemed like he had just closed his eyes when Angela jostled him. "Wake up."

Uzmahndey rose up from her shoulder. "Are we there yet?"

"We're approaching the Ecuador border."

Uzmahndey saw it was early dawn. They were on the side of the road at the edge of a small town. "If it's Tuesday, this must be Belgium."

"It's not Tuesday." Angela shook him. "Come on, Uz, wake up." She reached across him to open his door and shove him out.

Uzmahndey staggered upright.

Charlie, already out of the car, caught him to keep him from falling. "Can you drive?"

"Slap me."

Charlie grinned. "Gladly." She let him have it.

"Thank you." He fell in behind the wheel. "Where are we?"

"Not in Belgium." Charley helped him fasten his seat belt. "Tumbes."

Snugglesaurus got them across the border without incident, although not as smoothly as the last time. It took nearly an hour. At long last they were on their way again.

"How many more borders do we have?" Uzmahndey whined.

"One." Charley informed him. "Columbia."

"Columbia?!" Uzmahndey whined louder than before. "That's where all the drug cartels are. The country is full of guns. Everyone will be settling old scores, or making new ones, or..."

We'll kill whoever gets in our way.

"Will you take a valium, Angel. Better yet, I'll take one. Would that calm you down?"

As they passed another airport, Uzmahndey could only moan over what might have been. "We could have ended this by now."

"It's almost over, honey," Angela cooed from the back seat. "Hang on."

Turning off the Trans-American Highway, the road they were on veered away from the coast and improved to a limited-access highway. Uzmahndey sped up. "*Now* we can make some time."

"Do not speed," Angela barked. "We can't get pulled over."

The countryside through Ecuador was verdant farmland. There was much more development than Uzmahndey had seen in Peru. But it was no more peaceful. In the west toward the coast there was a tremendous explosion.

"What was that?" Charlie, rudely-awakened, screamed from the back seat.

"Maybe Russia is invading," Uzmahndey offered.

"Ecuador?"

"Why not. They invade everywhere else." Uzmahndey craned his head around. "If you want me to continue driving you have to feed me. Angel is likely to eat Good if I don't get some food in my body."

Uzmahndey pulled into the parking lot of El Bollo Rico, situated on the edge of a cloverleaf exchange. A small herd of goats were grazing in one of the grassy cloverleaves. As before, Charley and his sister went in to buy food for everyone.

While waiting, Uzmahndey looked Keanu over. His face was so livid it appeared to glow in the dark of the back seat. "Is he in a coma?"

"No," was Angela's deadpan answer.

"Maybe we can get him some good drugs in Columbia."

The brother and sister brought back several dishes. In one Uzmahndey saw an orange-colored stew, topped with avocado slices, quinoa, and seeds. "What's this?"

"Locro de papa," Charley answered.

"Potato stew," Charlie clarified.

"Is potato," Uzmahndey said with a poor stab at a Russian accent. "I told you Russia had invaded."

"The cook claims it's the most popular dish in Ecuador," Charlie said.

"It was either that or roasted guinea pig," Charley added.

"Is potato." Uzmahndey gobbled.

After finishing their meal, they continued northeast on the expressway. They passed through several large cities.

"Ecuador seems much more urbanized than either Chile or Peru," Uzmahndey observed.

Ecuador has a population of eighteen million in a country about the size of Colorado.

"I'm really not…" A passenger airliner passed directly overhead from east to west, drowning out the rest of Uzmahndey's comment. "Damn, he's low."

A moment later it crashed into a densely-populated area. The fireball startled him so much he nearly ran off the road.

"This is getting so bad," Charlie moaned.

"Let's hope they don't close the border," Charley said.

"What happens then?!" Uzmahndey erupted.

Angela shrugged. "Snugglesaurus will figure it out. Just keep driving."

Uzmahndey stayed behind the wheel until he got them through the tangled traffic of the sprawling metropolis of Quito, which took hours. Luckily, only a dozen or so corpses littered the streets. Eventually, he headed east out of the crazed city on another expressway.

At the first opportunity he pulled over. "I've had it. I'm seeing way more traffic than what's really out there."

He switched places with Charlie once more, she taking the wheel and he taking Angela's bosom. "Best pillow I've ever had," he mumbled before passing out.

"Wake up, Uz."

"I don't want to." He snuggled deeper into Angela.

"We're crossing over into Columbia. I want you behind the wheel." She pried his head up. "Get up there."

He did. Shortly after switching drivers, they pulled up to the end of a massive traffic jam. "What's going on?"

"Their computers at the border crossing are down," Angela reported.

Uzmahndey threw his arms wide. "Why not?" He looked back to Angela. "Now what?"

"We wait for the traffic to clear."

"That could take days. If ever."

"Look, Dad." Charley, seated in front next to him, pointed. "Cars are starting to move."

"Their computers are back online." Angela smiled. "And running better than ever."

Uzmahndey glanced at the stuffed dinosaur. "Snuggle-saurus?"

"Of course."

It took two hours for the jam to clear. Since it was such a mess, the border officials whisked everyone through as briskly as possible. They were in as sour of a mood as everyone else, and merely wanted to get their day in and get home to their distraught families.

Once they crossed the Rio San Miguel into Columbia, the expressway devolved to a highway, but it was still a good road. South American motorists proved to be no different than those in the states. As soon as the traffic jam opened up, everyone tried to make up for lost time. Naturally, there were two serious wrecks, but Snugglesaurus maneuvered them around these new jams. They continued, at a snail's pace, to the northeast.

Away from the border, the traffic jams eventually cleared. They passed through heavily-forested countryside with little development. Entering one major urban area, San Miguel, sporadic gunfire was heard all around as they crept through the dark city streets. Bursting out the other side, Uzmahndey sped back into forested pastures and farms. He studied the cultivated fields whizzing by.

"What does cocaine look like when it's growing?"

"Those aren't coca plants," Charley informed him. "You are more likely to see coffee plantations. Columbia grows some of the best coffee beans in the world."

"Thanks for reminding me." Uzmahndey pulled into the next restaurant they came to and dispatched his son to procure some coffee.

"Are you okay?" Angela asked.

"Yeah. We have to be getting close. I think I can go the rest of the way."

"Thank god," Charlie mumbled from Angela's shoulder.

Uzmahndey chugged coffee as they got underway again. They wormed their way through another city riddled with gunfire, La Hormiga, then ascended into mountainous jungle.

"Stay sharp, Uz." Angela cautioned from the back. "If anyone is going to waylay us, this is where they'll try it. We're deep into a national forest."

No one ambushed them. When they emerged from the jungle and drove into a city, Uzmahndey had a laugh when he saw its name. "Macarena? For real? Is this where the dance came from?" He began dancing in his seat.

"We're stopping here," Angela announced.

Uzmahndey was so slap happy he couldn't believe his ears. He kept driving and dancing. Not knowing the lyrics, he merely kept singing the name of the song, 'La Macarena,' over and over.

Until he saw a small airport. He stopped everything except the car to moan. "We could have flown here?"

"You saw that plane crash," Charley reminded him. "Do you really want to fly?"

"Why are we stopping?"

"We're almost at Canyo Cristales. We need to rest up before we go any further."

Snugglesaurus directed Uzmahndey to Hotel La Fuenta. Uzmahndey turned the engine off, laid his head down on the steering wheel, and passed out.

Chapter 38

Canyo Cristales

<u>Wake up!</u>

Uzmahndey jerked his eyelids apart. He found himself hard as a rock. Had he been dreaming of Eros? Again?

<u>No, it was me. I wanted to wake you up in a pleasant way.</u>

He was in a narrow single bed in a closet-sized bedroom with the door closed. "Angel?"

<u>Of course. I sure wouldn't do something like that to you. And Good could never even conceive doing something like that.</u>

<u>You wouldn't wake up.</u>

"Where am I?"

<u>In the Hotel la Cascada, in Macarena, Columbia.</u>

<u>Don't start singing the Macarena again.</u>

<u>You passed out at the wheel. Angela had to carry you in here. It was so embarrassing.</u>

Uzmahndey lifted the sheet and looked. "*This* is embarrassing. I don't know how you did this, Angel, just don't do it again."

The door opened and Charlie stuck her head in. "I thought I heard you talking to your xenobots."

Uzmahndey rolled over onto his side to hide the tent he made of the sheet. "What's going on?"

"Get up and find out."

"I will as soon as you get out."

"It's not like I haven't seen you before, Uz. At the Sunken Forest I saved your balls from freezing off." Despite saying this, she withdrew and closed the door.

Uzmahndey threw the cover off and sat up, staring down at his lap. "Why won't it go down?"

I could call Angela in here to help you with that.

No. She's too busy.

"Angel?"

Sorry. I was just trying to wake you up. I hope I didn't break it.

Uzmahndey rose and dressed. By the time he opened the bedroom door his discomfort had eased a little. He found Angela, Charley, and Charlie seated around a small kitchen table, upon which Snugglesaurus sat in the middle. "Where's Keanu?"

"In the other bedroom," Charley answered. While Charlie laughed.

Ignoring where her eyes were directed, he sat down at the table. At least it was out of sight. "What's the plan?"

"Canyo Cristales is in a remote part of Macarena National Park," Angela answered. "A tour guide will take us there."

"How is he getting us there?"

"By SUV most of the way. Then we'll canoe upriver."

Uzmahndey looked around for a clock. "How long was I out?"

"Just four hours."

He ran his fingers through his hair. "No wonder I feel so lousy."

Lousy? Really? I was feeling pretty good. Angel does have her uses.

I'll wring your pathetic neck.

"Shut up!"

All three at the table looked up at his outburst, but Charlie was the only one to laugh. "Still having a problem?" She ducked her head to look under the table.

Angela scowled at him. "Focus, Uz. This is serious."

Charley took up the tale. "The whole town has gone crazy. Gunshots, fires, looting. The Schumann Resonance must be up to an insane level." He looked out the window. "Macarena is a small town, only four thousand or so, and most of those are cattle ranchers living out in the country. But this place is mobbed now. People are flooding in from God knows where, many of them Gaia fanatics. They're as well-armed as they had been at Salar de Uyuni."

Uzmahndey looked at Snugglesaurus. "Have Snugglesaurus call in another drone strike."

"Won't work this time. There are a lot more of them. And the crazies are anticipating something like that, so they are not all ganged up together. They have spread out and en-circled our hotel. Besides, the U.S. has grounded its entire drone fleet until they figure out what happened in Bolivia."

"Go get Keanu up," Angela barked to Charlie. She turned to the other two. "Our guide just contacted Snugglesaurus. He can't pick us up. He can't get through to the hotel. We have to go to him."

"Where is he?" Charley asked.

"In Makalombia. An ecolodge on the edge of Macarena National Park."

"How are we going to get there?" Charley asked.

"When we're ready to go, Snugglesaurus will block the local cell traffic. The fanatics won't be able to communicate with each other. Their line is spread thin. For now. There are more headed here. That's why we can't wait. We've got to break through now."

Charlie dragged Keanu out of the other bedroom. He looked like death warmed over on power level ten.

"Can he even walk?" Uzmahndey asked.

"Are *you* able to walk now?" Charlie shot back with a smirk.

Uzmahndey glanced down. Thankfully, he was fully relaxed.

I've been thinking about Lake Kaindy. The memory of that icy water is enough to shrivel anything.

Uzmahndey looked out the second-story window at the town below while Charlie got Keanu ready to go, and Angela and Charley packed their backpacks. Columns of smoke rose from three different locations in the section of the small town he could see. Sporadic gunfire sounded from all around. His sharp eyes detected movement between the buildings; a heavily-armed man dashed across an alley. Drug cartel? Former FARC guerilla? Gaia fanatic? Opportunistic looter? Did it matter which? How were they ever going to get through to this last portal?

Look up.

Heavy clouds were massing above the small town. A sudden gust scattered detritus across the ground. Lightning bolts slashed at distant trees.

"Uzmahndey!" Angela barked. "We've got to move now!"

Uzmahndey snatched his backpack and followed the other four out the door. "What's going on?"

Charley smiled at his sister. "Help has arrived."

"What does that mean?" The brother and sister ignored Uzmahndey. Charley followed Angela's charge down the stairs, while Charlie shepherded Keanu down the hall behind them. Uzmahndey chased after.

Just as Angela reached a rear entrance to the hotel the entire building shook from a nearby explosion.

"Was that a missile?" Uzmahndey yelled. "A drone strike? You said they were all grounded."

"No drone." Charley turned a maniacal grin on him. "A lightning strike."

Before Uzmahndey could ask for more information, the black sky was ripped open and an ocean of rain crashed down. They all five ran into the drowning torrent. The building ablaze next door had been struck by lightning. As they dashed down an alley two more nearby lightning strikes rocked the lane.

Angela led them into a small café, where six men over-burdened with automatic weapons huddled in a corner peering out a window at the raging storm. She slammed two of them against the wall. As the others scrambled to their feet and attempted to raise their rifles, Charley took another two down. Uzmahndey knocked Charlie and Keanu to the floor then charged over top of them at the remaining two. One threw down his rifle and fled. The other fired. Uzmahndey had already juked, and the shot missed. He slammed into the man, smashing him into the wall so hard his skull cracked. He had never intentionally tried to give an opponent a concussion, but that didn't mean he didn't know how. As the limp body slumped to the floor, Uzmahndey turned to help his son. But Angela had already knocked one out, while Charley took the other man's rifle from him and bashed his face in with it.

"One got away," Angela yelled. "He'll alert others where we are. We've got to get out of here." She ran out the back. Charley chased right behind. Uzmahndey snatched up a rifle and ammo then turned to check on Charlie and Keanu. She was dragging him along at her side.

Uzmahndey yanked Keanu out of her grasp. "Go on!" When she started to protest, he slung his friend up across his shoulders in a fireman's carry. "I've got him. Go." She ran after her brother, while Uzmahndey staggered forward with Keanu.

Emerging from the back of the café, two more explosions directly ahead staggered him. After the blinding flashes faded, their afterimages washed out eyes already struggling with the black skies and the tsunami downpour. A gust of hurricane-force wind nearly toppled his top-heavy frame as he froze. He could see no one. He could see hardly at all through the black spots cascading across his dazzled eyes in the maddened rainfall.

Just keep running. We'll guide you.

Snugglesaurus is sending us directions. Go down the alley to your right.

**Ditch that loser you're carrying.**

"No way." Uzmahndey lumbered on with his load as directed. "Charlie would never forgive me."

At the end of the alley was their Jeep. Charlie sat behind the wheel, with Angela beside her up front and Charley in back. Uzmahndey dumped Keanu into the back then jumped in back himself. He slung the automatic rifle from off his shoulder. "We're in. Go."

Charlie skidded up the river flowing down the alley. When they rocketed out onto a main street, someone fired on them. Uzmahndey was surprised to spot the muzzle flash in a window of a corner building. His vision was clear. But he had no time to be amazed at what the xenobots could do with his eyes. Uzmahndey returned fire. The shooting stopped.

Charlie raced down the street. A Jeep erupted out of an alley she passed. A man in the front passenger seat stood and fired at them. Uzmahndey took aim, but never had the chance to shoot. A lightning bolt blasted the pursuing Jeep, obliterating it.

Uzmahndey was once again blinded. "Damn! Again! I was staring right at it!"

Charlie sped off the end of the paved street onto a muddy track into a dense grove of trees. They didn't give them cover for long. The Jeep burst out the other side of the grove into an open pasture. The tires bogged down into the slurpy bog. Charlie gunned the motor, and the tires dug in deeper and deeper.

Damn, Uzmahndey cursed to himself this time. He had never taught Charlie how to drive in these conditions. He rubbed his eyes furiously, trying to force them to function. They were sitting ducks there, stuck out in the open. With the rifle raised, he peered back at the murky trees they had just emerged from. His spastic eyes could hardly make them out. Any moment someone would come charging out after them. He hoped he'd be able to see them when it happened.

The Jeep lurched forward. Uzmahndey lost his grip and the rifle clattered out into the mud. But they were moving. The mud wasn't as deep. He felt the Jeep jolt across firmer ground. The wind had eased, also, and the rain lessened. Soon they were bouncing across dry land.

Amazed, Uzmahndey looked around. The clouds above were scattered, the sky lighter, the rain a mere drizzle. And no lightning. He looked back at the town they were fleeing. There the fury raged unabated, the howling wind bending trees to the ground, curtains of rain in the nearly pitch-black sky still flooding the streets.

"Why did you throw your gun down?"

The angry question from Angela pulled his attention back into the Jeep. "I dropped it. It was wet, and Charlie is bouncing us all over the place."

"I got us out of there!" she screamed.

Uzmahndey looked back to the wild storm hovering above the town. "How is that happening? I've never seen such a localized storm."

Charley smiled at him. "Our friends have come to help us."

"Ghost? No way. That's no hologram. That storm is real."

"It's not Ghost." Charlie turned around with a smile on her lips that matched her brother's. "Remember the dreams I told you about? One of them just came true."

Uzmahndey's gaze remained riveted on the unnatural disaster they were fleeing. "That was caused by aliens? Ones you dreamed about?"

"The lightning people."

"Watch where you are going!" Angela barked. Charlie turned back around. "Snugglesaurus is giving you directions, right?"

Uzmahndey finally turned back around to look up front. "Directions to where?"

"Makalombia," Charley answered. "Our guide is waiting for us."

Charlie slammed on the brakes, bringing them to a jarring halt. "My nerves are shot."

Angela spun around to the back seat. "Uzmahndey, can you see yet?"

He rubbed his eyes, blinked several times. He could see good enough. "Yes."

"Then get up here and drive."

He hopped out to trade places with Charlie. "You did good." He slapped her on the back. "I'm proud of you." Uzmahndey climbed in behind the wheel, while Charlie climbed into the back and settled Keanu into her embrace.

Uzmahndey spun out across the bone-dry field.

<u>Turn south.</u>

Uzmahndey did.

"Is Snugglesaurus giving you directions?"

<u>*Yes. We are on the east side of town. We need to go west.*</u>

Uzmahndey glanced back at Charlie. "You went the wrong way?"

"I went the *right* way!" she flared. "Away from the bullets."

<u>Swing far to the south. You want to stay away from the airport.</u>

Uzmahndey settled in for some hard driving through pastures and forests, keeping off roads as much as possible. Twice they were fired upon. Angela reassured them it was random violence sparked by the heightening of the Schumann Resonance and not attacks by Gaia fanatics.

Well south of the town and the airport, at Good's urging he turned north. At last they bumped out of a field onto Via Rio de los 7 Colores, which followed the Rio Guayabero. In the distance in the rearview he could see the roiling dark skies above Macarena. "That storm is still going on?"

"It's keeping the fanatics pinned down," Angela said.

"Yeah, Dad," Charley offered from the back seat. "They don't realize it's so localized. They're all half-drowned by now."

"Have you been having these dreams, too?" Uzmahndey asked his son. "About aliens?"

"Ever since Patagonia. Since I turned eighteen."

When Uzmahndey turned off at Makalumbia he found the place deserted. At the ecolodge their guide rushed out to meet them. "You still want a tour?" he shouted in disbelief. "The world has gone crazy!" He waved his arms all about the property. "Everybody is gone!"

Angela answered him by producing a wad of cash.

His eyes lit up as he counted it. He nodded his head, and it continued nodding as he ran inside to lock up the money. He returned driving a beat-up mud-caked ATV pulling a trailer with a long canoe loaded on it.

Angela herded everyone into the ATV, insisting Uzmahndey sit up front with their guide. They bumped back up onto the road then across the bridge over the Rio Guayabero into Macarena National Park.

Their nervous guide proved loquacious as he drove. "You come from Macarena?" When Uzmahndey responded only with a quizzical look, he went on. "Big storm there. You are all wet and muddy."

Uzmahndey gave a smile that did not ease the Columbian's nerves. "Yes. Big storm."

"Much lightning."

"Global warming."

"Yes, of course, you Americans cause this problem but don't suffer from it. The rest of the world suffers."

"We suffer." He placed his hand on their guide's right arm.

The Columbian yanked it free.

Uzmahndey attempted a reassuring smile. "I just wanted to see how hard you were vibrating."

Neither this response nor the smile reassured their guide. Smashing his lips together and forcing his eyes forward, he drove faster.

Not another word was spoken until their Columbian guide pulled over at the river access. He, Uzmahndey, and Charley unloaded the long boat off the trailer. Once they put in, Angela sat in the front, with Charlie and Keanu behind her. The other three shoved the boat out into deeper water then hopped in, with the guide taking the rear position. Everyone, except Keanu, who did nothing but sit quaking, took up oars and began paddling.

Motioning at Keanu, their guide leaned forward to whisper into Uzmahndey's ear.

"What's wrong with him?"

"He's vibrating too much."

The guide leaned back at that, as far back as he could get from Uzmahndey, and rowed in silence.

The first part of the journey upriver was uneventful.

"Stop!" Angela announced suddenly.

Everyone raised their oars. Their guide leaned around to look forward. "Why are we stopping?"

Angela pointed first to one side of the river, then the other. A dozen well-armed bodies, six on each side, were suspended in the trees ensnared in thick vines. Many of the vines had penetrated the bodies, emerging from their mouths, noses, eyes, ears, anuses.

Their guide moaned, crossing himself. "Guerillas. We must turn back."

"No!" Angela ordered in a voice not to be challenged. "Not guerillas. Look closely. These aren't Columbians."

Their guide did not want to look closely. He sat perfectly still with eyes closed, muttering what was most likely a prayer.

Uzmahndey couldn't take his eyes off the horribly-mangled corpses. "What happened to them?"

"The root people." Charley studied them in awe. "They live in the roots of plants and control them from belowground. All the roots are connected underground, like Aspen trees. They operate as one organism."

"More aliens?" Uzmahndey asked in horror as they drifted amid the carnage. "THIS is what is coming to Earth?"

"These people were here to ambush us," Angela said. "Our alien friends saved our lives." Angela resumed rowing. "Let's keep going." Everyone except their guide and Keanu lowered their oars back into the water. They continued upriver out of sight of the bloodbath.

<u>Look at the water.</u>

Uzmahndey had been ignoring all the sights, unable to get the image of the mutilated corpses out of his eyes. He focused on the river, as Good had urged. There were rivulets of red and pink flowing past. Was this blood? Were there more ripped-open bodies up ahead?

<u>No. It's caused by macarenia ciavegera.</u>

"Speak English, Good."

<u>*It's a tropical aquatic plant.*</u>

Uzmahndey looked up to the front. "Are we there?"

"Close," Angela called back. When a cascade came into view they all stopped rowing. It was an arresting sight. Along with the red and pink, black and yellow and purple and blue and green and many shades between rushed down over the rocks.

Mesmerizing. Also not navigable. She leaned around to look back at their guide. "How do we get around this?"

Their guide was a zombie.

Uzmahndey splashed a large quantity of water on him with his paddle.

Their guide jerked upright, looking all around. He pointed to a riverbank. They all, except him and Keanu, paddled the canoe over to where he had pointed.

Angela clambered out of the front and pulled the canoe up out of the river.

Their guide crossed himself as he watched a woman do this by herself, with five full-grown adults sitting in the canoe.

Everyone but their guide climbed out.

"Come on," Uzmahndey urged.

The Columbian sat perfectly still.

Uzmahndey looked at Angela.

"We can't leave him," she said. "He'll run off with the canoe."

Uzmahndey lifted him out of the canoe with ease.

"Either you come with us or we kill you. Your choice."

"There is a third option." Charlie pulled Uzmahndey back. "Watch."

Tendrils of mud sprouted from the ground at the man's feet and slithered across his shoes. Screaming in horror, he tried to pull his feet free, but couldn't. The snakes of mud writhed on up his pants legs all the way to his hips. He struggled in terror, but his legs wouldn't budge.

"He's not going anywhere," Charlie said.

"More aliens?" Uzmahndey asked.

"Microbial beings who live in the ground. Extremophiles who can exist just below the surface of a barren airless planet like Mars."

"Let's go." Angela walked upriver. Charley followed. Charlie dragged Keanu after.

Uzmahndey cast a final troubled look back at their guide. Mercifully, he had passed out. Or, unmercifully, he had suffered a heart attack and died of fright. Either way, his body was held upright by the alien microbial-infested dirt, which had by that time reached the man's shoulders. What had he done, Uzmahndey wondered, helping pave the way for these horrific monsters to come to Earth? As the writhing lines of mud wormed their way up across their guide's face and into his hair, Uzmahndey moved on after the others.

They trekked upriver until coming to a large pool. All the many colors swirled about the currents like a kaleidoscope. Angela stood at the river's edge staring out into the center of this psychedelic whirlpool.

"Gaia! This is your last chance to abandon the Earth peacefully. We offer you and all your people safe passage off-planet."

The water grew turbulent. One by one beings emerged from the churn.

Aetna, the fiery winged being Uzmahndey had glimpsed above Kilauea and had confronted at Blood Falls.

Crius, a young man with heavily-muscled arms raised high, spinning constellations of stars in each open hand, who had appeared in the night sky above Death Valley.

Pontus, the stocky bearded man with lobster claws on his head reaching out through his long hair, that had attacked them in Mono Lake.

Tartarus, the horned fire-blackened giant who had directed a scalding geyser and sulfurous fumes at them in Yellowstone.

Themis, the stoic white-robed young woman, standing erect with a legal scales in one hand and a sword in her other, who had risen from out of Spotted Lake in Canada.

Hyperion, the young man ablaze with blinding light who had struck Uzmahndey with a fireball at Eternal Flame Falls in New York.

Boreas, the winged blue-skinned man crusted with ice who had been lurking in a crevasse on Skaftafellsjokull Glacier in Iceland.

Aoide, the young woman who had played entrancing music on a lyre in the depths of Fingal's Cave in Scotland.

Oceanus, the massive muscular trident bearer who had ridden atop the rogue wave at Giant's Causeway.

Coeus, the blue-robed bearded man with an owl perched on his shoulder Uzmahndey had met in the Sahara amid the Richat Structure.

Nyx, the dark black-gowned beauty with flowing ebony hair who had brought on the sandstorm in Egypt that nearly destroyed Angela.

Iapetus, the fierce warrior in full metal armor wielding a battle-axe who had been lurking just below the rim of the Darvaza Gas Crater in Turkmenistan.

Tethys, the woman with a serpent wrapped about her neck who had tried to force Uzmahndey to remain with her in Lake Kaindy in Kazakhstan.

Eros, the mesmerizing seductress clad only in her long black tresses who had attempted to seduce Uzmahndey in the Stone Forest in China.

Pan, the horned goat-man with his pipes, and Tmolus, the white-bearded old man with a crown upon his white hair bearing a slender scepter, who had taken the children at Reed Flute Cave.

Mnemosyne, the pink-robed young woman surrounded by a hazy pink mist who had attacked their memories at Lake Hillier in Australia.

All the monsters encountered beyond the portal at Blood Falls - Erebus, Uranus, the trio of fifty-headed one hundred-armed giants, Phobetor, Hypnos, Geres, and the three Keres, one of which had torn open Uzmahndey's back.

This horrific horde of every creature they had contended with all around the world spread out, encircling the five.

Uzmahndey, Charley, and Charlie huddled in close to each other, back to back, with Keanu in the middle, ready to meet the onslaught.

Angela remained unmoved. "Gaia is still afraid to show herself?"

"My sister," Uranus roared. "My wife, is afraid of nothing!"

Tartarus advanced on Angela. "I will not abandon my underworld kingdom. I will drag all of you down there for my amusement. You will suffer eternal torture."

Tmolus stepped before Tatarus. "Except for this one." He pointed at Uzmahndey. "This one is mine."

Uzmahndey squared off to meet him.

Don't move.

"Why not? If they want to attack us one at a time, I'm good with that."

Yeah! Rip his head off!

Not this time, babe. Uz, stay still.

Uzmahndey heeded the warning. Assuming he was frightened, Tmolus strode imperiously forward.

He was knocked off his feet by an unseen force. He remained flat on his back, conscious yet unable to move.

All the other fantastical beings looked around in surprise. Or was that fear Uzmahndey saw in their eyes? What had happened to Tmolus?

In a second all the others, too, were felled, like Tmolus, and like him were pinned to the ground on their backs, unable to twitch a muscle.

Charlie burst out laughing at Uzmahndey's uncomprehending look. "The beings that dwell in deep space. The ones who ride gravity waves. They have pinned our enemies with waves of gravity. They could crush them into individual atoms, then smash their nucleus' into quarks. They could create mini black holes out of each of them. The negligible internal pressure of these beings cannot stand against such intense gravity. But our friends don't intend to harm them. They will merely hold them until we are done here."

That's why we told you to stay put. You could have been caught in those gravity waves.

We're always looking out for you, buddy.

It would have been more fun to rip their heads off.

Angela pulled a Cheerio from her Tupperware container. "Last chance, Gaia."

"It won't work, Angela."

Hearing the LSU head coach's voice, Uzmahndey realized Ghost had arrived. A FARC guerilla who looked like he had lived in the jungle for a decade stood next to Uzmahndey. "What took you so long to get here?"

"I've been busy transporting our allies here." Ghost strode up alongside Angela. "Gaia is not coming out to be trapped like the others."

Uzmahndey joined the two. "Can't we just seal her in there?"

"And let her continue to manipulate the Schumann Resonance? She'll drive the entire human race to an Apocalyptic war. We can't allow Mother Earth to remain in her lair."

Angela put the Cheerio away. "So I go in and drag her out."

Uzmahndey was aghast. "You're going with her, Ghost. Right?"

"I can't project myself through a portal. My influence is only good on this side. I'll stay here to watch over the children."

Charley charged forward. "She's not going in without me."

"Yes I am. You and your sister are too valuable."

"I agree." Uzmahndey stepped up alongside Angela.

She turned to him. "You don't have to do this. We've reached the final portal. You've completed the tour. You've honored your contract."

Listen to her, Uz.

No way! We're not missing out on this!

"Good?"

I'm willing to do whatever is necessary.

He turned back to Angela. "Three out of four accept being franchise tagged. We're coming with you."

What the hell, make it unanimous. Who wants to live forever?

"I do, Bad. Now that I know what it means to be human." Angela peered into Uzmahndey's eyes. "Now that I have something to live for I am prepared to die." She embraced him. Then shoved him away.

He fell back into the water.

Angela leaped through the portal in the middle of the river, disappearing from sight.

Uzmahndey rolled across the shallow pool after her. In a frantic splash he lunged through the rainbow water...

Chapter 39

Gaia

...into a pool even more resplendent than the one he had come from.

A Peter Max psychedelic fantasia ripped from a 'Yellow Submarine' storyboard. Massive lily pads sporting gargantuan blooms floated alongside him. At the pool's edge towering willow trees draped their languid green strands into the water. Vibrant neon pastels, exponentially more luminous than the water of Canyo Cristales, exploded all along the mossy edge in colossal bouquets. Dense tall grasses waved in the slight breeze, which carried earthly-scented bird song. A gentle sun radiated lightly in a pale blue sky buffered with cottony puffs of white.

Wow.

"Angel?"

What is this place?

"How are you talking to me? None of the others could in Gaia's realm."

"I told you when I gave her to you she was special."

Uzmahndey located Angela's dim form amid the brilliant colors engulfing them. He smiled. "How'd you like what I did? It's a football move. In the NFL you can hit the ground, and so long as no opposing player touches you while you are down you can still advance. I've scooted forward like that for a first down before."

Angela snatched him up out of the shallow water and flung him back out into the middle of the pool.

He splashed into the water and skipped across like a flat stone to tumble out onto the far bank. "What the hell, Angela?"

"I closed the portal." The voice was like a gentle spring breeze bearing a lilac scent through a robin's beak. "You can't send him back."

Uzmahndey stood, craning his neck all around. "Is that Gaia? I don't see her."

"We are standing in the midst of her."

Uzmahndey looked around with new awareness. Two huge blooms were her eyes, the willow branches her hair, the grasses her skin. "Where are the Blue Meanies and the Apple Bonkers?"

Angela gazed into the pair of multi-colored whirlpooling pupils. "It's over, Gaia."

"You will have to pull me out by the roots. That will kill the Earth."

"It will damage it, but this ball of rock is durable. The Moon didn't kill it. The Vredefort didn't kill it. The Chicxulub didn't kill it. The Sudbury didn't kill it. This resilient planet will survive you, too."

"But will you survive?"

In the blink of an eye the sparkling prismatic pool amid the resplendent floral garden grew dark, humid, fetid. Foul moss draped the limbs of bald cypress. Knotted skeletal mangrove roots clutched at mud-slick banks. Green slime ensnared deformed lily pads floating atop the stagnant dark water clad in thick duckweed. Rotted logs and sharp cypress knees jutted up out of the viscous slop.

A cloud of mosquitoes swarmed Uzmahndey. He swatted at them with both hands.

They won't bite you.

Realizing he wasn't being bitten, his swatting slowed.

We devised a scent in your sweat that repels them.

"We? Are Good and Bad..." Before he could finish his sentence his mouth filled with the bugs.

You can still swallow them. That can't be good for you. So keep your mouth shut and just listen. The others are here and functioning, they just can't communicate with you.

"What is the point of this, Gaia?" Angela was being swarmed by mosquitoes, also, but none could puncture her skin with their proboscis.

An old swamp hag lurched from out of the writhing dense shadows on the bank. "I have the entire world at my command."

One of the logs in the bog opened its gaping long reptilian mouth and locked onto Angela's leg. The alligator rolled onto its back, pulling her down out of sight below the muck.

Uzmahndey charged out into the black water. Two alligator heads surfaced before him, their cold eyes and countless sharp teeth gaped open in a grinning dare to Uzmahndey to keep coming. He pulled up short in water up to his knees.

Don't stop. We can take them.

A large snake dropped out of a low limb onto his shoulders. It sank its fangs into his neck.

Stay cool. If you panic your heart will pump faster and spread the venom before we can come up with an antidote.

Uzmahndey casually unwrapped the snake and pulled on it until it popped in two. "Was that calm enough, Angel?"

Angela exploded up out of the black water and flung the dead alligator into the dark shadows deep in the swamp. Trailing ropes of wet moss and with alligator guts dripping off her, she grinned at Uzmahndey. "Still glad you came?"

Uzmahndey tossed the gory snake halves off in opposite directions. "Wouldn't miss it for the world."

The old hag cackled. "How about for this world?"

Uzmahndey stood on soggy ground beneath the yellowish-green uplifting limbs of a fever tree. A few feet away Angela faced him beneath a towering baobab. The sky was lighter, although just as hot and humid. As before, not a breeze stirred in this jungle. Mosquitoes no longer tormented, but another cloud of insects engulfed him.

Tsetse flies.

Uzmahndey swatted wildly. "Seriously? Will they put me to sleep?"

Only tsetse flies infected with the Typanosoma parasite cause sleeping sickness.

"So I should be okay."

Most likely Gaia conjured up tsetse flies infected with the Typanosoma parasite.

Slap.

"You guys got this, right?"

Slap.

"An antidote?"

Slap.

Are you kidding? We're still working on the snake venom antidote.

Slap.

"Damn."

Slap. Slap.

"Are these bites fatal?"

If these flies are infected, for sure. But even if they are not, they can cause irritability, aching muscles and joints, swollen lymph nodes, severe headache, extreme fatigue, fever, and a skin rash.

"I really don't need to know all that.

Bad wanted to tell you that. I'm speaking for all three of us now.

"Just tell me if I'm going to die or not."

Don't worry. I am not dying in your sleep. No way for a warrior to go down.

Getting whacked in the head by a twenty pound sack distracted Uzmahndey from what were most-likely fatal bites. He fell to his knees as the huge long seed pod burst open, spilling a gooey muck all over him. "What now?!"

A woman up in that sausage tree just clobbered you with this giant fruit.

Before he could clean the pulpy mess off, another twenty pound sausage-shaped fruit staggered him. Uzmahndey looked up with slime-spattered eyes, trying to locate his attacker. He saw an olive-skinned young woman in a brightly-colored linen gown flowing from her waist down to her ankles perched high on a limb. Her upper body was bejeweled with lavish necklaces, leaving only her arms, shoulders, and painted breasts uncovered. She laughed as she reached for another large sausage fruit.

She's dressed like that to distract you.

"It won't work. Her tits aren't near as nice as Angela's."

Uzmahndey was ready when a third large projectile came hurtling his way. He caught it and threw it back. The giant fruit knocked the woman out of the tree.

Good catch and throw. You nailed her.

Before Uzmahndey could perform a celebratory end zone dance, a crashing in the quiver trees drew his attention. A white rhino charged Angela with lowered head. She dug her feet in and grabbed its large horn, slowing its charge but not stopping it. The three-ton beast drove her backward and slammed her against the baobab trunk. She was pinned. The rhino drug her stunned body along as it backed up, then charged, smashing her once again into the trunk. Angela held on, but seemed immobilized.

Uzmahndey ran over to help.

A male gorilla charged out of the marula trees and clobbered him. Uzmahndey sprawled on the ground at its feet, while the gorilla towered over him, beating his chest and roaring in victory. It stopped its rhythmic beating when Uzmahndey sprang to his feet and squared off to meet it. The gorilla lunged at him.

Uzmahndey dodged its clumsy arms, slipping under them and around, then slammed into it from behind. He grabbed the gorilla by its thick hair and shoved it forward ten yards. Unlike in a game, there was no penalty for blocking in the back or for holding. Uzmahndey drove the gorilla into the rhino.

The huge white rhino turned its wrath from Angela to the gorilla, goring it. Uzmahndey released the gorilla, spun around the two and grabbed Angela, pulling her away from the baobab tree. She nearly fell when he released her. Her back looked deformed from where the rhino had slammed her repeatedly into the tree trunk.

"Are you okay?"

"Are you? You feel hot, and you've got a rash on your face."

Uzmahndey touched the rash. "Come on, guys, you're not going to let those tsetse flies be the death of us, are you?"

This could be from that black mamba.

"You don't even know what kind of poison you're trying to devise an antidote for?"

"They're doing their best." Angela grabbed Uzmahndey by the arm and pulled him forward. "We've got to move."

He looked to see the white rhino had trampled the now-motionless remains of the gorilla underfoot and was eyeing them.

Climb up the leadwood tree.

Angela ran to a tall leafless tree, and he followed her up it. The white rhino charged, ramming the trunk. The entire tree shook.

"That living tank will knock this tree down in no time!" Uzmahndey yelled. "Why did you pick a dead tree for us to climb?"

This leadwood tree might be dead but it's still standing. Even termites can't bring this thing down. It's solid.

Another annihilating blow was delivered by the rhino. Uzmahndey dug his fingers into the bark. Two blows, and the tree wasn't even tilting. Maybe Angel was right.

The blazing sun burst through the jungle canopy. Only there was no longer a canopy. And it was no longer a dead tree he and Angela clung to. They were much higher up in the leafy branches of a live tree. All around them was eight-foot tall elephant grass so dense he could see nothing moving in it. "Where are we now?"

"Up an acacia tree in a savannah," Angela answered. "Be careful. We're fifty feet above the ground now."

What she didn't tell Uzmahndey was that the branches were full of wicked thorns. Tightening his grip in reaction to his sudden awareness of the height, he was pierced in dozens of places.

At the sudden unexpected sharp pain, Uzmahndey lost his grip and fell. He knew how to take a fall. He had been tackled hard many times and was used to being driven into the turf. He went totally limp, relaxing every muscle in his body, even his hands since he didn't have to worry about fumbling, and angled himself to land flat on his back. Still, it was fifty feet, and when he slammed into the ground the air was knocked out of him.

A lion approached at a cautious pace. Gasping for air, Uzmahndey couldn't move. He could only watch as saliva drooled across the wild animal's massive canines. The lion drew near enough he could smell its feral breath.

Angela landed on her feet between Uzmahndey and the lion. The big cat sprang. Angela caught it, but was barreled over by its charge. The lion mauled her with tooth and claw. Until she rolled it over onto its back. Mounting the tiger's chest, she ignored the razor claws ripping her arms as she grabbed both jaws, ignored the sharp teeth shredding her hands as she pulled with all her might. The lion's jaw snapped.

Angela rolled off the motionless big cat and crawled over to Uzmahndey. "Are you just going to lie there all day?"

He looked up to see shreds of cloth hanging from her shredded skin, electricity sparking over exposed broken wires. A fluid darker than blood, thick and viscous, oozed from several places. "You're leaking."

"If you can talk then you can get up." She stood and yanked Uzmahndey to his feet.

Only to face a variation of a centaur. Instead of a horse, the bottom half of the creature was a sleek black leopard; instead of a bare-chested man, the top half was a black bare-chested woman. Gaia laid a hand on the heads of the two tigers poised on either side of her. "I can do this for eons."

Uzmahndey and Angela both smiled in response. "We've already been around the world once fighting you," Uzmahndey said.

"We can go around again," Angela added.

The black woman–black leopard creature urged her two charges forward. The tigers sprang. Uzmahndey caught one, Angela the other. They slammed the two animal heads together so hard their skulls cracked, spilling blood and brains.

Look at her left shoulder.

Uzmahndey turned to Angela.

"What about it?"

Not Angela. Gaia. The leopard woman. Her *left shoulder.*

When Uzmahndey turned back to look he was blinded by snow and ice reflecting a brilliant sun. He threw his hand up in desperation, trying to shield his eyes. "Where are we now?"

"On her side of the Skaftafellsjokull Glacier portal." Angela stepped in front of Uzmahndey. "You are snow blind. Stay back until your vision clears."

"What about her left shoulder, Angel?"

No time for that now. We're about to be attacked.

"Can't you do something about my eyes?" As soon as he said that, his pupils returned to normal size.

Why do you think I have no time to talk? We're busy fixing the problem. And we're busy devising antidotes. The black mamba venom has been dealt with. Now we're working on the tsetse fly toxin.

"You haven't fixed that yet? Is that why I'm about to fall asleep on my feet?"

I won't let you do that. We've got a wolf and a polar bear to fight.

All Uzmahndey could see was a huge white blur charging them on all fours. "You call this fixing my eyes?"

Angela punched the huge bear on the snout. Its momentum carried it forward and felled her with the mass of its body, claws digging deep trenches across her already-mauled front.

Turning to help her, Uzmahndey never saw the gray timber wolf come at him from behind. Leaping onto his back, the snarling animal sank its teeth into his neck. Uzmahndey crashed flat on his face, with the big wolf chewing him up. He was paralyzed with pain.

Until he wasn't.

Good has your pain. Bad's got your adrenal glands. Reach back.

Uzmahndey reached back with both hands, grabbing the wolf's ears. He pulled with all the strength Bad could pump into his muscles. Both ears were ripped off. The wolf howled in agony, and sprang away. "So what are *you* doing?"

Finishing up with the tse tse fly poison. Now go help Angela.

Rolling over, Uzmahndey saw that Angela had the polar bear pinned to the ground on its back while sitting astride its chest, punching its face to a bloody pulp while its powerful deadly arms lay limp at its sides. "Doesn't look like she needs any help."

She's out of control. Go stop her.

Angela had only scraps of fabric and skin left on her. Her interior mechanism was deeply gashed, and whole sections of her had gone dark. The fluid leaking out before was now gushing.

"Angela."

There was no response as she continued to pummel the polar bear. The once-white pelt of the unresponsive animal was soaked scarlet.

"Angela!"

Still she punched its shapeless bloody glob of a face.

Uzmahndey crawled over to her and grabbed an arm.

Angela turned to him and raised her other fist high.

"The bear is dead! You can stop!"

The clenched fist jerked toward Uzmahndey, then faltered, then back, then toward his unprotected face again, then faltered. Finally, Angela froze.

Laughter drew Uzmahndey's eyes to an Inuit woman wrapped up in heavy animal furs sitting in the snow in front of him. "You two are nearly finished. One more biome ought to do it."

Uzmahndey floated in the water. He dog-paddled to stay afloat. He could see nothing but open sea. Including no Angela. He was alone.

Until a bare-chested beauty bedecked with shell necklaces and seaweed extensions woven into her hair surfaced ten feet away.

"Where is she?" he demanded.

"Where do you think? Robots don't float." Gaia dove, her scaly mermaid tail flipping high in the air like that of a whale.

Uzmahndey dove after her. The salt stung his eyes that he kept open. He could hardly see; what little he could see did not reveal Angela. He dove deeper.

Did you see her left shoulder?

Uzmahndey could not answer underwater.

No? I'll refresh your memory.

The image of the mermaid bobbing on top of the water appeared in his mind's eye. There was a livid bruise on her bare left shoulder.

You did that to her when you knocked her out of the tree with the sausage fruit. She can be hurt. You injured her shoulder. Go after it.

Uzmahndey had never played that way. If he knew a player covering him was nursing an injury, he did not try to aggravate that injury. But this wasn't football. He was fighting for his life. And Angela's. His vision at last cleared enough for him to see the mermaid swimming below him. A little further below her he saw Angela sinking. Gaia would have to wait. He had to get Angela. Uzmahndey dove for her.

A huge great white sliced out of the dark between him and Angela. Uzmahndey would never get to her in time if he had to fight that shark first. He didn't know how deep this water was, but he was already getting light-headed from holding his breath. Angela would soon sink down to pressures that could crush her damaged structure.

Forget the shark. Forget Angela. Get Gaia.

The monster shark swam straight for him, its rows of razor teeth gaping open.

Angela doesn't need you.

Angela appeared on the shark's back. She grabbed its dorsal fins and forced it away from Uzmahndey.

She was playing possum. Look behind you.

Uzmahndey glanced over his shoulder. The mermaid had swum up directly behind him.

The bitch wanted a front-row seat to your slaughter. Get her!

He spun and grabbed her left shoulder.

Gaia screamed!

Uzmahndey was back in the garden they had started from. Just inside the portal at Canyo Cristales. The shark, and the rest of the ocean world, was gone.

Except for the mermaid. She lay in the shallow pool with her left shoulder in his iron grip. Gaia screamed again! She thrashed about, trying to get free.

Uzmahndey tightened his grip. He looked madly about until he located Angela. She sparked in a jerking heap at the bottom of the pool in the deeper water in the middle of the river.

"Let me go!" Gaia screamed in agony as her scaly tail flailed about.

She couldn't fight free of his grip. Logan Wilson had once tried his mightiest to pull the ball out as he tackled Uzmahndey. He had failed.

No way was this creature breaking free of his grip. Uzmahndey squeezed her shoulder with all his might. "*You* let *us* go."

Pull her damn arm off!

Feeling the surge of adrenaline Angel flooded his system with, he squeezed harder.

The mermaid screamed so loud it deafened him.

Chapter 40

Interlude Nine

Uzmahndey heard a ukulele. It sounded like 'Over the Rainbow'. Then singing. It wasn't the little girl singing, from the old movie. It was a man. Who was that Hawaiian guy who covered this song? That deep masculine voice came out of a mountain of a man. He'd heard the singer had died. Must be a recording. Uzmahndey loved this version. It got played in Hawaii a lot. What was his name?

"Israel Kamakawiwo'ole."

"Coach?"

"Ghost."

The singing stopped, the ukulele faded away.

Uzmahndey squinted one eye open. Standing before him was the old Hawaiian guy he had seen in Angela's room at the Wild Ginger Hotel way back in Hilo. "Am I alive?"

"Barely."

"How?"

"Because of Good."

And me.

"Yes, Bad helped save you, too. As did Angel. But Good is gone."

"Did they take him? Why? Angela was here with the Cheerios!"

"No one took him. He overexerted himself."

"He had a heart attack?"

"More like he was used up."

"Angel?"

"She's okay, just too busy to talk to you right now. She is managing your pain."

"How could I talk with her in Gaia's realm?"

"She was an improved model. When I learned the xenobots couldn't communicate with you on the far side of a portal I modified one so it could. I sent it back with Angela after I repaired her."

"How is Angela?"

"A wreck."

"But you can fix her?"

"I don't know. This is much worse than the White Desert."

"Is she here? Can I see her?"

"She's in my lab. We'll check in on her later."

Uzmahndey cracked open his other eye. It looked like the delivery room Charley had been born in.

"Where am I?"

"At my base on the ocean floor at the Mid-Atlantic Ridge."

"What happened to Gaia?"

The old Hawaiian guy smiled. "She came through to our side of the portal with you. Screaming in agony. That's some grip you have."

"An elite receiver has to have a strong grip. After you catch a pass tacklers always try to rip the ball out of your hands." Uzmahndey held up his right hand, the one he had gripped Gaia's shoulder with. "I've never fumbled."

"Apparently Gaia has a low tolerance for pain. She came through the portal screaming for us to get you off her."

"Where is she now?"

"Under the watch of our allies."

"What will you do with her?"

"Banish her and her ilk from the Earth. After she adjusts the Schumann Resonance down to a proper level."

"So she could still escape back through the final portal."

"No she can't. We sealed the final portal at Canyo Cristales as soon as Charley and Charlie retrieved Angela from the other side."

"What about all the other monsters?"

"They are still held in a gravitational field that could crush them." The old Hawaiian guy chuckled. "They're our hostages. The reason Gaia became so cooperative. After we threatened to create some new black holes. With her people."

Uzmahndey mulled this over. "If you banish her and the others from the Earth, what's to keep them all from coming back?"

"Why would they want to? All the portals are sealed. There's no way for them to return to their realm."

"You're sure about that?"

"Snugglesaurus says there is a ninety-seven per cent certainty."

"How will you ensure that three percent chance doesn't happen?"

"I won't. You will."

"How will I do that?"

"By listening to Snugglesaurus. He will alert you if any of them return."

"You're leaving Snugglesaurus behind? With me?"

"If you accept the post of Earth Representative."

"What can I or Snugglesaurus do if they return? They're pretty powerful."

"You will notify our allies if the treaty is violated. They will come to your aid." The old Hawaiian guy smiled. "You saw what all *they* can do."

"Snugglesaurus can do interstellar communication?"

"No need for him to do anything other than monitor for Gaia's presence and inform you if she returns. If that were to happen it's up to you to call the other ambassadors on your phone."

"Damn, that's some coverage. What kind of a plan will I have?"

"A good one, along with a new phone."

Uzmahndey closed his eyes. He was not in pain, but he was exhausted.

"You need to rest."

"In a minute. How are my children?"

"They are both good."

"Keanu?"

"Good. Now go to sleep. I need to finish adjusting the Schumann Resonance with Gaia so I can start repairing Angela. Goodnight, Uz."

The old Hawaiian guy faded away, just like he had done back at the Wild Ginger.

I'm glad he's gone. What a wus.

Uzmahndey chuckled (which sounded like a death rattle). "Sounds like you're okay, Angel. Is Good really gone?"

Yes. He gave his all. But I think Bad will make it.

"Thank you for all you've done."

No problem. Now I'll play you a lullaby.

Israel resumed his song, strumming his ukulele.

Uzmahndey sighed (which sounded like he was expelling his last breath). "There aren't many chimney tops on the Big Island. And my troubles aren't about to melt away like lemon drops."

Why not?

"With the shape I'm in it looks like my football comeback is canceled."

I don't know about that.

Chapter 41

Cincinnati

The backdrop where Uzmahndey sat for a post-game interview was adorned with Cincinnati Bengals insignia. "I'd like to dedicate this game to Good and Ugly."

Several reporters laughed. "Is that a product endorsement?" one asked. "Some kind of licorice candy, like Good 'n Plenty?"

"No. Just something I wanted to say."

Another reporter spoke up. "You should be allowed to say whatever you want. That was an amazing game you played today. Over two hundred yards. Three touchdown catches. You were on fire."

"I threw some good blocks, too."

Genial laughter spread around the room. "Yes. You are totally selfless."

"I'm just one man. What matters is being part of a team. A winning team. That includes one of the best defenses in the league. Led by Logan Wilson. He is the best middle linebacker playing the game today."

Another reporter called out above the agreeable murmur. "You were out of football for three seasons. At some point you must have believed you were out of football for good. You even started your own business in Hawaii. What changed?"

"I found a woman who loves me. Who believes in me. And I never stopped pushing myself. You wouldn't believe how many mummy kicks I did these past three years."

"I don't know what that is."

"A rope-jumping exercise. I did a lot of rope work. To build up my knee."

"Your knee seems fine now. Any fear of re-injuring it?"

"In the NFL there is always the chance of serious injury. I suffered one. But I came back from it. With the big help of my little friends. So I'll take it one play at a time. For as long as I can perform at a productive level."

"You certainly did produce today."

After concluding the interview Uzmahndey was collecting his things in the locker room when Logan Wilson walked up to him.

"I heard what you said about me. I appreciate the plug."

"It's the truth. I'm just glad we're on the same team now and you won't be hitting me any more."

Logan Wilson slapped him on the shoulder.

"Only in practice." He walked away.

Or until we sign with another team. Then we'll knock your ugly head off.

Uzmahndey burst out laughing.

This caused Logan Wilson to look back. "I don't hit that hard in practice."

"I wasn't laughing at that," Uzmahndey covered. "I was thinking how much fun it's going to be to play in the Super Bowl."

"I've been there. I imagine it's more fun when you win."

Later that evening Uzmahndey walked into the crowded living room of his condo. Charlie and Keanu were there with their twins. Charley and his wife Amy were there, too, with their newborn. Angela was seated by herself in a corner wearing his jersey. Charlie dressed her in it every game day.

Uzmahndey went to Charlie.

"What did my granddaughters think of the game?"

Charlie nodded to the infant she held. "Ozzie slept through most of it."

Keanu nodded to the infant he held. "Kalani likes your touchdown dance." He set the little girl down on her feet before Uzmahndey. "TD dance, Kalani!" The little girl bounced from foot to foot.

Uzmahndey swept her up in his arms and danced with her. "That's my girl!" He danced her around the room and back over to her mother. "So how are my newest grandbabies doing?"

Charlie patted her large stomach. "The three of them are doing fine."

Uzmahndey lowered Kalani to the floor. "And your body is handling all this traffic through it okay?"

"Of course. You know how strong I am." She smiled at Keanu seated beside her. "Next time it could be quads."

Keanu shook his head. "*She* might be strong. If she keeps popping them out every five months all these kids will be the death of me."

"Be thankful your kids are growing at a normal pace. No growth spurts for this generation." Uzmahndey squatted down on the floor by Kalani. "It's a good thing your restaurant is doing so well. I told you there'd be a demand for good Hawaiian food here in Cincinnati."

"As long as Snugglesaurus keeps directing customers my way. Last week I had a family from Indonesia walk in asking for my mango lemonade." Keanu's face grew clouded. "How does he do that?"

"You're asking me? I have no idea how Snugglesaurus does what he does." Uzmahndey hopped up from the floor and walked over to where Charley and his wife Amy sat.

"Good game, Dad."

"Angel had fun." Uzmahndey squatted before Amy, who had their baby in her lap. "How is little Logan doing?"

The young mother appeared troubled. "He is the healthiest baby boy born last year."

Uzmahndey peered into her dark eyes. "That's a good thing, right?" When she didn't reply, he turned to Charley. "Right?"

"Of course." He rubbed his wife's shoulder. "Amy is just having a little trouble adjusting to the unusual family she has married into."

She looked defiantly from one to the other. "I love my son."

"Of course you do," Uzmahndey answered. "We all do."

Amy shot a furtive look to the side. Uzmahndey tracked her eyes across the room to the corner where Angela sat. Motionless, expressionless; even in the orange and black jersey she blended in with shadows that weren't even there. What blazed out were the many Hawaiian-themed tattoos that nearly covered her. Keanu had done his best to decorate the scars Ghost hadn't been able to repair, and this time it hadn't been prison tats, he had used his professional tattoo instruments and ink to do a colorful job. And Charlie had done a good job fixing her hair. Angela never bothered with it anymore. Yet all that failed to enliven. Angela's slack face reminded him of that first day she had walked into his office in Hilo.

Later that night after everyone had left the post-game party, Uzmahndey stepped out onto the balcony of his Mount Adams condo overlooking downtown Cincinnati. The lights of Paycor Stadium shimmered on the dark water of the Ohio River. It reminded him of Salar de Uyuni. The stiff December wind blowing across the hillside sure didn't. Yet there wasn't even a shiver. "Relax, guys. You don't have to work so hard anymore."

It's what we do.

"You did a good job in the game. That second touchdown catch was over the top."

Was that too much?

"It'll make this week's highlight reel for sure." He sighed as if he felt as tired as he should feel. "Next game let me play on my own."

What if your knee gets messed up again?

Uzmahndey considered. "Maybe let me play with my own natural abilities, but still protect my body from injury."

Does that mean let you feel pain?

He swore. "No. I don't know. Maybe."

Just lay out the game plan, Uz, and we'll try to stick to it.

"I'd just like to try one game on my own. Without being knocked out of the league again." He paused to consider. "And not hurting too bad."

How about exhaustion? Do we maintain your stamina?

"Damn, guys, why is this so difficult?"

We've been a part of you so long it's hard to separate us. Where do me and Angel end and you begin?

"I have no idea. Maybe hold off changing anything up. I need to think this over more."

He turned away from his view into Northern Kentucky. "We need to talk about something else. I've been having some weird dreams." Silence. "Any thoughts on this?" Silence. "Guys?" Silence. "Bad? Angel?"

You said guys.

He walked back inside. "Angel, you've never objected to me using that non-gender-specific term before. What's going on?"

She's dodging the question.

He slid the glass door closed. "Okay, Bad, since she's got no balls, you tell me."

We've been trying to be discreet. But with someone who doesn't know the meaning of the word, it's hard.

I know what discreet means!

"Discreet about what?"

Our relationship.

"Are you missing Good and Ugly?"

Stop beating around my bush and just tell him!

"You and Angel?" That was a loop-thrower. "How is that even possible?"

Do you really want the details?

"No!"

We spend an eternity together inside you. I guess it was bound to happen.

"Just knock it off!"

That's not fair!

We *have to suffer through what you and Angela do.* "That's sure not been much of a problem lately." Uzmahndey paced about the now-empty living room, which was still cluttered with the remains of the post-game family gathering. Angela would clean it up sometime during the night. "Having the two of you in my head is messed-up enough without me having to worry about what you're doing in there."

You didn't think it was messed up today while you were scoring three touchdowns.

Or when we ran over that safety twenty pounds heavier than you. He didn't even slow you down.

Uzmahndey jerked to a halt outside the closed door to the guest bedroom. "You're right. I'm not being fair. And you are also right about our relationship evolving. We're all three changing. You just surprised me. Give me a chance to get used to the idea."

Uzmahndey opened the door. This bedroom had been set up for the grandchildren to take naps and to spend the night. Soon they would have to buy another set of bunk beds. And another bed. Triplets. It wouldn't take long to repopulate the world with alien hybrids the way Charlie was going about it, even without the growth spurts and the twenty-seven hour pregnancy. It was only Angela who had been able to do that. He was glad Charley had sired only one child so far. His wife wasn't as strong as his sister.

Uzmahndey flipped on the light and walked over to peer down into the toy box. Snugglesaurus was buried beneath newer, cleaner, less-ravaged toys. His intense tutoring was no longer required since this generation aged at a normal pace. And the AI no longer manipulated financial markets like it once had. Not that Uzmahndey was aware of. It could be accumulating a fortune without anyone knowing it. Just as it could be enriching his grandchildrens' minds without being obvious about that, either. Actually, it could be taking over the world without anyone's knowledge.

The world certainly had changed. The entire human population had quickly calmed once Gaia dialed the Schumann Resonance back down. Since then world tensions had continued to ease. The planet's governments, under China's guidance, had even begun to get serious about protecting and repairing the environment.

Gaia's worshippers had dispersed. Without their goddess to stir their fanaticism they had calmed down. Snugglesaurus was keeping tabs on the ones still clinging to their old beliefs, but the misguided souls were causing no trouble. Hopefully, they would all find other religions to invest their souls in.

Snugglesaurus' glass eyes flashed. The AI had acquired a new function since the departure of Ghost.

"Guys, if you two aren't too busy..."

We're not now, but keep it up and we might be too busy during the Steelers game.

"Enough with the threats. Just relay the messages Snugglesaurus is receiving."

Graviton Grace congratulates you on your victory. She enjoys watching you play. She says if you ever need any help blocking she'd be glad to flatten some defenders for you.

"Thank her for her offer, but I enjoy doing that myself."

Actually, you don't do that by yourself.

Bad spoke up before Uzmahndey could answer Angel's snarky remark. Dirty Dave enjoyed your ground game.

"Tell him next time he's on Earth we'll go on another hike."

He'd enjoy that. He says there are some caves below Mt. Erebus no human has ever set foot in he would like to explore.

Rootless Ron wants to attend this Super Bowl he's heard so much about.

"Certainly. Maybe as a palm tree."

How would he do that?

"You don't think Snugglesaurus could influence the planning of the halftime show? Give it a Hawaiian theme? Maybe do a tribute to Israel Kamakawiwo'ole."

Time to get serious. Moving right along, Lightning Len wants to know when you play the lightning bolt team. He really likes their uniforms.

"Give Len the same answer I gave him last week. We don't play the Chargers this season, not unless we meet them in the play-offs. Any updates on Gaia?"

They haven't reestablished contact with her yet. They don't know where she's gone.

She won't dare come back to Earth. We kicked her butt.

"They are still monitoring our solar system?"

Surveillance has been set up just beyond the heliopause.

No way can she sneak back here.

"I'd feel better if I knew where she was." Uzmahndey set the toy dinosaur back in the toy box. "Tell them all I appreciate their congratulations. And tell Len he'll be the first to know if we meet the Chargers in the play-offs. And that whenever we do play them I hope he won't help them just because he likes their helmets. I don't want any sudden gusts of wind to blow any of our field goals or passes off-target, or for any of my teammates to get struck by lightning."

Not even Logan Wilson?

Uzmahndey couldn't stifle his laugh. "Don't tempt me. But we're on the same team now." He walked out, flicking the light off and closing the door behind him. "You two can go back to whatever you were doing."

That is so unfair! We're not obsessed.

We're just lonely and bored. There's not that much to do anymore.

Uzmahndey stopped laughing. "Damn, how does that even happen?"

We can show you sometime.

Yeah, next time we won't wait until you're asleep.

"Please don't. Just try to put me into a deeper sleep."

We had you practically in a coma. But Angel is so rambunctious.

What? Girls aren't allowed to enjoy sex?

"Okay! I guess I can live with it. I just hope you two are using protection." Once again, silence. "That was a joke."

That was a joke?

Oh. Ha ha.

"You thought I was serious? Why? I mean, how?"

We are physical beings.

"So you two are not just using my brain to fantasize?"

You fantasize about having a brain?

"You are actually...physically...for real..."

**Don't worry, we can't carry any diseases you don't already have in your body.**

"So there's no reason to use protection. Okay, sorry. Bad joke."

There is a reason.

"You mean Angel can get pregnant?! You could have babies? Inside my body?"

**Even on this backward planet xenobots can reproduce.**

Scientists have used frog egg cells to make xenobots that can bulldoze cells together to create a separate xenobot.

**Of course that's not how we'll do it. We are much more advanced.**

"Way too much information, guys. I don't need any more details. Just don't overrun my body with little baby xenobots."

Are you kidding? You can barely feed me and Angel.

"We'll talk about it some more another time. Right now I'm tired and ready for bed. Please do not disturb my sleep. I don't want to hear any headboards banging against the inside of my skull."

Uzmahndey walked into his bedroom. Angela sat in the chair she had settled in after everyone had left. It reminded him of how she used to sit up all night watching over the kids while they slept. It had bothered him, waking up in the middle of the night and finding her staring down at them. Sometimes now when the grandchildren stayed over he awoke in the night to an empty bed. He invariably found her in the other bedroom gazing down upon them as they slept, standing guard over the precious beings. Amy had seen her do this once. Logan had never spent the night again. Charley's young wife didn't understand. Angela would battle Heaven and Hell to prevent harm from befalling the children. Some imperative in her programming to stand guard at night, to protect her charges while they slept, ran in an infinite loop.

"Did you have a good time tonight?" Of course, she didn't answer. But that was no reason not to talk to her. Like someone in a coma, there was no telling how much she actually heard, or comprehended. "The babies are growing up fast. At least it seems so to me. To you it must seem like a snails pace. And so many of them. Charlie is having triplets this time, and talking about quads next time." He laughed. "I think Neo is getting overwhelmed. He'll have to open up a couple more restaurants to support them all. Which I'm sure would be successful, with the way Snugglesaurus helps his business."

Angela nodded her head to all that. Then she had a difficult time stopping it from nodding. Uzmahndey gently took her head in his hands and stilled it. "I hope Gaia does come back some time. I'd like the chance to kill her for what she did to you."

"It's...over."

Two words. That were nearly connected. With only a slight pause. She's getting better.

Uzmahndey smiled at Angela. "Can you believe how Angel has mellowed?" She merely stared in response. He didn't know if Angela could still hear the xenobots in his head. Most likely she couldn't.

A soldier needs to adjust to peacetime.

"And you, Bad. You turned out so pleasant."

I think some of Good rubbed off on me.

Good didn't rub anything off on me. I enjoyed running over that linebacker who tried to knock the ball out of your hands.

The corners of Angela's mouth turned up.

I think Angela enjoyed seeing that, too.

Yeah, Uz, maybe she can hear us.

The smile remained in place.

"Or maybe her face is just twitching." Uzmahndey pulled Angela to her feet to help her undress. Ghost claimed he'd done the best he could with her. He'd offered to build a new Angela from scratch, but Uzmahndey had turned him down. That wouldn't have been Angela. Uzmahndey set her jeans and jersey aside and helped her into her pajamas.

The first night in their new condo he had left her naked, only to be awakened in the middle of the night by the racket she made banging around looking for her pajamas. She had gotten into a routine of wearing them at night. It seemed established routines were all she had left.

Uzmahndey tucked her in.

"Time to sleep, Angela." She closed her eyes. He knew she didn't really sleep, but waking up during the night and finding her eyes open and locked on him kept Uzmahndey from a sound sleep himself. So she pretended to sleep until he was asleep. Then she would get up and take care of whatever she needed to take care of, or just go sit in her chair.

Uzmahndey stripped off his clothes. Since it was now just he and Angela there was no reason for him to keep his undershorts on. Yet he did. Established routines were hard for him, too, to break.

Uzmahndey raised his right arm and probed the armpit with the index finger of his left hand. It was always hard to find. Locating what felt and looked like a small mole, he pressed it for thirty seconds. The artificial arm came loose at the shoulder. It had gotten knocked a little crooked when he had been sandwiched between a safety and a linebacker after one of his catches. He twisted his arm into place then popped it back into its shoulder socket.

The alien tech was good. No doctor on Earth could tell which parts of him were real and which parts were prosthetics. His right arm and everything else that had been replaced meshed perfectly with what remained of his original body. Ghost had even scarred his new knee so it looked like his original injured one that had been operated on so many times. Uzmahndey was nearly as artificial as Angela. Two peas in a pod. He slid into bed and cuddled up to her.

Angela sighed.

Was that real? Had she really just sighed? With content-ment? Or was he merely projecting his hopes on her like so many times before? What did it matter, as long as he could hope. He had long ago accepted Angela for what she was. Like he would any woman he loved.

THE END